Also by Carla Sandrin

Uncorrupted

Katie's Heart (a children's novel)

A LICIT AFFAIR

a novel

Carla Sandrin

Sandrin Communications
Toronto, Ontario

To obtain print copies or eBooks, please contact Carla Sandrin at csandrin@rogers.com; or order through Amazon.com or the eStore at CreateSpace.com

ISBN 978-0-9868967-3-6

To Paul, my biggest fan and supporter

Chapter One

Viewing herself in the full-length mirror, Denise was struck by the vision of an imposter masquerading in somebody else's clothes. "At least I look the part," she said, straightening her visor. The stylist adjusted the collar and scrutinized her from every angle. "You're good to go."

Denise swung an imaginary golf club and gazed beyond herself in the mirror, as if watching the ball fly into the distance. "Appearances are everything these days," she said, her voice trailing off.

"Two minutes to showtime," the intercom announced.

As she approached the stage entrance, the producer gave her the thumbs up. He picked up the set of golf clubs leaning against the wall and placed them over Denise's shoulder.

"How much do these weigh?" she asked, slumping as if the weight of the world had been dumped on her.

"Need a caddy?" he quipped.

She turned to him with a furrowed brow. His sarcastic edge was not lost on her. "There's a good job for you, Gary." She peered at the audience from the stage side. A full house. Then she examined the set. No props, no coffee table with mugs of water, and no leather chairs arranged in fireside fashion. Even the elegant Persian carpet had been replaced by a fake green turf—an insult to the gleaming oak floor.

A young woman scrambled to her side. Grabbing Denise's arm, she said, "Thank you for letting me do this. I'm so excited...and nervous."

"Don't worry, Nicole, you'll be great out there."

"I hope so."

1

The stylist called Nicole over to fix her hair and Denise turned to Gary when she was out of earshot. "We have to talk about the show's direction. You know we're losing our focus here." Her tone was measured, her voice low.

With a half-smile he nodded, and motioned for her to get ready. Clenching her hands, she listened for the cue. It had been Gary's suggestion to bring Nicole on as a sidekick and Denise had finally agreed, with reluctance. After barely a year on the job, Nicole was just now becoming a proficient assistant and catapulting her on stage with no experience seemed risky.

A man's voice loomed across the studio. "Please welcome the host of *Montreal's Alive*—Denise Gagnon!"

The audience clapped with exuberance when she came on stage, the clubs banging against her hip as she walked, and Nicole prancing behind her. As usual, the crowd's energy was invigorating. Setting the heavy bag down, she greeted her fans in the studio and said, "I hope you're ready to play some golf!"

"*I* am!" Nicole blurted out, staring directly at camera 2. She took an iron from Denise's golf bag and swung wildly, almost toppling over. The audience howled.

"Perhaps we could all benefit from some lessons today," Denise said. She smiled at the expectant faces in the crowd, "You'll be pleased to meet our celebrity guest who has come to share her knowledge and to promote this fabulous sport. Please welcome the current LPGA champion, Sylvie Martin."

A lanky, broad-shouldered woman strode onto the stage, greeting the audience with a warm smile and a friendly wave. Denise congratulated Sylvie on her latest LPGA win and asked about her upcoming tour. They discussed how golf was not just a man's sport and why it was important for women to participate—not only for recreation, but to gain access to the fairway conversations that, nowadays, seemed to be replacing meetings in the boardroom.

"Why should women be excluded from these important discussions?" Denise said.

Sylvie raised her hands above her head and applauded. "No excuses, girls! Get out there and learn the game, and don't let the guys leave you at your desk while they're smacking balls and cracking deals." Loud cheers and clapping burst through the room.

Sylvie swung her club with the power of a three-hundred-yard drive. "Now you try," she said to Nicole, passing her a club.

Nicole bent over and wiggled her hips. Then she swung the club with exaggerated motions and a silly expression on her face. Laughter erupted. "Obviously, I have no idea how to play this game, but do you like my outfit?" She twirled around, displaying her snug little golf shorts, her thick ponytails flying in the air.

After trying a few swings herself, Denise invited volunteers on stage to practice while Sylvie gave pointers. There was a question and answer period, and then Sylvie passed out autographed golf balls to the audience. The show ended with Nicole holding up two golf balls and bellowing, "If you can't beat'em, join'em!"

Gary was still laughing from the sidelines when they left the stage and Denise strode past him, shaking her head.

"Did you hear the audience's reaction?" he said to her back. "They loved it."

She ignored his comment and kept on walking. Her show was degenerating, no doubt about it.

Denise listened to the fading applause as she entered her dressing room. The announcer's deep voice reverberated after she shut the door. "Thank you for coming to *Montreal's Alive*. I hope we'll see you again soon." More clapping.

For eight years she'd heard those exact words in the same generic voice. Sitting down at her dressing table, she rubbed her temples and kicked off the golf shoes. Either her feet had swollen over the last hour or the shoes were too small, but when she flipped them over, she saw that they were indeed size eight. She crossed her legs and massaged her heel. Today, the segment had gone all right in spite of her reservations; the audience was engaged and Nicole's buffoonery elicited some laughs. Nonetheless, the show's new track aggravated her. Sure, she'd agreed to mix up the content, to add more lifestyle-themed shows, but a disturbing trend was emerging—without her input. It was time to put a stop to this nonsense; she hadn't worked so hard all these years to host a fluff fest.

The light-hearted topics that Gary had recently introduced were undermining her original concept for *Montreal's Alive*: a daytime talk-show that would inform, stimulate, and broaden women's minds. There had even been discussion about American syndication. Why then, were the producers messing with the format? Denise pulled the file with the following week's schedule from her briefcase and grimaced as she reviewed the topics: Good-bye dog kennel—hello puppy spa; Mademoiselle Manners—the ultimate coach for unruly children; Family poker and other games to bring your brood together.

Asinine. All of it. She shoved the folder back into her briefcase.

The door opened before she registered the knock and Nicole poked her head in. "Cab's on its way."

Denise nodded. "I'll be out as soon as I've changed."

Attending a wine-tasting in Cleveland was hardly inspiring. She should be meeting with Gary to discuss the show's future rather than scuttling off to Ohio for the evening. When Gary had first suggested doing a segment on New England wineries, she'd been enthused. Why not explore what Quebec's American neighbours had to offer? She'd read that the north eastern states were producing some fine wines and she was anxious to try them. Touring the wineries and then inviting some of the top producers as guests on the show had been one of Gary's better ideas, a perfect opportunity to attract eastern state viewers. But then he'd changed the plan and made arrangements for her to go to this event in Cleveland instead.

Cleveland of all places.

Scrubbing the television make-up off her face, she noticed the fine lines at the corner of her eyes. The grey circles appeared darker today, and even the tiny mole at the right edge of her lips seemed unsightly. She cringed. After patting her face dry, she brushed on some powder and applied a thin layer of lipstick, finishing off with gloss. A little mascara and eyeliner picked up her weary eyes. Running the brush through her dark hair, she studied her face in the mirror. Good enough for an evening in Cleveland.

Her husband was supposed to accompany her on this trip, a rare occurrence given their hectic schedules. Everything had been arranged and their housekeeper had agreed to stay with the boys; in fact, Clara had urged them to take a trip together for months. "Couples need time away from jobs and children," she often told Denise. "It's essential for marital health." But when Francois found out that they would be going to Cleveland instead of New England, he backed out. "Sorry," he said. "Work is too busy and I can't afford to take the time."

Nicole could hardly contain her excitement when Denise had asked her to come along to take notes. She'd been clamoring to have more involvement in the development stages and Denise felt this would also be a good time to delegate some of the groundwork.

Denise took off the golf shirt and pulled a hanger from the closet. Where was her outfit? Oh, great. She'd forgotten her change of clothes at home. She could visualize the dry-cleaning bag hanging in the hall, exactly where she'd put it so she wouldn't forget. She quickly changed back into the black linen suit she'd worn to the studio, shoved several files into her briefcase and grabbed her carry-on. They would barely make their flight. Always running—and often in circles, it seemed. How did her life get so out of control?

In the taxi, Denise shifted her body to get more comfortable. The oppressive gray sky made it feel more like March than early May and she regretted not bringing an umbrella. Nicole brushed some lint off the shoulder of Denise's blazer and passed her a bottle of water.

"Wasn't the show awesome today?" Nicole said.

Denise yawned and nodded. "Yes, awesome."

"And Sylvie was so cool!"

"She certainly is an impressive athlete."

"How 'bout the way she got the audience involved? From the minute she came on stage..."

Denise stared out the cab window at the concrete wall lining the expressway and replayed the show in her mind. The vision of Nicole hopping around the stage like a zealous rabbit made her smile. The audience may have found her antics endearing but the novelty would wear itself out in no time. What bothered her most were the gratuitous humour and the slapstick banter. Sipping her water, she crunched the plastic bottle with her fingers.

As soon as she returned to Montreal she'd have it out with Gary.

Nicole's loud voice jolted Denise from her thoughts. Realizing that Nicole was still speaking to her, she nodded in agreement to whatever Nicole had said. "You took to the stage like a natural," Denise added.

"Thank you," Nicole said, blushing. "I loved it. I loved the whole thing." Then she gasped. "I forgot to check the messages before leaving. I'll do it now." She began punching numbers into her cell phone and Denise gazed out the window again. Traffic had slowed because of road construction and as the cab crawled forward, she surveyed the industrial scenery: decrepit factories boarded up, box cars stacked like children's blocks in colourful patterns, and hydro electric wires weaving through the sky. Further ahead were walls of newly-built houses rammed beside each other like the slats of a wooden fence. A tall concrete barrier attempted to shield the residential development from the highway's continuous hum. Perhaps she should do a show on revitalizing the industrial strip—an offensive thoroughfare that Montrealers and out-of-town visitors alike were forced to experience when entering and departing the city. Experts and lay people could share their ideas—a panel comprising architects, engineers, city planners and citizens presenting their arguments. Digging in her purse, she pulled out pen and paper to jot down her thoughts.

Nicole nudged Denise. "I just heard the messages and that journalist guy, the one who recently came back from Afghanistan, agreed to be a guest."

Denise sat bolt upright in her seat. "That *is* good news." Michel Beaudoin, the award winning journalist—she'd been after him for months to talk about the current plight of Afghani women. That would be an ideal segment to help upgrade the programming standards.

"And your mother called."

"Is everything all right?"

"I guess so. She wanted you to call her when you had a minute."

Sifting through her purse, Denise pulled out her own phone, and speed-dialed her mother's number. The answering machine picked up and her mother's warm voice chimed into the receiver: "Sorry to have missed your call. Please leave a message and I will get back to you as soon as I can. Have a wonderful day."

"Hi, Mother. I guess you're out. Did I tell you I'd be out of town tonight? If you need to speak to me, you can call my cell. Love you."

Before Denise had a chance to put her phone away, Nicole said, "Francois called too. He wants you to get back to him ASAP."

"We're almost at the airport. I'll call him from the gate."

"Seemed important."

"I'm sure it can wait." She leaned back against the taxi's cracked leather seat and closed her eyes.

"He'll get mad at me—he'll think I didn't give you the message right away."

"All right, all right, I'll call." She punched in his number.

"Oui?"

"Hi, it's me."

"Marcel called. A pipe burst at the cottage."

"Much damage?"

"I don't know, he left a vague message. Here's his number."

"Francois, I'm about to get on a plane. Can't you call him?"

"I'm busy too—meetings all day. It'll have to wait then."

"Fine," Denise said, clenching her teeth.

"See you when you get back."

"Listen, don't forget to—"

He hung up.

Damn. Always something breaking down.

"This trip should be fun," Nicole said. "Thanks for letting me tag along."

"You're welcome," Denise said. Nicole always tried to lighten a heavy moment; she was thoughtful in that way. Recently Denise had allowed Nicole to attend out-of-town meetings because she'd been begging for more involvement, and given how hard she worked, she deserved it. Besides, mentoring Nicole and helping her navigate through the cut-throat business gave Denise satisfaction. The girl had potential; she just needed to be reined in at times.

"I have to call the Get-Fit Foundation about the benefit next month," Nicole said. "Did you decide whether or not you'll give a speech?"

She'd forgotten all about it. "No, I'll have to give it more thought. Remind me again next week."

Nicole leaned toward Denise and looked at her with wide eyes. "Everybody wants you. You've got the best life. I would love to be in your shoes, even for a day—you're like the Queen of Montreal!"

Yes, everyone seemed to think Denise had a glamorous life, filled with never-ending excitement. In a recent piece for a national magazine, the interviewer kept reminding her how fabulous her life was. "What's it like to be the renowned and beautiful, Denise Gagnon?" the woman had asked. Now *that* was a loaded question.

After the flight, a taxi dropped them off at the Cleveland Museum of Art, where the wine-tasting event was being held. Denise planned to make the rounds, greet the key people and then slip out. Her reward at the end of the night would be a long aromatherapy bath. Naturally, Nicole would try to convince her to go out for dinner or to a club afterwards, but she'd stand her ground. It was already past 8:00 and the next day promised to be busy.

Nicole handed their V.I.P. invitations to a young woman at the entrance. "We're from QPN in Montreal." she said. "*Montreal's Alive*. We're here to scope out some wineries for our viewers."

"Welcome to Cleveland," the woman said, handing them a booklet, wine glasses, and a hard-covered book called *Sights of Cleveland*. She had a man take their bags and lead them into a large room where tasting counters framed the parameter. "I'll be right back with your host."

In the meantime, Denise and Nicole meandered over to a large round table with a spectacular floral arrangement in the centre. Hors d'oeuvres were artistically displayed around the table: towers of shrimp; radishes carved like roses; grape tomatoes, basil and mozzarella balls held together by toothpicks; gherkins and artichoke hearts; and bite-sized ham and pineapple skewers.

"Check it out," Nicole said, pointing at a giant ice sculpture in the shape of a wine bottle. "And look at all this food. I'm starved."

The woman returned with a middle-aged man and introduced Denise.

"Bonjour, Madame Gagnon," the man said, with a dreadful French accent. "At last we meet," he continued in a southern drawl. "I'm Jeb Porter." He reached for her hand and gently kissed it.

Before Denise had a chance to respond Nicole stepped forward and thrust the back of her hand in front of his face. "I'm Nicole Pelletier."

He kissed her hand and bowed. "Pleasure."

"Nicole is my colleague," Denise said. "We're very pleased to meet you too." She flashed her charismatic talk-show smile.

While they chatted, Denise noted her host's finely tailored suit and perfectly trimmed goatee. The incongruity between his southern accent and his appearance intrigued her. He sounded like George W. Bush but looked like a Parisian caricature—not what she had expected after speaking to him on the phone.

"You've done a tremendous job here, I'm most impressed," she said.

"Thank you. We've never done a wine-tasting of this magnitude before. Please, come and try some champagne." He turned to the young woman who had ushered him over. "Perhaps you'd like to give Mademoiselle Pelter a tour," he said. He then took Denise's arm and led her to the champagne section. "I think you'll agree that the Krug is one of the finest, smoothest you've ever tasted."

Jazz music played softly, mixing with the gentle murmur of the crowd; corks popped and glasses clinked, creating a symphony for wine lovers. The lights dimmed and groups of people clustered near the serving tables. Patrons milled around the counter and Jeb Porter bypassed the crowd, whispering into the server's ear.

Denise glanced around, feeling conspicuous in her conservative linen suit. Women wore mostly smart-casual outfits—capri pants with cotton tops and cardigans thrown over the shoulder, lacy blouses with breezy skirts and sandals. Occasionally a bright yellow or pink jacket burst out of the crowd. She spotted Nicole in spirited conversation with a wine distributor, her arms flying. The juxtaposition of Nicole in her bold go-go style dress and high boots next to the staid-looking man was quite a sight. But her joie de vivre was catchy and within seconds she had the man laughing. Nicole definitely had flair, no doubt about that.

Jeb Porter emerged with a glass and handed it to Denise.

"You're right," she said, after taking a sip. "This is sensational—it's rich and creamy with a somewhat nutty finish. I love the way the bubbles burst on the palate." From the corner of her eye, Denise noticed a man as he passed her—a tall man with glasses and dark wavy hair, graying at the temples—one of the few patrons wearing a suit and tie.

"You have good taste," Jeb Porter whispered, leaning towards her, "it's $450 a bottle. I was able to procure three cases for this event," he said with pride. "If you'd like, I'll put aside a bottle for you."

"Yes, please do." She didn't mention that Krug champagne was no novelty for her. When she'd lived in France she'd enjoyed it regularly.

"Now," he said, "I know you're anxious to try some of the wines we discussed on the phone. "You'll find the New England wines in that section over—"

A loud crash interrupted their discussion. Denise turned to see the man in the suit standing in a pool of wine. Attendants rushed to wipe the stains off his shoes and the bottom of his pants with white cotton napkins. "I'm terribly sorry," a woman cried out. "I didn't realize the bottle was so close to the edge of the table!"

"Not to worry," the man said, smiling at the woman who had knocked the bottled over, her face hanging like she'd committed the most terrible crime. "No harm done. A few splashes of white wine won't kill me." The man stepped out of the glass chards surrounding his feet and bent over to pick up the larger pieces. Two more attendants arrived with a broom and a mop and cleaned the rest of the mess.

"But your pants are all wet," the woman said, practically in tears. "Let me give you some money for dry-cleaning." She fumbled through her purse, but the man put his arm on her elbow to stop her.

"It's only clothing," he said, "please, don't worry about it."

"You're so gracious, most people would be furious. I could hug you!"

Denise sensed he was the kind of man one would want to hug— handsome, but not stiff, with a warm and sincere face. There was something familiar about him, but it was difficult to ascertain from a distance.

When the commotion died down, Jeb Porter continued his conversation. As he spoke, Denise peered discreetly over his shoulder at the man with the wine-stained pants. Someone had handed him a glass and he was taking a sip.

"Wonderful," she said, in response to Mr. Porter's remarks, although she'd only half-listened to him. "Then I'll leave you to sample at your leisure," he said. He bowed and walked away.

"There you are," Nicole said, jumping into Denise's line of view, her face flushed. "I've been working my way through the

Chiantis." She held up her glass, filled beyond a tasting portion. "Delicious." Pointing to a tray of sushi that a server was offering around, she said, "Let's get some of that." But the server disappeared. "Maybe not." She gestured toward the buffet table. "I'll clear the way and you can follow my path."

Denise laughed. "No thanks. I think I'll settle for room service at the hotel."

While Nicole barged through the crowd, Denise headed to the adjacent tasting table to try a newly released Chardonnay. As she waited in line to be served, she overheard a conversation taking place at another table. Two men were debating the vintage of a particular wine and she listened with interest while scanning the room for the familiar man. When she caught sight of him again, walking in her direction, he was still too far away for her to determine his identity. She tried not to stare as she became more convinced that she knew him. An unexplainable fretfulness tore through her, causing her chest to tighten and her hands to moisten.

"I'm positive this Burgundy is no younger than a '90," she overheard a gentleman from the group beside her say.

"Most likely between a 1975 and '80, I would say." The other man held his glass up to the light. "See the brownish tinge."

An intense woman with a boyish haircut charged over, waving an empty wine bottle and pointing at the label. "Didn't I tell you it's a child? See—1998!"

Denise laughed but then almost choked when the man she'd been watching was only about twenty feet away. He approached slowly, looking around the room nonchalantly, like he was taking in the scenery. She studied his tall frame, confident stride, and slightly stooped shoulders. Was it really *him*? Nicole arrived with crudités and napkins, and passed a plate to Denise. Suddenly, the man with the stained pants appeared in front of her—so close, she could almost feel his breath.

****

Montreal, Quebec – August, 1982

Denise fanned herself with her cigarette box; the crowded Montreal bar was stifling, even with the air-conditioner blowing.

The summer felt endless but it would soon be over, and she couldn't wait. In two days she'd be on a plane to Paris.

Everyone else was in such a good mood. Why couldn't she get into the spirit of the evening? She should be laughing and joking, enjoying the remaining moments with friends she wouldn't see for a long time. But she'd already said her good-byes the previous week at the surprise 'bon voyage' party they'd thrown for her, and it seemed anticlimactic to be hanging around still.

"Hey, Denise. Come and dance!" Joe called out from across the bar.

She waved and smiled, shaking her head, and mouthing the words, "Too hot."

"Come and dance with me," said Theresa, her best friend in the world.

"I'm sweltering," she said. "You go. Maybe I'll join you later."

Theresa shrugged and danced away. Denise ordered a gin and tonic at the bar and walked over to a round table where some friends were drinking beer and smoking. She sat down and pulled a pack of cigarettes from her purse. One of the guys passed his cigarette across the table for her to use as a light. She inhaled deeply.

She shouldn't have come out with so much to do at home: sort through her old winter clothes, pack, and clean her room, which her mother had been asking her to do for a month. She hadn't even selected her fall courses yet.

"So, Denise, what's the first thing you're gonna do when you get to Paris?" Vivienne asked. "Find a new man?"

"That's the last thing on my mind."

For months Mike had been trying to get her to cancel her plans for Paris. One late night, after a passionate kiss in his parent's Oldsmobile, he'd become emotional. "Why do you have to go away to study?" he said. "We've got great universities right here in Montreal, at your doorstep." Then he tried to guilt her into staying. "But I love you. I can't live without you. You're the best damn thing that's ever happened to me."

"I'll be home for the holidays," she told him. "And we'll write to each other. I'll write you every week. And you can visit me."

He'd even cried. "What's so frickin' great about Paris anyway? If you wanna learn about Paris, you can get some books from the library."

Nice.

Then last month he broke up with her. He had found a new 'love of his life.'

"I'm not talking about boyfriends," Vivienne said. "I'm talking about a lover. That's what I'd do—get myself a suave Parisian lover."

Everybody laughed. "No thanks," Denise said. "There's too much else to do in Paris." She sipped her drink and glanced at the bar, noticing a cute guy looking her way. He quickly turned his head. A few minutes later she spotted him eying her again. She smiled and then dropped her eyes before seeing his reaction.

The music had become louder, making it difficult to hear anyone talk. Her head started to pound; the cigarettes and the gin were not helping. Then Mike showed up with his new 'friend,' a slip of a thing with long blond hair and gold loop earrings. What bloody nerve. They stood at the other side of the table, his arm around the girl's waist, chatting with the gang. Every time he spoke, the girl flung back her hair and laughed. When Denise looked at him, he averted his eyes. What a jerk.

"I've gotta get going," she yelled to her friends over the blaring music. Before leaving, she scanned the bar, hoping to find Theresa, and caught another glimpse of that guy at the bar, whose attention was diverted by a red-head sitting next to him. Denise studied him from the distance and was captivated by the way he moved. His smile had a slight slant and when he laughed he lifted his chin. He seemed to be immersed in conversation with the red-head and had probably forgotten about her. Disappointed, she grabbed her purse and rushed toward the exit. When she passed through the door into the open air she immediately felt a sense of physical relief, but at the same time, the sadness that had taken hold in the bar intensified.

Walking towards Sherbrooke Street to get a cab, Denise heard a voice from behind. Her first impulse was to pick up her pace, but instead she stopped, and found the guy from the bar beside her. Seeing his striking blue eyes and slightly crooked grin up close brought on a strong sense of déjà vu. For the first time that night, her smile was not forced. "Do I know you? You look familiar," she said.

Chapter Two

Chris wiped his brow with a terrycloth towel as he and Tony left the squash court.

"I can't believe you got me again. That's three games in a row." He slapped the racquet against his hand and grinned at Tony.

"You're losing your touch, Lambert. Face it, you've got no hope."

Chris whipped the towel at him. "You wait. When you're least expecting it, I'm gonna go in for the kill." The two men laughed and walked over to the bar. "What'll you have?" Chris asked.

"The usual, but to celebrate my victory, make it a double."

Chris ordered a mineral water with two shots of lemon for Tony and a Coke for himself. They sat on a bench in the lounge area facing the glass walls of the courts, and Chris leaned forward to focus on a game in progress.

Tony nudged Chris and whispered, "Check that out." He pointed with his chin to two women who had sauntered by them.

"What?"

"Nice scenery, don't you think?" Tony said.

"Hard to tell from here."

"They sure scoped you out when they passed us."

Chris laughed. "Yeah, right."

"You still get the attention of the ladies. And me," Tony sucked in his oversized stomach and swept a hand over his balding head, "I'm the guy who isn't even here."

"C'mon. You're a hard one to miss," Chris said.

For eight years, they had played squash at the Cleveland Athletic Club, across the street from their office; the only time they could let their mutual competitiveness rage. Their squash matches had become a necessary weekly ritual; a fervent measure of their fitness and their wits. As partners at their merchant banking firm, they worked in unison to drive business and create deals. Over the years, business had prospered beyond their expectations and by now, they could practically read each other's minds when they handled clients. "No wonder you guys know what the other is thinking," Chris's wife had said more than once, "you spend more time with Tony than you do with me."

"What are you? Forty-five years old?" Tony said. "I'm not even forty yet, and available, but what do the women do? Gawk at the old married man with the gray hair."

"Hey, watch it there." Chris grazed his head with his hand. "I'm only forty-four, and at least *I* have hair."

Tony snickered. "True. Somehow the world has shifted and you're the one with the hair, the wife and kids, and the babes checking you out. There's no justice here."

Chris laughed. "You're sitting in the wrong car on the roller coaster, buddy." Not so long ago, Tony had brandished a healthy ego — and in the old days, he was quite the ladies' man. The divorce had changed him, brought him down a few notches, it seemed. "Don't worry," Chris continued, "things will work out in the end." Why couldn't he come up with something more inspiring? 'Work out in the end?' That's what people used to say to pacify him when his life was a mess, and here he was, using the exact same, inane words. He just didn't know what to say anymore. Tony would be better off if he lost some weight and cut down on his smoking and drinking. But there was no point lecturing him, not while he was still dealing with the blow of Melinda's departure.

He patted Tony on the back. "You smoke me on the courts every week. That's gotta give you some satisfaction."

"You better believe it! Killing you at squash is all I live for these days." They stood up and headed towards the locker room. "By the way, Peterson gave me a bottle of Chateau Margaux when we closed the Air Flamingo deal. A 1990, I believe. Should I drink it now or cellar it?"

Chris whistled and threw his hands in the air. "How'd *you* end up with that? Doesn't he know he gave it to the wrong guy? Talk about injustice."

Tony imitated an Italian accent. "Eh, I love my vino. Whaddo I do? I drinka or I keepa?"

Chris laughed. "You could drink it now, but it would definitely benefit from some more aging. I'd cellar it for another five years if I were you—maybe to drink with your future wife."

Tony guffawed.

"You're welcome to store it at my place. If you can trust me with it, that is." Chris had built an impressive wine cellar, which he'd designed and constructed with painstaking attention. Sometimes, when he needed to get away from the commotion in the house, or if he couldn't sleep at night, he reviewed his stock or reorganized the bottles.

"Sounds good," Tony said. "But if you drink it, Lambert, you're finished!"

"That reminds me," Chris looked at his watch, "I've gotta get moving. Laura and I are going to that wine-tasting event at the museum. Are you sure you don't want to come along?"

"Nah, but have fun." Tony waved him off. "I've got some things to wrap up at the office. But I'll be thinking of you chugging down those rare vintages."

"Don't forget to pass on that bottle so I can store it for you," Chris said, rubbing his hands together, as if he couldn't wait to get possession.

Chris headed to the locker room to shower and change. He glanced back at Tony and saw him slumped on the bench. Poor guy, he was sabotaging his own life with his workaholic tendencies. They'd already cost him his marriage; what would be the next thing to break down? His health? Chris thought about how lucky he was to have Laura and the children to keep him grounded. Otherwise, he could see himself on the same backbreaking treadmill as Tony.

****

Laura wiped the kitchen counter and checked the time. "OK girls, time to do homework. Jen will be here any minute. When she rings the bell, let her in. I'll be upstairs getting changed."

Thursday night was date night. Laura and Chris had made it a practice to devote one evening a week to each other. Life was hectic with their two young daughters, and if they didn't eke out this time for themselves, they would never manage to sit face-to-face and have a non-domestic conversation. And even though Monique was away at college, she still needed attention too.

Now, what should she wear? She shuffled through the suits and dresses hanging in organized rows in her walk-in closet. The work outfits from her management-consulting days took half the space. They had cost a fortune back then, a good chunk of her paycheck when she had started out. Maybe she'd wear them again someday if she went back to work. She sighed. Who was she kidding? They wouldn't fit her anymore, not with the extra weight she had gained since having children, and the styles were surely dated. She removed one of her favourite business blazers from its hanger. Did women wear pinstripes anymore? She noticed the boxy form — shoulder pads were definitely passé. Time to purge these relics of her previous life; perhaps Goodwill could do something with them.

Laura looked down at her figure and straightened her posture. How much had she gained? Fifteen pounds? Twenty? Good thing they didn't own a scale. And diets were impossible. She and some neighbourhood friends had periodically attempted various 'proven diets': Weight Watchers, The Protein Diet, the Grapefruit Diet, and even that new Fiber-Fling Diet. Nothing worked, so what was the point? Chris was a sweetheart; he never mentioned her weight. She secretly hoped he hadn't noticed the surplus pounds. More exercise, that's what she needed to do — and to drink more water. But she hated water; it made her feel bloated. And where would she find the time to exercise the recommended forty-five minutes a day?

She selected her grey dress-pants with the matching jacket, her standard outfit, and a favourite because the tapered seams masked her imperfections. Pulling her red silk camisole top off the hanger, she held it against her chest and looked in the mirror. Yes, a little punch was definitely needed.

Hearing the babysitter arrive, Laura dressed quickly. And with practiced speed, she brushed her hair and pulled her highlighted curls back with a hair band. Maybe she should get a new, shorter style; didn't people say that women over forty shouldn't wear their hair long? Never mind, she wasn't quite forty...soon, but not yet. The phone rang.

"Hello."

"Hi, Hon," Chris said, "I'm about five minutes away. Are you ready?"

"Just about. I'll meet you outside."

Chris no longer came into the house on date-nights because the girls and the dog would be all over him, excited to have him home and unwilling to let him go.

Laura slipped on her black pumps and went downstairs to kiss the children good-bye. The moment she was in the front yard she began to relax. She loved her nights out with Chris; sometimes they were the only escape from her mundane routines. Checking her purse to make sure she had the tickets, she sighed. Truth was, she'd much rather have gone to a movie, feeling more like escaping in fiction than standing all night in a crowded room with a group of boring wine enthusiasts. Not that she didn't enjoy her wine, but she preferred drinking at home, over a relaxing dinner, or at a restaurant. Chris deserved a night of his choosing, though; when was the last time they had done something he really wanted to do? His wine hobby was a good diversion from the stress at work and the girls' constant nattering at home. At least the wine-tasting event was being held at the Cleveland Museum of Art, a lovely setting. And they had good food. Yes, they always had good canapés.

Chris pulled into the driveway and Laura got into the car, welcomed by soothing classical music. She sank into the comfortable leather seat and indulged in a moment of serenity. The immaculate car was a pleasant relief from the clutter and spills in the SUV.

Chris greeted her with an affectionate kiss. "Guess what?"

"You're whisking me off to Hawaii?"

"No, just thought I'd mention...I love you."

"You're happy today. Is it me that brings you such joy, or is it those new wine releases that you can't wait to get your hands on?" she said.

"Only you can make me truly happy, my darling. However, the wine may bring me an ever-so-small touch of joy, I have to confess."

"And pain to our pocketbook," she said, laughing.

"Don't despair. I'll keep my meager wine budget in mind and try to restrain myself."

"I don't care what you spend as long as it's on wine and not on women!" she said, a teasing glint in her eyes.

Chris laughed. "You mean I'm not allowed to spend anything on my mistress?"

"I'd rather your mistress spend money on you." Laura enjoyed starting their date nights with playful banter. It always set the mood for the evening and by the time they got home she'd feel reconnected and amorous. Date night was sex night. At least, that was the expectation.

****

The function was underway when they arrived at the museum. Chris's eyes lit up when he read the list of new wine releases presented on a large board and he pointed to the vintage he'd been hoping to try. "Here's the Bordeaux I was telling you about. We better get to it right away — before it sells out." They handed their tickets to a woman at the door, picked up their tasting glasses and notebooks, and headed to the museum foyer. The room had been transformed into an elegant wine-tasting venue, creating the impression of a grand European-style winery, with antique wooden tables, fine crystal decanters, and servers dressed in dark suits. Chris scanned his surroundings, energized by the buzz in the room. After a stressful day at work and that grueling squash game, an evening like this was exactly what he needed.

Laura pointed to the champagne section. "Shall we start over there?"

"Superb idea." Chris took her hand and led her through the crowded room.

Before taking a sip, he inspected the golden hue in the glass and made a toast. "To my beautiful wife, who lets me drag her out to these dull occasions when she could be at a fine restaurant, dining on filet mignon instead." They clinked glasses and enjoyed their first taste of the evening.

"This is incredible," Laura said. "We should get a case."

Chris laughed. "You have excellent taste. Only $450 a bottle!"

"On second thought," she said, "Do they have any sparkling wine here?"

This was the Laura that Chris loved. He was never quite sure what mood would await him when he got home from work, especially when he arrived late, but tonight she was happy and carefree. He'd better not blow it and ruin his chances for later on. "Did I mention how gorgeous you look tonight?" he whispered. "I love it when you wear red." He leaned over and kissed her on the cheek.

"There's the McDermotts. Let's say hello."

"You go ahead." He gestured toward the Bordeaux section. "I want to put my order in before everything's gone. I'll meet up with you later." Walking toward the tasting table, Chris passed by a woman who looked vaguely familiar. She was engrossed in conversation, but he did not want to stare. When he was far enough away, he turned around to glance once more and saw her profile. No, it couldn't be. After so many years, Denise was practically a figment of his imagination. More than two decades had passed since they had been together. The Bordeaux that he was interested in had such a long line that he moved on to the next table where there were fewer people. As the server filled his glass, the woman next to him, reached for her own glass and knocked over a bottle of wine, sending it flying to the floor. Crashing at his feet, red wine sprayed his shoes and ankles and he found himself standing in a red puddle with pieces of glass surrounding him. The woman let out a yelp and looked like she was about to cry. She was so contrite that Chris felt sorry for her and tried to appease her by making light of the event. After the situation had been dealt with, he finally had a chance to try the wine. Taking a sip, he noticed the woman he had seen earlier, looking his way. He quickly turned his attention to the wine agent and asked about the vintage.

Thinking he should find Laura, Chris headed toward the other side of the room, but then he diverted his direction, propelled by a commanding need to know if that attractive woman was indeed Denise.

She had moved on to another wine table, waiting her turn, with notebook and wine glass in hand. Suddenly, she turned his way and he stopped walking, almost paralyzed on the spot. He pretended to scribble something on his notepad and then resumed walking, one hand in his pocket. He glanced at the tasting tables and considered sampling something else, but his desire to taste wine had vanished. All he wanted was to know if the woman was who he thought she might be; perhaps his eyes had tricked him. Moving forward, he snatched surreptitious glances, stopping now and again, one moment egged on by determination and the next, repelled by nerves.

Before his trepidation could change his mind, he found himself in front of her, face to face, body to body. But when he tried to say something, he couldn't. The moment froze and he was left lingering in it, immobile. They stared at each other, dumbfounded.

Her companion made the first overture. "It appears that you two know each other, or at least you think you know each other." She laughed. "Should *I* make an introduction here?"

Denise came to life and smiled at Chris, ignoring the woman. "I think I got stuck in a time warp for a second. Chris, what a surprise! How long has it been?"

"Twenty, maybe twenty-five years?" He tried desperately to remain composed. "You look exactly the same. It's uncanny." Should he kiss her European style, shake hands? He did nothing.

"It didn't take me long to recognize you either. You'd think twenty-five years would have done more damage to us," she said with the same alluring smile that he remembered. Even her enigmatic eyes were unchanged, although more striking it seemed.

"This is my assistant, Nicole Pelletier," she suddenly announced.

He had barely noticed the girl until the introduction. The camera lens in his mind had only fixated on Denise; he wasn't ready to broaden the aperture, but he had no choice. Amazing that he had missed the wild curly hair and bold-patterned dress. They shook hands.

Nicole flung her hair to one side and said, "I'll let you two get reacquainted." She grinned at them both and winked at Denise. "See you later."

"It's good to see you, Chris. I never expected to see you again."

"Me neither." He coughed and looked down at the floor, suddenly conscious of his wet, wine-stained pants. When he looked up he said, "What are the chances...I mean, how strange to...I mean...wow." He spoke in a low, barely audible voice.

"The only thing different about you are the glasses," Denise said, "and a gray hair or two. She lifted her hand as if to touch his hair, but instead, she swept her own black strands behind one ear.

Chris adjusted his glasses' frames. He felt nineteen again, his self-confidence and healthy ego suddenly obliterated. His brain was blocked, his body numb.

"Do you live in Cleveland?" Denise asked.

He tried to act composed. "Yes, I've been here about twenty years. I came after finishing my degree out west."

"I thought you'd settle out there. I remember you telling me that you'd either become a ski bum or a mountain banker." They both laughed.

"You have a good memory, but no, it didn't work out that way. How about you? Where are you living these days?" Was it possible that they lived in the same city? His heart pounded with such force that he wondered if Denise could hear it.

"Montreal. I host a daytime talk-show on one of the local TV stations."

"And what brings you here?" He hoped his disappointment wasn't pasted on his face.

"This wine event. I'm researching Eastern State wines for my show — we're planning to invite a few vintners to speak about their regional wines."

God, was she ever stunning. "And what about Paris? How was Paris?" What a ridiculous question. Denise had gone there years ago, not last month. Nothing seemed to come out right.

"That was eons ago. Paris was an experience. I thought I'd stay forever but I left after twelve years."

"How come?" He crossed his arms, almost dropping his wine glass.

"Circumstances."

Chris nodded as if he understood. He looked down at her hand and noticed a wedding ring. Then he remembered Laura. She'd be wondering where he was. There were so many things he wanted to say to Denise, to ask her, but this wasn't the time or place.

"Are you still in town tomorrow?" he asked.

"I have meetings with some wine producers during the day and I'm leaving in the early evening."

He couldn't let her go that easily. All he wanted was an hour with her, maybe two. "Do you think we could meet at some point for a coffee?"

"I could steal some time first thing in the morning...if that works for you."

He'd have to reschedule a few things and get Tony to cover for him, but he'd make it work. "Sounds great."

They agreed to meet downtown at a coffee shop at 7:30 a.m. Everything had happened so fast that he hadn't had a chance to process his reaction: excitement, anxiety, stress, guilt. Why was he feeling guilty? He was going for a coffee, not some clandestine rendezvous. But he wasn't sure about telling Laura. What would be the point of bringing up a youthful romance, one that was practically forgotten?

He found Laura soon after, engaged in conversation with a new group of acquaintances and she beamed as he approached. "Did you get your Bordeaux?" She turned to the group and said, "I bet he bought a few cases and blew his whole budget."

Chris laughed. "No, not yet, there were too many people in line."

She nudged him affectionately. "Let's check again. I don't mind waiting in line while you do some tasting."

Chris lifted his glass to the friends as Laura led him away. Her enthusiasm was sweet considering how these functions were not her thing. Walking toward the Bordeaux section, Chris caught himself keeping an eye out for Denise, desperate for another glimpse. He came upon her at the Finger Lake tasting area, where she was talking to a man. She was still as slender as he remembered and was dressed in black, the only colour he'd ever seen her in. She appeared poised and self-possessed, a depiction of understated glamour — the same nineteen-year-old girl he had known, but wrapped in an extra layer of sophistication.

Laura tapped him gently on the back. "The gentleman asked what you would like to try, Chris — the '82 or the '86?"

"Oh, sorry. How 'bout you try the '82 and I'll take the '86?"

They made the rounds, visiting several more tasting stations, taking notes and discussing their assessments. Sporadically, Chris glanced around the room searching for Denise, but to no avail. He bought a few cases of wine, a bottle of the expensive champagne that Laura had raved about, and was ready to leave. The packed room, the stuffy air, and the crowd-induced heat were stifling.

Chris was quiet in the car. He said he was tired but his mind kept wandering to the encounter with Denise. Their short exchange had left him unsettled, needing more. What was it about Denise that produced such visceral unease? Perhaps telling Laura about running into her would defuse his anxiety. They'd make light of the incident and have a laugh over the notion of old flames. Laura had dated lots of men over the years and had been left with a bruised heart once or twice. She'd understand.

But Chris said nothing. He put on a Sinatra CD and rested his right hand on Laura's thigh. She covered his hand with her own and squeezed.

At home, they checked on the girls and went to bed. When Chris didn't make romantic overtures towards Laura, she snuggled up closer and began to kiss him. He gently changed his position and moved away.

"I'm bagged tonight, Honey. I had a really intense day." He shifted again, close enough to kiss her and put his arm around her. "Good night," he whispered.

Sleep eluded him. His mind churned over the memory of that summer evening with Denise, twenty-five years ago; one night of passion that had evolved into a recurring fantasy. He had thought of her frequently as a young adult, and in later years the memory would visit him unexpectedly, sneaking into his mind. The passage of time could not completely repress the lingering impact stamped on his life by that one night. Seeing Denise again had made the recollection as clear as if she had been in his arms tonight. The passionate floodgates of his youth opening up in his mature consciousness frightened him. What was *she* thinking? Did that night leave a lasting impression on her, or had it merely been a casual fling, soon forgotten? He had been certain that she had felt the same way back then. But now, he was unsure if that flame had ever burned in her the way it had in him.

Chapter Three

When Chris woke up, diffused light seeped through the blinds. He tossed around in bed hoping to snatch at least another hour's sleep, but Laura stirred and he didn't want to wake her. With careful movements, he untangled himself from the sheets twisted around his legs and slipped out of bed.

In less than two hours he would be having coffee with Denise. If he weren't an alert morning person he would have considered last night's encounter a dream. What were the chances of bumping into an old flame like that? But then, could he place her in the category of an 'old flame?' Old girlfriend would not describe her either, nor would lover. Those terms would imply something more. He couldn't think of any words to capture the essence of their relationship, not that they'd had a real relationship.

Chris had promised to make the girls breakfast and see them off to school, to make up for missing them the night before, and he knew they'd be disappointed to find him gone. He wrote a note and left it on the kitchen table:

Hello my sweethearts,
I'm sorry but I can't have breakfast with you this morning because I have to get to work early. I promise to make it up to you tonight. Have a great day.
Hugs and kisses, Daddy.

Taking extra care with his grooming, Chris had a long shower, shaved meticulously, and clipped his fingernails with precision. Laura had given him several after-shaves and colognes over the years that he had rarely worn, and two of the expensive bottles had never even been opened. He removed the cellophane packaging from a blue box with a picture of tennis racquets and soccer balls, but when he unscrewed the lid from the bottle, the scent was overpowering. The cologne with a deer on the label looked less appealing, yet the scent was much more subtle; oaky with a hint of musk. That one would do.

Chris entered the walk-in closet and sifted through his suits and shirts, all organized according to Laura's meticulous plan—jackets and slacks in one row and shirts underneath. The sky-blue shirt and the sleek tone-on-tone blue tie was Laura's favourite combination. That, with the navy suit, should work. After getting dressed, he removed his black oxfords from the shoe rack and noticed a few scuff marks. He usually had his shoes shined downtown, near his office, had never thought about doing them himself. Where was that shoe-shining kit Laura had given him for Christmas one year? He found it on the top shelf of his closet and polished both shoes, giving them a swift brushing to finish off. Perfect.

Examining himself in the mirror, he straightened his tie. The last time he had given such careful attention to his appearance was on the day he married Laura, eleven years ago. In the mirror, he saw a man who appeared successful and confident. What would Denise see?

Arriving at the coffee shop a few minutes early, Chris scanned the crowd to make sure Denise hadn't arrived yet. The workday bustle was underway and a long line edged the serving counter. He picked up a newspaper and read the headlines while waiting to place his order. Usually he'd get a tortilla breakfast roll or a muffin along with his coffee, but he was not hungry and ordered only a double espresso. With his coffee and paper in hand, he sat down at a table by the window. People came and went with typical haste, muttering a few words of greeting to acquaintances and placing their regular orders. For everyone else, today seemed an ordinary day.

Chris read the same article on the front page of the business section three times. The words floated around in his consciousness without taking hold. He checked his watch; where was she? Whenever the door opened, a waft of air brushed his face and he would

28

look up, only to be disappointed. What if she couldn't make it? They hadn't exchanged cell numbers and she had no way to contact him. What if she had changed her mind? He recalled last night's conversation. He'd been the one to suggest getting together — perhaps she'd agreed out of politeness and had no intention of coming. How could he assume that she would be as eager as he was to reconnect?

****

Montreal – August, 1982

When his shift was over, Chris ripped off his shirt and wiped his dripping body with the sweaty garment. The loading doors had been open all day in the warehouse and the large industrial fans had been blowing at full force, but there had been no escape from the heavy humidity. Usually, the temperature dropped by evening, but not today. All he could think of was getting home, taking a shower, and cooling off before going out. The guys wanted to meet at Winston's, which was fine with him; he didn't care where they went, as long as they caught the action. Chris jumped in his rusted Chevy and rolled down the windows. He'd have just enough time to drive home, shower, and grab a bite before meeting the gang downtown.

The hot streets of Montreal came alive in the summertime, particularly as night approached and the students hung up their summer-job hats to join their friends for a night of mindless, unbridled fun. Crescent Street was the place to be — a guaranteed good time. Chris and his friends cast off their insecurities when they came into contact with the contagious energy in the downtown streets. For a few hours, they could evade the bridge to maturity and allow themselves a brief escape from their uncertain futures. Chris reveled in the last few nights of his carefree summer. Soon he'd be swamped by demanding university courses and dreaded domestic chores. Gone would be the days when home-cooked dinners would be placed before him, when clean clothes would miraculously appear in his drawers, and when accommodation would be free. Chris's mother had even tried to teach him some household skills to prepare him for his new life, but he'd simply laughed and said, "Don't worry, Mom, I'll figure it out," his outward confidence masking his inner doubt.

Winston's rocked. The music, the people, and the general rowdiness of the place appealed to Chris's group. They had to wait forty minutes to get in, but no one complained because half the fun was socializing in the streets. Chris bumped into friends and acquaintances, and the time passed quickly as they horsed around with each other under the commercially lit sky.

The Montreal night-scene opened the gate to uncensored freedom. Bars were like high school dances with no chaperones, no curfews, and no protection from the consequences of over-drinking and reckless behaviour. The risks were ever-present, barely acknowledged. Chris and his buddies had been lucky; they hadn't smashed their cars after a night of drinking or landed unconscious after a street brawl like some of their peers — sometimes Chris wondered how they'd made it through their teens unscathed.

By the time the bouncer waved them in, Chris's friends were already high, having smoked a few joints in the line outside. They sat down at the crowded bar, ordered beers, passed cigarettes around, and flirted with a female bartender. Chris watched and listened with amusement; his friends' audacity amazed him.

Taking a drag from his cigarette, Chris scanned the bar for people he knew. Across the room he spotted an alluring girl who looked familiar; where could he have met her before? He feigned enthusiasm in his buddies' conversation by laughing and joking with them while glancing in her direction. She smiled as she mingled with her friends but Chris saw something sad in her eyes, or was it his imagination? Her mahogany shoulder-length hair was parted in the middle and hung straight down either side of her face. She was wearing all black, unlike most of the women in the bar who wore bright summer colours. When she smiled her face softened, but her eyes appeared wistful, even from a distance. Chris tried not to stare, but he couldn't resist — she was so damned attractive; the type of girl the guys in high school would consider untouchable, too pretty to dare ask out. Sometimes those girls would end up with no date at all to the dances because nobody would risk being humiliated by rejection. It was always safer to pursue the ordinary girls, nice enough and not out of their league. But this was not high school, this was the real world, and perhaps it was time to grow up and take a chance.

"Hey Christopher, you're not listening!"

"Back to earth, buddy, we need your input here."

His friends were bantering about who had the best chance to win a woman's attention across the bar. She was much older, probably thirty, and provocatively attractive. Chris joined in the speculation while stealing looks at the girl who had captivated him. Was this the *coup de foudre* that hopeless romantics referred to? Couldn't be. Love at first sight was a ridiculous concept that only happened in the movies, not something that happened to real people.

The music increased a notch in volume and the lights dimmed; an indication that midnight was approaching. He picked up his beer, his third, stopping short of taking a drink. He'd had enough. From the corner of his eye he saw the girl get up from her table. Should he ask her to dance before somebody else did? Approach her and make conversation? If he was going to do anything, this was his chance. Her back was to him, exposing her toned shoulder muscles as she spoke to the group. She had a tennis player's physique, or a swimmer's. Was she taller than him?

Chris summoned his courage and got up from his stool. Thankfully, the redhead was busy talking to the guy on her left and he could steal away without seeming rude. But the girl he had his eye on removed her purse from the back of a chair and headed toward the door. Shit. Without a word to his friends, Chris navigated his way through the crowds toward the exit, hoping to catch up with her. What would he say? Would she think he was harassing her? If he let her sail out that door he would always wonder what she was like, what he may have lost. Her face was already imprinted in his mind and erasing it was unimaginable. She darted through the maze of people and Chris had to pick up his pace to avoid losing her to the night.

When he reached her on the street he was almost out of breath. "You leaving too?" he said, trying to sound nonchalant. "It was getting really loud in there, wasn't it?"

She seemed surprised or perhaps annoyed; then a slight smile emerged. He grinned because he didn't know what else to say.

"Do I know you? You look familiar," she said.

"I've been asking myself the same thing. Maybe we met in a previous life." Oh brother, why did he have to go and say such a stupid thing?

"You never know."

A group of boisterous young men passed by, singing and laughing like drunken fans at a ball game. Someone yelled, "Hey wait up," and knocked Chris's back with a thud as he scrambled to get ahead on the busy sidewalk. Chris rubbed his shoulder but didn't let on how much it hurt.

"I'm Chris Lambert." He held out his hand. She must think he was such a fool, with his exaggerated formality.

"Denise. Hi." She shook his hand. "You're right about the bar, it was way too loud in there."

When she spoke she tilted her head in a way that invited further conversation. At least she hadn't rebuffed him. "Do you come here often?" he asked. What a stupid, stupid thing to say. He hoped it was too dark for her to see him blush.

"Kind of. It's fun coming downtown. Besides, there's not much else to do in Montreal at night."

"I know what you mean." The day-time heat had succumbed to night-time dampness and Chris noticed Denise shivering. Fighting the urge to put his arm around her, he pushed his hands deep into his pockets. "It's not too late. Do you want to go somewhere quiet for a drink?"

She hesitated. He hadn't lost her yet. "C'mon, we could try to figure out how, or if, we know each other."

"OK, but only a quick drink, I have to get up early in the morning for work."

Chris took her arm, shocked by his own boldness, and to his amazement, she didn't resist. They walked down Crescent Street and stopped at a quaint bistro-style restaurant with a yellow awning over the entrance. Through the window they saw an intimate setting with a few diners lingering over coffee.

"I've had dinner here with my parents," Chris said. "It's a good spot and they're still open."

They sat at a small table by the window, which was set for dinner with a white linen table cloth and a small vase of flowers. A tea-light candle burned on the side.

"Would you like some wine?" he asked.

She nodded.

Chris requested the wine list, self-assuredly, like his father would have done. He didn't know much about wine but he perused the list with great concentration. The bottles were all expensive and he didn't have much money. Never mind, this was not a time to skimp. He recognized a type of wine his parents drank and decided to splurge, ordering a bottle. Denise's eyes came alive, they almost glistened. Was she laughing at his awkwardness playing the grown-up or was she genuinely pleased to be there sitting with him? She looked stylish in her black outfit, in contrast to his khaki pants and faded blue polo shirt. Why hadn't he worn a nicer shirt? He had a closet full of decent shirts at home that his mother always pestered him to wear. The worn edge of his sleeve suddenly bothered him and he rolled it up, trying to hide the imperfection.

"So," she said. "Where could we have met before?"

"Where are you from?" he asked.

"The West Island. How about you?"

"South Shore. Couldn't have met through school then."

"I've only bypassed the South Shore on my way to the Townships."

"And I only go your way to get to the airport," he said.

Denise laughed. "I guess we don't know each other then."

"Now we do."

"We do?" she said.

"You're so pretty." The words had slipped out unexpectedly and she'd probably think he was hitting on her. Why didn't he think a minute before opening his mouth? What a moron.

She fiddled with her necklace, her eyes hinting pleasure. "Thank you."

The waiter served the wine. What should he say now? What should they talk about? God, this was unnerving. He was miles out of his element; he never should have brought her here. In the bar, all he had wanted to do was to talk to her, to be close to her, and now that they were here alone, he couldn't think of one damn intelligent thing to say.

"Summer's almost over," she said. "What are your plans?"

"I'm going to the University of British Columbia to study business," he said.

"Vancouver's beautiful."

"Yeah, and I wanted to be close to the mountains. I love skiing. If I could find a career on the slopes, I'd be in heaven." In fact, if she were with him, then he'd definitely be in heaven. "How about you?"

"I'm going to Paris in a couple of days."

"Wow. Paris."

"Yeah, I'm pretty excited."

"For how long?" Paris was too far away to fathom.

"Four years. Or more. I'm studying at the Sorbonne."

"Great." But what could he expect? He lifted his glass. "To our adventures."

"Yes, to our adventures," they said, clinking glasses.

"You leaving anyone behind?" he asked.

She raised her eyebrows.

"Boyfriend, I mean."

Her eyes sank. "Nope. My boyfriend and I broke up last month. I don't have to worry about that."

Chris felt elated and deflated at the same time. She was unattached yet on the rebound...and she was going away. But then, he was leaving too; hooking up was impossible anyway. "I've always wanted to go to France, myself."

Her face lit up. "It's something I've been dying to do since I was twelve. I can hardly believe I'm going and..."

Chris imagined himself walking down the streets of Paris holding her hand. How cool it would be to travel around Europe with her. They could get Euro-rail passes and backpack their way around, like many of his friends had done. And skiing together in the Alps would be amazing. If she didn't ski, he could teach her. They could meet at Chamonix or somewhere like that during the holidays. Was he crazy? What was he thinking, getting carried away like that? She was still speaking and he had completely zoned out. Man, was he ever dense.

"Do you think you'll ever come back here?" he said.

"Who knows? I'll see where life takes me."

The more they talked, the more he was drawn to her. But what could he do about it? A few glasses of wine together and some friendly conversation would have to be the extent of his fantasy.

At 2:00 a.m. the restaurant was closing and the waiter gave him the bill. Chris paid it with the last few dollars in his pocket — the best expenditure he'd made all summer. Outside, the vitality in the street felt invigorating. The alcohol combined with the physical chemistry, and the emotional connection that Chris felt, spurred on his courage. He put his arm around Denise's shoulders and said, "Is there any chance you'd come home with me tonight? I mean, so we can talk some more. My parents are in the country and the house is free."

Her body stiffened. He prepared himself for rejection. She didn't respond right away and for a long moment Chris hung onto a fragment of hope.

"Don't feel any pressure, I just want to spend more time with you. You can sleep in my bed and I'll sleep somewhere else."

She'd likely decline, but he couldn't say good-bye without trying. She rambled on about having to work in the morning and how much she had to do to prepare for her trip.

There was still a chance.

"We can have some iced tea, listen to music, and fall asleep in the living room, or wherever. I'll drive you to work in the morning."

"Hmm. I don't think it's…well, all right."

He couldn't believe it. She had said yes! "Great…super. My car's a few blocks from here. Do you mind walking?" He was talking a mile a minute. "That's great," he said again, his voice deeper than usual, in an effort to conceal his astonishment. The idea of surging in an unknown, precarious direction with Denise charged him. He wanted to pull her close and kiss her; all jumbled into one thought was the desire to make love to her and to be with her forever. Such powerful feelings were new to him and he felt foolish for allowing himself to venture there.

Someone called his name from a distance. He turned his head and saw his friends from the bar approaching.

"You took off on us, Lambert! What's the deal?" Bob said. He looked at Denise. "Who's your friend?"

Chris glared at them and made a quick introduction. They all said hello without shaking hands.

"Where you guys goin'?" asked Jonathon.

"Nowhere," Chris said. "How about you?"

"Don't know," Bob said, staring at Denise. "We'll probably hit Craven's for one more beer. You wanna come?"

"No thanks," Chris said. "We're getting some air."

Denise remained silent, looking embarrassed. Chris stabbed his friends with a deadly stare, hoping they'd get the hint; he didn't want his magical moment with Denise to be blighted by their presence for one more second.

The guys staggered away and Bob said, in a sing-song tone, loud enough for them to hear, "Chris is gonna score tonight!"

****

Chris felt a tap on his shoulder. When he looked up, he saw Denise.

"Hi," she said. "Sorry for being late. I got held up by a phone call." Her smile was dazzling.

He stood up. "No, no, don't worry. I just got here myself. What can I get you?"

"A regular coffee, please. With cream." She started to remove her raincoat and Chris reached over to help, placing it over the back of an extra chair.

"Have a seat," he said, pulling out the chair for her. "I'll be right back."

The coffee shop was still busy but it seemed like they were the only ones there. Chris watched her read the newspaper while he waited in line. Her dark shoulder-length hair covered her face as she leaned forward. Then she looked up and caught his furtive glance. She smiled and he smiled back.

Chapter Four

Denise read the same headline about twenty-five times: 'Parents to be held accountable for the misdemeanours of their children.' It was like her brain had frozen, preventing the words from penetrating. All she could think about was how strange it was to be with Chris again. Such an unlikely thing to happen—what was the meaning behind their coincidental reunion? Chris arrived with her coffee and placed it on the table. "Thank you," she said, picking up the cup between her palms.

"Has life been good to you these past two-and-a-half decades?" he asked as he sat down across from her.

"Hmm, how does one summarize twenty-five years? Overall, I would have to say, yes, life has been good. There have been ups and downs, but I can't complain."

"That's how it goes, I suppose." Observing her hand, he said, "You're married, I see."

"As are you." She pointed to his wedding band. "Do you have any children?"

Chris nodded and took a sip of his espresso. "We have three girls. Our eldest is twenty-one, from my first marriage, the other two are ten and seven. And you?"

"Three boys," she said. "Eleven, nine and six."

"You have your hands full," he said.

"So do you." She wanted to ask him about his first marriage; what had gone wrong, but it was none of her business; this was merely a friendly chat, not an interrogation.

"Tell me about your kids," he said.

She dug into her purse and pulled out their wallet-sized school pictures. "This is Thomas, my eldest. He's into computers and woodwork. This is Luc. He's the sports fanatic. And this is my baby, Martin, the wild and adventurous one."

Chris looked at the pictures, at Denise, and once again at the pictures. "I see you in all of them, especially the eyes."

The coffee shop was no longer as busy and Denise lowered her voice. Not that anyone was listening to her conversation, but she was accustomed to strangers stretching an ear out of curiosity. "What about your family?"

"Monique's at college and the two younger ones keep my wife and me running. They're spitfires," he said, breaking into a smile.

"You would've been a young man when you had your first child," she said.

"Twenty-three."

She never would have expected Chris to settle down at such a young age. What about all those ski-bum dreams? Back then he had remarked that he didn't see himself married until at least thirty. The fact that he had changed his mind aroused in Denise a strange sense of betrayal.

"How did you make that leap from studies to marriage to baby so fast?" she asked. Bracing herself, she waited for him to say, 'I fell in love.'

"It's a long story and a rather sordid tale."

"I've got time if you do. I'd love to hear your sordid tale."

****

"You asked for it." He took off his jacket and hung it on the back of his chair.

Where should he begin? Years had passed since he had told anyone the circumstances of his marriage to Kendra, a topic he usually avoided.

"I should start by saying the marriage was a mistake right from the beginning." He'd have to be careful not to sound too negative; this was Monique's mother after all. "I got married because the woman I was dating one summer got pregnant."

"So you dropped everything and married her. Very noble," Denise said.

"But also naive."

"How's that?"

"It was a loveless marriage and a disaster from the start."

"At least you gave it a try."

"I felt I had no choice. Kendra wanted to keep the baby and I couldn't, in good conscience, leave her to raise our child alone."

"So you came to Cleveland?"

"He nodded. I quit my graduate studies and moved here to join her."

"The marriage was short-lived?"

"Yes. I tried hard at the beginning to make it work, and she did too, in her own way. But I was so busy with my job and trying to support the family that I didn't even realize how miserable I was."

"And Kendra?"

"I think she was even more miserable than me. Kendra had been a waitress when we met and was a very social person. After the baby came, she stayed home and tried to play house but she felt trapped. I encouraged her to find a job if that would make her happy, or even go back to school. She had no interest."

"An impossible situation."

"And she despised me, no matter what I did."

"What about your daughter?"

"I think she loved Monique, but didn't know how to be a parent. She was young—barely nineteen when Monique was born."

"And you weren't much older."

"No. I was a kid who had led a pretty cushy life." Chris looked in his paper coffee cup and saw that it was empty. He brought it to his lips anyway, hoping for one more drop, but it was completely dry. He was getting too personal. This was not how he had intended their morning discussion to go; instead of learning about Denise's life, he was carrying on about himself.

"What happened?" Denise asked, luring him back to the conversation with her inquisitive eyes.

Chris could feel his body tensing while he talked about his ex-wife. He told Denise how Kendra blamed him for her unhappiness and how erratic her behaviour could be. At times she'd play sweetly with Monique and at other times she'd ignore her completely. She would go out a lot, leaving the baby with neighbours, and at times, refused to speak to Chris for weeks. He found himself juggling both the job and the parenting role almost single-handedly.

"But you hung on?" Denise said.

"I didn't want to fail."

"It's hard when a relationship ends, no matter what the circumstances," she said.

"The final catalyst was finding out, when Monique was five years old, that she wasn't my biological child." His mouth was parched and all he could think of was water, but it didn't occur to him to get some.

Denise gasped. "How did you find that out?"

"Inadvertently — through a blood test one day when Monique had an accident and needed a blood transfusion."

"You must have been livid."

"I was, at first. My life had been completely sabotaged by this lie." Chris pressed the coffee cup between his palms and flattened it.

"A nightmare," Denise said. "And that was the end?" She shook her head sympathetically.

"It didn't simply end. It crashed through the ground. Ironically, I think Kendra was relieved. The deception must have been eating away at her and was probably fuelling her hatred toward me." He slowly rolled up the paper cup like a cigar.

"What about your daughter?"

"The only bright light in my life was Monique." His face lit up when he said this. "She was an absolute joy. I never would have thought a child could bring that much happiness into my life."

"And when you found out she wasn't your child?"

"Nothing changed. She would always be my daughter."

"Did Monique know the truth?"

Chris nodded. "But I tried to make her feel as safe as possible. I told her that blood couldn't link us together any more tightly because she was permanently attached to my heart."

Denise leaned into the table. "What happened to Kendra?"

"I don't know. She left us both."

"Disappeared? She didn't even maintain contact with her daughter?"

"She'd send the occasional present on Monique's birthday and a letter from time to time, but basically, yes, she disappeared."

Denise frowned. "How could a mother ever leave her child?"

He couldn't explain it. Kendra had told him that she was sinking and had to claw her way out. Escape meant survival. But to Chris, Monique was the trade-off to freedom, and she was worth it. "I don't know," he said.

"And how did Monique cope with all of this?"

"She was incredible. She never gave me a second of trouble. I think she knew as well as I did that it was sink or swim for both of us."

"She sounds courageous...and strong."

"I'd love you to meet her some day." What a strange thing to blurt out, and how presumptuous. He imagined the introduction: 'Monique, I'd like you to meet the love of my life, Denise. She's the one that got away.' He cleared his throat.

"That would be nice," Denise said.

Denise swept her hair behind one ear, a habit he remembered from the past. The image of that very motion, all those years ago, played back in his mind. She watched him with intensity, like she understood his relinquished pain. Could the soulful connection he felt with the woman in front of him be authentic? For a man who considered human relations a matter of practicality, including matters of the heart, he was amazed by this revelation. He didn't know what to say next.

"Sounds like you got over the bridge and it didn't collapse," she said.

He nodded. "Life is much better. You fumble along until you figure things out."

"And sometimes that takes a lifetime," Denise said.

"Sadly, yes." He excused himself and went to the counter to get some water. The dryness in his mouth was making it impossible to speak clearly. He took two large gulps. Why the hell had he launched into this whole Kendra episode? It was uncharacteristic of him to carry on like that, but Denise had been so inquisitive and gracious.

When he returned to the table he said, "I've monopolized this entire conversation. I still don't know anything about you." He wanted to know everything about her: her job, her children, her life in Montreal, and her adventures in Paris. "When can we see each other again?" Perspiration seeped from his body.

"I'm supposed to fly out this evening, but I may be able to change the ticket to a later flight. Would you be able to meet for a drink after work?"

He ran through his commitments in his mind. The girls had soccer and he'd promised to take them—Laura would do it if necessary. "Yes," he said, "drinks after work. Sounds good." He gave her the address of a place a few blocks from his office and they agreed to meet at 6:30. After a hasty good-bye, she flew out the door.

Chris watched Denise cross the street. She hadn't changed much over time; or was it how she affected him that hadn't changed? A quarter of a century had passed, yet he was drawn to her in the exact way he had been when they first met. What was he doing seeing her again that evening; what was he launching into? But it didn't take much to convince himself that these rendezvous' were harmless, that there was nothing wrong with two old friends getting together to reminisce. Besides, she was leaving that evening, returning to another life in another country.

****

Montreal—August, 1982

By the time they arrived at Chris's parents' house it was almost 3:00 a.m. Denise was surprised at herself for having agreed to come, never having done anything that impetuous before. Her mother would have a fit. But she had a good feeling about this guy—a really good feeling. Chris put a record on and got some iced tea while Denise walked around the living room looking at the photographs. It was like viewing a gallery of his family's life: baby pictures, birthdays, school portraits, graduation, first communion, and Christmas scattered throughout the room. A picture of Chris when he was a young boy, perhaps seven or eight years of age, caught her attention.

"Soooo cute!" she said. "And you've hardly changed."

"Embarrassing," he said. "My mother has us on display like some sort of china collection."

Denise laughed. "I love family photos. They give me a sense of history." She studied a large family portrait displayed on the grand piano. "Are these your parents and your sister?"

"Yeah, about ten years ago."

"Your parents look like nice people." She suddenly missed her own father who had died when she was eight.

"Thanks." Chris took her hand and led her to the sofa. They sat down and he put a cushion on his lap, motioning for her to lay her head on it. They reclined quietly and Chris stroked her hair while she lay motionless listening to the music. Carole King's mellow voice soothed her nerves. "Where you lead, I will follow," the song went, "anywhere that you take me to…" Happiness surged through her core, a feeling she had long forgotten, or had never truly experienced.

Chapter Five

Laura was in the basement organizing the girls' craft room when she heard the phone ring, and she raced up the stairs to answer it before the machine did.

"Hello," she said, panting.

"Hey, Laur. How's your day going?"

"Oh, Chris, I thought you might be the school calling. Sophie was coughing this morning and I don't know if she'll manage to get through the whole day."

"Fever?"

"No, no fever."

"Good. I wanted to check with you about this evening. I know I said I'd take the girls to soccer but a business thing's come up."

"Shoot," Laura said. "With Sophie feeling crummy I thought she could stay home with me while you took Tanya."

"Couldn't Tanya go with a friend?"

"I guess that's the way it'll have to be. But she'll be disappointed."

"She'll be fine."

"When will you be home?"

"Eight, nine—not sure."

When the conversation was over, Laura made several calls before finding someone who could take Tanya to the game. Having to juggle plans at the last minute because of Chris's unreliable schedule was one of her biggest gripes these days. 'Sometimes I really hate his job,' she said to herself as she lugged a load of laundry to the basement.

Laura waited eagerly for the girls to arrive home from school, anxious to find out how Sophie had made out and feeling regretful for having sent her at all. The school bus arrived at 4:00 sharp and she watched the girls trudge to the door from the hall window. Sophie lagged a few steps behind her sister, her head drooping. As Laura had expected, Sophie's nose was dripping and her cough had deteriorated.

"Sweetie, why didn't you tell your teacher you were sick? She could've called me to come get you," Laura said, removing the backpack from her daughter's shoulders.

"I didn't wanna make you drive all the way out there, Mommy. And I'm not that sick."

Laura felt her forehead. "Oh, yes you are. I want you to go upstairs, get out of your uniform and crawl into bed."

She coughed. "Can I watch TV in your bed?"

"Yes you may."

"Yay!" she yelled out, which prompted a coughing fit. She coughed the entire way up the stairs.

"No fair!" said Tanya. "Why does *she* get to watch TV?" She threw her backpack on the floor.

"You know why, young lady. I'd like you to get changed and when you come back to the kitchen I'll make you a snack. Then homework."

"Not if Sophie's watching TV. I'm not gonna do stupid homework."

Laura ignored her remark and went to check on Sophie. She was already in pajamas, her clothes strewn all over the floor. "Get under the covers, sweetie, and I'll be back in a few minutes with some hot lemonade." Sophie pouted endearingly. Amazing how adorable they were when they were sick. If the roles had been reversed and Tanya was suffering with the flu, Sophie would be the one downstairs fussing about the injustice of it all, as if being sick was such a great privilege.

"Time for homework," Laura said, entering the kitchen.

Tanya scrunched her face. Laura was about to tell her that she'd be going to soccer with the Jamesons instead of her dad, but then thought better of it. Chris coming home late had sure messed things up.

"What's for dinner?" Tanya said.

"I don't know yet."

"Can we have pizza?"

"No."

"Why not?"

"Because I said so." But then she reconsidered. Maybe pizza would circumvent the tantrum that was sure to erupt. And the whining and complaining was wearing her down.

"When's Daddy coming home?"

"Late."

"Why?"

"He's working."

"What about soccer?"

"You're going with the Jamesons."

"Noooooo!"

Laura left the room.

When the Jamesons came to pick Tanya up, the house had recovered its equilibrium. Tanya had had her pizza and finished her homework, and Sophie was dozing. Laura had forgotten to ask Chris if he would be eating out. She called him on his cell phone to check, but there was no answer. She made some chicken, rice and zucchini and prepared a plate for Chris to heat up in the microwave if he hadn't eaten. Her own dinner consisted of a skinless chicken breast, zucchini and salad—no rice; avoiding white carbs was her latest strategy for weight loss. Some wine would be nice. She found half a bottle left in the fridge from the other day. A glass of wine might relax her. The moment she sat down to eat her dinner Sophie called out, her tearful cries interrupted by a hacking cough. Laura left the meal on the table but brought the wine glass with her.

"I'm cold, Mommy."

"It's because of the fever. I'll get you some medicine."

"No," she cried, "I hate that stuff."

When Laura finally returned to her dinner, Tanya arrived home. She was filthy from the soccer game and needed a good scrub in the bath. By the time the bath was done, teeth were brushed and she had tucked Tanya in bed, it was after 10:00. Laura poured herself another glass of wine and sat down to eat. Already reheated twice in the microwave, the chicken tasted like plastic and the zucchini had lost all semblance of itself. The crisp salad, which she had tossed with a light vinaigrette, had shriveled into an unpalatable green mush. Starving, she finished the entire meal and then had three scoops of maple walnut ice cream for dessert.

By 11:00, Chris still wasn't home. Laura settled into bed with a new book and was getting into it when the phone rang.

"Hello."

"I hope I'm not calling too late."

"Monique, hi. No, no. It's not too late. I'm reading in bed." She propped herself up against the headboard.

"How is everybody?" Monique asked.

"Sophie has the flu but otherwise we're good. How are your exams going?"

"Not bad. I've got one left and then I'm coming home."

"We can't wait to see you. The girls have been asking daily when you're arriving."

Whenever Monique went back to college after a visit, the entire family would go into a slump. The girls worshipped their older half-sister and Chris adored her. Laura was never able to formally adopt her because Kendra was roaming around somewhere, but right from the beginning she had considered Monique like her own daughter.

"Five more days and counting," Monique said.

"Do you need help packing up? Your father said he'd be happy to come out and get you."

"Actually, I already have my transportation organized. A friend here has a van and he's offered to bring me."

"Excellent. When can we expect you?"

"Saturday evening."

"Will you be here for dinner?"

"I think so."

"Then tell me what you'd like. We'll have a special meal. And invite your friend too."

"You're the best, Laura. Hmm. How about your yummy roast pork, baked potatoes, and that cheesy broccoli dish, with the crispy bits on top? The girls like that, don't they?"

"Your dad does too. And for dessert?"

"Pumpkin pie."

"You've got it." Monique always chose pumpkin pie, no matter what time of year it was and Laura loved to make it for her. "I'd pass you on to your dad, but he's working late. Any message?"

"Just give him a big hug for me."

Laura put down the receiver and nestled into the covers. Having Monique home would bring some welcome cheer to the household. She was such a pleasure to have around and always helpful with the girls. When Laura first met Chris, Monique was only nine years old. They had made it through all the stages, even the teenage years, without any difficulty. She was always such a reliable and responsible girl and had never given them trouble. Considering her younger daughters' penchant for histrionics, Laura wondered if they would pass through adolescence with as little drama. Monique was a perfect role model, a treasure, in fact.

Chapter Six

Denise paid the driver and got out of the cab. An expansive purple awning flashed the name of the restaurant in bright white letters. *Fizzazz.* She looked through the window and saw a long, narrow bar with a glass counter and black leather high-back barstools. Glancing at her reflection in the sheen of the glass door, she made a quick adjustment to her hair. She opened the door and let two people out before entering herself. Then she let the door shut without going inside. Did she really need to do this? They had had their chat in the morning, learned about each other's lives — what more was there to say? When the door swung open and a woman exited, Denise took a deep breath and slipped in. Music played softly, soothing her nerves. A model-esque hostess wearing skinny black pants and a fitted black tee-shirt with a wide belt approached. Denise smiled at her and said, "I'm meeting someone here." She scanned the bar area, hoping to be there first so as to have an opportunity to freshen up, but Chris was sitting at the end of the bar waiting. "There he is." She straightened her posture and headed his way, flashing her trademark 'Montreal's Alive' smile.

Chris jumped down from the stool and greeted her with a kiss on both cheeks. He took her carry-on, placed it on the floor between the seats, and motioned for her to sit down.

"I'm glad you could come. No problem changing flights?"

"Not at all." Actually, she hadn't booked another flight because she had no idea how long their tête-à-tête would last. She'd take her chances at the airport.

Chris ordered drinks, a scotch for himself and a martini for Denise. They positioned their barstools, which swiveled, partially facing each other, partially facing the bar.

"How was your day?" Chris asked.

"Lots of running around, but productive." In reality, it had only been semi-productive. The earlier meeting with Chris had thrown her off and she had found it difficult to focus. Thank goodness Nicole had been there to take notes. "How about you?"

"Hectic, but also productive."

"What business are you in?" she asked.

"Merchant banking. My partner, Tony Salvo, and I set up a firm together about eleven years ago."

"Do you like what you do?" she asked. The next question slipped out before he had even answered the first, "Successful?" Denise grimaced at her tactlessness.

"We're doing all right. We've been fortunate. And yes, I enjoy my job."

Then Chris asked her a strange question, out of the blue. "Are you happy, Denise? Is your life everything you had hoped it to be?"

How on earth would she answer that one? "Yes. Absolutely. I'm very happy—my life couldn't be happier, really."

"Good," he said. The bartender delivered their drinks and Chris picked up his glass. "To our reunion. And to your happiness."

"Likewise," she said. She felt like a schoolgirl—awkward. Her job was to make other people feel comfortable and to ask questions, to entertain. But here she was, stumped for words and utterly self-conscious.

"How was that trip to Paris in...?

"August, 1982," she said.

"Yes, that's right, twenty-five years ago. You were excited about starting a new life in a new place. I remember how animated you were when you talked about your upcoming adventure."

"Paris was indeed an adventure." She took a big sip from her drink.

"Tell me everything." He leaned back in his chair and crossed his arms as if ready to hear a dissertation.

Did she really want to rehash those nasty memories? Perhaps she could gloss over the unpleasant things and concentrate on the positive; yes, that's what she'd do.

"The city absolutely lived up to my expectations. It's fabulous. Have you been to Paris?"

"Never. I'd like to take my kids some day, do the whole European thing."

"Me too. Francois and I have talked about bringing the boys. France, Germany, Switzerland, Austria...such beautiful countries. And the skiing—"

"Skiing in the Alps has always been a dream of mine," Chris said.

"When I lived in France I skied a lot. We had a chalet in Chamonix and...well...I'd think of you because I remembered how passionate you were about the sport."

"What was it like over there—in the city, on the slopes, at the university?"

She paused. "Long story."

"I'd like to hear it, from the beginning." He playfully pointed his finger at her. "It's your turn now."

She paused. "OK. I'll try to give you a simple recap, from what I remember. When I first arrived, I stayed with a French family in the suburbs and took the train to school."

"At the Sorbonne, right?"

"Yes. Art history and Literature. I loved it. And I earned my room and board by working part-time as a nanny."

Chris's eyes widened. "I can't imagine you as a nanny. How long did you do that for?"

"The plan was to stay with them for three years, until I finished my degree."

"Sounds like a good arrangement."

"It was. Until..." She asked the bartender for some water. Why was she getting into this? She proceeded to tell Chris about the family she had lived with. The workload had been minimal and she had been generously included in holiday gatherings, and even in the couple's social events. She didn't feel at all like an 'au pair,' which was her official title. The mother treated her like a sister and the father was a helpful advisor; the children were respectful and appreciative. Her situation couldn't have been better.

"Near the end of my second term, in the spring, the youngest child became ill and was hospitalized with a serious infection that became untreatable. That's when everything fell apart."

"How old was the child?"

"Only five. It was heartbreaking. For weeks no one knew from one day to the next if he would survive."

"And did he?"

"I don't know." Denise's eyes welled up. She cleared her throat and sipped her martini.

"How come?" Chris said.

Denise told him about the terrible stress in the house and how the mother spent most of her days and often nights in the hospital with her little boy. Denise tried as best she could to keep things running normally in the home and even put her studies on hold while helping out. The father became depressed because he felt helpless and Denise would try to console him by making nice dinners and listening to his problems. He would tell her about his work, his dreams, and about private marital issues. One day, when the child's condition had deteriorated, his father came home from the hospital in a disturbed state. He embraced Denise with desperation and groped her uncontrollably. Shocked by his sudden aggression, she tried to push him away; but before she knew it, he was ripping off her blouse.

Denise stirred her martini. "I can't believe I'm telling you all this."

"What a frightening situation for a young woman."

"It was horrifying."

"What happened next?" Chris asked.

"I locked myself in the bedroom and waited until morning to come out."

"And the father?"

"He was in the kitchen when I came down and his eyes were bloodshot. Like he hadn't slept all night." Denise clasped her hands together beneath the bar, trying to stop their trembling.

"Were you afraid of him?"

"At that point I only felt pity. His son was dying and he was beside himself with grief. He was so vulnerable and I expected him to apologize, to be remorseful. I thought he'd try to set things right."

"And?"

"No apology. He told me to pack up my things and leave, that I wasn't needed anymore."

"Bastard," Chris said.

"The worst thing was that he commanded me not to contact his family ever again, and if I did, he would tell his wife that I had been trying to seduce him in her absence."

"That's harassment. No worse—abuse!"

"My mistake was trusting him, not seeing this coming. I never even found out what happened to poor Stephan. When I called the hospital they told me he had been moved somewhere else, but they wouldn't tell me where. I checked the obituaries daily but never found his name. I still think of him sometimes, and pray that he's all right." Emotion surged through her and Denise blinked hard to keep the tears from escaping.

"Sounds like a helluva first year in Paris. You didn't consider going home after that?" He reached out his hand as if to take hers but they were still clasped under the table. He picked up his glass.

"Never. I couldn't let that man destroy my dreams."

The bartender approached and asked if they'd like to move to the dining room.

"Shall we?" Chris said.

"I should get going soon." In fact, she should have already left. She'd said too much as it was. "I'll stay for a quick bite, but then I have to run." The martini had gone to her head and she was hungry. Some food would settle her down before leaving.

When the plates were placed in front of them, Denise smiled at the waiter and then at Chris. "Lovely," she said. The pink salmon filet and the asparagus bundle tied together with ribbons of yellow and red pepper strips, presented like a picture. Miniature new potatoes had been cut into spirals, and a golden puree adorned the edge of the plate. Chris had ordered the same thing along with a bottle of California Chardonnay. "This looks too good to eat."

"It's the first meal we've ever shared," Chris said. He held up his wine glass. "To our first dinner together."

For a fleeting moment, Denise didn't breathe. In front of her, she saw a young man, barely nineteen years old, who was telling her about his hopes and dreams for the future. The years in between didn't exist, yet Chris's graying hair and his seasoned skin proved otherwise. She picked up her fork and broke off a piece of salmon, but when she lifted it to her mouth her hunger was gone. Chewing was difficult and every subsequent bite of her meal was harder to ingest. Why had she told Chris about the French family? She'd made herself sound vulnerable and naïve — definitely not how she wanted to be perceived.

"Tell me about your job," Chris said.

Denise noticed that Chris redirected the conversation back to her, no matter what they discussed. Generally, she avoided speaking about herself and let others do the talking, but Chris had somehow managed to reverse the roles.

"I love my job," she said. "A lot of pressure comes with being in the public eye, but I thrive on it."

"Are you a big television personality?"

"I wouldn't say big, but I do have a certain following, particularly among women. It's a daytime events show that covers a range of topics, from gardening and decorating to local events and international concerns."

"Sounds interesting." Chris topped up their wine glasses. "How did you get into that?"

"I fell into it. When I came back from France I needed a job and my mother happened to know someone who worked at the station. For eight years I worked as an assistant to the host of a similar show, and when she moved on to other things the network hired me to take her place. I was lucky."

"I don't believe in luck," Chris said.

Denise shrugged. "I did work hard, there's no question, but at the same time I was at the right place at —"

"I see a woman who's strong and determined. You created your own luck, I'm convinced of that."

"Thanks for the vote of confidence," she said. Interesting that her husband, Francois, had never used the words strong and determined to describe her. Her mother was the only one among her intimates who attributed those characteristics to her.

"We create our path," Chris said.

"Not always."

"I'm not saying that we can control everything that happens, but self-determination has a big role in who we become and what we do with our lives."

"I agree…to an extent." She thought about some of the choices she had made in her life. Going to Paris, her various relationships, getting married, children—and then she thought of the choices she didn't make, like maintaining contact with Chris. What would have happened if they had kept in touch? Where would she be?

"For instance," he said, "you went to Paris and lived there for…"

"Twelve years."

"You are who you are, partly because you went out on a limb, left a familiar world behind, and broadened your mind. You wouldn't have the job you have, or the family you have, if you hadn't taken that big step."

"That's true. But we can say that about anyone's track. If they hadn't done A then they never could have achieved B."

"And if I hadn't chased you in that bar twenty-five years ago, we wouldn't be sitting here tonight having dinner together." He laughed.

Denise couldn't stop herself from thinking about other hypothetical situations in her life. If she had kept in touch with Chris perhaps she'd be sitting here as his wife, not as a remote memory. If she hadn't found out the truth about Jacques, her long-time boyfriend in Paris, she could still be there living with a liar and a fraud. "You don't believe in fate?" she asked.

"No. You?"

"I'm not sure." The waiter removed their dishes and offered coffee. It was getting late. She should go, should have left a long time ago.

"Do you think fate brought us together last night?" he said.

"I haven't figured that out yet."

"Whether it was by fate or by coincidence, I'm glad that we've had this chance to reconnect."

Was he saying, 'It's been swell, have a nice life?' Denise picked up the napkin from her lap, folded it carefully and placed it neatly on the table in front of her. "On that note, I think I'd better be going. I don't want to miss my flight."

Chris insisted on taking her to the airport. She crossed her legs in the roomy car and stared straight ahead. Her fatigue had lifted during their conversation in the restaurant but now she felt drained. Soon she would be on an airplane, heading back to the life she had painstakingly crafted, one stitch at a time. She watched Chris drive, eyes focused in the darkness, hands grasping the steering wheel, lips taut. Why did she have to bump into him yesterday? Now she would have to say good-bye and sprint off to her future, exactly as she had done twenty-five years ago. Then, the future had been filled with possibility, but this time, it was filled with scripted certainty. Certainty that she would keep doing the same thing every day, certainty that she would watch her kids grow up, only to leave her, and certainty that old age would leave her with an empty shell of a life, one that she had worked hard to enrich with meaning. No, she wouldn't get depressed; she didn't have time to flounder in speculation about the 'what ifs' of life. Her life was full and she was fortunate. She couldn't complain about her lot.

When they arrived at the airport, Chris stopped at the Air Canada entrance and got out of the car. He collected her things from the back seat and helped her with her jacket. "You're shivering," he said.

"It's cool tonight," she said as she pulled her jacket closed. The air was actually quite warm for May and she knew her chill was inflicted by nerves.

Then he said, "I guess this is it. Again."

She smiled. "Yes, I guess it is."

"I have to tell you, I'm loath to say good-bye. We hardly touched on the events of our lives."

"That's true. But the stories could go on and on."

"Or they could come in pieces."

"Easier to process that way."

"We could keep in touch," he said.

"We could send e-mails—"

"Periodically. To say hello—"

"To check in."

"Why not?"

"Why not."

They exchanged business cards. Chris leaned towards Denise to kiss her on the cheek but the kiss turned into a hug. She sunk into his embrace, lingering an instant too long. She detached herself, shuddering.

"It was great to see you, Denise. Please do keep in touch."

"Absolutely," she said. She waved his card in the air and put it in her purse.

He walked backwards towards his car. "Next time, I want to hear about the rest of Paris. We didn't even get past your first year."

"Perhaps," she said, and blew him a kiss. She didn't want to talk about Paris anymore. What she wanted was to learn more about *him*.

Chapter Seven

When Denise arrived home, the house was dark except for a faint glow coming from the dimmed pot-lights in the foyer. She hung up her coat in the hall closet beside the skirt and jacket she had intended to wear at the wine-tasting event. Climbing the stairs in her stockings, she was careful to avoid the steps that were creaky. When she checked on the boys, she found them all sleeping so soundly that tiptoeing had been unnecessary. That night, they all slept in Luc's room, which they only did when either she or Francois was away. The eldest of the three, Thomas, was on Denise's yoga mat, on the floor. Scruffy, the family cat, was curled snuggly in Thomas's duvet, her head barely visible. She didn't budge when Denise rearranged the cover, but her motor-like purr gave life to the dead quiet of the room.

After Denise kissed her children, she stood back to observe them for a moment. Thomas, with his cool demeanour, was still unsure of his bearings, while Martin, the youngest of the three was devilishly independent. And Luc, the middle child, was consumed by sports. Anything that involved a ball, a stick, a racket, and running shoes excited him. Her active brood transformed into tender souls in their serene and motionless state. What would become of them; what kind of men would they grow into? How much longer could she and Francois influence them? They were growing up too fast. Perhaps she should be more tuned into their world and less frantic about her own.

Denise peered into the master bedroom before entering and saw Francois sitting at the small writing table, in his pajamas, working on his laptop. His thick blond hair was tussled. She glanced at the bed; the covers lay in a turbulent heap.

She closed the bedroom door and walked over to him, the thick wool carpet absorbing her gentle tread, and put her hand on his shoulder from behind, trying not to startle him. "Hi."

But he was so engrossed in his work that he flinched at her touch. "Oh, hi. You're later than I expected. Problems with the flight?"

"I got held up at my meeting and had to take the next flight...which was delayed. Sorry, I should have called." She bent down to kiss him.

"How was the trip?"

"Good. I met with some interesting winery owners and invited a couple to come on the show." Should she mention bumping into Chris? No, it was past midnight — too late to get into that; perhaps another time.

"And how was the wine party?"

"You mean the tasting? Interesting. I think you'd have enjoyed it." She removed her jacket and hung it on the back of his chair.

Francois stood up and put his hands on her waist, looking into her face. "I'm sorry, my love, I should have come with you. But work is revving up again and I would have been stressed."

"It's OK," she said.

"I called Marcel about the pipes at the cottage and he's taken care of it." He began to unbutton her blouse.

"Thanks for arranging that." She backed up, yawning, and undid the rest of her buttons. "How'd it go with the boys?"

"Great. Thomas had a big math test yesterday and thinks he did all right. Luc had karate today."

"Did you take him?"

"No, Clara did."

"And how was Martin?"

Francois threw his hands up in the air and grinned. "Up to his usual tricks."

Denise's smile transformed into another yawn.

"Time for bed," Francois said. "I'll finish on the computer while you get ready."

Denise slipped on her pink satin negligee and went to the bathroom to wash up. After removing her make-up and cleansing her face, she stared at herself critically in the mirror. Wrinkles, a few stubborn gray hairs, and bags under her eyes cruelly confronted her. She frowned. Hideous. When she was younger, she had seldom worn make-up because she thought it was unnatural, that it distorted rather than enhanced; funny how her views about beauty had changed. Chris's repeated compliments about her appearance were reassuring, yet unsettling. Was the image he had of her at nineteen deluding reality? Surely he must have noticed a big difference. How would he react if he saw her like this, without make-up, without clothes?

She applied her night-moisturizer and dabbed some horrendously expensive eye-cream under her puffy eyes. Forty-four years old and here she was, already in disrepair. A few years ago she would never have considered cosmetic surgery, but because of her profession, she was forced to re-evaluate. Perhaps she should bring the issue to the forefront—do a show about the pros and cons of artificial beauty.

Francois was waiting for Denise in bed when she came out of the bathroom and she slipped under the sheets, snuggling beside him. While her head was nestled against his shoulder, his hands swept her torso. But she was not in the mood for romance; her mind was too crammed with thoughts of Chris.

"I'm exhausted," she said, "I don't have the energy tonight for…I need to get some sleep." She pulled up the covers and moved away from him.

For a moment, Denise thought he hadn't heard her because he edged closer and began brushing wisps of hair from her forehead. Her body tensed. "It's all right," he whispered, "good night."

Denise relaxed and within minutes Francois was asleep. She tried every sleeping position she could think of and still couldn't get comfortable. The more she tried to push thoughts of Chris out of her mind, the more they insinuated themselves. What if she had sought him out when she had first come back from Paris? Apparently, they were both single then. She had considered trying to locate him at the time, but she hadn't seen him for over a decade and felt awkward about it. Besides, she had been such a mess after the nightmare in Paris with Jacques. She had needed to get her life back in order and to rebuild her confidence. But, what if...

Her thoughts drifted back to the night she had spent with Chris twenty-five years earlier at his parent's house, when he'd been so tender, so loving...

****

Montreal—1982

Chris had switched records and the soothing music permeated her consciousness like a drug, her body melting into the moment. "Do you want to go upstairs?" Chris whispered. She opened her eyes and smiled dozily. Taking her hand, he guided her to his bed-room.

In a way, being with Chris felt surreal, but at the same time, luscious and natural. What had she been doing with that idiot, Mike? When she had been with him, they were two bodies con-torted into one, both inhibited, both desperate for mutual approval. Now her body hovered and drifted into oblivion, connecting and surrendering with blissful acquiescence to this stranger's touch. She was lost in sensations that she didn't know existed. Words floated around: soft, perfect, succulent, dreamy...who was saying these things? Was it Chris's voice she heard or her own? Perhaps her mind spoke in a state of transcendence, while her body heaved in delight. After making love, neither of them spoke; they lay curled up together for a long time, exhilarated and exhausted, drifting in and out of consciousness. Then they made love again, with even more intensity. When it was over, they clung to each other and fell into a deep, resurrecting slumber.

A short time later, Denise jumped from the bed as if she'd been frightened by an explosion.

"Oh my God! I've got to be at work in forty-five minutes. How long does it take to get to McGill from here?" She was working at the university library for the summer, cataloguing and re-shelving books.

Chris gave her a towel. "I'll get you something to eat while you shower. Don't worry. I'll get you there on time."

Denise didn't know what to say or how to behave in the car. Part of her wanted to hold his hand, to feel his touch one last time, but another part of her wanted to escape. She was leaving in four days and there was no point hanging on to a romance that had no potential. When would they ever see each other again? Realistically, never. The night had been like a sweet dream but it was over and she felt disheartened, crushed by its intensity. Dreams end when reality barges in and she needed some time to process what had happened. Clutching her purse, Denise swallowed hard to hold back tears and she looked out the window to avoid Chris's face.

Their conversation was banal as they passed the time en route. When they were almost at the university he said, "Will I see you again, Denise?"

"I'm leaving in a few days. Does it make sense for us to start something now? You're an amazing guy, but we're both going away and I don't see how we can go anywhere with this."

"Will you write to me from Paris and let me know how things are going?"

"Sure." But she wasn't sure. She couldn't let a new relationship come between her and Paris. Why cling to something that had barely begun, that was more a fantasy than anything else? She bit her tongue to stop herself from crying.

When they arrived at the library, Denise was anxious to get out of the car. Chris grabbed a pencil, jotted an address and phone number on the back of a receipt, and handed it to her.

"My parents' address," he said. "Best way to find me."

She slipped the paper in her purse without looking at it.

"I'm glad I met you," he said.

"Me too." She leaned over and brushed his lips with a kiss.

"We should —"

"I have to go, I'm already late." She didn't want to hear it; she knew she wouldn't last another second without bursting into tears. Clutching her purse, she got out of the car and ran to the entrance of the library without looking back.

****

Slumber pushed Denise into an enormous crevice, where she is sinking further and further into darkness. Something pulls her deeper into the abyss, her arms are flailing and she's gasping for air. Chris's voice calls from above, quietly saying, "Don't worry, I've got you, I'll pull you out." Where is he?

The cat jumped on the bed and woke Denise from her strange dream; her heart raced as she recovered from the realization that Chris was not asleep beside her. Scruffy slinked around her body, as if aware that something was amiss. Sitting up in the bed, Denise held the cat in her arms, stroking her silky fur. Francois was hidden by the darkness, but she heard his heavy, even breathing. He was a good man, not always easy, but decent. And he was a devoted, attentive father. What about Chris? What kind of husband and father was he? He seemed content with his life — certainly his due after all he had been through. Her own past difficulties were minor in comparison. Yet she felt a kinship with Chris. Years ago, they had both left their comfort zones of familiarity to explore the terrain of unknown possibilities. For her, Paris. For him, British Columbia. But they had both been yanked away for reasons beyond their control. She had often heard the adage, 'you can't always control what happens to you, but you can control your attitude about it.' Chris's ability to lunge ahead with a positive mindset was admirable. Had she dealt with her own setbacks as commendably? She thought not.

Fatigue beleaguered her, but her mind would not give in to the forces of exhaustion. Half of her being lay in a semi-unconscious state while the other half churned relentlessly. The interminable silence finally induced sleep at the cusp of daylight.

When Denise woke up she didn't hear the usual Saturday morning commotion. She drowsily turned towards the clock on her bedside table and was shocked at the time. 11:18 a.m. Francois must have taken the boys out. One streak of light, forcing its way between the slats in the blinds, flashed across the floor like a laser beam. She continued to lie still, reveling in the luxury of such rare solitude, and stared up at nothing. But it was too tranquil. She should get up and occupy herself. Her body seemed weighted down by an imperceptible force, and her consciousness was unwittingly driven back to thoughts of Chris. She had hoped that a fresh day would leave ruminations of him behind, that there would be no more room for him in her overloaded mind. Not so.

What would Chris be doing? Probably enjoying a leisurely morning with his family, perhaps engaging in a flurry of domestic activity. What *she* should be doing. Was he thinking of her? She imagined the two of them as a couple, with a houseful of happy children. Denise pinched herself hard enough to leave a small welt in her skin, the sharp pain delivering her back to reality.

Dressed in jeans and a tee-shirt, Denise came down to the sun-filled kitchen, which was blinding after the darkness of the bedroom. Dregs of coffee steamed in the pot that Francois had left on for her. She opened the glass sliding door to the backyard, inviting the spring smells and cool breeze into the house. The chill in the air passed through her bones, producing goose bumps all over her body, but she didn't bother to get a sweater. The phone rang.

"Hello."

"Hello, Dear. I hope I'm not interrupting anything."

Denise's mother was always concerned about intruding. "Not at all, Mother. Francois has taken the boys out and I'm puttering around in the kitchen."

"How are you all?" Her tone was warm, as usual.

"We're great. How about you?"

"Wonderful, but I have a favour to ask you."

Her mother hardly ever asked for favours. "I'd be happy to help. What can I do?"

"I thought I'd take a trip to visit Camille and the children in Wisconsin for a few days, and I wondered if you could pick up the mail and water the plants while I'm gone. Only once or twice would be fine."

Her mother still lived in Denise's childhood home, only fifteen minutes away. "Of course, I'll do that for you." She hadn't watered her own plants or retrieved her own mail for years because she had Clara.

"If you're too busy, I can ask a neighbour."

Her mother hated asking people to do things for her. She was fiercely independent, always had been. "No problem. I'd be happy to. When are you leaving?"

"Monday. I'll be gone a week."

Denise heard the boys charging into the house. "Mother, the gang is home and I have to run. We'll talk later?"

"Give them monster hugs for me."

"I will. Love you." She hung up the phone.

The children flew into the kitchen, leaving a wake of jean jackets, caps, and shoes behind them.

"Hey guys," she called out. Only the six-year-old, Martin, ran into her outstretched arms. Thomas and Luc spoke simultaneously, each trying to talk over the other.

Francois came in last, his arms full of groceries. "We went to the Atwater Market," he said. "We bought lots of good stuff."

"And we had *pain au chocolat*," Martin shouted.

Chocolate croissants were a big treat in their home. Denise licked her finger and dabbed away the evidence from the edge of Martin's mouth.

"And Dad let us each get a smoothie with ice-cream," said Luc. "A smoothshake!"

"We got you some Cambozola cheese and some Roblochon," said Thomas.

"How thoughtful, my favourites. Thanks, guys."

"And a baguette," Martin said. "It's still warm."

Francois gave her a kiss. "I hope you won't mind, but I have to go to the office for a few hours."

He had given her the entire morning to herself; how could she protest? "Go ahead. The boys and I have lots to do."

Francois waved and left as quickly as he had come.

Damn. She hadn't expected this; she had some work of her own to do. Perhaps she could settle the boys with a movie and steal away to her study for a couple of hours.

"I guess that means Dad won't be able to come to our swim meet this afternoon," Luc said.

"What swim meet?"

"You wrote it on the calendar, Mom. From 2:00 to 6:00 at the Aquatics Centre."

She had forgotten all about it.

"I'm not going," Thomas said. "There's no way I'm going to sit through another stupid meet."

"You can't stay home alone all afternoon," said Denise. "You can bring your homework or something to read."

"No way. It's too hot and crowded. You can't make me go."

"Yes, I can!" But was it worth the battle? Denise dialed her mother's number. Thank goodness she was still at home. Her mother agreed to meet them at the pool and bring Thomas home with her. They didn't have much time.

The children's sports were always a chore for Denise. Well-intentioned strangers addressed her as a friend because she was a regular household face in Montreal. And those who didn't watch *Montreal's Alive* recognized her nonetheless and felt compelled to say hello. She rarely had a moment's peace, even to watch her own children compete. People would actually stand in front of her to talk to her while she tried to maneuver around them to see. Today, she didn't have the energy to deal with over-zealous fans. But what else could she do? Her boys had an important meet and she was their mother.

After lunch, Denise went to her study to check her e-mails. Over thirty messages awaited her. She scanned them with her usual sharp eye, looking for anything urgent. One message jumped out at her. Taking a deep breath, she double-clicked.

Denise,

It was great to see you yesterday. How remarkable to bump into each other after all these years. I feel like we didn't have a chance to finish our conversation, perhaps the opportunity will present itself again some time. You've obviously had an interesting life so far, I'm glad that your journey has brought you to a good place. Write me back when you have time – I'm still curious about those years in Paris.

Regards,

Chris

She let out her breath. Now what? Should she write back immediately, or wait a day or two?

"Mom, Mom—we have to go!" Luc shouted from the hall.

Denise checked her watch. They should have left already. She ran to the basement, where all their sports gear was kept, and shoved towels and bathing suits into a sports bag. Snacks—they would need something to eat. She scrambled to the kitchen, searching for appropriate refreshments. Where did Clara keep the juice boxes? She tossed packages of cookies and crackers into the bag, and at the last minute, a block of cheddar cheese. They'd have to buy drinks at the pool.

The kids were ready and waiting for her in the car by the time she had assembled all the paraphernalia. The most important items, their goggles, were left hanging on a hook in the basement, next to where the bathing suits had been.

Chapter Eight

On Sunday morning, Chris woke before the birds began to sing. His internal clock never allowed him to sleep late, no matter how few hours he had slept. The rest of his family usually dozed longer and today, even their dog Pepper, lay comatose. Lifting his head wearily, Pepper looked at Chris with a half-open eye, shifted his position, and then dropped his chin, reclaiming his slumber.

Chris brushed his teeth and combed his hair before putting on his running shorts and tee-shirt. He'd given up his goal of running the New York marathon long ago, the demands of work and family life left no time for training. But the dream was not dead, merely set aside for a time when life would allow him the luxury of such indulgences. Golf was the other sport he had to put on hold for the future, but every time he saw his clubs leaning against the wall in the furnace room, he felt a pang of regret. The two rounds a year he played with clients, and perhaps a third with Tony, didn't do justice to his love for the game. Neighbourhood jogs and his weekly squash games were the only two forms of exercise he could justify at this stage in his life.

Chris drank a glass of orange juice and started a pot of coffee before heading out. Pepper appeared, wagging his tail, surprisingly frisky for the time of day. Chris opened the back door to let him out but he didn't budge.

"You want some attention don't you?" He rubbed behind the dog's ears, which prompted Pepper to flop over on his back. The dog reveled in delight as Chris rubbed his stomach. When he was satisfied, he hobbled to the door, panting to go outside.

Pepper had come into the family when Laura was first pregnant, as a companion for Monique. Chris had been worried that she would be jealous of the new baby and had thought that a dog would be a good diversion. As it turned out, Monique was ecstatic about the new baby and hardly interested in the dog. He was a straggly black mutt spotted with patches of white and a lopsided gait. In no time he'd become attached to Chris (and vice-versa), and the family jokingly called him 'the shadow' because he was always at Chris's heels. Pepper lay by Chris's bedside at night, saw him off to work in the morning, and greeted him at the end of the day.

Chris went outside and did some stretches in the front yard, resting his foot on the wrought-iron railing for balance. The day was perfect for a run. No rain, no fog, no people, and barely any traffic. After his warm-up, he ran to the end of the driveway, then changed his mind and returned to the house. Running would not be thera-peutic if he'd be wondering the entire time whether or not Denise had responded to yesterday's message. He had purposely avoided the computer earlier, hoping to escape this preoccupation, but the more he tried to ignore the possibility of a message waiting for him, the more he thought about it. He'd allow himself one look today, and only one. If she hadn't written, then so be it, he would get on with the weekend and carry on with a clear mind.

When he scanned the computer screen in his study, he found nothing from Denise. Maybe she hadn't received his e-mail. Should he resend it? But then, only a day had passed, better to wait. Chris rushed outside and began to run along his usual route: up the street to Shaker Boulevard, turning right and running past the stately homes lining the street. The early spring shrubs were in bloom and the fresh buds on the mature trees were on the verge of exploding into leaves. He inhaled, taking in the strong, refreshing smells. His pounding feet on the concrete and rhythmic breathing were the only sounds that reverberated around him. Sweat trickled down his back as he increased his speed. He turned down a winding street that looped through the neighbourhood and would bring him back to his house. The circuit usually took half an hour.

A runner, whom Chris had seen before, jogged towards him from the opposite direction. He recognized her by the black baseball cap with a bright pink band around its edge and the same coloured insignia across the front. *NYM*: New York Marathon. With winter running gear shed, replaced by shorts and a tee-shirt, he could see the woman's muscular legs and strong arms—a serious runner. They passed each other and she flashed a wide smile, lifting her arm in greeting. He returned the gesture. Her intense focus and solid pace revealed an admirable determination.

Half a block later, Chris heard the screeching of a car's wheels and a loud thud behind him. He turned around and saw a body sprawled in the middle of the intersection. His legs raced towards the fallen woman where he saw a young man get out of the car and wander toward the motionless body. When Chris arrived at the scene the poor man appeared paralyzed as he gazed down at the inanimate woman, splayed in a pool of blood. The black cap with the pink trim lay on the concrete about ten feet away and the woman's long blond hair, previously hidden under the cap, was tousled around her face. Scrapes and cuts marred her body and dirt from the road was smeared across her silken skin. She looked like a discarded doll. A Ford stopped near the commotion and an older man got out, offering assistance.

"Do you have a cell phone?" Chris called out.

"No," the man said.

"Go to that house and pound the door until someone answers." Chris pointed to a clapboard house at the corner with two cars in the driveway. "Have them call 911."

The man lifted his arm in a saluting motion and ran to the front door.

Chris kneeled beside the victim. Blood poured from a gash in her left leg and her right shoulder was dislocated. She was unconscious. The young man who had hit her sat on the edge of the sidewalk and covered his head with his arms. He rocked back and forth in silence. Chris took the woman's pulse, which was faint. He tore off his shirt, rolled it up and placed it under her bleeding leg for elevation.

The man driving the Ford returned from the house, breathless, and said, "The ambulance is on its way."

A woman came running out behind him in her dressing gown. Chris shouted to her, "I need a blanket, jackets, anything warm — and towels." She ran back to the house.

He pointed to the vehicle that had hit the runner, "Cut that car's engine." Then he addressed a bystander, "We need some ice."

Thanks to Chris's experience as a ski patroller many years ago, he knew how to respond in an emergency. And nobody questioned his calm authority. The lady in the housecoat emerged from her house a few minutes later with an armful of blankets and towels. A tall man with grey hair and a grey beard, dressed in a suit, followed with a bag of ice. Chris used one towel to put pressure on the wound and another as a tourniquet. He covered the victim with blankets and gently placed ice around her shoulder. Sirens shrieked in the distance and then an ambulance arrived. While recounting what had transpired to the paramedic, Chris kept an eye on the woman as two other paramedics moved her to a stretcher.

The man who had driven into her was still sitting on the curb with his head down and his face buried in a crumpled towel. Muffled cries emanated from his smothered mouth. Globs of vomit pooled around his feet and on his shoes. When a police car came, Chris and an officer helped him up and escorted him to the cruiser. Noticing the runner's baseball cap on the road, Chris picked it up before getting into the car himself. He'd been asked to go to the station to give a formal statement, and with all the commotion, it hadn't occurred to him that his family was waiting for him at home.

****

Chris still wasn't back from his run and it was getting late. Laura and the girls ate breakfast in their church clothing because they couldn't wait any longer in pajamas. They rushed through their pancakes and sausages, now dry and chewy after keeping warm in the oven. Today was the first day in weeks that Chris had promised to go to church with them rather than to the office after his Sunday morning run. Laura had prepared a special breakfast for the occasion and now she found herself checking her watch repeatedly as they ate in unusual silence. Where on earth could he be? Even if he had had a late start he should be back by now.

Sophie had insisted on strawberry sauce for her pancakes and, naturally, some had dribbled down her blouse. Laura could not remove the stain by spot-cleaning and the only other appropriate blouse was wrinkled, but there was no time to iron. She hurried the girls, soiled blouse and all, into the car and sped off. How she hated arriving at church after the service had begun; the muscles in her chest began to ache with tension. Where the hell was Chris? She didn't know whether to worry or to be angry.

Immediately after the service, Laura rounded up the girls from Sunday school and told them to get their jackets.

"But, Mom. What about the cookies?" Normally, she would stay for coffee and mingle with the parishioners, while the girls feasted on cookies and played hide-and-seek with their Sunday school friends.

"Not today. We have to get home." She was in no mood for chit-chatting and forcing herself to be congenial. Even the service hadn't engaged her, and she could hardly recollect what the sermon had been about. Smiling and exchanging niceties would require too much effort in her state of mind.

The girls climbed into the car, their faces downcast. "Why do we have to miss the fun part? You're mean," said Tanya.

Laura ignored the complaint and drove homeward, while Tanya and Sophie argued in the back seat. Chris had promised to spend the day with them, but here she was again schlepping the girls to church on her own. Perhaps he'd forgotten about church and had gone to the office after all. She hadn't thought to check the garage to see if his car was gone. But hadn't she seen Chris, in her sleepy state, slipping out of the bedroom dressed for a run earlier on? She wondered if she'd been dreaming or if she'd misunderstood his intentions. Second guessing herself seemed to be a recurring theme these days.

From two blocks away, Laura noticed a police car parked by the curb near their house. As she got closer, she realized it was parked in front of their house. She covered her mouth with one of her hands, as if to stifle a scream. "No, no, no, no," she repeated quietly, in a voice she barely recognized. The car was practically driving itself; she had lost all sensation in her limbs. But when she arrived at the house she saw Chris sitting in the passenger seat, calmly talking to an officer. The cruiser door was open and he had one foot on the pavement. Laura jumped out of the SUV and dashed towards him, noticing blood stains on his hands when she got closer. Chris got out of the police car when he saw her, wearing an over-sized police shirt and holding a black baseball cap with the bright pink initials *NYM* embroidered on the front.

"Thanks for your assistance today," she heard the officer say. "You did a helluva job, keeping your head like you did."

"I'm glad I could help. I hope that woman will come out of this all right." Chris removed the shirt and tossed it onto the front seat of the police car.

"Yeah, let's hope," said the policeman.

The girls ran up to Chris but they didn't hug him. Instead, they inspected him tentatively.

"What happened, Daddy?" asked Tanya.

"I'll tell you inside," he said.

Fighting back tears, Laura followed them into the house. But the huge relief she had instantly felt upon seeing Chris unharmed did not completely override her annoyance. Lately, something always disrupted their plans and kept him away from home. Her jaw tensed as she tried to dispel such thoughts. She should be grateful...and proud.

Chris relayed the entire sequence of events. The woman, Sonya Foster, turned out to be an acquaintance from their children's pre-school days; a pleasant woman, always friendly and quick to volunteer when help was needed. Because the children attended different schools, Laura didn't encounter Sonya often anymore, but they   occasionally crossed paths at the grocery store or at community functions.

"I'll call her husband tomorrow to find out how she's doing," Laura said.

"Good idea. I'm trying to be hopeful, but I tell you, I've never seen anyone so mangled," he whispered, keeping his voice down even though the children were watching television in the family room, out of earshot.

"What about the guy who hit her?"

"I guess he'll be charged. Depends on the extent of the injury. Worst case is vehicular homicide."

Laura gasped. "She might die? And he'd go to jail—a convicted felon?

Chris nodded. "He was speeding. Says he didn't see the stop sign. Eighteen years old."

Laura slapped her hand against her heart. "So many lives could be destroyed by this." She shook her head. "What a terrible tragedy."

Chris crossed his arms over his bare chest and nodded. "It's tragic all right. Life is bloody fragile."

Laura noticed Chris's glassy eyes. "You're shaking," she said.

"I'm cold. I'd better get a shirt."

When Chris was upstairs, Laura checked the thermostat; it was seventy-four degrees in the house, but she was shivering too.

Wearing a fleece sweatshirt, Chris came back into the kitchen. Laura wrapped her arms around him. "You could have been the one who was hit. I don't know what I'd ever do without you."

"I suppose it could have been me crushed by that car." He hugged her tight. "But it wasn't."

The doorbell rang. Neither of them moved.

Sophie ran into the kitchen. "Uncle Tony's here!"

"If you want to shower and change, I'll talk to Tony."

"OK. I won't be long." He ran up the original servant's stairway that connected the kitchen to the second floor.

Laura greeted Tony and ushered him into the kitchen, offering him a cup of coffee.

"Sure, thanks, if it's already made."

"I was about to make a fresh pot."

Tony put the bottle of wine he was carrying on the kitchen counter and hung on to a file in his other hand. "Chris said he'd store this bottle for me in his cellar. Thought I'd drop it by before I broke down and drank it."

Laura smiled at him and nodded. "Chris will be down shortly. We've had quite a dramatic morning." She told Tony about the accident while she cleaned up the breakfast mess.

"Brutal," Tony said. "In a matter of seconds, lives can be blown to smithereens."

"No kidding," Laura said.

Chris came down and gave Tony a pat on the back.

"I heard about your heroic morning," Tony said.

"I wish I could have done more." He noticed the file in Tony's hands. "What's that?"

"It's the Anderson deal. I wanted you to go through it before I presented tomorrow. Would you mind reviewing it today?"

"No problem."

Laura stopped slicing bread and glanced at Chris. He had promised he wouldn't work that day.

"In fact," Tony said, "if you have some time we could go through a few points together."

"We'll talk in the study." Chris gave Laura an apologetic shrug.

"Tony, would you like to stay for lunch?" Laura asked. "We'll just be having cold cuts, but there's plenty." She couldn't cast him off now. Where else would he go? Either back to work or to an empty house. The least she could do was invite him for a meal; besides, he was easy company and the girls loved him.

"Thanks, that'd be great," he said.

When the men were gone, Laura checked her phone messages.

"Hi, Honey, it's me. I'm sorry I missed breakfast and church. I got caught at the site of a car accident. I'll explain later. Be home soon...bye." His voice sounded tense, and sad.

****

Chris sat behind his large walnut desk and Tony dragged the leather armchair from its place by the window over to the desk.

While Tony reviewed the papers, Chris checked his e-mails. The one he had been anticipating was wedged between others, as if it had been there all day. He opened it and read:

Dear Chris,

Thanks for your message. I enjoyed seeing you in Cleveland too – one doesn't often bump into friends from the past like that. You seem happy. Your life has been filled with interesting experiences and you've come out of your hardships a great success. Bravo to you for your steadfast commitment to both your family and your career. But then, I'm not surprised. When I first met you, you struck me as a winning kind of guy.

Take care,
Denise

75

PS. As far as Paris goes, that's a whole other chapter. I think it's your turn to reveal the next chapter of your life!

Tony relayed the critical aspects of the deal to Chris, his head immersed in papers.

Chris reread Denise's message.

"How do you think we should structure this offering?" Tony said.

But how would they move on to the next chapter?

"Chris, any thoughts?" Tony repeated.

"Uh. Sorry. What were you saying?"

"The way I've structured the deal. Do you agree with the format?" Chris noted the frustration in Tony's voice. "I'll have to go over it again. I can't remember the details."

"I just read the whole damn thing to you. What were you doing in the meantime? Having cyber sex or something?"

"Funny. I was reading the legal piece from Grayton. You know, on the Dorset file—you were copied on it too. Sorry. Let's start over."

Tony leaned over the desk and spread the relevant sheets out in front of Chris. Chris nodded and agreed to almost everything Tony suggested. Frustrated, Tony said, "I'll leave these with you this afternoon. Why don't you call me when you've had a chance to study them on your own, all right?"

"Yeah, absolutely."

"I think your head's still stuck in that accident. Must have shaken you up more than you realized."

"You're probably right. Let's see if lunch is ready." He glanced at Denise's e-mail one more time. *A winning kind of guy.*

Chapter Nine

Denise had read Chris's e-mail response at least a dozen times during the past few days. Every time she checked her messages she took another surreptitious glance. She had learned to be more careful since Nicole had appeared in her office, unannounced, two days ago. Nicole said she had knocked, but Denise hadn't heard a thing, and suddenly, there she was, peering over her shoulder. She hadn't even noticed the overpowering designer scent wafting across the room until Nicole had left. Nicole must have been standing at her side for some time because her eyes were glued to the screen when Denise detected her presence. How much had she read?

This time Denise had closed her office door before rereading Chris's note:

Hi Denise,

How are you doing? Thank you for your e-mail. I've been swamped with work and family busyness. How is spring in Montreal? I'll be out your way at the end of next week — would you happen to have some time for a glass of wine, or another cup of coffee? Perhaps you can regale me with more tales of Paris.

All the best,
Chris

Three days had passed and she still hadn't responded. What was holding her back? She'd love to see Chris again, but she had no desire to talk about Paris. She had already said too much. Those years were buried in the recesses of her consciousness and were landscaped over. To dig into that part of her past would be like destroying a beautiful garden to get to a useless relic buried underneath. But weeds were emerging—small ones, harmless probably. Was she calling Chris a weed? And his curiosity about her life a threat to her little patch of peonies? How silly.

Chris,

Thanks for the message. Is business bringing you here, or family? Are your parents still living in Montreal? We have a lot of catching up to do. I would love to see you again. I could manage Friday afternoon – about 5:00, after my show. If you can squeeze it in, you're most welcome to attend. We tape at 4:00. Should be an interesting segment: 'Women in Afghanistan.' But if you're busy, we could meet for a drink afterwards.

Hope to see you Fri. – Denise

Perhaps she should say that she was busy next week, or would be out of town. She read her message several times before making a decision. By the last reading, she could barely make out her own words. Why such trepidation? Their communications were harmless; simply a pleasant diversion from the spinning sensation she had been experiencing lately. She pressed send and watched the words vanish into oblivion.

The house was quiet when Denise walked in the door. Clara greeted her from the kitchen entrance, her hands busy, drying a salad bowl. She wore a red and pink striped apron and her graying shoulder length hair was tied back with a clip. Clara's exact age was an enigma but the family speculated that she was in her late fifties. Every day of the week she wore a different apron over her black polyester slacks. Denise called her the most fashionable housekeeper in town.

"How was your day?" Clara asked in her usual nurturing and relaxed tone—as if running a household and caring for three boys was an easy undertaking.

"Wonderful. The show went without a hitch. Our guest today was a master gardener—there's no end to what you can learn about spring planting." Denise followed Clara into the kitchen. She removed a pair of bright orange clog-like plastic shoes from a gift bag with a garden motif and held them up for Clara to see. "Today's audience give-away—gardening shoes."

"Cute," Clara said.

"Do you want them?"

Clara smiled. "Thanks, but I don't think they'd be necessary for watering the planters on my apartment balcony."

"Maybe my mother would like them. You know how she loves her garden."

"Oh, she called today. From Wisconsin. I left a note." Clara pointed to a pad on the kitchen counter. "She asked me to remind you to put out the recycle bin when you go over."

"I forgot that I'd promised to check on the house. Where has the week gone?"

"It's always the way," Clara said.

"Where are the boys? It's awfully quiet."

"Upstairs. They've finished their homework and are all ready for bed, so I let them watch that DVD."

"Excellent. You go home, Clara. It's been a long day for you too."

Clara removed her apron, folded it neatly, and placed it in her special drawer. She opened the refrigerator and showed Denise a platter with pork tenderloin slices, sweet potato and green beans. "Dinner for you and Francois. It needs four minutes in the microwave."

"Clara, you're wonderful. Thank you."

The boys reluctantly turned off the television when Denise came upstairs. Settling them in their rooms, she spent a few moments with each of them trying to learn about their day. But not allowing them to finish their movie had annoyed them, and nobody felt like talking. She was too tired to keep prodding, so she said good night and went back downstairs.

Had Francois mentioned when he would be home? She couldn't remember. She couldn't even remember if they had spoken during the day. She filled a glass of water from the cooler in the kitchen and stared into the backyard while she drank, trying to appreciate the spring flowers emerging from their winter beds. The cat swirled its tail around her legs as it circled her feet. Denise put her glass on the counter and picked her up like a baby.

"You happy to see me, Scruffy?" The boys had come up with the name, which really didn't suit the regal-looking Persian-Tabby mix. "Let's go to the study and review tomorrow's program," she said, as if speaking to a person. Putting the cat down, she went to the front hall to get her briefcase, which contained her laptop and the program notes. The cat followed at her heels and jumped on her lap as soon as she sat down. She stroked Scruffy for a moment and then put her back on the floor.

When she reached for the file in her case, she found herself removing the laptop instead. How long had passed since she had e-mailed Chris? Three, four hours? Would he have read her message yet? She turned on the computer and checked. Only work-related items. And those, she'd leave until tomorrow. The topic for the next day's show was interesting—*Women and Technology – the Fear Factor*. The guest was a female engineer who had built a consulting business in technology awareness. Denise wanted to help women, especially those of her generation and older, to overcome their insecurities and inhibitions around technological tools. Nicole had argued with her about the topic. "Boring," she had whined. "Nobody wants to sit through an hour of tech-talk." But Denise had insisted and Gary had agreed that it was an important and informative subject. Nicole had yawned. "Here we go again," she'd said, "yet another wonderfully entertaining segment." As efficient and energetic as Nicole was, she was beginning to get too brazen. A serious talk was due.

Denise didn't know that Francois had pulled up in the driveway until she swiveled her chair around to face the window. She saw him talking intensely on his cell phone, the car still running. Ten minutes passed before he finished his call and turned off the engine. When he came into the house she greeted him at the door.

"You won't believe this," he said, hyped like a kid who had scored the winning goal of an important game. "You know that restoration project I've been talking about, the old bank building on Sherbrooke?"

She nodded, but had to think hard about what he was referring to.

"They're going ahead with it and they want me to be the chief contractor. And I'll be working with Pierre Leblanc."

Pierre Leblanc, the most prominent architect in the city, was an acquaintance of theirs. "What a coup. That's fantastic. You're the perfect man for the job." She extended her arms to embrace him but he was taking off his jacket and didn't notice.

He barreled past her and headed straight for the kitchen. "I've had my eye on that building for three years. It'll be a challenge to get it back to its former glory but thank God they didn't tear it down to build something hideous."

Denise could see where this was headed. Once Francois got his mind wrapped around a big idea there was no letting go. He'd immerse himself to such a degree that nobody and nothing else would exist—for a while.

"It irks me how quick developers are to demolish a perfectly sound structure—it's happening too often these days. You wouldn't believe how close this one was. If it weren't for Pierre, there'd be a gaping hole in the ground with another condo in the works."

Denise watched Francois pour himself a beer. His movements were precise and intense. Even the way he removed the jar of roasted peanuts from the cupboard and tipped some into a bowl was subconsciously methodical. He didn't waste a movement or a breath when he was revved.

"In fact, I've decided to get on the Heritage Board. I'm tired of standing by and watching greedy developers undermining the system. They find a loophole, and suddenly a beautiful heritage property is demolished and a flashy condo building appears." He scooped a handful of peanuts from the bowl and dropped them into his mouth. "This city is becoming another generic place—might as well call us city #8 or #25 or whatever. Nobody has foresight anymore. At the current rate, by the time our boys are grown, there will be no character left in Montreal."

Francois flung his arms into the air and spilled his drink on the floor, on his shirt, and down his pants. "Oh shit! I'm sorry. I guess I got carried away. No, no, I'll clean it," he said, as Denise mopped up the spill with a rag.

"It's all right," she said. She was grateful for the disruption. Francois' diatribe could carry on for the rest of the evening and she was too weary to appreciate his zeal.

"If the project goes ahead—and it's not final yet—I'll be out of commission for a while at home. The work will be intense." He wiped the beer off his shirt with a wet paper towel, leaving large water marks and little bits of paper from the disintegrated tissue.

"I'm sure we'll be able to work something out with Clara," Denise said. She rinsed the cloth at the sink and wrung it out.

"I'll still be in town and can see the kids at night. Weekends might be tough because I'll have to be on site most of the time."

"Don't worry, we'll manage. It's a great opportunity, I'm happy for you." Denise kissed him on the cheek.

Pulling her close, Francois kissed her on the lips. His yeast infested shirt seeped into her blouse as they embraced. The sticky, smelly beer residue seemed to penetrate her skin.

"I wasn't expecting such an easy sell. I thought you'd get all anxious about your schedule and the logistics with the boys, since a lot more will be on your plate if and when this happens."

Denise was surprised at her reaction as well. She was used to Francois' flexible schedule and often counted on him to drive the boys to their activities. And he frequently took on the evening load when she had late meetings or was out of town. But this would be good for Francois because he needed a big project, something new to delve into. And she needed some mental space.

This project could be good for them both.

That night, Denise lay in bed staring at the blank ceiling. Turning to her side, she looked at the digital clock on the bedside table. 2:47 a.m. She squinted to make sure she had read the time correctly. Nothing had helped her fall asleep: drinking hot milk, reading the instruction booklet that came with her new cell phone, and an hour ago, taking half a valium. Francois slept like a bear in hibernation and she watched his chest rise and fall, hoping that the rhythmic movements would somehow lull her into slumber. Eventually, she threw off the covers and sat up at the edge of her bed. Enough. Putting on her robe as she left the room, she headed downstairs.

The street light in front of the house shone through the bay window, illuminating the living room enough to see most of the furniture. Denise peered out at her manicured front garden, willing the calmness outside to penetrate her agitated mind. She dropped down on the sofa and scanned the room. It felt foreign in the dim light, like she was sitting in somebody else's house. High ceilings, crown moldings, and gumwood wainscoting suggested old-world European elegance. The silk taffeta drapes, falling like puddles on the hardwood floor, looked more burgundy than terracotta in the distorted light. As her eyes became accustomed to the semi-darkness, Denise glanced around at the precious items that Francois and she had collected together over the years. She tried to relax, breathing deeply, as she fixed her eyes on the Quebec winter land-scape painting hanging over the fireplace. But her mind would not rest.

She began rearranging accessories in the room, moving two topiaries from the mantle to the shelf by the bay window and re-placing them with two silver candle holders. The trophy-sized Henry Moore sculpture of a mother cradling a baby in her arms seemed strangely out of place on its mahogany pedestal. Denise picked up the valuable carving and examined it, as she often did, marveling at the artist's ability to capture the essence of maternal love from a stone. She ran her fingers over its smooth contours, imagining the creative energy that had produced the piece. Fran-cois' parents had given them the sculpture, a prized possession, as a wedding gift. "You can buy a house with this thing," Francois' fa-ther had said. "Don't you dare sell it," his mother had countered, "this sculpture will bring you luck and lifelong love as long as you own it."

Denise walked towards the fireplace, having decided to pair the candleholders on one side of the mantle and place the sculpture on the other. Her foot caught the edge of the Persian carpet and she reeled forward, dropping the carving head first onto the marble tile at the base of the hearth. She picked it up and gasped. The mother's arm, although not broken, had a large visible crack where she was holding the child. Denise hyperventilated and collapsed on the floor, cradling her head in her arms. How could she do such a care-less thing? Breathing deeply, as she had been taught in yoga, helped calm her body but not her nerves. Eventually she pulled herself up and placed the figure where she had intended, turning it enough to hide the fracture. Why did she have to go and fiddle with the sculp-ture? She should have left it be, intact and untarnished. A numb pain pressed through her chest and worked its way to her feet, as if her own body was slowly cracking.

She fumbled her way to the study, sat down at her desk and stared at the computer screen. Fragmented memories of Paris had been appearing in her mind since Chris had asked her about those years. She'd see herself walking along The Champs-Elysées, popping into a favourite café, or having words with Jacques at the dining room table in his grand Parisian apartment. Like scenes in a movie, she'd see shots from different angles, and different perspectives. She'd had a dream the other night, full of close-ups. Her face was contorted with negative emotion—tears streaming down her cheeks, twisted anger in her eyes, and sallow skin with protruding cheek bones highlighting her despair. Were these haunting visions stealing her sleep? Or was the upcoming rendezvous with Chris the cause of her agitation? Inviting him to her show-taping had been a bad idea. But the stage had never intimidated her before; in fact, that's where she came alive. A few months prior, the Premier of Quebec had attended a show on multi-culturalism, and she'd been thrilled to have him in the audience. They'd even had a drink afterwards and enjoyed a relaxed conversation. But the thought of Chris sitting in the studio, watching her every move and listening to her every word, made her nauseous.

If they had drinks afterwards, he'd be apt to prod her about Paris. Did she want to open that can of worms? She opened a fresh document on her computer. Maybe she needed to write about those years in Paris, as if she were talking to Chris, telling him about it. She had never kept a journal or even written about her life experiences; she had left that job to others, like journalists who interviewed her. What had happened in Paris after her ordeal with the French family was personal, a story she had shared with few people. If she wrote it all down, like a memoir, then perhaps her mind would settle down and the nasty flashbacks would disappear.

Where was her stationery? She rummaged through her desk drawers until she found exactly what she was looking for—the soft ivory paper that her mother had given her for her birthday last year, with the gold initials *DG* embossed on the top left corner. As she wrote, she would imagine herself sitting across the table from Chris, sharing a piece of her life as he listened with great attention. But instead of talking she'd be writing, using a cursive voice.

When she finished writing, the morning light was filtering through the blinds. Soon the boys would be getting up. Denise folded the letter and tucked it in a drawer, under some documents. Maybe she would give it to Chris to read one day, maybe not. Now, she needed a strong cup of coffee.

Chapter Ten

The boys piled into Denise's car and climbed over one another until they landed in their seats. Having run out of time during the week to do the promised chores at her mother's house, Denise was compelled to bring the children with her on Saturday. Thomas could have remained at home alone — he was old enough at eleven — but that would have resulted in protests from the other two boys who were already incensed at being torn away from their favourite Saturday morning cartoon. Denise pulled out of the driveway and headed down Silverbrooke Crescent.

"Give me that!" screamed Martin. He kicked the back of the driver's seat with force, sending a jolt down her spine.

"I had it first," yelled Luc.

"Thomas, do me a favour," Denise said, raising her voice, "get that thing, whatever it is, that they're fighting over." She gritted her teeth and spoke in an authoritative and controlled tone, "Boys, stop fighting." Why hadn't she made the time earlier in the week to water her mother's plants? She could have slipped away from the studio on Thursday and gone to her mother's place in peace.

Stopped at a red light, Denise turned toward the boys. "Give it to me!" she yelled, over the continued shrieks. She snatched the small plastic unicorn whose horn had long since been ripped from its head. "Thanks for your assistance, Thomas," Denise said.

9:30 in the morning and already she needed a Tylenol. "When we get to Grandma's, I don't want you all to tear around the house. I need to check on a few things and water the plants. Thomas, you take out the recycle bin from the garage, and you two," she glared at the younger boys in the rearview mirror, "can play in the backyard...quietly." No one listened to a word. The younger boys were slapping each other and laughing, while Thomas was gazing out the window, day-dreaming. She turned on the CD player and the song, "Puff the Magic Dragon," helped quiet them down.

Pulling into her mother's driveway, Denise was surprised to see several days' worth of newspapers strewn around the front entrance. Surely, her mother would have cancelled the paper; the mistake must be on the distributor's end.

"Luc, pick up those newspapers," Denise said, once the children were unloaded. She unlocked the front door with her key and gathered the scattered mail from the entranceway floor. Several letters had made their way down the hall in a straight trajectory. How they could be propelled through the mail slot such a distance was a mystery. She sorted through the items and gave Luc the junk mail to dump in the recycle bin outside. She placed the rest in the catch-all basket on the hall table and automatically dropped in her key chain. There had been a time during her youth when there would have been five sets of keys in that basket. Her mother had taught all her children to put them in the same place when coming in the door—a habit that still remained.

When Denise entered the kitchen, she stopped short. Dirty dishes covered the counter and a coffee pot, with its dried residue, needed a good soaking. A pint of milk sat out the counter, now spoiled of course. Why was the kitchen in such disorder? For such a fastidious housekeeper as Denise's mother, this disarray was uncharacteristic. After Denise's father died, her mother began working outside the home, and out of necessity, she devised a strict cleaning schedule to keep the house spotless at all times. Denise and her siblings were assigned a room each week and that room had to be tidied, swept, dusted, and scrubbed until it glistened. The children would joke that their mother was running a domestic boot camp. To this day, Denise's mother kept a rigorous cleaning schedule for herself. And she had always been particularly finicky about leaving the house tidy when going on a trip.

Denise found an elastic band in the miscellaneous drawer and looped her hair through it twice. Few things had changed in this house over the years. Even the old wallpaper with the climbing green vines remained. She remembered Mr. Johnson, one of the neighbours, coming over one morning to help her mother hang the paper. When Denise had returned from school that day, the kitchen walls were covered with simulated foliage.

She washed the dishes, dried them, and put them in the cupboard. Then she scrubbed the coffee pot, forgetting to use rubber gloves, her freshly manicured nails chipping in the process. Through the window over the sink, she watched her younger boys playing in the backyard. Luc directed Martin as they climbed the lower branches of the enormous weeping willow that dominated the yard. Denise and her siblings had spent many joyful hours playing around that tree. Her father used to join in their games under the pendulous branches, and she remembered him placing her high up on one of the strong branches, urging her to leap into his arms. She couldn't have been more than three years old. Was this a true memory, or a re-enactment of a photograph she had seen in one of her mother's family albums? She could even hear his strong confident voice, "Don't worry, DeeDee, I'll catch you—jump! Jump!"

When she finished cleaning the kitchen, Denise found the watering can under the sink and filled it to the top. Wandering from room to room, she gave each plant enough water to revitalize it, but not so much that it would over-saturate and begin to rot. "Plants are like people," her mother would say, "give them too much of anything good and they'll begin to self-destruct." The plants were her mother's glory, bringing much pleasure and serenity to her life. Why couldn't she—Denise—find something like that, something to placate her soul? She had occasional meditative moments, like at the cottage, when she woke at dawn to the shimmering, still lake; but as soon as a boat, or even a canoe glided by, the water's glassy surface would be defaced and that feeling would be lost.

The African violet in the den had black dots on its leaves and no blooms. Wasn't this plant almost always in flower? Unsure whether it needed water or not, Denise gave it a few drops. Thomas was watching a show, snug in a chair, covered by his grandmother's hand-crocheted afghan. Denise remembered her mother making that blanket about a decade ago, after Thomas was born. She envisioned the different shades of blue wool balls lying at her mother's feet, while she crocheted in front of the television. She called it her evening news blanket because she had done most of the work while watching the news.

Thomas, engrossed in a National Geographic-type show about Ancient Egypt, did not acknowledge his mother as she moved about the room. She sat down on the loveseat and watched the re-enactment of Egyptian labourers hauling massive stones up a steep ramp towards the top of a pyramid. "Isn't this fascinating?" she said. He didn't answer, didn't seem to hear her speak.

Denise heard laughter coming from the kitchen and went down-stairs to check on the younger boys. Tracks of mud led from the front door to the kitchen, where Luc and Martin were helping themselves to cans of ginger ale from the fridge.

"Whatever has gotten into you boys?" she shouted. "Since when do you *not* remove your shoes when coming into the house? And since when do you take something from Grandma's fridge without permission?"

The boys looked at each other and giggled. They put the drinks back into the fridge.

"Grandma always gives us a ginger ale when we come here," said Luc.

"And cookies," said Martin.

"Well, Grandma's not here." Denise grabbed several sheets of paper towel, wet them, and got on her knees to clean the soiled floor. "Take off your shoes and don't move."

The boys did as they were told.

When she had finished, Denise corralled the two children to the door and called upstairs to Thomas.

"Is he watching TV?" Luc asked. "You said we couldn't watch TV. No fair...," he whined.

"Get in the car, boys," she said, and nudged them forward.

Outside, the next-door neighbour scurried toward Denise as she was getting in the car. The woman was short of breath. "I'm glad I caught you. Is Marie away?"

"Hello, Mrs. Peterson. Yes, Mother has gone to Wisconsin to visit Camille for a few days."

"Why didn't she tell me she was going? I would have been more than happy to keep an eye on her house. If I don't know she's gone, how can I help her?"

Denise knew exactly why her mother hadn't mentioned that she was leaving. Perhaps Mrs. Peterson had good intentions but she was more than her mother could bear. And being obligated to Mrs. P. was not a good thing. She'd have you hanging out her laundry if you owed her a favour. Many years ago, Denise had occasionally hung out with her daughter, who was a year younger and always up to tricks. Mrs. Peterson had always found a way to twist the circumstances of Becky's misdemeanours and put the blame on others. Denise had been a victim of her manipulation more than once.

"I suppose Mother didn't want to bother you. Besides, I told her that I'd come out to check on the house."

"She left the sprinkler going, you know. It almost drowned my garden. See?" She pointed to the damp ground by the side of her house, her permed hair-do stiff like a bird's nest as she flapped her head about. Denise recalled the old days, when Mrs. Peterson used to traipse around the neighbourhood with curlers in her hair, and the kids calling her Curler Queen behind her back.

"So sorry about that," Denise said. "It's very unlike my mother. She must have left in a hurry."

"Marie should communicate better. I could be a tremendous help to her if she'd only let me. And I would have been more than happy to take her to the airport."

To be confined with that woman for any length of time was torture for her mother. And driving in the same car would have been intolerable, even for twenty minutes. As patient as she was, she could barely abide Mrs. Peterson's incessant chatter, which was only getting worse with age.

"That's kind of you, but I'm sure she had everything organized." One aspect that struck Denise as rather odd about Mrs. Peterson, was how she never mentioned Denise's show. In spite of the fact that she spent hours in front of the television set, (Denise's mother could see the screen flashing through the living room window and could even hear the droning television sounds well into the night) she withheld any remarks she may have had. Whatever it was that kept her from spewing her opinions was fine with Denise, and she didn't even mind the way Mrs. Peterson patronized her as if she were still a child. "Maybe she doesn't follow the show," Denise once said to her mother. "Nonsense," her mother had replied, "she just doesn't want your boots to get too shiny for Dahlia Crescent."

It was almost noon when Denise and the boys arrived home. The excursion had taken twice the time Denise had expected, causing them to be late for swim-team practice. She hadn't even thought about lunch.

By the time Luc and Martin were at swimming and Thomas had been dropped at a friend's house, Denise's head was throbbing. She took two extra-strength Tylenols and warmed up a bowl of macaroni and cheese left over from the boys' lunch; four mouthfuls were enough to reduce the sharpness of her headache.

She brought her laptop to the kitchen table where the sun streamed in through the large picture windows. Chris had e-mailed early in the week and she re-read his message.

It's all booked. Will try to make it to your show after my meeting. I have your business card with the address, but how do I obtain a ticket? In case you don't have my cell number and need to get a hold of me (it's also on my card) I'll give it to you again: 216 849 7732. Looking forward to seeing you.
Chris

Then she read her response:

Chris,
Am glad it's all arranged. I will leave word at the entrance that you may be coming. The person at the desk will usher you to a seat. If you're not able to make the show, we can meet afterwards at the Realitz. How's 5:00 at the bar?
See you soon,
Denise

His reply:

Sounds great. See you then. Chris

All week, she had been vacillating between wanting and not wanting him to come to the taping. Normally, she felt empowered on the stage and in complete control. But with the possibility of

Chris watching, a nagging sense of foreboding kept taking over, catching her off-guard and chipping away at her nerves. She chastised herself for her insecurity — Chris probably wouldn't make it to the show anyway, and her silly ruminations were simply a waste of energy. "Get a grip," she told herself. But the knots in her chest tightened.

Denise went online to check the forecast and the news headlines. Then she looked over her shoulder, almost expecting Nicole to be standing behind her, watching. She typed "Chris Lambert" into the search engine. A number of items appeared with his name. She clicked on, 'Lambert & Salvo Capitol Incorporated — Merchant Banking,' and read the company profile.

Lambert & Salvo Capital's seasoned team of investment managers adds value and aggressively expands each portfolio. We seek to acquire mid-sized businesses with revenues of $25 million to $200 million. Our aim is to offer unique strategies to create competitive advantage and add value through acquisitions or divestitures.

She clicked on 'principals':

Mr. Lambert has been co-president of Lambert & Salvo Capital since 1996. Previously he held a senior position with First State Investments and sat on the boards of several corporations. He earned his BCom at the University of British Columbia and an MBA at Case Western Reserve University, Cleveland.

Chris's business success was evident on the screen, but in conversation, she had detected a humbler version of the man. The discrepancy made him even more alluring. Sometimes company profiles showed a picture of the principals, and she was disappointed that this one didn't.

The phone rang and Denise jumped.

"Thought I'd check in," Francois said. "What are you all doing?"

"Luc and Martin are at swimming and Thomas is at a friend's." She checked her watch. Thank goodness Francois had called; she had lost track of the time. The boys' practice was almost over.

"Are you all right with me being out a few more hours? We're wrapping up the design discussion, but still have to cover construction procedures."

They had made plans to go out for a family dinner that evening. She could bring the boys herself, but after the morning's disastrous outing, the idea was not appealing. "No problem. Do what you need to do. We're fine." She'd make grilled cheese and let them watch a movie.

"Thanks. I'll be home by 9:00 or so."

If she'd known that he'd be gone all day and evening, she would have taken the children to the cottage. Their family outings were becoming increasingly difficult to arrange.

Denise put the phone down and picked up the cat, fast asleep at her feet. She leaned back in the chair and stroked its soft fur. "Time to go, Scruffy." Closing her eyes, she listened to the cat's soothing motor while she continued to pet her, unable to move.

Chapter Eleven

L aura wondered if she was in the right place when she entered the hospital foyer; the marble floors, the contemporary artwork, and the glass-topped reception desk seemed to belong more in an office building than a healthcare facility. She approached a young woman wearing a bright orange happy-face button, with the words 'Can I Help?' framing the circumference.

"Hi. Can you tell me where I might find Sonya Foster?"

"Let's see." She checked her computer, "Ms. Foster is on the tenth floor, in room 1028." She pointed to the vase of flowers Laura was carrying. "Those are pretty."

"Spring blooms to cheer her up."

"I'm sure they will. Says here that she was moved out of intensive care just yesterday."

"Oh my, a whole week in the ICU?"

"Not to worry, I'm sure she's past the worst."

Before Laura could thank the woman, an elderly lady was asking questions in what sounded like Chinese. The receptionist nodded, but obviously hadn't understood a word. Laura took her flowers and headed to the elevator. The doors were glass, as was the ceiling of the atrium. Large palm trees and a fountain created a tropical atmosphere. Because of the brightness, Laura didn't take off her sunglasses until she reached Sonya's floor. When she arrived at room 1028, she found the door wide open. One of the beds was empty and the other was concealed by a navy blue curtain. An older woman sat in a chair at the base of the bed, speaking quietly. Laura was about to knock but her hand froze in mid-air. She had come here intending to offer support, but now she felt like an intruder.

They weren't good friends after all, barely even acquaintances; Sonya might not even recognize her.

The woman in the chair noticed Laura before she had a chance to change her mind. "Can I help you?" she asked, her tone indifferent.

Laura stepped into the room and smiled at the lady, who appeared sullen. But then, this was a hospital, and not a place to come for the joy of it. "Is this Sonya Foster's room?" she whispered.

"Come in, come in" the lady said, motioning with an impatient wave. "Sonya's right here. I'm her mother, Erika."

Laura walked in, shook Erika's hand, and introduced herself to both women. Sonya lay motionless, an intravenous hooked to her hand. "I heard about the accident from my husband, Chris. He was at the scene." She handed the flowers to Erika.

A strained smile appeared on Sonya's face. "They're beautiful, thank you," she whispered. A tan bandage, wrapped around her head, made her look bald. Laura wondered if her hair had been shaved for surgery, but she couldn't bring herself to ask.

"I want thank him for everything he did," Sonya said in a strained voice. "Please tell him how grateful I am."

"Chris was extremely concerned. We both were. It's good to see that you're out of intensive care." Laura was glad that she had come but did not want to overstay, given Sonya's condition.

Erika dragged a chair from the other side of the room. "Please, sit down. My daughter gave me a huge scare. But she's going to be fine, the doctor says. She'll need some physiotherapy and lots of time to recuperate, but there were no permanent head injuries, thank God."

Laura pulled Sonya's baseball cap from her purse and placed it at the end of the bed. "Chris wanted me to give you this. He says to wish you the best and to tell you that he hopes to see you on the 'Shaker' running circuit soon."

Sonya's eyes brightened. "I'd like to think that would be possible," her voice was barely audible.

Erika's body stiffened as she shook her head. "Not for a long time, my dear—not until you are one hundred percent." Then she said to Laura, "I have to keep an eye on this girl, she's likely to sneak out the door and go racing off long before she's been given the go-ahead. Same as when she was a child."

"Once a mother, always a mother," Laura said.

"Sonya has been through enough havoc lately. She didn't deserve a blow like this." Erika motioned for Laura to sit down.

"I haven't seen her much since the kids were little," Laura said. "I didn't know there were difficulties." She anticipated a reaction from Sonya, but her eyes were closed.

"No, she would never let on, doesn't wear her emotions on her sleeve. But since Jack left, life's been a struggle for her...for us all."

"I'm sorry," Laura said.

"Mother, please let's not get into this," Sonya whispered, her weary eyes now open.

Laura could see that she didn't have the energy to argue.

"Good old Jack," Sonya's mother said, "nobody saw it coming." She moved the angle of her chair to face Laura. "For Christmas last year, I offered to come up from Houston to look after the children while they went away together. They'd been married almost ten years and decided on Bermuda—the same hotel they'd stayed at during their honeymoon."

Sonya's closed her eyes again and her drawn face revealed no emotion.

"They seemed happy when they came back. All tanned and relaxed." She looked at her daughter and shook her head. "I stayed on a bit to visit with Sonya, and Jack went back to work. When I left, I had this warm feeling in my heart. You know...the feeling a mother has when all is good with her kids."

Laura could hear her own mother's voice, "A mother can only be as happy as her most unhappy child." Laura remembered feeling guilty many times in her youth because whenever she was going through a bad patch, she knew she was dragging her mother down too.

Sonya shifted in her bed, as if to find a comfortable position.

"She's on painkillers," her mother said. "Not only does she have stitches in her head but they had to operate on her leg. Lots of broken pieces in there."

"Perhaps I should leave," Laura said. "I don't want my visit to be a strain."

"No, no. Don't go. Sonya appreciates your company."

The nurse came in to check on Sonya's intravenous and Laura stood up. Sonya opened her eyes and pointed to the flowers that her mother had placed on the window sill, and mouthed the words, "Thank you."

"I'll see you out," her mother said.

They walked down the corridor and Erika took Laura's arm. "It's just as well that I didn't tell you the whole story in there."

She proceeded to tell Laura how three months after she had returned to Texas, she got a phone call from Sonya telling her that Jack had left the family. There had been no words, no forewarning, only a feeble note saying he had met someone at work, and there was no point prolonging their marriage when his soul-mate had turned out to be someone else.

"And now this." She wiped the wetness under her eyes.

"How awful," Laura said. "Poor Sonya."

"It gets worse. Jack wanted to sell the house to get his share of the equity, but Sonya thought a move would be difficult for the children, so she got a job and bought him out. Now she has a huge mortgage. It's been difficult, very difficult indeed."

"I can imagine." But Laura could not imagine being in Sonya's shoes. To go from a happy, stable family life to one of loneliness and worry was frightening. How was it that she never knew that this was going on in her own neighbourhood, only a few blocks away?

"I try to help her," Erika said, "but I don't have much money myself and my arthritis is getting worse. I can't even do laundry the way I used to. And I'm lonely here without my friends. I hate to miss my activities: my walking club, bridge, bingo…you know, the things that old ladies like me do."

The lamenting put Laura off for a moment. Sonya's mother was hardly an old lady, and who was the one lying in the hospital bed, after all? But then, it must be difficult to watch a grown daughter suffer so.

When the elevator doors opened, Erika let go of Laura's arm but her face was downcast, as if she were being abandoned.

Laura plucked weeds from the flower bed in the front yard while she waited for Chris to arrive home. He had called to say he was five minutes away and Laura had slipped out the door, as she did every Thursday night. They hadn't made specific plans for the evening, but the fresh spring air made her feel like going for a stroll in the village, followed by dinner at one of the quaint country restaurants.

Chris's car appeared on the driveway and he joined her on the front lawn.

"Hi," he said, and kissed her gently. "Your tulips are sensational. I didn't realize we had so many."

"I planted a bagful of bulbs last fall before the ground froze. I guess they liked the warm weather today." She stepped back, observing her handiwork with pride.

"You ready to go?" Chris asked.

Laura dropped the weeds into a basket at the side of the house and removed her gardening gloves, while Chris opened the passenger door. "Ah, feels good," she said, sinking into the luxurious leather seat. "Let's open the sunroof."

"Where to?" Chris said.

"How about Chagrin Falls?"

"Good idea. Dinner and a movie?"

"I was thinking of a walk and then dinner."

"Walk where?"

"Around. I don't know. Through the town, on the trails by the falls."

"Hmm."

"You don't feel like walking?"

"Not in my suit and work shoes."

"It's not like we'd be walking through the woods."

"I'd be more comfortable in casual clothes. I can go inside and change."

If the children saw him, he'd never get out of the house. "No, never mind. We can go to a movie."

Chris put on a CD and they drove in silence for the first few minutes.

"Are you hungry?" Laura asked.

"I could eat. How about the Ranch House?"

Red meat, fries, salad drenched in heavy dressing…"I feel like something healthier tonight. How about the Corner Café?" She had lost about seven pounds in the last few weeks but Chris hadn't mentioned it. How much would she have to lose before he noticed?

"That'd be fine."

They were early enough to get the best table in the restaurant, overlooking the falls. The sun was setting and an orange glow shone over the horizon. Chris ordered a bottle of wine.

"I went to see Sonya Foster at the hospital today," Laura said.

Chris looked puzzled.

"The runner who was hit by the car last week. I mentioned I'd visit her."

"Oh, right. How is she?"

"Broken leg, head laceration, mild concussion…but she'll recover."

"She's lucky. It could've been much worse."

"Her mother was there. She updated me on Sonya's life."

The waitress came to pour the wine and they placed their dinner orders. Chris offered Laura some bread from a basket and she declined, picking up her wine glass instead.

"Her husband left her for another woman about a year ago." Laura leaned into the table and lowered her voice. "I had no idea. I've bumped into her enough times that you'd think I'd have known something, but she never indicated that anything was wrong."

"Nasty stuff," Chris said.

"Her mother told me it came out of the blue. One day they were a happy couple, the next day they were history."

"Probably more going on behind the scenes."

"I don't know. I'm just grateful for what we have." Laura reached across the table and took Chris's hand. "You're such a wonderful husband, and the best father. Seeing Sonya today made me appreciate *us*." She removed the wine bottle from the canister and poured herself some more. Chris's glass was untouched. "I can't imagine what wretch of a man would up and leave a woman with two small children. Her mother indicated that there were financial stresses too."

"What about the running?" Chris asked. "Will she be able to run again?"

"I don't think they know yet."

"How were the girls today?"

Why was he changing the subject? Men were strange the way they didn't want to hear about people's problems, or relationships.

The waitress arrived with the food. She placed a bowl of steaming mussels and a green salad in front of Laura and a strip sirloin and baked potato in front of Chris.

"The children were fine. No disasters, no meltdowns, no crises at school. A good day."

Chris didn't seem to be listening. Laura watched him gaze out the window in deep thought; pressures at work most likely.

"Won't it be nice to have Monique home this weekend?" Laura said.

"That's right—I forgot she's coming this weekend. What time on Saturday?"

"No, Friday. Remember? I promised her a special dinner, and she's bringing her friend."

"I didn't realize Friday was the day. I won't be here. I've got meetings in Quebec all day and then dinner afterwards. I won't be home until Saturday."

"But we discussed this and I even reminded you last week. She'll be disappointed if you're not there."

"Nothing I can do, my plans are set. Can't we have the dinner on Saturday?"

"We made all the arrangements for Friday and I don't know her plans after that."

They spent the next few minutes eating in silence. The waitress poured the rest of the wine into Laura's glass and she drank it like water.

"You did a good job with that bottle," Chris said.

"Excuse me?"

He laughed. "You polished off almost the whole thing yourself."

"What do you mean? You've been drinking too."

"Barely."

She beckoned the waitress. "I'll have some coffee please, no dessert."

"What movie would you like to see?" Chris asked.

"I don't care."

"When we get to the theatre we can check the listings and decide," he said.

They hurried to the car, not wanting to be late for the 9:00 show. The temperature had dropped since the sun had set, and a frigid gust pushed through the streets. Laura stumbled on the uneven sidewalk.

"You all right?" Chris asked.

"I think I twisted my ankle."

He took her arm. "A little too much wine?"

"It has nothing to do with the wine. I'm perfectly sober." How dare he keep remarking on how much she had to drink. She gave him a cutting look.

"Can you walk on it?"

"It's fine."

She shook off his arm and tried not to limp.

When they got to the theatre they couldn't agree on which movie to see. Chris had no interest in the romantic comedy that appealed to Laura, and Laura had no interest in the action thriller that appealed to him. Unable to settle and unwilling to concede, they decided to watch different movies.

Chapter Twelve

Usually Chris was so busy that each day melded into the next and by Friday he could hardly believe that another week had whizzed by. But anticipating his rendezvous with Denise, the days crept along like a car in rush-hour traffic, reminding him what it had been like as a child anxiously awaiting the distant weekend. Finally, he was on the plane to Montreal, only a few hours away from seeing her.

At the airport, he rented a car and headed into the city. Not having been back to Montreal for some time, Chris felt like a foreigner. Dorval Airport's name had been changed to Pierre Elliot Trudeau International and the all-French road signs took some adjusting to. When he arrived downtown, he noticed that many new buildings had sprung up from past parking lots and Dorchester Road had been renamed Boulevard René Lévesque. Chris parked near his client's office building on University Avenue and grabbed his briefcase from the trunk. Arriving twenty minutes early, he decided to kill time in the underground shopping mall, which connected many of the office buildings in Montreal. After descending the escalator, he walked along the maze-like corridor of stores. A card and gift shop caught his attention and he went in to browse, hoping to find something to bring home for the girls.

Sifting through a rack of cards, he picked out a card that said, *Life is Love & Love is Sustenance.* A blurred picture of a couple embracing was superimposed by floating roses. He put it back.

"May I help you?" a woman with a red pixie cut asked.

"No thank you."

"Our Mother's Day cards are over here," she pointed to the section.

"No, that's not what I'm looking for."

"A birthday card? Female or male? How old?"

"No, I'm fine."

She hesitated, as if about to say something else, and walked away.

Chris selected a card with a black and white photograph of a sailboat on a lake, the sun setting beyond a forested mountain—a scene that reminded him of his childhood cottage. Then, from a shelf crammed with plush toys, he picked up a small Beanie Baby alligator for Sophie, who was into reptiles at the moment, and a mouse for Tanya, who was into rodents. He paid for the items, slipped the card in the inside pocket of his jacket, and tossed the animals into his briefcase.

The elevator took him to the thirty-second floor, where he was greeted by an effusive receptionist sitting at an oversized desk, flanked by floor-to-ceiling glass doors. She stood up and greeted him, "Monsieur Lambert?" He nodded. "Entrez, s'il vous plaît." A miniature plaque on the desk introduced her as Marsha Brady, a throw-back to his adolescent memories. Her auburn, shoulder-length hair bobbed as she led him to the board room. The serious business suit that she wore did not hide that fact that she looked no older than eighteen. Marsha ushered him to the boardroom and introduced him to the clients.

"Thank you for coming today, Monsieur Lambert, it's a pleasure to meet you," the president of the company said in French. "We convened a few minutes early to review the agenda." Everyone stood up to shake Chris's hand and exchange pleasantries. Having lived in Montreal during his formative years, Chris had learned French as a second language and although he didn't speak it often, he could still communicate with fluidity, albeit with an English accent.

In the past, Chris had sent his junior manager to meet with this group, because the potential business was not substantial enough to warrant his time. Nothing had changed, but he knew that his presence today would create an expectation and he'd have to express a sincere interest in getting involved himself. The meeting was conducted in both French and English, Chris shifting languages with ease.

By 2:00, they had finished their discussion and he accepted an invitation for a late lunch. The president, the financial officer, and the in-house lawyer accompanied him down to the lobby. They decided on a restaurant and walked along St. Catherine Street in the balmy weather. Chris removed his jacket, threw it over his shoulder, and loosened his tie. The Montreal streets were bustling with folks of all kinds—students in denim, seniors wearing hats, women clad in stylish outfits with modish haircuts, and men wearing sporty leather jackets and designer suits. In Cleveland, the human landscape along the downtown streets was more staid, generic. There was vitality in Montreal that Chris had long forgotten or dismissed. It was good to be back.

Talking as he walked, Chris hadn't noticed turning up Crescent Street, the active bar district of his youth, until they stopped in front of the restaurant. The brownstone entrance and the yellow awning over the doorway were familiar. He stepped back and looked up at the name. *Panache*—the very restaurant he had come to with Denise the night they first met.

Not much had changed in twenty-five years; the same name, the same awning, and the same cobalt blue door. The interior décor had been updated, but the galley-style design of the small space remained. Tables lined the side walls with a narrow path in between, and each one was covered by a white linen tablecloth with a small vase containing one tulip. As skeptical as Chris was about fate, and as pragmatic as he was about life in general, the fact that he was in this restaurant at this very time was too bizarre to be mere coincidence.

While they ate and talked, Chris could not stop glancing across the room at the table he had shared with Denise when they were nineteen years old. Snippets of their conversation passed through his mind as if he were back in time. With half an ear, Chris listened to the discussion at the table, and he participated when appropriate, but he couldn't avoid the other conversation going on in his head. The vision of a youthful Denise floated around the table and details of their conversation that night were as clear as if she was talking to him now—her siblings' names, where she went to school and her plans for Paris. He checked the time. Denise's show would be starting in less than an hour.

"We'll be waiting to hear from you then," the president said, as they shook hands in front of the restaurant.

"Bien sûr," Chris said. You bet.

"Thanks for coming up here today," the financial officer said. "I think we've made some progress."

The lawyer spoke intently. "I don't think there will be any serious impediments. I've worked on American placements enough to know we can work within the legal confines." She shook his hand with a firm grip. He made a mental note to follow-up when he returned to Cleveland.

Relieved that he was free to go to Denise's show, Chris hustled to find a cab. When he arrived at the television studio, he found an attendant and was ushered into a room that seated about three hundred people.

"We have open seating but because you are a special guest of Madame Gagnon, you may sit in any of the reserved seats up front." She pointed to the empty seats in the first row.

He looked around and noticed all the women in the audience. The few men in attendance wore casual clothes, not one was in business attire. "No thanks, I'm fine here at the back, I may have to leave early." This was untrue of course, but sitting in the front row would make him feel uncomfortably exposed.

The woman said, "As you wish," and left him standing at the back of the room, briefcase in hand. Like a salesman at a funeral, Chris couldn't imagine feeling more out of place.

When the theme music began, the audience's murmurs subsided. A woman wearing a lime green mini-skirt and a tight black top appeared on the stage. Her thick brown curly hair was tied back by a bright green ribbon and she waved to the audience, smiling with such exuberance that Chris couldn't take his eyes off her teeth.

"Welcome — bienvenue — to *Montreal's Alive!*"

Chris watched with amazement and puzzlement. Who was this woman? Where was Denise? He leaned against the wall and crossed his arms.

"We have a very interesting show for you today — a rare appearance by one of Canada's top international freelance journalists. He spends many months of the year racing from one side of the globe to the other, reporting on issues beyond our imagination." The woman's tone had changed from giddy to contemplative.

Chris suddenly remembered her—the assistant who had accompanied Denise at the wine-tasting in Cleveland. What was her name again?

"Please welcome Michel Beaudoin, who is here to talk to us today about the current plight of women in Afghanistan."

A man walked out on the stage and bowed his head to the audience. He wore blue jeans and a tweed sports jacket. His hair was about chin length and he wore John Lennon-type glasses.

Chris scanned the stage and then the audience. Where was Denise? Camera people hovered by the large equipment but filming hadn't begun.

Nicole ushered the man to an armchair facing the audience and sat down in a matching chair to his right. "Now," she said, "tell me, how was your trip?" She sounded like she was asking him about his holiday.

"Both encouraging and discouraging," he said. He was not smiling.

"I understand that women are free once again, now that the Taliban is less powerful."

"No, that's not necessarily so. Certainly their situation has improved but the country still has a long, long way to go." He crossed his arms in front of his chest.

Nicole grimaced at the audience. To Chris, she appeared more interested in connecting with the spectators than with the guest.

"And that awful burka, do women still have to wear it?"

"You would be surprised how many women do continue to wear the burka, despite the fact that they are no longer forced to."

"Why would they choose to cover up when they can dress as they please?" Nicole stood up and posed for the audience. "What is more appealing? This (she pointed to her own outfit) or that?"

Bright camera lights beamed toward the side of the stage. Chris heard a stagehand yell, "Action."

Nicole pointed to the right of the stage where a woman in a full burka was shuffling towards them. The audience fell silent. Grinning, Nicole said, "May I present, a current fashion piece from

Afghanistan, worn by the one and only, Denise Gagnon." The audience applauded.

Chris noticed a vacant seat in the back corner of the studio and dropped into it. He released his grip on the briefcase he had been clutching and slid it under his seat. His hand throbbed and his tense shoulders ached. Through the mesh covering her face, Denise introduced the guest and the day's topic to the television viewers. Chris watched her take the seat beside Michel Beaudoin. "I'm certain you'll agree," she said, "that we cannot, as a society, sit idly by and ignore the plight of these innocent victims of political instability."

"Yes," Jean interjected, "Afghanistan has the worst education system in the world, the worst social inequalities for women and children, and unfathomable poverty."

Denise faced Jean. "I've been wearing this burka for less than ten minutes and I already feel oppressed."

"You've hit the nail on the head. Women in Afghanistan have suffered terrible oppression for many years. And persecution. To unveil themselves, even though they technically have the freedom to do so, is frightening and risky."

"I feel like I don't even exist under this heavy cover—like I'm anonymous. And it's terribly uncomfortable."

Jean nodded. "Yes, the burka is a strong symbol of the ongoing plight of Afghani women. During the 1996 to 2001 Taliban rule, women were treated like non-entities. They were forbidden to work, study, seek medical help from a male doctor, or leave the house without a male escort. Some women were forced into degrading activities in order to feed their families."

"What kinds of things did they have to do?" Denise asked.

"Street begging and prostitution were not uncommon. Women were forced to cover their bodies while being stripped of their humanity."

"Horrifically ironic," Denise said.

The audience was silent, as if the room was empty.

Denise removed the head piece of her burka, revealing her beautiful face and striking eyes. "I could hardly stand it under there," she said. "Phew, I can breathe."

"That's the point," Jean said. "Women were, and still are subjugated to miserable conditions."

Now that Chris had seen Denise's face and could truly experience the power of her presence, he felt a heightened awareness of his own physicality. He didn't want to share her with the strangers in the room or with the man speaking intimately with her on the stage. He wanted that intimacy for himself, bodies close, breaths colliding.

For the rest of the hour, Denise and Jean talked about the slow progress in Afghanistan since the end of the Taliban rule and the ongoing prevalence of repression in the rural areas. Then Denise removed the entire burka and women from the audience came on the stage to try it on. Mesmerized by her transformation, Chris didn't hear anything else that was said. All he could think about was how beautiful she was and how she had hardly changed in twenty-five years. Loud clapping jolted him from his fixated state and he clapped along, half-heartedly, trying to convey appreciation in case she saw him. They hadn't made eye contact at all during the show, which made him feel like an intruder rather than a guest.

Chris stood with his hands in his pockets while the predominantly female audience paraded past him towards the exit, and he smiled when his eyes met someone else's. Unsure how he would find Denise once she left the stage, he waited for the studio to empty. When a crew member, clad in jeans and a tee-shirt, walked up the aisle, he intercepted her.

"Excuse me, I'm looking for Denise Gagnon? I believe she's expecting me...I'm a friend."

The woman, caught off guard, said, "Sorry, I don't know anything about that. Hey, Danny," she shouted to a man across the studio, "Do you know if Denise is expecting a visitor?"

The man turned toward Chris. "Oh yeah, she mentioned the possibility. Mr. Lambert?"

Chris nodded.

"Take him to Denise's dressing room."

"Sorry about that." The young woman said. "It's chaotic after a taping. Please, follow me."

They went through an obstacle course of wires and props as they made their way across the building. He stood at the door for a moment before knocking, engulfed by trepidation. What was he doing? Why had he come here? Perspiration trickled down his face and he wiped it with his sleeve. Perhaps he should leave. He removed the card he had purchased earlier from his jacket pocket and thought about writing Denise a note, explaining that he had seen the show but couldn't stay. But when he saw the image on the card, a boat sailing against the sunset, a gentle wave of calmness rippled through him. He knocked on the door and Denise promptly opened it, welcoming him with a hug.

"I'm delighted you came. I didn't know if you'd make it."

"I'm glad I did. It was great to see you on stage like that, doing your thing."

"I only noticed you near the end, sitting at the back."

"To be honest, I felt more comfortable there."

She laughed. "Oh, I'm sorry! I should have warned you. It's a daytime show and the audience tends to be mostly women. But we do get lots of male television viewers."

Who wouldn't tune in to watch Denise's show? She was entrancing. "You were fantastic out there, completely in your element."

"I'm comfortable in front of the camera, comes with experience. But the human interest stories, the personal struggles, are what drive my passion for this job."

"You must meet fascinating people."

"Yes, and I'm blessed to have this opportunity to learn from them—even if it's from a mere snapshot of their lives. Sometimes I feel like I'm entertaining guests in my living room and a simple conversation turns into a great discovery."

"You're very talented, a complete natural. It's a skill that few people have."

"Thank you." She sat down at her dressing table and shuffled make-up products and hair brushes.

"You could do much bigger things, I'm convinced of it—go national if you wanted...and they'd love you in America. You have this quality...this incredible appeal." Did he sound like an over-zealous fan?

"I appreciate your vote of confidence." Chris watched her face flush in the mirror and she leaned over to remove her shoes.

Did his opinion matter enough that he could make her blush like that? "Are you still available to go for a drink?" he asked.

"Of course. In fact, I've cleared my schedule to allow for a longer visit, if you're not heading back early, that is."

"I'm all yours tonight," he said. "I mean, I didn't make any plans because I was hoping to see you...to spend some time with you." A few hours ago he had spoken with ease and confidence to a group of people he had never met before and now, like a buffoon, he was stumbling all over his words. "Shall we go to the Realitz, like you suggested in your e-mail? I'm staying there." Another stupid thing to say—what if she thought he was implying something else?

"The Realitz is perfect—on Fridays, they usually have a jazz band playing in the bar. If you don't mind waiting a few minutes, I'm going to have a quick shower and change my clothes. Those bright studio lights are very hot, especially with that burka on."

Chris recalled the morning after they had been together twenty-five years earlier, when Denise had rushed to have a shower before work. They had just spent an intimate night together and he hadn't wanted the day to begin. The memory emerged with such clarity that he felt like he was reliving those moments, like he was nineteen again...

Wearing jeans with no shirt, he stood in front of the bathroom door of his parent's house listening to the water pounding against the tiles. He imagined Denise's naked body being cleansed of their night together, the soap lathering her hair and running down her back. He wished he had the nerve to open the door and to say to her, "Don't go to work today, stay with me for one day." Maybe she would have invited him join her in the shower, forgetting about her job and indulging one more time in the deep pleasures they had discovered in each other. But he didn't have the nerve, didn't dare to intrude. Instead, he had gone downstairs to make coffee.

Now, as he listened to the shower through the dressing-room walls, Chris couldn't help but wonder what if...what if he had had the courage to turn the door knob that day, to poke his head inside and ask, "Can I come in?" He grabbed the newspaper from a side table and forced himself to focus on the headlines. The words melded into each other and the photographs became caricatures — nothing made sense.

Denise returned to the room refreshed and glowing. She wore a simple black dress with a silver-grey shawl draped over her shoulders. Having removed the heavy television make-up, she looked more like herself, her dark eyes striking against the contrast of the shawl, even more beautiful than he remembered. An intense, melancholy expression swept across her face when she looked at Chris, the exact image that had captivated him all those years ago.

Outside, Denise led Chris to her car, which was parked behind the building. Neither spoke as they drove the short distance to the hotel.

Chapter Thirteen

D enise received celebrity treatment by the staff at the Realitz, and she was courteous and friendly in return. For the first time ever, Chris was completely overshadowed by his date, and he wasn't sure how he felt about it. Heads turned as they made their way across the bar area, while whispers hardly concealed the excitement in the room. Denise seemed oblivious to the attention, but Chris was well aware of peering eyes along their path. He wished he could shield her from the communal gaze, but there was nothing he could do. Until now, Chris hadn't thought about her public persona; when they had met in Cleveland a few weeks ago, there hadn't been any great fanfare. Of course, no one knew her there.

The hostess appeared and she ushered them to a quiet table at the back of the room where they would have privacy. "You're quite the celebrity here in Montreal," Chris said. "People can't stop gawking at you. You're a moving magnet in this town."

"I barely notice anymore. Most people aren't intrusive, only curious. They see a familiar face and try to figure out how they know that person."

"What about your husband? Does it bother him to see all these people cranking their necks when you walk by?"

"He gets plenty of attention himself. In fact, he's got his own contingent of admirers. As one of the top contractors in the city, he's made many appearances on those renovation shows and people tend to recognize him too. Occasionally he comes on as a guest on my show, and the audience loves him."

"A celebrity couple."

"To some, I suppose."

The waiter arrived with two glasses of champagne that they hadn't ordered. "Compliments from the bar," he said.

"How lovely," Denise said, offering one of her charming smiles.

Chris watched the waiter practically trip over himself as he walked away. "People adore you. The audience couldn't get enough of you today. And champagne on the house?" Perhaps the affinity he felt with Denise was not unique. But then, here she was, alone with *him*. "How do you feel about all this attention?"

"It's flattering, sometimes annoying, but it's part of what I do. My job is public, and people who tune into the show regularly feel like they know me. I'm not an actress, I'm a regular person who asks a lot of questions."

Chris noticed Denise fidgeting with her napkin. "Are you uncomfortable to be here with me?"

"Oh, no! Why would I be? I meet with all kinds of people here; it's not unusual for me to have a friendly drink with a man in the evening."

That's right, he was just a man having a harmless drink with a woman — nothing wrong with that, nothing out of line. To be considered another old acquaintance, another friendly rendezvous, was humbling. But is that how she saw him? He didn't want to fall into that category, nor be dumped into a pool of male admirers. A silent moment pushed its way in. For a while they watched the jazz band and Chris tapped the table to the beat. The waiter came to check on them.

"A cosmopolitan for me please, Robert — not too strong," Denise said.

"I'll have a Glenfiddich please." Chris said. "With ice."

The dimly lit room provided an invitation for intimate conversation and the sharing of secrets, but a chasm had emerged across the table.

Denise reached over as if to take his hand. But she picked up a cardboard coaster and played with it. "It's good to see you again, Chris. I've thought a lot about you since Cleveland."

He cleared his throat. "Me too. Seeing you again has conjured up a lot of memories. I'm not prone to reflecting on the past and I'm kind of surprised at myself. Spilling my guts and dumping my whole life story in your lap was not the smoothest move on my part."

"I found your story fascinating. And I've been thinking about all those things that happened to you, especially learning how you'd been duped into early fatherhood. What a cruel injustice." Denise became more and more animated as she spoke. "How could you ever forgive someone who lied to you like that?"

"My anger towards Kendra didn't last long. Once I was able to dig deep and see things from her perspective, I began to forgive her. She played tough but she was way too young and vulnerable when she got pregnant." Chris paused and sipped his scotch. "The baby had to have been either mine or this other guy's and she made the assumption that I was the father, prayed that was the case. I don't see it as a malicious act anymore. It wouldn't help to stay bitter. Besides, Monique could have been my child, given the timing."

"That's huge, to have such a capacity for forgiveness. I think most people would feel a tremendous sense of betrayal and would harbour resentment forever."

"I don't know. What good would that do? Carrying that kind of anger wouldn't help anybody, and Monique had been exposed to enough dysfunction already. When Kendra and I split up, we could breathe normally again—I wanted us to have a positive beginning, a fresh start that wouldn't be weighted down by past mistakes."

"Great attitude," Denise said. "Laudable."

Chris shrugged. "Enough about me, tell me more about your life. What happened after that incident with the French family? You mentioned a long-term relationship."

Denise stiffened. "I have to confess, I'm not quite as forgiving as you. I was betrayed too. It's been thirteen years since I left Paris, but when I think of him—all the lies, I still feel guttural hatred. I don't think my anger will ever go away."

Finally, he was getting her to open up, to show some emotion. "You don't strike me as a bitter woman."

"My saving grace is that I was fortunate enough to build a new life, a great life that has allowed me to move ahead of those memories."

"What happened over there? What did the guy do to you? Considering the previous episode with that father, you don't have good luck with Frenchmen!" Chris flinched, realizing her husband, Francois, must also be French.

Denise's body became rigid as she crossed her arms. Chris wanted to pull his chair beside hers and put his arm around her. This was supposed to be a pleasant evening, not one that would call to mind painful memories and cause her stress. He ordered a bottle of sparkling water and asked if she was hungry, but she wasn't. Chris felt a sudden protectiveness toward her, much like he felt for his daughters and wife when they were troubled; he wished he could banish her past and annihilate her pain. What if he and Denise had maintained contact after the summer of 1982, even loosely? He could have visited her in Paris during those early years and she could have come to British Columbia to see him, or they could have met up in Montreal after completing their degrees and made plans from there. Surely, her life would have been better with him by her side, with his support. One hypothesis after another bombarded Chris's mind until Denise's voice nudged him back to the present.

"Do you remember that night we met, when we sat at the restaurant and talked and talked?"

"I remember it clearly. In fact, I had lunch at Panache today. My clients brought me there for a bite after our meeting. It hasn't changed much."

"How strange for you to end up there. I haven't been back there since our night."

Chris swiveled the melting ice cubes in his scotch glass. She had said, 'Our night.' Not, 'that night' or 'the night we met', or even 'since then.' *Our night.* What did she mean by that? He drank from his glass, almost choking on one of the bits of ice. He cleared his throat and said, "Sitting near our table at the restaurant earlier, and knowing I'd be seeing you shortly, was weird."

"Do you think there is some larger plan for us to reconnect like this, or do you think it's all a big coincidence?" Denise asked.

"Who knows?" Chris picked up his cocktail napkin and tore a piece off the corner. "I'm not a big believer in providence. I tend to be more of a here and now kind of guy."

Denise gave him a dubious look. "You don't think, in any remote way, that fate has brought us together?"

"What does 'fate' mean anyway? Destiny, doom, God's hand? I prefer to view life as a series of random events—some things that we have control over, some that we don't."

"Hmm. My view of the world is somewhat different," Denise said. Her eyes met his over the top of her martini glass. "I believe things happen for a reason."

"And the reason we met again is…"

"I haven't figured that out yet, but I'm glad we did."

"Me too." Chris shifted in his seat and watched the jazz musicians scatter for their break. He faced Denise again. "I have great memories of our first evening together, but I've always wondered what it meant to you?" There. He'd asked the question that had plagued him for many years.

Denise's image created a serene portrait across the table in the soft light. Pondering her answer, she twisted the ends of her hair around her finger, a habit Chris recalled from when they were nineteen. He wondered if she would evade the question or simply tell him it was too long ago to remember. If she shrugged it off, as a youthful fling, that would probably be for the best; his life could return to normal and he would no longer feel out of control. Yes, it would be much better to learn that he had merely been a passing romantic experience, one to build upon. Waiting for Denise to answer, Chris felt that same churning anxiety he'd felt when he'd asked her to come home with him for the night all those years ago.

Denise lowered her chin, leaned forward and spoke almost inaudibly, as if she was breaking a confidence. "That was the most beautiful, most powerful, most incredible night of my life…though I didn't know it then."

Chris's lungs felt like they were constricting. He took a deep, quiet breath. "Why didn't you contact me again? You had my number; I left our future completely up to you."

"It was a strange period in my life, Chris. I had just broken up with my boyfriend and was feeling pretty crushed." She coughed, and took a drink of water. "I was vulnerable and needy when I met you. You helped me escape from my sadness, you made me feel cherished and you repaired some of my broken self-confidence. I felt safe with you, and although it was naïve, because I hardly knew you, I trusted you completely."

"Why then, did you disappear like that? You could have called me to say good-bye, you could have written me from France. I got the impression that I had misread the whole thing, that I was a total idiot to think that what we shared was special. I know we were kids, but even then I could tell the difference between lust and love." He lowered his voice, "The intensity of that night still resonates with me."

Denise's eyes glazed over with what Chris came to realize were tears. He didn't want to upset her, but he couldn't backtrack, he needed to hear it all.

"My feelings scared me and spurred me to flee. I remember being confused, I couldn't even articulate the emotions to myself. And I was embarrassed. I had never done anything like that in my life."

"You didn't commit a crime," he said.

"What I mean is…I wasn't that kind of girl. I didn't have one-night stands. You were the second guy I had ever slept with and I'd only just met you. I was shocked at myself…more like mortified. But during that night I could break away from my confusion for a while. I remember feeling comfortable with you—this stranger. That night was thrilling and frightening at the same time."

The music resumed and the words 'Since I Fell for You' floated through the room, the raspy voice of the vocalist lured Chris and Denise away from their conversation. Time had no meaning then, nor did the air they were breathing. What was passing between them was weightless and obscure and they observed each curiously, as if to inquire, "Who are you? Why are you sabotaging my life?" Denise pulled her shawl tightly around her shoulders.

Chris stripped their silence. "What about the next day? Do you remember? You were so withdrawn, and reserved. You hardly said anything when I drove you to work."

"I was self-conscious. I was afraid you'd think I was loose. I don't know—it was awkward. My instinct was to run, to run into the future, to my new life overseas."

"Gone, just like that." He snapped his fingers. "And you never have the urge to contact me?"

"Yes I did, but I was afraid to. I never really knew what you thought of me, so I resisted. Our lives were going in such different directions, and practically it didn't make sense." Her voice began to trail off. "I guess I should have...oh, I don't know."

The conversation had taken on a life of its own. What was he doing there, sitting in the Realitz bar, having cocktails with Denise? Chris was elated by the developments, but at the same time, threatened. His current reality was ideal—like quintessential ski conditions, when the sun is shining and the hills are covered abundantly by well-groomed snow. There may be an icy patch here and there, a small crevice to avoid, an errant cloud overhead, but overall, everything is good. Denise's presence was a menace, a violent storm. But he had invited this tempest into his life. He could have let things be, he didn't have to pursue this friendship. Chris thought of his hotel room upstairs, comfortable and enticing. With discretion, they could make their way there, separately, and recapture that blissful feeling of absolute intimacy. But the days of the carefree, go-for-it kind of attitude were long over. Everything had consequences; every move could impact other people. Chris had never cheated on a woman, even in his youth when he and his friends were up to all kinds of tricks. He recalled his mother saying to him one day, "The thing I know for sure about you, is that you will always have high principles. You will never lie, cheat, steal, or be unfaithful to a woman." They had been doing dishes and she had said that out of the blue. He told her she was right.

Denise continued, "For years I kept the slip of paper with your address and phone number in the pocket of my purse," Denise said. "Sometimes I came upon it accidentally and sometimes I consciously pulled it out. I could never bring myself to throw it out because that was my only memento from the time we shared. And it was a symbolic link to you. Sounds silly, doesn't it?"

"No I don't think it's silly, it's heartwarming. But if you kept my address all that time, why didn't you drop me a note?"

"I figured it wasn't possible to hold on to what had transpired between us. And we were across the world from one another, what would be the point?"

Denise had been close to his grasp, yet so elusive. What would have happened if he had tried to track her down? But he hadn't even known her last name and it would have been difficult if not impossible. During the years, he had chastised himself over and over for not getting her address. Everything had happened so fast that morning when she left.

"Tell me," he said, "what happened to you in Paris that's so difficult for you to talk about?" Whatever went on over there must have contributed to their displaced romantic destiny and he needed to know the facts.

"I don't want to talk about that. I'm having such a pleasant time with you and I don't want to spoil the evening. But I will tell you one thing—I had to leave France suddenly, and when I came home to Montreal, I thought of you."

Denise's demeanour appeared fragile again, as if she was delving into some dark, unsafe place in her soul. How quickly her manner had transformed from a state of self-confidence to self-doubt. If only he could reach out to her, take her in his arms.

"Then why didn't you try to locate me when you were in Montreal?"

"Because I was in an emotional crisis and crumbling inside. I could hardly face my family, let alone a one-night lover from the past." She broke her pensive expression with a demure smile.

"I'm sorry you were that unhappy. Maybe I could have helped you," Chris said.

"When I came home, I considered trying to locate you. Maybe deep down I craved the same kind of comfort and reassurance you had given me before, which was selfish."

"I wish you had tried." Damn it. All it would have taken was one phone call.

"I found my old purse and checked the pocket, but the paper with your address was gone. I couldn't imagine how it had simply disappeared. I took it as a sign to leave things alone."

Chris figured out which year that was and ascertained that he was single then, living in Cleveland with Monique. Laura hadn't entered his life yet, and he was working hard to build his career while raising his daughter. "My parents were still living in the same house. You could have easily reached me through them."

Denise looked down at the table and then slowly lifted her eyes to meet his. "Yes, I probably could have tracked you down. I knew your last name was Lambert, but I didn't have the nerve. Like I said, I was such a mess back then. And for all I knew, you were happily married with children, a golden retriever, and a white picket fence. Besides, what's the point of speculating? Life is what it is."

"You're right, there's no point." Chris wanted to go back in time and make everything all right for Denise, to be the one to help her recover from her despair. He noticed her rubbing her cheek, as if it hurt.

"Are you all right?" he asked.

"I'm fine. I just have a small ache in my tooth."

"You should get it checked out." Now he wanted to fix her physical pain too.

"I suppose I should — eventually. Who has time for the dentist?"

Chris laughed. "Nonsense! Health comes first." He knew he sounded exactly like Laura reprimanding him for not tending to his various complaints.

They continued chatting into the late evening, but veered away from the previous topics. Chris wanted to delve more deeply into Denise's personal thoughts, but sensed that she was becoming uncomfortable and the last thing he wanted to do was drive her away. Sharing stories about their children and their work was much safer. For a while they also talked about wine, a common interest.

Denise looked at her watch. "I can't believe how much time has passed. I feel like we just sat down."

"I feel like a cad," Chris said, "I haven't offered you dinner." While talking to Denise for the last few hours, he had lost sight of all else. He'd hung on to her every word and watched her movements as if he were filming her in his mind. "Would you like to eat something?"

"It's getting late, I should go." She stood up, smoothed out her dress, and picked up her purse. "I've been so immersed in our discussion that I didn't even think of food."

Chris left some cash on the table and walked her through the hotel lobby, again conscious of people's gazes. He slowed down as they passed the elevator, and chastised himself for wanting to invite Denise up to his room. What was wrong with him? For the first time in his life, Chris was afraid of himself, what he was capable of doing if given the chance.

He walked Denise to her car and opened the door for her, stepping away so he wouldn't be tempted to engulf her in his arms.

But she moved towards him and kissed him on both cheeks. "Lovely to see you, Chris."

"You too."

She got into the car, but before closing the door, she pulled a white envelope from her purse and handed it to him.

"What's this?"

"My life in Paris — actually, it's a tale of failure and disappointment."

"I was starting to think you'd keep me in suspense about your Paris days forever."

She laughed nervously. "Now I'm embarrassed. There's no mystery involved, only a sad story about a gullible Canadian girl who went abroad with big dreams and came home with nothing but an empty, angry heart."

Chris leaned over the car door and said in a low voice, "There's nothing gullible about you, and there never was. I have a feeling your story is more about a young, idealistic girl whose heart was damaged and has never quite healed." God, he wished he could press his body against hers, feel her heartbeat, smell her skin. Why was this happening; how could he let it?

He shut the car door and stood alone in the parking lot, watching her drive away.

Chapter Fourteen

Chris hung up his jacket when he entered his hotel room. He removed his shoes and tie, and observed the lavish furnishings. High ceilings, antiques, and luxury fabrics gave the impression of old-world charm. Chris had been to enough five-star hotels that he barely paid attention to the finer details, but he knew Laura would appreciate this room. One day he should bring her to Montreal and they should stay at the Realitz. She had only been to Montreal to visit his ailing mother and had never seen the sights as a tourist. Yes, she would love it here, especially Old Montreal with its cobblestone streets and quaint shops.

The evening had ended rather abruptly and much too soon. But what had he been hoping for? Denise had a family to get home to, and more important things to do than idle away time with him. A pang of guilt struck him for not having flown back to Cleveland; he would have arrived home late, but at least he'd have been there when the girls woke up.

Calling room service, Chris gazed out the window at the busy street below. He ordered a club sandwich with a salad and asked to have his suit and shirt picked up for laundering. Then he changed into the white terry robe in the bathroom. It was only 9:10. Under normal circumstances, he would have rushed to the airport after his meetings to catch the first flight back home, but then, this was not a normal day.

He poured himself a scotch from the mini bar and removed Denise's letter from his jacket pocket. Sitting down in a comfortable armchair, he hesitated before opening it. What could this letter contain? And why couldn't she tell him about Paris in person? She was probably embarrassed, perhaps even traumatized by the events of her past. When he unfolded the pages he was surprised to see her handwriting. The flowing script on personal stationary induced a visceral sensation; he could almost feel the blood flowing through his veins. He had never considered the power of the cursive form before.

Chris, I'm going to tell you what happened in Paris after I finished my studies. I don't know how it will come out, so please bear with me as I try to piece together these fragments of my past. I think I left off telling you about the incident at the Duval's country house and then moving in with a couple of good friends from school. During my last year at the Sorbonne, I fell in love.

Chris took a large swig of his scotch, emptying the glass, and then went to the mini bar to pour himself another. He looked out the window again, squinting to decipher the forms below. Sherbrooke Street was splattered with rain and the domes of open umbrellas hovered over pedestrians, hiding their bodies underneath. A colourful mosaic danced beneath him like a kaleidoscope. He drew the curtains and sat down to resume reading.

I'd been working part-time at a wine store, where I'd occasionally have contact with one of our biggest suppliers. His name was Jacques. He was several years older than me and although I found him attractive, I didn't think of him as a prospective boyfriend at first. We used to talk to each other during his visits and I suppose we flirted a little. A couple of months after we first met, he invited me to lunch.

A knock at the door startled Chris and he almost dropped his drink. Oh yes, the food. The hotel server said, "good evening," and entered with the tray.

"Thanks," Chris said. He took the plates and dismissed the man with a nod.

"You have some dry-cleaning?"

"One moment, please." He put the food down and fetched his clothes. Handing over the laundry bag, he said good-night and abruptly shut the door. Only after he'd sat down again did he realize that he'd forgotten to tip the fellow. Tomorrow he'd make up for it.

He was sophisticated and wealthy, owning his own vineyard and several other businesses. When we met, I was twenty-three and he was thirty-nine; the age difference didn't bother either of us. I was impressed by his success and captivated by his charm. He pursued me aggressively, as intensely as a business acquisition, I later learned. Initially his tenacity scared me, but eventually I gave in to his unyielding attention. It was flattering, and I was quickly swept into his life. He took me everywhere, to exotic places like Monaco, Rome, London, Prague, and Vienna, and my world opened up in a way I never could have imagined.

At the beginning my life was truly a fantasy, and since school was almost over, I was ready for new adventures. I didn't expect or plan for this, but the excitement suited me well at the time. My student visa was about to expire and because of Jacques, I could stay longer in France. He arranged a work visa for me and I became his employee, working as a sales agent for his winery. My passion for wine developed from there.

Jacques owned a luxury apartment in Paris and I soon moved in with him. What a contrast to my simple student life. Mahogany, oak, granite, marble, crystal, and opulent fabrics surrounded me. There were fresh flowers in every room and the ceilings were at least twelve feet high. I felt like I was living in a palace and I sometimes had to remind myself that I was the lady of the house, not one of the staff.

For special dinners, Jacques brought in his favourite Parisian chef along with his sous-chef. This was a wonderful learning experience for me. Any opportunity, I would be in the kitchen, observing and assisting. I had great fun working with these talented and entertaining gurus of French cuisine, much more fun than playing hostess in the evening, which brought me stress rather than pleasure.

Surrounded by company, I felt like I was on show, perceived by others as Jacques' latest conquest. When I mentioned this to him, he tried to appease me by saying that his past exploits with women meant nothing since he had found me. He said that I was the love of his life, his eternal passion.

At the time, many people lived as common-law partners in France and we didn't feel the need to marry. I thought we were committed to one another, bound for life, and didn't consider it necessary to make our union official. Jacques said we were more married than all the married couples he knew and being gullible, I believed him. He used to tell me that if I ever left him he would die, that I was the breath for his soul, the fuel for his life. He was a romantic and I had fallen under his spell.

So many people came and went in our lives that I could hardly keep track of who was a friend and who was a business associate. I often entertained the wives while the men conducted business and I was always available to accompany Jacques on his travels. I became his personal assistant of sorts and he jokingly called me his biggest asset, his most important investment. I can't say that I reveled in this role, but I did accept it as part of the relationship.

Jacques' business interests were far-reaching. He owned a few magazines, an investment company, many properties, several restaurants, and the vineyard – his favourite enterprise. It was his father's great passion and when he died, Jacques stepped in. Under his guidance the winery attained the status of a highly prized label – his greatest pride. I loved the vineyard too. When I accompanied him there, we'd walk amongst the grapevines, inspecting the grapes and tasting their sweet juice. The peace and beauty of the countryside made me never want to leave; it was paradise to me. But the vineyard was far from Paris and Jacques always had to rush back to the city to tend to other business… so I was told.

During those years I explored Paris in a way I never could during my student days. I went to the theatre, the opera, shopped in the most elegant boutiques, and dined at Paris's finest restaurants. Life was good. I thought I was happy.

Chris's cell phone rang, causing him to jump. He reluctantly answered it.

It was Laura. "How are you?" she asked. "Is everything all right? You said you'd call after your meetings and it's getting late."

"I'm sorry." He lowered his voice as if he were among other people. "I'm still tied up at a business dinner. Can I call you in the morning?"

"OK. The girls send hugs and kisses. We miss you. I'll talk to you in the morning."

He hesitated before signing off. He was a liar. What had gotten into him? Couldn't he have come up with another excuse—a less blatant lie? And he hadn't even asked about Monique's arrival. Tomorrow. He would make up for everything then.

"Are you still there?" she asked.

"Yes, yes. Sorry. Uh, I'll call you around 8:00 in the morning, OK?"

"That's fine. Have a good night."

After hanging up, Chris leaned back in the chair and closed his eyes. He massaged his scalp as if trying to activate his brain. What the hell was he doing delving into another woman's life while neglecting his own family back home? He hadn't even bothered checking his e-mails or touching base with Tony. Leaning forward, he picked up Denise's letter and continued reading.

Jacques traveled a lot but I didn't always accompany him because he needed me to stay behind to deal with business in Paris. When he was gone I'd spend time with my girlfriends from the university who led more conventional lives. Some of them had children and I'd visit them out in the suburbs, which would bring me back to earth for a while. In the city, I'd go to museums and sometimes to the ballet or the opera. Jacques's absence also gave me time to write letters back home and to read.

Starting a family became increasingly important to me, but Jacques kept dismissing the idea using the excuse that our lifestyle was not conducive to having children. For the first few years I agreed, but as time passed, and after my thirtieth birthday, I became restless. I suppose I was waiting for him to change his mind, but he never did. Occasionally, I broached the subject with him but he was unresponsive, leaving me feeling empty. I couldn't understand why he had no desire to have children with me; we were in love, and as far as I was concerned, the timing was perfect. But I couldn't force the issue, wouldn't dare.

I respected and admired Jacques for his drive, his work ethic and his integrity — he seemed to be a man of honour and I was proud to be his partner. However, he was extremely intense and could be volatile, which sometimes scared me. I learned to live with his outbursts because they would pass as quickly as they came.

I don't know what happened to the good years; they ran away from me somehow, but it wasn't until the end of our relationship that I realized how terribly unhappy and empty my life had become. The early years with Jacques were filled with enriching worldly experiences, but over time I had become a worn-out, hollow shell with no sense of who I was anymore.

Jacques never mistreated me yet I came to the realization that he never fully acknowledged me either. He loved me, that I believed, but it was a selfish kind of love. He loved what I brought to his life, how I made him feel. He didn't love who I was or what I was about. In fact, he didn't know me at all. I was a valuable accessory to his life, one that met his needs and fed his ego. During those years I lost my identity and my self worth began to erode. Ironically, I didn't realize this until after I had left him and left the country. During my relationship with Jacques I was spiraling downward; had I not learned the truth about him I could still be there, a mere shadow of my former self.

Chris stopped reading. Denise's story had flowed like fiction, like a tale of shattered hopes and disillusionment. How could life have gone so wrong for Denise? How could her young passionate spirit be crushed like that? Chris went to the mini bar and poured himself a Perrier. He tossed the green bottle in the trash with force, causing it to shatter. Some of the glass shards rebounded over the edge of the can.

Who was this character, Jacques, who abused the gentle nature of this exceptional woman? If he himself had been Denise's boyfriend back then, he would have cherished her, not used and discarded her like this swine had done. What a great life he could have given her; what a great future they could have built together. Chris picked up a section of his sandwich, brought it to his mouth, but didn't take a bite. Setting it back on the plate, he sat down and read some more.

We had been together for eight years when I got wind of Jacques' secret life. I still can't believe how utterly naïve I had been — I had never had an inkling of his infidelity. I had trusted him and revered him throughout our entire relationship. He was larger than life to me and I never doubted his devotion. Yes, he was away for long periods but he phoned me every day, no matter where he was in the world. Being such a powerful person, he had enormous demands placed on him, and I knew from the beginning that I would not have him entirely to myself. But I never thought for one minute that I had been sharing him with another woman.

As it turned out, he wasn't having an affair with another woman. I was the affair — I was the mistress! I found out, after eight years of committing my life and soul to him, that Jacques was married and had two children. And it wasn't a case of Jacques' marriage going awry and his finding solace in a new love; he was still living as husband and wife with this woman and leading a double life. If it hadn't been for his private chef, who inadvertently let it slip out, I wonder how much longer I would have remained the unwitting mistress. Maybe my whole life.

Jacques' wife and children lived on the vineyard estate, which had been in his family for generations. He had actually spent many of his supposed travels at his home in Bordeaux with them. Apparently his wife didn't like to come to Paris and was content living her life as a 'country gentlewoman.' The children would have been teenagers when I found all this out and if his wife knew about me, I will never know. Maybe she accepted the fact that he had a mistress in the city, but for me, this deception was something I could not get past. Jacques was shocked and distressed when I found out because he had done such a good job concealing the truth from me for so long — not one person had even hinted about his married status during all those years. Perhaps they thought I knew, or perhaps no one dared to cross him.

When I confronted Jacques, he tried to downplay the relevance of his family. He said, "I have a responsibility toward them, can't you see? But my marriage has been long over, I tell you!" He tried to appease me with more lies. "You are the most important person in my life. Yes, I have spent time there, but it was necessary to oversee the vineyard." When I asked if he slept with his wife, he didn't respond. He evaded the question by saying, "I have children, I have to look after them, and they need their father. Can you not understand that?"

Can you believe it? He was trying to make me feel guilty for keeping him away from children I didn't even know he had. I asked him again if he slept with his wife and when he didn't answer the second time, I knew the truth. I could see it in his face, in his eyes that wouldn't meet mine. He tried to embrace me, to calm me down, but by then I was out of control. I hit him with all my might. "You are blowing everything out of proportion," he yelled. "You are breaking my heart."

I felt sick. It was the worst thing that had ever happened to me. My life had been smashed into pieces and I felt incapable of carrying on. I wanted to leave but there was nowhere to go. When I asked him to leave, he refused. That night, I stayed in the bedroom as he slept on the floor at the door. I remember him saying, "My darling, I am here waiting for you, I will not leave you." I think he was physically trying to prevent me from leaving. The next day he begged my forgiveness. He told me that he had wanted to tell me the truth but was protecting me by keeping me in the dark. He said the fact that he was married didn't change the way he felt about me, that everything he had ever said was sincere. When I told him I could no longer be with such a deceitful and egotistical brute, he was aghast. He said, "In time you will understand that what we share is too important to throw away." What __we__ were sharing! I was the one who was doing the sharing — with another woman! When I told him that, he shouted, "Grow up," and left the apartment, slamming the door. That was the last time I saw him.

I contacted him a few days later to ask how we should work out financial arrangements, at least until I got back on my feet, and he laughed. He said I wasn't entitled to anything, and since I no longer had a job, I no longer had a visa and couldn't stay in France. He told me I was an illegal resident and because we weren't married, I couldn't fight him for a financial settlement. "You wanted out and you've got it," he said. "Don't come crying to me for help. You've made a choice and you have to live with the consequences." I was amazed at how quickly I could go from loving Jacques to hating him. I had never felt so vulnerable in my life. Fortunately, my mother sent me money and paid for my plane ticket home. This is how I returned to Montreal and back to my mother's house. Thank God for Mother — she was my rock; without her, I don't know how I would have carried on.

Why am I telling you all this, Chris? I suppose because I haven't entirely dealt with all those emotions and seeing you again has opened up my soul and somehow given me permission to spill out this part of my past. Please keep my story between us — few people know about it and I prefer to keep it that way. I apologize for my long-winded monologue; I guess I got carried away. I don't mean to make myself sound like a victim here and I certainly take responsibility for the choices I've made — choices that have taken my life in unexpected directions. You know this better than anyone, I expect.

The good thing about my experience is that I learned from it, and gained a greater appreciation for family and friends. For a while I thought a part of me had died, but over time I realized that I still had a fighting spirit and I needed to channel it in a positive way. I now have a fabulous family, a satisfying and challenging career, and enriching friendships. I consider myself a fortunate woman.

You asked about Paris and I delivered much more than you bargained for. I hope I didn't bore you silly with these melodramatic details. But thank you for asking and taking such an interest. I'm the one who usually asks the questions — such is my profession; I'm not accustomed to talking about me.

I consider myself privileged to have you, Chris, such a fine person, among my family of friends.

Affectionately,
Denise

Chris put the letter down and leaned back in his chair. Wow. Denise sure went through the wringer back then. But he was not surprised that she hadn't let the ordeal hold her back in life. Even when they had been together at nineteen she had a fearless quality that he admired — going off to school in a foreign country where she didn't know anyone, leaving her family and all that was familiar. Notwithstanding her courage, Denise did have a vulnerable side, which he couldn't help but be attracted to. And sharing this information with him must have been a big deal for her; it indicated that she trusted *him*, that she was letting *him* in. A nice gesture. Very nice indeed.

Chris read the last paragraph of the letter again. Friends, she said. Yes, at the end of the day, a friend was what he was to her and all he could ever be. He turned on his laptop and stared at the screen for a long time. How could he express all that he was feeling without coming on too strong? Before going to bed he wrote Denise a note:

Dear Denise: I read your letter. What a story! We have to talk. Chris

Chapter Fifteen

Monique was on the phone in the kitchen when Chris arrived home, and her eyes lit up when he came in the room. Ending her call, she flew into his arms.

"Hey, Dad!"

"How are you, Chickpea?"

"Super. But it's great to be home. How was Montreal?"

"Pretty good. Listen, I'm sorry I couldn't be here for your dinner last night."

She waved dismissively. "No probs."

"Where's the rest of the gang?"

"Shopping. Laura said they'd be home around lunchtime." Monique poured them each a cup of coffee. "How's work going?"

She looked like his little girl in her old robe covered with kittens, and fuzzy yellow slippers on her feet. But her comportment, her easy maturity, shook him into the realization that Monique was not a child. Stray hair strands fell around her face, framing the strong features that had no semblance to his. The rest of her wavy hair was tied back in a messy ponytail, another picture of childhood.

"Work's fine. But I want to hear about you." With his arm around her shoulders, he led her to the family room. Reclining in an armchair, he inspected her face. "I can see that you're spent. How were those last exams?"

"One was a killer but the other was OK. I'm just glad to have them behind me so I can have some fun, fun, fun." She plopped onto the sofa and hugged a throw cushion.

Monique deserved the break. Always a conscientious student, she attacked her studies with such intensity that he often worried about her health. And she was too thin. "When was the last time you had a proper night's sleep...and a proper meal?"

"Dad, I'm tired 'cause I pulled a few all-nighters during exams. Don't worry; I'll catch up. And yes, I am eating enough, lots of healthy stuff."

"No more jujubes and popcorn for dinner?"

"No. My jujube days are long over — since I overdosed on them. They've been replaced." She grinned mischievously. "By chocolate chip cookies and M&M's."

Chris grimaced. "Don't tell me that, I can't stand to hear it." He threw his hands over his face.

"Kidding! Lots of fruit and vegetables, and occasionally a balanced meal."

"That's better, but you've got to eat properly — you need to feed that brain as well as that skinny body."

"I know, I know, I know."

"And when do you start your job?"

Monique had worked as a swimming instructor and life guard at the local pool for the past few summers, and this year she was to be a supervisor.

"Not for two weeks. Thankfully, I have some free time. I told Laura that you guys should take off on a trip together. I'd be happy to look after the girls."

"That's a kind offer. I'll check my work schedule." His mind roamed to Denise. What would a romantic getaway be like with her? Where would they go? St. Bart's, Hawaii, Bermuda? He imagined walking together, barefoot on an isolated white sandy beach, hand-in-hand; a scene from their romantic destiny that had never materialized.

"Dad, yoo hoo! Are you listening?"

"Sorry, what's that?"

"I asked if you wanted to play tennis this weekend." She sprang from the couch and pretended to serve the ball.

"I'd love to. Go ahead and book the court for this afternoon. But you gotta take it easy on your old man." Chris stood up and yanked Monique's ponytail. "It's great to have you home."

Chris went to his study to check in with work. He hadn't reviewed his e-mails since yesterday and, as usual, an accumulation of memos and messages awaited him. He scrolled down, hoping for a word from Denise. What was he expecting? That she would rush home and write to him immediately after having seen him the day before? He leaned back in his chair and clasped his hands behind his weary head, yawning. In spite of the dark, quiet hotel room, and the comfortable king-size bed, he had hardly slept.

Denise's image appeared in his mind and he smelled her perfume, sensing her lips brushing his cheeks. He thought about their conversation at the Realitz and then her letter. Perhaps he should e-mail her again or call her, comment on what he had read. No, not yet. He'd come across as anxious, overzealous. Besides, she might still be reluctant to talk about that period of her life. And he'd have to be careful how he handled things going forward, considering that they were both married. The smartest, safest thing to do would be to lay low for a while because a friendship between them could only work if he respected personal boundaries, for everybody's sake.

Maybe he should send her flowers, a small gesture to convey his appreciation for their resurrected friendship. Roses would be nice. He could congratulate her on the success of her show and tell her how much he enjoyed their conversation. Rifling through his desk drawer, he found the business card of a florist he used to call when sending flowers to his mother in Montreal. When the woman answered the phone he almost hung up. Clearing his throat, he mustered the nerve to follow through.

"I'd like to order some flowers for delivery."

He ordered two dozen long-stemmed roses in a variety of colours, and then changed his mind. "Make it twenty-five please, and don't include any red ones." Chris remembered how Denise once told him that she thought red roses were a cliché, given by men with no imagination. He took a deep breath, then said, "The note should read, 'Dear Denise: a rose for each year I missed knowing you. XO Chris.'" After paying by credit card he hung up, shocked by his own nerve.

Chris plowed through his work, addressing the critical issues with focused determination. In work mode, he could accomplish a lot in a short time. Laura and the children would be home soon and he had to make efficient use of his time. Once he'd completed the most urgent action items, he called Tony.

"Hey, it's me. Any bombs while I was gone?"

"Yeah, you lost the Kramer deal."

"What?" The Kramer takeover was Chris's biggest prospect at the moment.

Tony laughed.

"Very funny."

"Don't worry. Everything's under control. How was Montreal?"

"Good. Worth the trip." Tony had no interest in pursuing Montreal because he didn't speak French. Chris could do whatever he wanted there without Tony's involvement, but he'd better drum up something concrete if he wanted to go back. "You going to the office today?"

"I'm already at the office."

"Ged outta dare," Chris said. "Go for a run, fly a kite, do something outdoors."

"I'll be heading home soon. Listen, can you to go to San Francisco next week?

They'd been working on a big deal out west that was near completion. "One sec, let me check my agenda." He pulled up his calendar on the computer and studied his commitments for the following week. "The end of the week could work."

"Good. A couple of days should do it. I was gonna go myself but now that the Carmichael mess is erupting again and —"

"No problem. I wanted to meet with the San Fran guys anyhow." Chris thought about Monique's offer to mind the girls. Laura would be thrilled to meet him there for the weekend; she'd been itching to get away for some time.

"I'll leave it with you then," Tony said. "Thanks."

Chris heard commotion coming from the kitchen. After wrapping up his call, he went to greet his family.

Laura unpacked groceries while the girls battled over donuts.

"Hey, hey, what's going on?" he said, entering the kitchen.

The girls stopped bickering and ran to him. He picked them up together and hugged them. "That's better. No more fighting please."

They ignored his comment and fired a rapid succession of inde-cipherable words, competing for his attention.

Laura glared at the girls and then at him. "They were like this the whole time you were away."

"I think you two spitfires had better settle down." Chris said. "I brought you something from Montreal and if you go to your rooms to play quietly, I'll bring you your presents. Mommy and I need a few minutes to talk."

"What d'you get for us?" Sophie asked.

Chris pointed to the old servants' stairs. "The faster you ske-daddle, the faster you'll find out."

Tanya raced up the stairs with Sophie following, trying to grab onto her foot.

Laura sighed. "Ah, some peace." She turned to face Chris, "Good trip?"

"Not bad." He kissed her on the lips. "How about you? The girls giving you a hard time?"

"We've had our moments. But they're excited to have Monique home."

Chris picked up a case of water bottles from the kitchen floor. "Where do you want this?"

Laura motioned to the utility closet.

"You should have left them in the car for me to bring in. They're heavy."

"I didn't know you were home. You didn't call to say what time you were coming." She continued putting groceries away in the cupboard, her back to him.

Shoot, he'd forgotten to call again. "I'm sorry, I meant to call at the gate, but I was late checking in at the airport because of the rental car, and by the time I arrived, the plane was boarding and —"

"It's hard to plan the day when I don't know what's going on." She glowered at him. "You were so vague last night."

The edge in her voice struck him like a sharp jab. "I'm sorry. I was planning on the early flight but didn't know if I'd need to stay for a breakfast meeting." Why was he creating this jumble of untruths?

She began to unload the dishwasher and Chris reached over to help. She handed him the rack of cutlery.

"I have some good news. At least, I hope you'll see it as good," he said.

"What's that?" She unloaded plates while he spoke.

"How does California sound to you?"

"What do you mean?"

"I mean San Francisco."

"When?"

"Next weekend."

Her face softened. "Really?"

"I need to be there for work on Thursday and Friday. I thought you could meet me there for a long weekend. And with Monique here to watch the girls…"

She put the plate she was holding on the counter, the tension melting from her face. Her eyes gleamed. "I've always wanted to go to San Francisco."

"I know," he said.

She put her arms around him, holding him tightly. For the first time in days, his body relaxed. He had always found it difficult to contend with Laura's quiet wrath—it was good to see her happy again.

Monique burst into the kitchen, dressed in skinny jeans and a lacy blouse. Her hair was pinned up by a funky rhinestone barrette. A young man followed at her heels.

Chris and Laura disengaged from their embrace.

"Andrew came to pick me up for a matinee and a bite to eat," Monique said. "Dad, this is my friend, Andrew, from school."

They shook hands and he glanced at Monique. She hadn't mentioned anything about an Andrew.

"He came for our family dinner last night," Monique said. Andrew brushed his long bangs aside and waved to Laura. "He helped bring my stuff back from school."

"What about our tennis game?" Chris asked.

"Tomorrow?" she said.

"Sure."

Monique described the movie they were going to see and then the two rushed out the door. Chris couldn't peg the guy…was he a friend, a new boyfriend, or what? He looked at Laura, perplexed.

"I'm not sure what's going on with those two," she said. "He was polite at dinner and helped with the dishes, seemed nice enough. But the way he cozied up to Monique all evening makes me guess that he likes her a whole lot more than she likes him."

Chris couldn't ask Monique straight out about her love life, no matter how curious he was. His humourous probing sometimes led to interesting accounts of her college dating scene, but she didn't include much detail. In spite of Monique's good judgment, he couldn't avoid feeling uneasy about this guy with the long hair.

"So, what do you want to do today?" he asked Laura. "Your wish is my command."

Laura beamed. "Anything. I'm just happy you're home."

Chapter Sixteen

Denise left the dentist's office and walked to her car rubbing her left cheek, still numb from the freezing. It felt like a balloon but when she looked at her reflection in the car window, the inflammation was minor. Even so, she shouldn't go back to the studio, not while she was slurring her words like a drunk. There would be no show-taping that day and meetings weren't scheduled until the afternoon—why not give herself the morning off? And what a glorious day to be outside; a hot summer day in mid-May was highly unusual, a gift to enjoy. She opened the passenger door and tossed her jacket on the seat. For the first time that season she was outside in short sleeves; how soothing to feel the sun's rays caressing her face and covering her shoulders like a shawl.

Checking her cell phone for messages while she walked, she listened to voicemails from Nicole, her mother, the show's producer, and a magazine editor requesting an interview. Nothing from Chris. They hadn't made plans to be in touch when they had seen each other the week before, but she could not shed the nagging desire to hear his voice and discover his reaction to her letter. His last e-mail indicated that he wanted to talk, but who should be the one to call? She put the phone back in her purse and looked at the storefront window beside her. Bright summer clothing almost leapt through the glass, beckoning her to come inside, but she continued walking down the boutique-lined street.

Denise seldom came to this section of the city, a district further east than she had reason to go. She passed clothing boutiques, shoe stores and gift shops interspersed with quaint coffee shops, bakeries, and restaurants bustling with morning customers—an enchanting world, hidden from her busy life. She felt like a tourist in her own city.

A small clothing boutique called 'Soleil du Printemps' — 'Spring Sunshine' — caught her attention. Artificial tulips and daffodils sprung from the ledge behind the window, and mannequins, wearing pastel spring coats and floral hats, idled in the imitation garden setting. The door chimed when Denise opened it and a grey-haired saleswoman looked up from behind the counter. In a singsong voice she said, "Bonjour. Beautiful day, yes?" She had a thick indiscernible accent. A large white open collar exposed grape-sized glossy pearls draped around her wrinkled neck.

"It's like summer," Denise said. A spa-like fragrance permeated the store, drawing her in.

The woman removed the glasses sitting on the tip of her nose, and let them drop to her chest; a thin silver chain held them at the top of her bosom. "Can I help you find something today?"

"I'm browsing, thank you."

"Please, take your time." She put her glasses back on, and returned to her task.

Denise sifted through a row of blouses, pleased that the sales-lady didn't recognize her. The colourful garments blended one into the next, against a backdrop of green foliage painted on the wall. A lifelike cardinal, perched on the branch of a potted tree, chirped when she passed it. She stopped at an interesting outfit, navy slacks and a bright pink blouse, hanging on display.

The woman interrupted Denise's moment of serenity. "That fuchsia shade is in style very big this year. You have the perfect complexion for it."

Denise removed the silk blouse from its hanger. "Hmm. It's a bit bold for me, don't you think?" She held it against her torso.

"No, no. You must try it on."

Denise checked the tag. Size six. Why not?

The woman pulled a slim navy skirt, with a long slit up the side, from a rack. "Perfect combination. You try this too." She handed the skirt to Denise.

When Denise emerged from the fitting room she looked around for a mirror.

"Beautiful," the woman said, exaggerating the syllables. She pointed to a full-length mirror in the back corner of the store.

"This is not me," Denise said. She turned sideways to see the outfit from a different angle. The form-fitting blouse accentuated her breasts and waist, and she wondered if it was too tight. "I think it's too much, too attention-grabbing—not my style."

"Nonsense," the woman said. She removed her reading glasses again and marched toward Denise. "You are stunning, like a model." She steered Denise closer to the mirror. "I be honest. When you came into the store, I thought, what a beautiful woman. But when I see you in this outfit, I think, she is magnificent."

Denise examined the back. "I don't know." She swept her hand across the smooth fabric. "Feels luxurious," she said.

"I not show you anything else," the woman said. "This outfit you must buy."

The style did flatter her figure. A departure from her usual conservative tastes, but why not be adventurous? If she changed her mind, she could always return the clothes. "All right, I'll take it."

The woman hung the clothing with care in a garment bag and told Denise that she had made a wise decision. When she handed over the outfit, she said, "Merci, Mme. Gagnon. One day you come back here and tell me what your lover thinks."

Lover? What on earth was she talking about? Denise looked at her hand to see if she had forgotten to put on her wedding ring. There it was, large and glistening and impossible to miss.

On the way back to the car, she checked her phone for missed calls. There were two: one from Nicole and one from Chris. She skipped Nicole's message and went directly to Chris's. Listening to his voicemail, she held her breath.

"How are you? I wasn't sure whether to call you – how we should go about corresponding. But I wanted to let you know that I appreciated your shar-ing all that Paris business with me. I know it was hard to rehash. I'm uh, uh, going away next week for a few days...to San Francisco. Well, (long pause) maybe when I get back we can arrange a time to see each...I mean to talk. Take care."

She exhaled. Should she call him back? She wanted to talk to him, but not about the letter. Why had she given it to him? Now she felt exposed, and embarrassed. Perhaps she should wait until he got back from his trip. How long did he say he'd be gone? She got into the car, sat for a minute with the engine running, and dialed.

He answered on the first ring. Her mind went blank and she almost hung up. "It's Denise. I got your message."

"How are you?" they said in unison.

"Did I call at a bad time?" she asked. "Are you busy?"

"No, no. It's fine."

"I'm just calling…I thought I'd…well, I'm returning your call."

"I'm glad you're calling."

How to break the cycle of awkward pleasantries? She cleared her throat. "So, you're going to San Francisco. For business?"

"Partly. Laura is meeting me for a few days at the end."

"How nice." Her body tensed as she gripped the phone.

"Yes."

She waited for him to continue.

Chris said, "I uh, I uh, well… I was thinking, when I get back, will you be around?"

"I think so."

"I might have another meeting in Montreal. Could we get together, for dinner, or something?"

"I'd like that."

"We could talk about your story."

She had to think for a second. Story? Oh yes, her letter. "You mean Paris?"

"You had some ordeal over there."

Suddenly, Paris seemed like more than a lifetime ago. "There's not much to say now that you know all about it—more than you could possibly want to know. I'd much rather hear about San Francisco. It's one of my favourite cities."

He laughed. "I'm sure we'll have a lot to discuss."

Her heart fluttered, a sensation she hadn't experienced for years. In less than two weeks, she would see Chris again.

Denise drove toward downtown, and although the temperature in the car was comfortable, her hands were clammy and her body was overheated. She could almost hear the sound of her heart beating. A high-school giddiness took hold and she drew several deep breaths to calm herself. When she stopped at a red light, she phoned her mother.

"Hello, Mother," she said, her voice too cheerful for her own liking.

"Denise, darling, where are you? You sound far away."

"I'm in town and wondering what you're doing for lunch."

"I haven't thought about it. I was about to do some gardening."

"Can I come over for a bite?" Her mouth still hurt from the dental work but she was getting hungry.

"Of course. How lovely to snatch you away from work during the day. What a pleasant surprise."

She was the quintessential mother — never too busy to tend to her children. Raising the four of them single-handedly after their father died had been difficult for her, often working overtime to make ends meet, but she always seemed to find time when she was needed. Denise never figured out how she'd managed, where she'd found the resources. Her mother called it the 'mystery of mother-hood' — you do what you can, and *you can do* what is necessary.

Denise's mother was kneeling on the ground planting annuals when Denise turned into the driveway. The rim of her straw hat was as wide as a serving platter and she wore beige cotton pants with a long-sleeved white shirt, leaving little of her sensitive skin exposed to the elements. Denise remembered how her mother had made her slather on sun screen at a time when her childhood friends were using baby oil to achieve the darkest tan. Of course, her mother was wise for her day, and a decade later everything she had said about the dangers of too much sun exposure was true.

Denise walked up the front path and listened for a moment to the cheerful melody her mother hummed as she planted the red, white and pink impatiens. "Hello, Mother," she whispered, trying not to startle her.

"Hello, darling, you're here already. I didn't hear you drive in." She used the spade to help her stand up, wincing as she struggled for balance.

Denise ran to her aid.

"No, no. I can manage," her mother said. Over-sized sunglasses covered much of her face and droplets of perspiration moistened her skin.

An image of her mother on the beach during a family holiday sprang to Denise's mind. As the children splashed in the ocean, played in the sand, and collected seashells, her mother sat under a gigantic beach umbrella, covered from neck to toe in her flowing beach dress. Her brown hair was tucked under the same straw hat that she was wearing now, and 'Jackie O' sunglasses shielded her eyes from the glaring sun. Denise recalled her encouraging voice, "What a beautiful castle! Oh, let me see the shells you've collected." And her gentle orders, "Now, Tom, take your little sister for a splash in the waves, will you?"

Denise's mother linked arms with her and led her into the house. "My goodness, this is indeed a wonderful surprise. To what do I owe your unexpected visit? Is anything wrong?"

Denise laughed. "You think something has to go wrong for me to barge in on you?"

"No, but it's the middle of the day, on a...heavens, I don't even know what day it is!"

"It's Friday. I had a speck of time and thought I'd come to see you without my brood for once."

Denise often dropped in with the boys on the weekends, or her mother would join them at the cottage, but they seldom had the chance to visit with just each other alone.

"Why were you out in the midday heat?" Denise said.

"You know me, I can't take the sun but I love the warm weather. I was planting in the shade, so no need for concern." She removed her hat and sunglasses, an elegant portrait in her gardening clothes, with a pretty blue kerchief around her neck. Always dressing simply but with flair, she added modest touches like scarves and smart bits of jewelry and the subtle adornments made all the difference. Her hair was pearl white, thick and straight like Denise's, but cut short, almost to her chin, a style she'd worn since Denise could remember. She had an attractive face, well-worn with wisdom. Warmth, compassion and empathy spilled from her eyes. And at seventy-five, she had more energy than her four children put together, they often joked.

At the cottage a few years earlier, Denise had forbidden Thomas to play with the firecrackers that he had mysteriously acquired. She was making dinner when she heard loud cracking sounds, like mini explosions coming from the forest. With a sense of dread she raced toward the direction of the noise. But what she had found, in a little enclave in the woods, was her own mother, squatting with eight-year-old Thomas, lighting the firecrackers. The mischievous expression on her mother's face was hilarious. Denise had chastised them both, fighting the urge to laugh, and walked back to the cottage with the image of her mother's devilish expression, one of her favourite memories, imprinted in her mind.

"What do you feel like eating?" her mother asked.

Denise rummaged through the fridge. "Hmm, something soft because of my teeth. How about a tuna salad sandwich? You sit, Mother, I'll make it."

Her mother washed her hands and sat down at the kitchen table where the five of them had shared hundreds of meals over the years. Not much had changed in that room, other than the wallpaper once or twice. The cabinets, the furniture, and even the avocado-green refrigerator were the same as when Denise was a young girl. But the laminate floor sparkled and the Formica countertops gleamed; not a single errant crumb or a greasy spot would ever be found in her mother's home. When she could finally afford some cleaning help, she'd refused to even consider the idea because she was used to doing it all herself.

"If you insist on making lunch, I'll accept the offer. Tuna would be fine. I need to rest this leg. It's a wee bit sore from kneeling in the garden."

Denise found a can of tuna and the mayonnaise, and removed a loaf of whole wheat bread from the breadbox.

"Did I thank you yet for checking on the house while I was away?" her mother said.

"I was happy to do it." Denise used the old electric can-opener to open the tuna. "But I've been meaning to ask you about something. You left the sprinkler on out front and the kitchen wasn't as pristine as usual. Is everything all—"

"I'm sorry, dear, I didn't mean to leave the mess to you. I simply couldn't get going that day. With the packing and all, I was slower than usual. But I'm fine."

"I think you should go for a check-up, just to make sure."

"Heavens, no. I'm as strong as a horse. Sometimes I forget my age, that's all." She stood up and went to the counter. "What can I do here?"

"Please, leave this to me. You relax." Denise gestured toward the chair. She emptied the tuna into a bowl and dropped in some mayonnaise. "Mother, do you remember me telling you about that boy I met, before I left for France, back in '82?"

"Hmm. Do you mean Mike, who drove you crazy with his constant phone calls and jealousy...and then left you broken-hearted when he started up with another girl?"

"No, not him. Chris, the guy I met a few days before leaving."

"I vaguely remember the name. Why?"

"We had a brief...friendship. I barely got to know him, really. And then when I came back from France, I considered looking him up."

"Now I remember. You were frustrated because you had lost his address."

"I bumped into him recently." Denise tossed the sandwich filling together, her eyes glued to the mixing bowl.

"Oh?"

"In Cleveland, on a recent business trip. It was quite strange, after all these years, to see him."

"And?"

"There isn't an 'and'. Don't you think it's a strange coincidence though? I felt like I was reconnecting with a long lost friend who fell from the sky." She seasoned the filling with salt and pepper and spread it evenly on the bread.

"Are you renewing this friendship?"

"Loosely. We had a brief visit when he was in town for a meeting last week. Nice man. He's married, has three daughters."

Denise's mother looked at her with a penetrating gaze. "Careful, now."

"What do you mean, careful?" Denise's voice went up an octave.

"I think you know what I mean."

"Mother, I may have made some bad choices in my life, but I'm not foolish." She could feel her face getting hot. Why had she mentioned Chris? Her mother was reading all kinds of ridiculous things into the relationship. She set the sandwiches on the table with a thud. When she got the milk out of the fridge, she closed the door with more force than was needed.

They ate in silence at first. Then Denise said, "I think you should fix up this kitchen. Look how tired it's getting."

"But I like it this way. I'm used to it. Besides, I'm too old for renovations."

"I'll help you. We can make a project of it."

"No thank you." She smiled, "When you're my age you'll understand."

Chapter Seventeen

Silence greeted Denise when she walked through her front door at the end of the day. No Clara, no kids, no Francois. Where was everybody? She was looking forward to winding down with the boys, having hardly seen them during the week. Francois' car wasn't in the driveway, perhaps he'd taken the boys to the park, taking advantage of the unseasonably warm day. She checked her e-mails in the study before doing anything else. Nothing of consequence, nothing from Chris. Hanging her purse over the back of the chair, she stood motionless for a moment, as if waiting for something to happen.

When she went to the kitchen to check for a note, she saw Francois and the two younger boys through the sliding glass doors, playing catch in the backyard, wearing shorts and tee-shirts. She watched them toss the ball around, laughing at their own fumbles. The sight warmed her heart because neither Francois nor Luc enjoyed playing catch. Martin must have coerced them into it.

By the time she came downstairs in her jeans and tee-shirt, they had come inside for lemonade.

"Hey, guys, I was about to join in your fun." She rarely played sports with her children but the premature summer warmth had inspired her.

"We're done playing," Luc said.

"Martin wore us out," Francois said, ruffling the boy's hair.

"They're boring," Martin said. "They never want to play for long."

"What do you mean? We played catch for over an hour," Francois said.

Denise laughed. "I'll play with you. Let's go." She headed for the door, expecting Martin to scamper after her.

"No thanks. I think I'll play inside now."

Denise looked at Francois and he shrugged his shoulders.

"What's for dinner? I'm hungry," Luc said.

"Hmm. I haven't thought about it." Denise checked the refrigerator.

"Clara made up some burgers for the barbeque," Francois said, "to celebrate this summer day in May. How about ice cream cones for dessert?"

"Yeah!" the boys shouted in unison.

"But for you, Madame, the chef will prepare a feast of grilled lobster tail." Francois opened the fridge to show Denise the fresh seafood he had purchased from the market. "With caesar salad and crusty bread. Does that entice you?" He wrapped his arms around her waist. "Champagne is chilling in the fridge."

"Marvelous. What are we celebrating?"

"Partly my new project, and partly this sensational day."

"Sounds good to me." She picked up the baseball and tossed the ball in the air.

"In fact, I even had the roof down on my car today — the first time this year," he said. "Let's see how long this weather lasts."

"You watch, "Denise said. "It'll probably snow again." She'd been wondering where his car was, but he must have put it in the garage in case it rained. So far, the spring weather had comprised of snow, sleet, much rain, and only hints of warmth. The perennials didn't seem to know whether to push through the ground or hunker down, waiting for warmth and sunshine.

"No way," he said. "Summer is here!" He put a hand on her shoulder and kissed her cheek. "You go relax in the garden while I get the champagne."

"Where's Thomas?" Denise asked.

"He's at Michel's for a sleepover. He'll be home around lunchtime tomorrow."

"I see."

Why was everything happening without her knowledge? She supposed she should be grateful, but they could have checked in with her, at least as a courtesy. What happened to the days when they communicated about everything? Not long ago, Nicole was sticking posted notes all over her computer with messages from Francois and the kids: 'Could Martin miss karate to play at Robbie's? Could they have pizza for dinner? What time was she coming home?' But lately, their lives seemed to proceed smoothly without her.

Denise sat with Luc and Martin while they ate their burgers.

"Tell me about your day, boys." Neither responded. "How was school, Martin?"

He took a big bite of his hamburger. "Good," he said, as mustard and ketchup oozed down his chin.

"And you, Luc? How was your day at school?"

"Fine."

"Was Mrs. Stevens in a better mood?"

He nodded.

Denise cleared the table when they were finished eating and then sent them upstairs to change into pajamas. After the children were settled with a movie, she went to get the outfit she had purchased earlier in the day and tried it on again. Not bad. She checked the back. Yes, it was rather flattering, dazzling even. And she did have a youthful figure; why not show it off like the lady at the boutique had suggested? She refreshed her make-up, dabbed on Francois's favourite perfume, and went downstairs for dinner. Francois was bringing out the garden chairs when she approached.

"Whoa!" he said. Then he laughed. "That's some outfit."

"You don't like it."

"I didn't say that."

She waited.

"It's different. I like the shoes."

"Why don't you admit that you hate it?"

"It's a little vampy. But you look great. You always look great." He wore a face that Denise knew distinctively: tilted head, lopsided smile, serious eyes. To others, that facial expression would be charming; warm even, but to her it spoke of masked displeasure. He applied that expression to people he disliked, to slackers at his building sites, and to the kids when they interrupted him.

Denise brought some popcorn up to the boys, both happily watching television and playing with their Gameboys. She changed back into her jeans, thinking her first impression had been right; the outfit was hideous. She hung it back in the bag. Clara had left the bedroom window open and now that the sun had set, summer warmth had vanished and the spring dampness reappeared. The draft made Denise shiver as she looked down at the backyard, watching Francois putter back and forth, setting the table. When he came out carrying a small vase of flowers and some candles, she was surprised. Romantic dinners were not usually his thing.

When she came down, Francois handed her a glass of champagne and served the appetizer. She closed her eyes while she sipped and the sensation of bubbles popping on her tongue brought her back to the recent evening at the Realitz with Chris. Soon he would be in San Francisco with his wife. Denise hadn't been there since her Paris days, when Jacques had taken her on a whirlwind trip to California almost twenty years earlier. They had visited Napa Valley, Sonoma, Carmel, San Francisco and San Diego. But the trip had not been filled with romance. In fact, she was hard-pressed to remember if they had been alone at all, other than in their hotel room at night. Business had always been Jacque's priority. A trip to California with Chris would be different, much more enjoyable. Denise felt a jealous pang as she imagined Chris and his wife strolling along the charming streets of San Francisco.

"Sit," Francois said, and pulled the chair out for her. "I have a few more things to do inside but I'll join you shortly." He pointed to the appetizer. "Please start eating." She could see that he was proud of his culinary achievement and she was supposed to be impressed.

Denise scrutinized the first course that lay before her — smoked salmon with asparagus spears and capers. As delicious as it looked, she had no appetite. She created geometric designs with the pumpernickel triangles and lemon wedges, and distributed the capers around the circumference of her plate.

Francois returned with his Norwegian ski cardigan, draped it over Denise's shoulders, and sat down. "Why did you change?"

"Because you said I looked like a whore."

"I did not. I meant you looked sexy. The neckline was a bit low, but hey, why not? And I'm not used to seeing you in wild...I mean...strong colours. I could get used to it."

The damage was done. She'd never wear that outfit for him again. "Don't worry, you won't have to."

"You're making way to big a deal out of this." He took her hand. "You're beautiful, no matter what you wear."

Was she over-sensitive? Francois had been nothing but pleasant since she'd come home and she was giving him a hard time. Guilt shrouded her conscience. "I think we should go away somewhere for a few days — for a change of scenery," she said. "And to make up for our botched trip out east."

"When?"

"Now. Soon. To Bermuda. Let's go to Bermuda," she said, buoyed by the idea.

"What about *Montreal's Alive*? You've always said you need to plan for weeks before taking time off."

"Yes, but Nicole's getting comfortable on stage. She could fill in for a couple of shows. I'd keep in touch, daily. I think I could manage it."

"A terrible time for me, I'm afraid," Francois said. "The heritage project is getting into gear now."

Denise stared at the back of the garden, seeing only darkness.

"Remember our earlier conversation?" Francois continued. "About how busy I'd be?"

"Yes, I do. But I didn't realize things had progressed at such speed."

"We're in the planning stages, but as soon as we get the building permits, we're off and running. Could happen any day."

"Oh."

Francois told Denise about the project, repeating much of what she already knew, speaking with energy that she only witnessed when he plunged into his creative mode. His hands soared while describing how he planned to transform the building and his voice blared with enthusiasm as he explained his vision. Denise tried to force herself to focus on the conversation but her mind was navigating the streets of San Francisco.

"How do you like the smoked salmon?" Francois asked. "It's wild, from the west coast."

She had been struggling to swallow the smallest of bites. The tension in her body had undermined her ability to derive enjoyment from the delicacy that lay before her. "It's delicious." She mustered up a smile.

Denise had an equally difficult time eating the lobster tail and salad that Francois had prepared. But she ate her serving, feigning delight. Afterwards, she insisted on cleaning the dishes in spite of Francois' offer to help; she needed some time alone, a break from his exuberance. When she was done, she slipped into her study to check her e-mails again, finding a message from Chris. Goosebumps emerged over her body and she pulled François' thick sweater tighter around her torso. She checked the time the e-mail had been sent—9:58—about the time he had appeared in her thoughts at dinner. How strange.

She opened the document.

Nine days is too long.

She pressed reply.

Yes.

The following week, Denise immersed herself in work and accepted more speaking engagements than usual. She'd given the Get-Fit speech at the launch of a new fitness institute for women and had agreed to speak at an upcoming Cancer Research benefit. While sitting at her office desk, reviewing the show schedule one day, Nicole came in carrying stacks of files.

"Thanks, Nicole. You can leave them here." She cleared an area of her desk.

Nicole spotted a bright yellow garment bag hanging on the outside of the closet door. The words 'Soleil du Printemps' were inscribed on the bag in a bold, decorative script. "I love that store. What did you buy there?" She unzipped the front and looked inside.

"A mistake. I changed my mind. It's going back."

"Can I see?" Nicole removed the blouse.

"What a fabulous top. Why aren't you keeping it?"

"It doesn't feel right on me."

"I think it would look awesome on you." She pulled the skirt off its hanger. "And this skirt, it's beautiful," she said, holding it against her waist. "Can I try it on?"

"Go ahead."

When Nicole returned, wearing the outfit, Denise nodded. "Not bad. Much better on you."

"Too tight and kind of conservative for me," Nicole said, "but I love the lines. Can I see it on you?"

"Why not?" Nicole had vastly different taste but she usually had a good sense of what suited Denise.

When Denise walked into the office wearing the outfit, Nicole gasped. "Wow. I can't believe you don't want to keep it — you look amazing." Nicole walked around her, examining the outfit from every angle. "It's made for you. You can't take it back."

"When would I wear it?"

"Anytime, anywhere — out to dinner, to a party, an evening function. You've got those sleek high-heeled patents that would go perfectly. All you need is a purse." Nicole was familiar with Denise's entire wardrobe and was obsessed with fashion and shopping.

"If you find me a suitable purse, I'll keep the clothes," Denise said.

Nicole laughed. "Deal!"

Nicole was a dynamo with a heart — zany at times, but sensible. And Denise could count on her for almost anything; how fortunate to be surrounded by people she could count on.

By the end of the week Denise had recovered her equilibrium. The programming had been successful and the show ratings continued on their positive course. Francois had begun his work on the heritage project and, as he had warned, was consumed by the job. Denise decided to take the boys and her mother to the cottage for the weekend and leave Francois to his business. Thomas was busy with a project of his own for school, and was invited to stay with a friend in the city to work on it.

During the week, Denise had managed to push thoughts of Chris out of her mind while darting from one thing to the next, at work and at home. Yet, she was well aware that next weekend Chris would be in San Francisco with his wife. Jealousy crept into her psyche in the most intrusive and unforgiving way. She hoped that spending time at the cottage would derail such inscrutable feelings.

Denise dragged the two boys grocery shopping, drove to get her mother, and headed up north. En route, they sang road songs, played car games, and listened to kid-friendly CD's.

They arrived at dusk and the boys scurried off to explore, a ritual they never tired of, no matter what time of year it was or what the weather was like. The dense forest separated their cottage from the next, creating the impression that they were alone in the wilderness. Only when facing the picturesque lake was there evidence of other dwellings. Denise inhaled deeply as she got out of the car; the scent of the evergreens and the purity of the air provided instant relief from the urban stress. She paused to admire the natural surroundings and her entire body suddenly relaxed.

Martin came from nowhere and knocked her as he hid behind her back. He laughed nervously. "We found a snake in the woods and Luc says he's gonna put it in my bed tonight."

"First of all," she said, "those are harmless grass snakes, and they don't bite. Secondly, I'd be astonished if Luc could catch one, they're so slithery and quick."

Martin stepped out from behind her, looking relieved. "I don't care, anyway. I'm not afraid of snakes." He ran back into the forest.

Denise and her mother began unpacking the car. Holding groceries in one arm, Denise's mother grabbed the stair railing with her free hand, gasping for breath.

"Mother, are you all right?" Denise dropped her bag and ran to her. "You need to sit down and put your head between your knees."

Her mother put down the grocery bag, sat on the wooden step, and wrapped her arms around her chest. "I'm fine. I need to catch my breath, that's all."

Denise stiffened when she saw her mother's strained, pale face.

"There. I'm all right. I just needed a moment."

"Go inside and lie down," Denise said. "I'll finish unpacking."

Her mother used the railing to pull herself up and stood erect, her face still white. Denise approached to help, but her effort was rebuffed by a stubborn, "No."

When Denise entered the cottage with the last load from the car, she was surprised to see her mother putting the groceries away. "Mother, what are you doing?"

"I think you can see what I'm doing, dear. No need to fuss over me."

The next morning, when Denise awoke, the air had a sharp, chilly bite and she saw faint clouds of breath when she exhaled. She had forgotten how cold the nights could be up north at that time of year and she turned on the electric heater. Removing the blanket from her bed, she wrapped it around her shoulders and went to see who else was up. A warm fire blazed in the living room when she came out, and she was met with the inviting smells of bacon and coffee. Her mother and the children were busy playing cards and they didn't see her standing in the hallway watching them.

"Now, listen carefully. We each have nine cards, twenty-seven cards in total. How many pairs would that make?"

"Thirteen," said Luc without hesitation.

"And how many cards are left once we gather up all the pairs?"

Luc was about to respond when Denise's mother signaled not to speak. Martin thought hard.

She said, "Thirteen pairs equals twenty-six cards, but if we had twenty-seven cards in all, there would be how many left?"

"One!"

"Very good. And that one card is called the 'Old Maid.' She showed them the queen of clubs."

"What's an old maid?" Martin asked.

"I guess it's an old lady who's not married."

"Like you." he said.

Denise's mother laughed. She pulled him to her side and hugged him hard. "You're absolutely right, just like me."

Denise retreated without being seen. She swallowed to fight the tears but they drizzled out against her will. Her mother had never complained about the sacrifices she had made for her children, not once had she outwardly lamented the fact that she didn't have a man in her life. How hard life must have been at times, and how lonely.

Chapter Eighteen

Chris didn't notice Monique standing behind his chair, hadn't even heard her come through the front door or go to the kitchen to get a drink.

"What are you watching, Dad?"

He jumped up, rattled. "Monique, it's 4:00 a.m. Why are you coming home so late?"

"I was out with Andrew."

"Till four?"

"What are *you* doing up at this hour, and what are you watching?" She plunked herself down on the sofa and focused on the television. "A talk show?"

"I'm a...it's a..."

"A show about interior decorating or something?"

Chris wanted to turn the television off, but the remote control was out of reach. "What were you doing with Andrew all this time?" he asked.

"Hanging out."

"And what kind of friend is this guy?" Chris tried not to be conspicuous as he studied Monique's appearance—tight, low-cut jeans with a thick leather belt and a fitted T-shirt, exposing her midriff. A string of large, colourful beads encircled her neck. Her platform sandals added about two inches to her height. Chris much preferred her fuzzy slippers and flannel pajamas.

Monique shrugged. "He's just a friend, more or less."

"I see."

Monique picked up the video jacket that was lying on the coffee table. Then she noticed all the others. "What *are* you watching?"

Chris got up and turned the TV off. He couldn't evade the question any longer. "It's a kind of current events, general interest show from Montreal, called 'Montreal's Alive.'"

She lifted her eyebrows, as if waiting for further explanation.

He uttered the first thing that came to mind. "I've been asked to appear as a guest, to talk about wine collecting. They want to do a segment on building a personal wine cellar and um…collecting."

"And they called you?"

"Yes."

She looked skeptical.

"The host of the show is an old school friend of mine. We bumped into each other at a wine-tasting function and we got to talking. She invited me to come on the show and share my knowledge." Was he going overboard? Could she possibly buy this malarkey?

"Oh," was all she said.

"Anyway, they sent me these tapes to check out the show, to give me a sense of the format." He was falling deeper and deeper into a quagmire of lies and couldn't get out.

"Are you gonna do it?"

"I don't know, I haven't decided yet. Not sure if I can take the time."

"I think it would be cool. You should go for it. That could be your fifteen minutes of fame. Or hour, or whatever." She turned the TV back on.

"Monique, it's late. Let's get to bed. We'll watch this another time." To Chris's relief, she yawned and turned the TV off.

"You're right. It's getting late. I'll see you in the morning."

She gave him a sleepy kiss and he watched her drag herself upstairs. Chris gathered up the videos and put them back in his briefcase. How stupid could he be? It hadn't occurred to him that someone might find him watching at this hour. He felt like he'd been caught watching pornography by his daughter. On a whim, a few days earlier, he'd called the station in Montreal and had the video transcripts couriered to his office. When they'd asked which episodes he wanted, he'd been stumped. "A transcript from each year since the show began," he'd spat out. "The ones with the highest ratings. I'm doing a comparative analysis with daytime talk-shows in the American Midwest." The person had responded with disinterest, simply asking where to send the videos, and for his credit card number.

When Monique arrived, he'd been watching a show on the perils of home construction and renovation. To his surprise, the guest was Denise's husband, Francois. He wasn't anything like Chris had imagined. For some reason he'd expected a more burly kind of guy— heavy set with big hands. On the contrary, Francois was tall and lean, and wore dark-rimmed glasses, appearing more bookish than contractor-like. He seemed at least 6'2 and was fair, almost Scandinavian-looking. Monique had startled Chris at the beginning of the show and he didn't get a chance to hear the man talk, but he imagined a French accent and a laconic speaking style. Chris was anxious to get back to the tapes but wondered when he'd have the opportunity. He couldn't take another chance watching when his family was about.

On Saturday morning, Chris woke up with a headache. He'd planned to go to the office at some point during the day. To have slept in until 10:30 was highly unusual; he couldn't recall the last time he'd slept that late. When he went downstairs he found an empty kitchen and a note on the counter:

We've gone to riding lessons. You were sleeping soundly and I didn't want to wake you. I hope you're feeling all right. We'll be back around lunchtime.
XOXO Laura

Damn. The girls' first riding lesson and he'd promised to go. Laura was thoughtful to let him sleep—she must have sensed how drained he was. After pouring himself a cup of coffee from the pot Laura had left brewing, he leafed through the newspaper laid out on the kitchen table. Pepper stood at his feet waiting to be noticed, and Chris crouched down to rub behind the dog's ears.

"You're a big pest," he said, as Pepper nuzzled against his knee. Chris spoke to him like a child, "What do I do with such a demanding, slobbering creature?" The dog stood up on his hind legs and licked Chris's face.

Did Denise have a dog? She'd probably have a lapdog like a Maltese Terrier, something dignified and dainty. Temptation nudged him to watch the videos again, but he refrained; Monique was probably still asleep and could come down any time, and he certainly didn't want a repeat of last night. Instead, he went to the study to check his e-mails, finding only work-related messages. Without thinking about what he'd say, he opened a new e-mail page and typed:

Hi Denise,

I'm enjoying a quiet, lazy morning at home today and am about to do some work. I know we said we'd talk after California, but I find myself wondering about you, and how you're doing. Did you go to the cottage this weekend? How was the rest of your week? I enjoyed our visit in Montreal – I almost felt nineteen again. Drop me a line when you have a moment.

Take care, Chris

What he wanted to say was, "I miss you...I wish I could be with you." Where was his head taking him? He went to the window and looked outside, then sat down at his desk and stared at the computer screen, unmotivated to enter the realm of proposals and high-powered deals. Perhaps another cup of coffee would get him going.

The morning serenity transformed into mayhem when Laura and the girls arrived home. From the study, it sounded like a gaggle of children swarming through the house. But only Sophie and Tanya were there, running like horses through the living room, dining room and kitchen, playing some kind of galloping tag.

"Dad, Dad, we brought you lunch," Sophie shouted, when she saw him approach.

The greasy smell of deep fried fast food attacked his senses as he entered the kitchen. Wrappers strewn across the floor, along with squished french fries and ketchup smeared across the table, made the kitchen look like a school lunchroom.

"Here's a Big Mac," she continued, following him into the kitchen.

"No thanks, not today, I'm not hungry."

He could see her disappointment and knew that he should at least pretend to be enthused.

"We got milkshakes too, do you want some?" Tanya asked.

He picked up the clutter from the floor. "This is ridiculous, all the greasy, messy food. What was your mother thinking?" he said, under his breath with clenched teeth.

"I thought you liked McDonalds," Sophie said, taken aback.

"No, I don't like it. In fact I can't stand it. It's pure junk, full of trans fatty…whatever." What's wrong with a sandwich and a glass of milk?" he said with irritation.

The girls stared at him but didn't flinch. He could see that they weren't going to let him destroy their dining pleasure. Sophie started blowing through her straw, causing the chocolate milkshake to overflow.

Laura popped her head into the kitchen. "Oh, there you are. Don't forget, we're dropping by to see Sonya and her mother this afternoon for tea. Could you help me out and do something with the girls while I make her a casserole and a rhubarb pie? In fact, I think I'll make a pie for tomorrow night's dessert too. My parents are coming, remember?"

"Oh, right. You did mention that. The girls can help me do some garden work." The last thing he wanted to do was have afternoon tea with the ladies, especially with ladies he didn't know. But how could he bail out? Sonya was apparently intent on thanking him for helping her after the accident, and this was her way of doing it.

Remorseful for having been so cranky with the girls, Chris sat down at the table and told them a joke. They giggled with pleasure even though they had heard him tell the same joke before. He couldn't let his inner turmoil overflow into his domestic life; his daughters were innocent after all. "Now, girls, let's clean up this mess," he said.

****

"Thanks for watching the girls," Laura said to Monique. "We shouldn't be more than a couple of hours."

Monique looked up from the coffee table in the family room, where she was playing Clue with the children. "No problem. Have fun."

Laura was grateful to have an excuse to get out of the house. The girls had worn her down in the morning, fighting and carrying on about every little thing. Horseback riding had been a disaster, with Sophie refusing to get on the horse and Tanya fussing because she wouldn't be taught to trot for some time. And Chris had been no help at all. She'd considered talking to him about giving her more support, but he'd been so busy lately, and distracted. Perhaps she'd raise the subject at night, when the girls were in bed.

Chris carried the chicken divan casserole to the car, still hot from the oven, and Laura carried the pie. She wore her beige pleated pants and an aqua sweater set, with a matching silk headband. Chris wore the navy pants and yellow button-down shirt that she had picked out for him. At the last minute she'd suggested he throw on his blazer, out of respect for the hostess, given all that Sonya had been through lately. She'd almost suggested he wear a tie too.

"You might not need the blazer," Laura said, when they were backing out of the driveway. "I don't know how fussy this will be. But it's always better to dress on the side of formality, don't you think?"

"It's not like we're in England going for High Tea," he said.

"There's a nice idea. Will you take me to London for tea some day?"

"Absolutely."

"How about when we're in San Francisco? Let's have it there." Laura lifted the pie that was sitting on her lap to make sure it hadn't made any marks on her pants.

"Sounds good."

She loved fancy tea sandwiches—cucumber and watercress in particular. And scones with clotted cream were a decadent treat. The last time she and Chris had had High Tea together was in New York at some fancy hotel, years ago. She reveled in the thought of four romantic nights alone with Chris in San Francisco; they would benefit from spending time together—to talk, to laugh, to play—like in the old days. She hadn't worn a negligee in years; perhaps she should slip out to the mall during the week and find something sexy. Chris used to love her in silk teddies and skimpy nighties, but since she'd had children it hadn't occurred to her to wear them anymore, especially with her extra bulges and cellulite. Flannel and cotton pajamas had somehow become her standard sleeping apparel. And sleeping naked was a rare occurrence given the girls' habit of crawling into bed with them in the middle of the night.

"Oh my gosh," Laura said, as they pulled to the curb in front of Sonya's house. "She's got her house up for sale."

"It's a big place for a small family," Chris said.

"Yes, but she loves that house, and it's the only home the kids have ever known. Why would she be selling it now?"

Chris opened the back door of the car to get the casserole. "You'll find out soon enough."

They walked up the cobble-stone path towards the front entrance of a charming two-story Tudor home. The leaded windows and a half-timbered gable conveyed an English cottage feeling, not formal, but distinguished. "Such a beautiful house," Laura whispered. "Too bad they're moving."

Sonya greeted them at the door, balancing with a cane. Her mother stood behind her, appearing anxious.

"Look at you," Laura said to Sonya, kissing her on the cheek. "Who would have known that you'd recently undergone major surgery?" Sonya's hair had not been shaved after all, or if it had been, there was no sign of stitches. Her lean frame made Laura feel fat, in spite of her recent success at losing weight. Sonya wore a mid-calf, A-line crimson skirt with a wide belt. A fitted white shirt, tucked into the skirt, revealed slim, toned arms and shoulders, which had been hidden under the hospital blankets when Laura had last seen her. She'd forgotten how stunning Sonya was.

Introductions were made and Sonya's mother took the casserole from Chris. Laura followed her to the kitchen with the pie.

"You're an absolute doll to do this," Erika said

"It's nothing—a pleasure."

Erika lowered her voice, "I suppose you noticed that the house is up for sale?"

Laura nodded. "I'm surprised."

Erika shook her head. "It's terrible, just terrible. Sonya can't go back to work because she has trouble with her balance — dizziness — and there's some internal damage, and well, she can't afford to stay here. That's the bottom line."

"What a shame," Laura said.

"And that's not all." Erika's voice had become a loud whisper. "Her ex-husband, Jack, won't help out one iota, although he certainly can afford to. Seems he's starting a family with that girl and they've bought a new house themselves."

"Poor Sonya," Laura said. "She must feel awful."

Sonya came into the kitchen at that moment, stepping awkwardly with her cane. "Mother, would you mind bringing in the tea?" She addressed Laura. "Please, come and join us in the living room." Then she shot a piercing glance at her mother.

Laura sat beside Chris on the chintz sofa and the other women sat across from them in matching striped tub chairs.

Chris crossed his legs and then his arms. "You've made incredible progress since the last time I saw you. From what I witnessed, it's remarkable that you've recovered like you have."

Sonya laughed. "I may have been crushed like a bug, but my will is somewhat stronger."

"Your fitness level must have had a lot to do with your ability to withstand the trauma. When I saw you running that day, I could tell that you were a serious athlete."

Laura became conscious of her own body; no hard muscles would be found on her soft physique. Sports activities had become part of her pre-motherhood past, unless she could count running up and down the stairs with laundry and walking the dog.

"The doctor did say that my heart was strong, but I was still very lucky. And lucky that you tended to me after I was hit. In fact, I wanted to thank you for that…to let you know how much I appreciated your help." She picked up a gift bag from beside her chair and handed it to Chris.

"What's this?"

"A little something. Go ahead, open it."

He removed the tissue paper and then the object within — a black baseball cap with the letter's NYM inscribed in front, like hers,

163

but in grey. He put it on his head and grinned. "Fits perfectly. Thank you."

"I won't be running the marathon myself, but hopefully I'll be cheering you on."

He laughed. "You give me too much credit. I'm not the runner you are. I wish I could say that I'm up for it, but I'm way behind the pack when it comes to training."

"One of these years, perhaps," she said.

"How about training together when you're ready to run again."

Laura looked at Chris, trying to decipher if he was serious. When did he think he'd have time to train for a marathon? She took a sip of her tea.

Waving her hands in the air, Erika blurted out, "Oh no. I'm afraid Sonya's running days are over. Did you see her limp?"

"Mother, the doctor didn't say running was out of the question."

"Don't get your hopes up, dear."

Sonya leaned over and poured more tea. "Please, help yourself to some sweets."

Two platters of pastries, squares and cookies sat on the coffee table — enough for a crowd. Laura reached for a plate and served herself. Unable to choose between the lemon meringue tarts or the pecan squares, she took one of each. Chris selected an apple tart, Erika picked up a shortbread cookie, and Sonya had nothing. In spite of all the turmoil in her life, she was a composed hostess, holding up as if nothing was amiss. Laura wanted to ask her about the house and where she was planning on moving, but couldn't bring herself to raise the subject.

"Where are the children?" Laura asked.

"With their father for a few days."

"And when they come home, they'll be surprised to see the house up for sale," Erika said.

With a disheartened sigh, Sonya said, "I had to do it quickly, the real estate agent said the spring market is already petering out and I'd barely catch the end of it if I didn't act immediately."

Laura watched Chris remove his jacket and place it over his baseball cap on the chesterfield's arm. "Where will you move to?" she asked.

"Close by, I hope. You see, this home is too big for us. As much as I love it, there's no sense in staying in a house with much more space than we need."

Her mother coughed.

Sonya glared at her.

Sensing a confrontation coming, Laura piped in, "There are many lovely houses in the neighbourhood, and I'm sure you'll find one to suit your purposes. I can help you search."

"Thank you, I may take you up on that. My mobility is rather compromised." She pointed to her cane.

Chris shifted in his seat and crossed his legs the other way. Laura helped herself to another pastry. They talked for a while longer about current affairs and then about the children. Sonya offered a glass of wine to everyone and when her mother didn't budge from her seat, she struggled to get up herself.

"Thank you, but I think we should get going," Chris said.

"Are you sure I can't convince you to have one glass of wine?" Sonya asked.

"I'll have some," Laura said. She noticed Chris wince when she accepted the offer and was about to retract her words, but suddenly changed her mind. Why should she have to leave because he was restless? They hadn't even been there an hour. "Chris, why don't you go home and relieve Monique while I stay for one glass of wine?"

Chris stood up. "Good idea, take your time."

"You take the car. I'll walk home later since it's a great afternoon for a stroll."

Chris thanked the women for their hospitality and Sonya saw him to the door. They chatted at the entrance for some time and Laura could hear laughter erupting intermittently. What could they be talking about that was so funny? Erika chattered on about her life in Houston and then reverted to the topic of irresponsible men. Laura only half-listened to her diatribe.

"You, on the other hand, have a good man there," Erika said. "You hang on to him."

Sonya came back to the living room, scowling. "Mother!" she said, with exasperation, "Please."

"I'm only complimenting Laura on what a fine man she has."
She cocked her head, as if she had been slapped in the face.

Sonya perked up. "Mother, would you do a huge favour for me
and bring out some cheese and pâté from the fridge? And the wine.
It's in the refrigerator door." Turning to Laura, she said, "I guess I
got it backwards, I should have served the savory things first. I'm
not the best hostess."

"Nonsense," Laura said. "It's all wonderful, in whatever order."

Erika wasn't budging and she had a sour expression on her face.
Sonya asked again, "Mother, are you going to get the cheese or
should I?"

Erika headed toward the kitchen without responding.

"I have to apologize for my mother," Sonya said. "Sometimes
she gets over-involved in situations and she thinks the world has
come to an end." She leaned toward Laura and whispered, "And
now she's mad at me because she's missing out on our conversation."

"I think she means well," Laura said. "She's concerned about
you."

"Jack may have screwed us, and this accident may have set me
back, but I'm not going to succumb to misery. I'll survive this, we all
will."

Erika returned with an open bottle of Sauvignon Blanc and two
wine glasses. She poured the wine, gave Sonya a sharp glance, and
walked out of the room.

"My mother is supposedly here to help out, but then she resents
it when I ask her to do anything," Sonya said. "The sooner I recover,
the better—for many reasons."

Laura gave a sympathetic nod and took a substantial sip of her
wine. "I must say, you certainly appear collected in the face of all
this adversity, Sonya. "I don't know how you maintain such a positive attitude."

Sonya smiled. "It's all about survival."

"Yes," Laura said, "I suppose it is." A part of her wished that
Sonya was falling to pieces, that she wasn't so courageous in the
face of her misfortune. Instead, Erika appeared to be the one in
crisis.

"You have every reason to pull through this, Sonya. I'm sure you'll manage very well." Laura said this knowing that if she were in Sonya's shoes she'd be devastated. She nibbled on the last bits of crust from her lemon tart.

"You're sweet. Thanks for your support."

Laura had come to Sonya's that day intending to cheer her up, to help her through her hardship. But she was evidently fine, and in control of her life despite the challenges. Why did she, herself, feel deflated and useless? She finished her glass of wine and was grateful when Sonya filled it up again.

Erika brought in a cheese platter and this time sat down.

"We'll find a cute little bungalow with a small, manageable garden, and before long I'll be back at work." She smiled at Laura in a reassuring way.

Laura almost envied her. Sonya had such confidence and determination. Nothing was going to stop her from succeeding in her new life. Undoubtedly, she'd be married again before long; a woman with such striking characteristics and self-assurance would not be ignored.

"Mother is right about one thing, though, you're very fortunate to be married to a man like Chris. I can tell that he's devoted to his family."

"Yes, he is a great husband. I couldn't be happier." Truthfully, she'd be a lot happier if Chris worked less, if he helped more at home, if he was more supportive of her dreams. But then, what were her dreams? She'd been so immersed in renovating the house and raising the girls for the last few years that she couldn't begin to think of what they might be.

"Help yourself to some cheese," Sonya said. "Thank you, Mom, for bringing it out."

"You're welcome," Erika said, in a sociable tone, apparently recovered from her earlier annoyance.

Laura served herself some grapes, then crackers, and then cheese—too good to resist. She noticed that Sonya wasn't eating much—a few grapes, a nibble of cheese. Perhaps her appetite had been curtailed by the stress. That must be it—she appeared composed on the outside but inside she was reeling. Laura's sudden speculation was strangely uplifting. Perhaps she would be needed after all.

"Tell me, how are you coping? I know you're resolute to move forward, but in the meantime, how do you manage?" Laura asked.

"For one thing, I've learned to rely on myself and myself alone. From now on, I count on no one, trust no one."

"Is that so? Erika said with a furrowed brow.

"I'm referring to men, Mom. You know I appreciate all you do."

Laura must have projected a surprised expression because Sonya went on to elaborate.

"And I don't mean people like your husband—Chris is a gem. I mean the world at large, the people who appear sincere, who use and abuse others and think all is for their taking."

Sonya spoke in such a poised manner and with such conviction that Laura found herself nodding in agreement. She popped a cracker loaded with brie into her mouth. Erika refilled her wine glass to the top.

"In fact, it's not just the men," Sonya said. "For every unfaithful man, there's a woman who's seducing him away from his commitments. Men are such weak, egotistical children. They'll lose their heads almost every time a woman pays them the least bit of attention, especially in midlife. It's sadly predictable."

Laura drank more wine. She didn't know what to say. Marriages were breaking apart like old book bindings these days and if she took a count, she could come up with at least a half-dozen casualties. Thank goodness her own marriage was well bound—she and Chris may have had their conflicts but for the most part, they were stuck together indelibly. Chris would never check out of his life like Sonya's husband had.

By the time Laura stood up to go, it was well past dinner time. She was unsteady on her feet and not keen on walking home, but Sonya couldn't drive because of her condition, and Erika was uncomfortable driving on streets she didn't know. "I only drive in Houston," she said, "where the roads don't play strange tricks." Laura called a cab, citing a cramp in her leg as the reason for not walking. When the taxi dropped her off at the house it was only 7:30 p.m., but she was exhausted. She snuck past the den where Chris and the girls were watching TV, through the kitchen, and up the back stairs, without being noticed. Dropping her clothes on the ground, she slipped under the bedcovers, hoping that an evening nap would clear her head.

Chapter Nineteen

Once again, Chris couldn't fall asleep that night. Laura nestled against him, her leg flopped over his lower body. For a long time he didn't move because he didn't want to disturb her heavy slumber. Monique hadn't come home yet and though he wasn't worried, he didn't like her gallivanting with Andrew until all hours of the night. What could they possibly be doing? Well, he knew what they could be doing, but hoped that wasn't the case. In his mind, the relationship was casual, not a deep involvement; maybe they were watching movies and talking, or were out with a group of friends. She had said they were hanging out. What did that mean? And she'd become evasive when he asked questions. This new side of Monique was making him uneasy.

An hour later, Chris sat up in bed and switched on the light to read. Laura's laboured breathing was getting worse. He read a few pages of the Kennedy biography he'd started a while ago, but the words, as inspiring as they were, did not engage him. At 3:00 a.m. he went downstairs to get a drink of milk and something to eat. Tempted to watch the videos again, he went to the family room but then turned back. Not a good idea. Instead, he went to the study and unfolded the letter from Denise, which he'd already read numerous times. Why was he so intrigued by her past? Could he be searching for some understanding as to why she would choose the Parisian over him? Sitting comfortably in the wing chair with his feet on the ottoman, he read the pages again, not fully concentrating. The hand-written words made him feel closer to her and in a strange way they were comforting. She had beautiful penmanship; the letters were formed with precision but flowed with elegant ease.

If he brought the letter to someone who analyzed handwriting, what would they say? He must be losing his mind to be thinking of having Denise's writing psycho-analyzed.

He heard clattering at the front door. This time it was *he* who startled Monique.

"Dad," she whispered, "You're still up?"

"And you? You're still up too, I see."

"Yeah, but I'm twenty-one. I'm supposed to be out late having fun."

"And what does your 'fun' consist of?" he asked.

Monique kicked off her shoes, and headed up the stairs.

"Excuse me...I was talking to you."

She shot him a look of annoyance.

He became acutely aware of his ruffled hair and wrinkled pajamas as he stood at the bottom of the stairway with arms crossed, waiting for a reply. He tried to compensate for his less-than-commanding appearance with an authoritative voice. "Where were you exactly?"

"Out with friends."

"With Andrew?"

"Yeah, him and some others."

"Till 3:30 a.m.? Again?"

"Things don't get going until at least midnight—in case you don't remember."

He didn't like her sarcasm. "What about Andrew? He breezes in and out of here with you but hardly speaks. Where does he live? What do you like about him?"

Monique sat down on the stairs and sighed heavily, like a teenager. "I don't know what your problem is. He's a friend from school, he lives here in the States, and he's a good guy. What else do you need to know?"

"You're spending a great deal of time with him and staying up to all hours, which concerns me, Monique." He hated sounding like an overbearing parent scolding an adolescent, but he was trapped in the never-ending role of fretful father, one that he'd long ago assumed as his prerogative. When she was away at school, that was one thing, but now that she was home and he was part-witness to her escapades, he couldn't refrain from commenting. Laura would never delve into Monique's personal affairs; she wouldn't cross that boundary, but someone had to.

"Sheeesh…, Dad. You're blowing this out of control. I'm going to bed." She got up and stomped up the stairs, leaving him with no more knowledge about her life than before they'd had the conversation.

In the morning, Chris woke at his usual time, having slept a mere two hours. When he walked into the kitchen, he found Sophie and Tanya preparing a breakfast tray.

"Morning, girls. What are you doing?" He kissed each daughter on the top of her head.

"We're making breakfast in bed for Mommy," Tanya said.

"She'll love that."

"What did you get her for Mother's Day?" Sophie asked.

Mother's Day! Shit. He knew it was coming up but then he'd completely forgotten about it. "Flowers. I'm getting her flowers. I'm heading out to get them right now."

"Are you going to give her a necklace like last year?" Tanya asked.

Damn, damn, damn. "Yes, I'm giving her jewelry, but don't tell her. I want it to be a surprise." He winked at the two girls and they giggled, happy to be part of the conspiracy.

"See what I made for Mommy." Tanya showed him a cardboard picture frame containing an old family picture. Sparkles and glitter decorated the frame.

"It's beautiful," he said.

"And this is what I made," Sophie said. She presented a glass jar with scraps of coloured tissue paper glued around the outside. "It's a vase."

"Mommy will love it," he said, and hugged her. "Now, girls, I have to go to the store for the flowers, wait till I get back before making breakfast. When I come home, we can surprise her together."

"Can we watch cartoons until you get back?" Tanya asked.

"Of course."

Wearing sweatpants and an old tee-shirt, Chris headed out. The only store open that early was a 24-hour grocery store about five miles away. He drove well over the speed limit, in spite of light rain, but couldn't bring himself to slow down. Presumably, the faster he got there, the less guilty he would feel.

The only flowers at the store were carnations and mums. He bought three bundles of white carnations and two bundles of long-stemmed yellow mums and had them wrapped together. They may not be roses but they would have to do. He looked for specialty chocolates but didn't find any and bought two boxes of heart-shaped gingersnaps instead. Fresh-squeezed orange juice would be a treat, he thought, and he found a bag of oranges from Florida.

When he got back home, the girls were in the kitchen again, fixing breakfast. "I thought I told you to wait," he said.

"But we want everything to be ready as soon as Mommy wakes up," Sophie said.

They had made toast, which was cold and dried out, and were attempting to make scrambled eggs. The frying pan contained a yellow mess, resembling a pancake, with hard white specks poking out.

Chris laughed. "You have to stir the eggs, that's why they're called scrambled, Honey."

"Oh," Sophie said. "Can you do it?"

"Of course." Chris found a tall vase and arranged the flowers as best he could. He started a pot of coffee and the girls pressed the orange halves on the juicer machine, and arranged the cookies on a plate.

Laura came into the kitchen, bleary-eyed. "What's going on?" she said in a groggy voice.

"No, you can't come in here," shouted Tanya. "Go back, go back!"

Appearing confused, Laura looked at Chris.

"Happy Mother's Day," he said.

When they finished preparing breakfast they all traipsed upstairs, Chris carrying the tray, Sophie the gift bags, and Tanya the flowers. The girls plunked themselves on either side of Laura and Chris sat at the end of the bed. They watched her open her gifts and talked to her while she ate her breakfast. "My gift is still coming," Chris said.

"Can we do something special for Mother's Day, like go to a movie?" Tanya asked.

"Is that special for you or for Mom?" Chris asked.

"You could take us, and Mommy could have a break," Sophie said.

"Oh, I like that idea," Laura said.

"The problem is that I have to go to the office for a few hours this afternoon."

"For how long?" Laura asked.

"A few hours, three, maybe four." Chris went to the window and opened the blinds. Grey clouds shrouded the morning sky and rain thrashed against the pavement.

"I see." The disappointment in her voice matched the weather outside.

"I'm sorry, I would have gone yesterday, but we had to go to that tea at Sonya's."

"My parents are coming for dinner, don't forget."

He had known that yesterday too, but had already forgotten. "I'll be back by then, when are they coming again?"

"5:00. I planned for an early dinner."

"Need anything from the store?" he asked.

"No thanks." Her voice had a cool edge. "I'm all organized."

Monique poked her head in the door and sang out. "Happy Mother's Day!"

Laura beckoned her in with a wave.

She pounced on the bed wearing an oversized tee-shirt and plaid boxers. Her uncombed hair spilled from a sloppy ponytail, remaining from the day before. "I have something for you," she said.

"What is it?" the girls cried in unison.

Monique handed Laura a tiny pink velvet bag with a draw-string.

"Open it. Hurry." Sophie said.

Laura untied the bow, taking her time admiring the delicate case, and then removed a small item wrapped in purple tissue paper. Sophie and Tanya crowded around her, almost crushing her against the headboard. Inside was a sterling silver pendant in the shape of a heart. She placed it in the palm of her hand and held it out for all to see. "I love it, Sweetheart," she said to Monique.

"It's to go on your silver chain. The one I got you for Christmas."

Laura handed the ornament to Tanya and leaned over to hug Monique. "Thank you."

"Well, girls, I'd better get moving," Chris said, hoping the commotion had distracted everyone from his non-existent gift. He'd have to go to a jewelry store to get Laura something before the day's end. In a low voice he said to the girls, "Don't forget to clean the kitchen mess."

"Sure," Laura said. "Leave the clean-up to a seven and nine-year-old." She was not amused.

"Don't worry, I'll do it," Monique piped in.

"Thanks, Honey," Chris said. He turned to Laura. "I'll try to be back before your parents arrive, to help you get ready." He kissed her warmly and in return, she gave him a feeble smile.

By the time Chris got to work he could hardly concentrate. He usually functioned well on little sleep but today the adrenalin didn't kick in. The financial statement he tried to decipher became a big blur of numbers and rubbing his eyes made things worse. His head throbbed but he hadn't thought to take any aspirin before leaving home. Making a mental note to keep some at the office, he pushed his chair back and leaned back, lifting his feet up on the desk. Within seconds, he fell asleep.

At 2:00 he woke with a start. The rain slammed against his office window and the ominous clouds looming overhead made it feel like night. He turned on the light and forced his mind into motion. The task at hand, although tedious, engrossed him to the point of losing track of time and when he looked at his watch again, two hours had passed. The stores would close soon, damn it. Why hadn't he gone to the jewelers to buy Laura's gift before coming to the office? He continued his number crunching, hoping to finish within the hour. By 4:30 he was done, but it was too late to get to the store and be home in time to help Laura, as he had promised. Before leaving, he checked his e-mails and found a full page of new messages — nothing from Denise.

Chris drove home at a faster-than-safe clip on slippery roads. When he arrived, he saw his in-laws' sedan parked in its usual spot, several feet past the fire-hydrant, in front of the house. The only sign of life came from the front light in the living room, which shone from the darkness like a single star in the sky. Chris mustered up his son-in-law congeniality and straightened his posture as he approached the entrance. His head didn't ache anymore, but the mid-afternoon nap had left him feeling sluggish.

Laura's parents greeted Chris with friendly cheer, but Laura didn't utter a word. In fact, she barely looked at him. Resentment radiated through narrow pupils when their eyes met, and her pronounced wooden movements conveyed pent-up hostility. Chris figured he'd have to spend the rest of the evening making up to Laura for his delay and for messing up the day, but dispelling his wife's wrath was never an easy endeavour.

"Can I refill your drinks?" he offered.

"Dinner's ready, we've already had second rounds," Laura said.

"Let him relax a bit before we eat, Laura," her father said. "Can dinner not wait a few more minutes?"

Laura threw up her hands in frustration and left the room. Chris poured himself a double scotch and refilled everyone else's glass with Sherry.

"Sorry to keep you all waiting. I'm inundated at work," Chris said to his in-laws, loud enough for Laura to hear from the kitchen. "It's been a busy month and I'm scrambling to keep up. Business is rolling in faster than Tony and I can handle these days."

"When it's booming you've got to pounce. Who knows when the markets will clobber us all again," Laura's father said. A retired stockbroker who had faced many ups and downs in his career, he loved to share his insights. Chris appreciated his good intentions and respected his knowledge; Laura's father had been a good mentor over the years and a tight bond had developed between the two men.

"Will you be hiring new people?" his mother-in-law asked.

"Probably. But it takes time to figure out what our exact needs are."

His in-laws nodded with understanding. At least they acknowledged his work pressures; they never passed judgment and stayed clear of interfering. Laura returned to the living room and sat rigidly on the edge of the sofa, with no signs of understanding coming from her.

"Now then," Laura said. "Can we eat?"

Laura had set out the good china in the dining room, and the girls had helped lay the table, apparent by the crooked display of cutlery, and the way the napkins had been stuffed in the wine glasses like scrunched paper balls. Dinner consisted of a delicious prime rib with roasted new potatoes, cauliflower gratin, and steamed green beans. High praise was offered from around the table and Laura accepted the compliments with grace. But she didn't speak to Chris, barely even acknowledged him throughout the meal, and at the end of the night, after he'd single-handedly cleaned the entire kitchen, she went to bed without saying a word.

He'd screwed up royally—late for dinner and no gift. Thank goodness the girls hadn't mentioned it. All night he'd been waiting for one of them to say something, but they hadn't, and fortunately, he'd averted embarrassment. In San Francisco he'd buy Laura something sensational, the nicest piece of jewelry he'd bought her yet, and she could pick it herself. That might get him out of the doghouse.

Chapter Twenty

On Sunday morning, Denise woke to her alarm clock's piercing ring at 6:00 a.m. Since it was Mother's Day, she wanted to do something special for her mother — breakfast in bed and then queenly service for the rest of the day. She and the boys had concocted their plan the day before, when her mother had taken a nap.

The children wanted to be woken up early too, insisting that they partake in the breakfast preparation. With sleepy eyes, Martin helped make raspberry pancakes, his grandmother's favourite, and Luc went outside in his pajamas to pick some wild flowers for the tray.

When Denise's mother poked her head into the kitchen, Martin shrieked, "No, Grandma, you can't be here. You have to go back to sleep." He took her hand and led her back to her bedroom.

Luc carefully carried the breakfast tray and Denise brought a mug of coffee and a glass of orange juice. Martin followed with the giant Bristol board Mother's Day card that they had created for her.

"How lovely," their grandmother said when the boys entered her room. She put down her book and opened her arms wide, inviting them to plunge onto the bed and snuggle in her embrace.

Denise watched as they presented the card, now bent from lying on top of it on the bed. The boys had drawn pictures of what they perceived her favourite things to be: flowers, frogs, rainbows, birds, and three stick-children at her side with a big heart floating above them. The colourful pictures were superimposed by a giant sun.

"This is magnificent," she said. "I'm going to have this artwork framed and I'll put it up in my kitchen where I can see it every day."

Denise placed the breakfast tray on the bed and kissed her mother's cheek. "Happy Mother's Day."

"And to you, my darling." She nodded to the boys.

"Oh yeah," Luc said. "Happy Mother's day, Mom." He gave her a hug and Martin followed suit.

In the afternoon, the boys pestered Denise to hike with them to the modest country store, a small wooden hut perched on a hill at the intersection of the main road and the unpaved lake road. The mile-long trek was always worth the reward at the end—a treat chosen from several shelves of chocolate bars and candies. Once the onslaught of summer vacationers arrived, the ice-cream shop next door would be open, an even greater enticement for the boys. Inspired by the sunshine and fresh air, and desiring the exercise, Denise and her mother agreed to accompany the boys on their first hike of the season.

The midday sun was strong and Denise regretted making the children wear jackets. After walking a short distance, they had already tied them around their waists. Her mother wore her big sombrero-style hat, while Denise and the boys wore baseball caps. Not much traffic passed as they walked along the dirt road, roaming from one side to the other. Dawdling as they walked, the boys collected stones on the dirt road, shoving them in their pockets, and Denise and her mother lagged behind, giving the children some independence.

Denise's mother inhaled deeply. "I love the spring country air. It perks up my lungs and makes me want to sing."

"Spring and fall have always been my favourite seasons," Denise said. "But summer and winter have their virtues too," she said, laughing.

"Ah yes, you always were a four-seasons gal. I remember when you were little, you couldn't wait for summer, but when the blossoms fell off the trees and the tulips died, you cried, because spring was over."

Denise had always lamented the end of nice things. The prospect of a new beginning excited her, but at the same time, she'd be disheartened because one day that too would end. Her father came to mind; after he died, everything changed. She was eight when her hero disappeared from her world, ending her life as 'Daddy's girl,' and leaving her with a lifelong void.

"Mother, how many years would you and Dad have been married, if he were still alive?"

"Fifty-one years," she answered, without a second's thought. "Wouldn't that have been something?"

"Do you think you would have lasted together all those years? I mean, been happy all that time?"

"He was the love of my life."

"Is it because of Dad that you never remarried?"

"No. Because of you kids." She picked a blossom from a shrub and pressed it against her nose. "Lovely," she said.

"You thought we couldn't handle it?"

"No, I thought *I* couldn't handle it. I had enough going on with my job and the family's needs when you were children. I couldn't spread myself any thinner."

"But what about later, when we were grown?"

"By then, dear, I was set in my ways. I enjoyed my friendships with various gentlemen who crossed my path, but I was comfortable with my life as it was."

"I don't know how you did it, Mother. The things that stand out from my childhood are you working and studying and studying and working. Yet you never got impatient with us, and you hardly ever yelled. And you must have been overwhelmed during those years."

"I had no choice back then. Without insurance money and no viable profession when Dad died, I had to forge ahead. It was a matter of survival." She linked her arm with Denise's. "Ah, but what a good life we've had. Everything worked out, didn't it?"

Denise's mother had become a nurse and then a teacher at nursing school. When she retired, she'd received accolades from past students and colleagues, and was honoured for her contributions by the institution at which she had taught for many years. Denise remembered all the cards and flowers she'd been given, and the gold watch, which her mother still wore with pride.

"I wish I had your strength, your wonderful attitude."

Her mother patted her hand. "You do. I *know* you do."

"Luc caught a frog," Martin shouted from somewhere in the woods. The boys had found a creek and when they emerged, were smothered in dirt. Luc came out with the slimy creature trying to escape from his grip.

"He's humungish!" Martin said, barely able to contain his excitement. Luc calmly brought his reptilian prize to the women. Denise recoiled but her mother held out her hands.

"Can I hold him?" she asked. Luc carefully passed the frog into his grandmother's wrinkled palms.

"He sure is a big fellow," she said. "What should we do with him?"

"Keep him, keep him." Martin said.

"No, I think we need to give him back to nature," Luc said.

"Good idea, let's take him back to the pond, to his home," their grandmother said.

Denise, who was not a fan of slimy creatures, waited by the side of the road while the others entered the woods with the frog. She pulled the needles off a pine tree branch, one by one, listening to the laughter through the trees. Her mother's clear voice rang with delight. "There he goes, see him jump?"

Denise loved the warm and loving way her mother interacted with the boys; playing cards, telling them jokes, handling reptiles — why couldn't *she* relate to her own children that way? Impatience often hampered her ability to connect with them in the city, but in the country she was in a calmer state of mind. Wouldn't it be nice to be able to enjoy her children like her mother did, naturally and unencumbered.

The sun's heat had intensified by the time they were ready to go back to the cottage. The kids had had their treats and were less enthused about walking the distance home. Dragging their feet, their young bodies were slumped over like old men as they headed back.

"Can't you go to the cottage and get the car?" Luc asked.

Denise stopped in her tracks and glared at him. "This was your idea, young man. Do you not recall begging me to let you go to the store? In fact, you wanted to go alone. Whom would you have complained to then?"

Martin began to cry. "I have a stone in my shoe. Owww..."

She pulled off his shoe and shook it. No stone.

Denise's mother said nothing. They continued walking, an occasional groan emanating from one of the children dragging behind. Denise ignored the sounds and increased her pace. Her mother kept in step until, suddenly, she stopped and gripped her arm. Her breathing became laboured and she bent over, one arm covering her chest.

"What is it Mother?" Is it your heart?" Her own heart lurched.

"I…yes I think…I don't know."

Denise guided her to the side of the road. "You have to lie down." She gathered the jackets hanging from the boys' hips and laid them out on the ground, in a shady spot on the edge of the road, and then rolled up her own jacket to create a headrest. Her mother didn't resist as Denise gently lowered her onto the makeshift bed and checked her pulse. If there were any beats at all, they were impossible to detect.

Panic gripped her. "Mother! Mother!" she cried. "Oh my God, oh my God!" She started to cry. "No, no, no."

Her mother lay still, unconscious, or worse.

Denise attempted CPR, meticulously following the instructions she had learned on one of her shows. She put her ear to her mother's chest. Nothing.

Luc said, "We need help. I'm going to find a cottage with a car so she can go to the hospital. Martin, you stay here with Mommy and hold her hand."

Before she could respond, she saw Luc running along the dirt road, as fast as he could. No matter how hard she tried to compose herself, she couldn't stop shaking and crying. Her mother was sheet white and her lips had turned purple. Denise held her wrist, praying for the slightest flicker of a pulse and pleading that this was merely a fainting episode because of the heat. "Please, please, please," she said, in a whisper. "Don't let this be a heart attack."

Martin sat on the ground beside his mother and put his arm around her waist. "It's going to be OK, Mom," he said, in a small voice.

Denise wiped her wet face with the front of her shirt, but the tears kept streaming down. "Don't die. You can't die," she said. Her voice trembled as she quietly begged for help. If there was a God, couldn't He help her at this time? She had never asked for anything before.

When a van pulled up beside them with Luc in the passenger seat, Denise had no idea how much time had passed. A man wearing jeans and a sweatshirt got out and ran to her side. "Your son told me his grandmother was unconscious."

Denise nodded, unable to speak.

"I called 911 and they said to bring her to the hospital immediately. Waiting for an ambulance would take too long."

Denise tried to stand but couldn't, and her muffled sobs hindered her efforts to speak.

"I'll put down the back seat and we can lay her down." He worked quickly and the boys tried to help.

Denise watched, paralyzed, as the man carefully lifted her mother under the arms and the children lifted her legs. They carried her to the van and with great care placed her inside. Denise crawled into the back and kneeled beside her. Without being told, the boys jumped into the middle seats and fastened their belts. The man got in the car and started the engine; a cloud of dirt surrounded them as the car sped toward the hospital.

When they arrived thirty minutes later, paramedics were waiting with a gurney at the emergency entrance. Someone ushered Denise and the boys to a stark waiting room where long-faced people sat on hard institutional chairs, awaiting news of their own loved ones. Luc and Martin sat in silence on either side of Denise, their earlier boyhood impishness transformed to grave maturity. They didn't ask for vending machine money, for their Game Boys, or for the channel to be changed on the television, which droned on with the news in the corner of the room. Like Denise, they stared ahead as if suspended by fear. The kind man who had brought them to the hospital had vanished as suddenly as he had first appeared.

When the doctor came to get Denise he told the boys to wait with the nurse, a kindly woman. The nurse handed them each a sucker, which they put in their pockets. Compassion poured from the doctor's face and he gently touched Denise's shoulder as he directed her to a private room. She sensed doom. Moving his chair from behind his desk to face the other chair directly, he asked her to sit down. The blood rushed from her head and her body went limp as she slumped into the seat. If she had still been standing, she would have passed out.

"I'm sorry," he said. He sat down and shook his head, sadness in his eyes. "Your mother had a massive heart attack. There was nothing we could do to revive her."

Denise lurched forward and the doctor caught her before she collapsed on the floor. She started to convulse as silent sobs gripped her throat. He held her against him as the initial shock pulverized her body, and then he reached for the phone on his desk.

The last thing she recalled before waking up on a gurney in the hospital corridor was a gentle voice telling her that everything would be all right, and a needle piercing her thigh.

Chapter Twenty-one

Laura checked her watch while waiting to disembark the plane at San Francisco Airport. They had landed fifteen minutes earlier but were still sitting on the tarmac. The late afternoon sky, barely perceptible through the misty windows, hinted at evening, but it was only 5:00. Making a mental calculation, she realized she'd be pressed to get to the hotel before Chris if they were stuck there much longer, especially with the rush-hour traffic.

The man standing behind her in the aisle said something and when she turned around she realized he was speaking to her. "They could at least let us know what the problem is," he said. He dropped his bag on the floor, causing a loud thud, and plunked his large frame into the seat.

"Yes, it's taking forever. Perhaps it's a security issue. I don't know what's normal these days."

"This is definitely not normal. Even with all the extra security, they shouldn't be this slow to get us off the plane." His eyes darted around impatiently.

She gave him an empathetic nod, determined not to let a short delay interfere with her cheerful mood, not on this precious holiday. She still had to collect her bag and then find a cab, but as long as she'd arrive to the hotel before Chris, she'd be fine. Her heavy shoulder bag dug into her skin, causing her back to ache and she placed it down in the narrow space in front of her. The bottle of champagne, packed in ice, along with the Beluga caviar, were heavier than she'd realized. Maybe she had used too much ice, but she had been adamant that everything be properly chilled. They'd planned on saving the expensive Krug for a special occasion, and as far as she was concerned, this trip warranted celebration. The last time the two of them had been away together was too long ago to recall. Five years ago, Laura's parents had offered to watch the girls while Chris and she went to Spain for a week, but that trip hardly counted because after two days in Madrid, they had to rush back home when Tanya's appendix erupted and she had to have emergency surgery.

Laura planned to greet Chris with pomp when he arrived at the hotel — as a kick-off to their luxurious mini-getaway: a glass of champagne, some caviar, and a little romance if they had time. She'd want to shower and slip on her sexy lingerie before he arrived. The thought excited her; too many years had passed since she'd greeted him with sex on her mind. After making love they'd dash off for dinner at that phenomenal restaurant they'd heard about. Hopefully, Chris had remembered to make the reservations.

After finally deplaning, Laura went to the baggage claim area and was relieved to see her black suitcase amongst all the others on the luggage carousel. The red ribbon she'd tied around the handle turned out to be a clever idea; she didn't have to waste time trying to identify her bag like others were doing. She lifted her bag and helped an older lady remove hers.

"My son is supposed to be here waiting for me," the lady said. She sounded fretful.

"I'm sure he'll be here shortly," Laura said.

"Maybe he left because we took forever coming out." Her voice trembled.

"He may have gone to get a coffee or to check the screen for information, but I doubt he'd leave," Laura said.

"But what if he doesn't come. I don't know what to do. I don't travel very much, you see, and my eyesight is poor. He told me he would be right here and that I didn't need to worry about a thing," she repeated. "I knew I shouldn't have come. I'm too old to travel."

She couldn't have been more than eighty and, in Laura's view, appeared in good health. "Not to worry," Laura said, and patted her gently on the arm. "I'll wait with you until he comes." She checked the time. Damn, she was late herself, but how could she leave the poor woman in such a state?

"You're a dear." Her eyes darted around the terminal as if keeping a vigilant watch for danger.

"Let's sit down over there, where we can have a good view." Laura led the old lady to a row of unoccupied seats. "What does your son look like?"

"He's gorgeous. Tall, with dark brown hair and brown eyes." With shaky hands, she removed her wallet from her purse, and took out several worn photographs. "This is him," she said, and pointed to a photo of three college-aged people standing in front of a church. A man stood erect, his arms flanked across the shoulders of two women on either side of him, laughing. "This was taken at my nephew's wedding a few years back." The photo was out of focus, making it difficult to determine the man's features. "The girls are my daughters." She gently touched the image of the woman to the left. "Sandra died five years ago of cancer."

"How sad," Laura said.

The other photos were of various grandchildren, and the woman rambled off their names.

"Shall we call your son?" Laura asked. "You can use my cell phone."

She shook her head. "I only know his home number and he's coming from work."

Laura looked around. A few stragglers remained in the baggage claim area, but the luggage had been collected and the carousel had stopped moving.

"We can call his workplace if you tell me the name of his company." I'll get the number from 'information.'"

"I don't remember the name, it's a new job, he's in electronics. What if something's happened to him? What will I do?" She became teary.

"Don't worry. I'll stay with you until we have this resolved." Trying to be inconspicuous, she checked the time.

"I never should have come. I told him, 'it's not a good idea, Harvey. I'm much too old to travel.' But he insisted. He said, 'Ma, you have to come to San Francisco, it's your one and only chance.' He's only here for a year, you see. Then he goes back to Boston. He wants to show me around, give me the tour."

A man came rushing towards them. In his late fifties, Laura thought. He was practically bald with a rotund physique, and certainly not tall. Laura smiled as she recalled the lady's description.

"Ma," he said, as he hurried over to them. "Did your plane arrive early?"

She stood up and they embraced.

"No, at 5:00, like I told you."

"You told me 6:00, Ma. I even came ahead of time to make sure I'd be here when you came out."

The trepidation in the lady's face had vanished, replaced by jubilation. "Never mind, Harvey, you're here now." She hastily introduced him to Laura and then they trundled off. Laura collected her belongings and hurried towards the exit. A short while ago she had been engulfed by a torrent of people dashing in every direction, but now she found herself alone in a sterile, abandoned place. She couldn't wait to get to the hotel.

Stepping out into thick fog, Laura looked up at the sky, a soft drizzle brushing her face. The sun had been shining when she left Cleveland and she hadn't thought to check the weather forecast, or to bring a raincoat. The humid air penetrated her clothing and her cotton turtleneck clung to her body like cellophane. Why had she worn the light wool pants with the polyester lining? A loose fitting skirt and blouse would have been much more comfortable. The two light layers of clothing suddenly felt oppressive in the damp air, even though it wasn't hot. Water seeped from the bottom of her carry-on as she stood on the curb waiting for a taxi. Maybe it hadn't been such a good idea after all to fill freezer bags with ice. She opened the carry-on and rearranged its contents, hoping the leaking would stop once she had straightened the melting bags of ice. She considered dumping the water on the road but then a cab stopped in front of her and before she knew it, the driver was putting her suitcase in the trunk. She climbed into the car, carefully placing the carry-on upright at her feet. At last, thank goodness, she was one drive away from her destination.

"The Grand Hotel please. At Union Square."

"You're not from here, are you?" The cab driver said. "With your beautiful curly blond hair I thought you were a California girl."

Laura didn't like his bluntness but she was stuck with him. "No, I'm from the Midwest."

"Been to San Francisco before?"

"No."

"Most beautiful place on earth."

"I'm looking forward to seeing it."

"Best thing to do is drive along the coast."

"Yes, we plan to."

"Only problem is...earthquakes. They say we're gonna get one any time. A big one, maybe the biggest yet."

"Really?" Laura said.

"Yup. I built an earthquake shelter in our basement. I've got water and canned food to last for months. Every day when I go to bed I pray, please don't let it happen today."

"Maybe they're wrong, maybe there won't be one for a long time," she said.

"Oh yeah, it's guaranteed. I hope for your sake it don't happen when you're here. I'll pray for you too."

"Thanks," Laura said. "Do you know the weather forecast?"

"Nope. Here, you get what you get. I don't pay attention to weather. It's the earthquakes you gotta worry about."

Laura hadn't considered earthquakes when they were planning this trip, not being one to dwell on doom. But what if something did happen to them? The girls were practically babies; their lives would be ruined. Maybe she shouldn't have come. "Will we see the Golden Gate Bridge on our way to the hotel?" she asked, hoping to veer him off the subject of earthquakes.

"No, but it's a beauty. Did you know that the Bay Bridge is made with more concrete than the Empire State Building? These bridges are meant to withstand earthquakes, but I hope I'm not driving on one when it happens."

She stared out the window, unable to see much because of the fog. When she used to travel for business she enjoyed the approach into the city from the airport and taking in the urban landscapes. But here she had no sense of location because the hazy fog interfered with her view. "How much longer before we get to the hotel?" she asked.

"About fifteen minutes."

Darn, Chris would be arriving around the same time. "I'm going to make some calls," she announced. Chris didn't answer his phone but she left a quick message saying that she was on her way, and then made imaginary calls for the rest of the ride to avoid the cab driver's banter.

At the hotel, a valet took Laura's suitcase and opened the door for her. Enormous vases of exotic flowers and potted hibiscus trees created an intimate garden-like ambiance in the expansive hotel lobby, and the tension in her body melted away, serenity taking over. Luxurious velvet covered couches provided a lounging area where some people drank cocktails and conversed quietly, while others read the newspaper or studied maps, planning their itinerary. She observed a group chatting with animated enthusiasm—a mother, father, and three adolescent children. One day, she'd love to bring the girls to California, and in a way, she wished they were there with her now.

She checked in at the reception desk and a porter helped her with her bags. Did he notice the leaky carry-on? The only sign of Chris when she entered their suite was his book on the night table. Good, she had arrived before him. The deluxe room contained a king-size bed that faced a large window overlooking Union Square, and the bedroom opened to a cozy den with a sofa, a chair and a writing desk. She tipped the porter and hurried to the bathroom to unpack the dripping bag over the sink. Phew. The caviar, swimming in a pool of icy water, was still well-chilled. Even the champagne had remained cool. She checked the time. 6:50 p.m. If she rushed, maybe she could still be ready by the time Chris arrived.

Laura showered, put on her lacy red panties and matching bra, and then her new dress with the pink and white floral pattern and scalloped hem. She tied the matching pink cardigan over her shoulders, sprayed on some perfume, and applied her make-up. Too bad there hadn't been enough time to get her hair done before the trip. Pulling her hair back, frizzy from the rain, she secured it with a pink hair clip. Not bad for a rush job she thought, as she changed her earrings to the small diamond studs she'd carried in her purse. Chris liked her in pink; he often commented how feminine the colour was. Would he notice that she had dropped a dress size? She had been thrilled when she tried on her usual size twelve at the boutique and the dress had been too big. For the first time in years she could fit into a size ten.

By 7:30 Chris still hadn't arrived but the extra time provided an opportunity to prepare the caviar and champagne. From the ice machine down the hall, Laura filled a metal bucket and immersed the bottle in it. She laid out the toast triangles that she had brought from home on a pretty paper plate. The hotel wine glasses on the dresser would have to serve as champagne glasses and she pulled out two white linen napkins from her suitcase. Laura surveyed the self-catered caviar picnic and was satisfied with the result. There was nothing left to do but wait. At 7:45 she tried Chris's cell phone, but again no answer. She called home.

"How was the flight?" Monique asked

"Uneventful. I'm at the hotel waiting for your dad. He didn't call by any chance?"

"No."

"Can I have a quick word with Sophie and Tanya?" She held the phone away from her ear as they screamed in the background.

"Me first."

"No, me first."

Laura heard Monique negotiating with them and then Sophie came on the line; she always managed to finagle her way.

"Hi, Mommy. We went to Pizza Hut for supper."

"Lucky you."

"Tomorrow we're gonna play hopscotch with Monique. Bye."

Tanya came on next. "Monique said Katie could come over tomorrow and if we're good, she'll take us to the mall."

"That's wonderful. I miss you already, but I'm glad you're having fun," Laura said. "But listen to Monique and don't give her a hard time. Remember, she's the boss."

"OK. Love you, Mommy." Tanya hung up the phone.

Laura turned on the TV and flipped channels. Nothing caught her attention and nothing was remotely interesting. Why hadn't she brought another book? The one she did bring she'd finished on the plane. Nibbling on a toast triangle, she eyed the champagne, chilling in the bucket, waiting to be opened. Perhaps a small glass while she waited for Chris would settle her down. With gentle prodding, the cork exploded out of the bottle and hit the   ceiling, leaving a small mark. Oops. She had no idea where it landed. To prevent the bubbles from fizzing over the top of the glass, she poured with caution. Then, closing her eyes, she took a sip. Delicious. If she opened the caviar and prepared it nicely on the plate, everything would be ready for Chris when he arrived. She took the small jar off the ice in the bathroom sink and twisted the lid until it popped open. Lifting the container to her face, she examined the tiny black eggs and sniffed. With a plastic knife, she spread a small amount on a piece of toast and took a bite, closing her eyes to focus on the subtle flavor; savory, but not too salty. And not at all fishy tasting. Chris would love it. She had some more and then sat on the sofa, flipping through the "San Francisco Life" magazine   lying on the coffee table. The champagne complemented the caviar perfectly—smooth and dry. She got up and poured herself another glass and also one for Chris, intending to hand it to him when he walked through the door.

She dialed his cell phone number and left another message on his voicemail. "Chris, it's 8:00, where are you? You said you'd be here by 7:00, latest. I'm beginning to worry about our dinner reservation." She hung up the phone and went out to the corridor, hoping to see him coming. Empty. The elevator door opened and she ran out to greet it, convinced that he would be there. But a family of four poured out, laughing as they disembarked, the young son shoving his sister who tried to block his way.

Back in the hotel room, Laura helped herself to more caviar and finished her second glass of champagne. Maybe she should order up some food. Not having eaten since noon, she was ravenous. As she searched for the room service menu, she stubbed her toe on the foot of the bed. "Shoot!" Limping around the room, she grabbed the menu and picked up the champagne bottle on the way to the sofa. She sat down and held the cold bottle against her throbbing toe. Then she refilled her glass. The menu offered a decent selection and she read the choices several times. Mixed salad with balsamic vinaigrette, shrimp cocktail, smoked salmon tartar—yum. It all sounded scrumptious. Considering they'd be eating out soon she should order something small, something light. Deciding not to order food after all, in case Chris arrived before the room service did, she snacked on more caviar instead. As she lifted a piece of toast heaped with caviar to her mouth, some dropped on her dress. Damn. She stumbled to the bathroom and tried to remove the stain with a soapy cloth. To Laura's dismay, the dress had a big, ugly blotch right in the middle of her stomach. Tears of frustration welled in her eyes as she aimed the blow-dryer against the damp spot. As the patch dried, a grey stain highlighted by a water ring appeared.

Sitting on the edge of the bed, Laura watched television and drank what was left in the bottle and eventually, the glass she had poured for Chris. At 9:15 she lay down on the bed and fell asleep.

****

Chris checked his watch as the meeting was coming to a close. 9:00 p.m. He hadn't expected complications to arise. Tony had implied that the deal was pretty much wrapped up, but the client almost backed out at the last minute and he'd had to fight hard to keep to it alive. The client kept throwing new issues on the table and at one point Chris lost his cool, coming close to storming out the door. One hundred million dollars almost blown to smithereens. But he had met with these types before, posturing for more concessions when the details had already been agreed upon in principle. Fortunately, he'd been able to salvage the near wreckage and had procured something significant to bring back to Cleveland.

He shook hands with everyone but declined a dinner invitation. "My wife flew in from Cleveland today and she's waiting for me at the hotel," he told them. One man patted him on the back and winked, as if to say, 'yeah right, buddy — I know what you're up to.' Chris couldn't wait to get out of there.

He called Laura from the cab but she didn't answer her cell phone. After listening to her messages, he called the hotel and asked to be connected to the room. No answer. Strange. Where could she be? Perhaps she'd gone for a walk or was investigating the shops around the hotel. She'd been looking forward to checking out the great stores around Union Square. Hopefully she'd have assumed that he'd been stuck in the meeting and would understand; it wasn't the first time he'd been held hostage by a client. He called the restaurant to push out the reservation, but was told by a contemptuous employee that he'd forgone his table an hour ago. When Chris arrived at their room he found Laura fast asleep, breathing heavily, snoring irregularly. He sat down on the bed and gently rubbed her back.

"Laura," he whispered. He stroked her hair. "Laura, wake up." She rolled to her side and muttered something unintelligible. Then he noticed the empty bottle on the table. He quietly walked over, picked it up and inspected the label. She had drunk the entire bottle of Krug, the champagne they'd purchased at the wine-tasting last month. Then he noticed the caviar jar. All eaten. Feeling like a louse, he plunked himself down on the sofa and rubbed his temples. It had been a brutal day, and now this. He wrote Laura a note on the hotel stationary and placed it on her bedside table.

Sweetheart,

I'm sorry to have kept you waiting. The business meeting got out of hand and was almost a write-off. I'm going down to the restaurant to grab a bite. Haven't eaten all day. If you wake up, come join me.

Love, Chris

He covered her with a blanket and turned off the lights. When he came back an hour later, he found her sleeping in the exact same position.

Chapter Twenty-two

Laura woke to rumbling sounds coming from the vent. She pulled the covers to her chin and scanned the room, looking for Chris. If the other side of the bed had not been disturbed she would have panicked, fearing that something terrible had befallen him. But the pillow had an imprint of his head and the bedding was left in the same state as at home, sheets and blanket neatly folded down, as if he'd be coming back soon. The digital clock on her bedside table indicated 9:36 a.m. She couldn't have slept twelve hours straight...could she? Throwing the covers away, she found herself swathed in her dress from the night before, the soft flowing fabric crumpled like an overused gift bag. Standing up was onerous; on the first try she felt lopsided and had to sit down on the bed. Why had she drunk so much? Her head swirled but somehow she mustered the strength to drag herself to the bathroom. Grateful to find some Aspirin in her toiletries bag, she popped three into the back of her throat and swallowed without water. The mirror gave her a shock — spastic hair, raccoon eyes, and pasty skin. What a vision of loveliness. Thank goodness Chris wasn't there to see.

On the desk she found two notes from Chris, one from the previous night, and one from that morning.

Dear Laura,

Thought I'd let you sleep. Looks like you had a rough time last night. It's my fault, I know I kept you waiting too long (but there is a reason). I'm really sorry and I'll make it up to you, I promise. I don't want to wake you so I'm going downstairs to have breakfast and read the paper. Come meet me when you're up. Love Chris

Everything came back to her after reading the note. Yes, he should be sorry. He hadn't shown up on time and hadn't even bothered calling. Looking down at her dress, she saw that it was disheveled and stained with caviar. Ruined. She ripped it off her shoulders, stepped out of the wrinkled mess, bunched it in a ball and threw it in the trashcan. Chris came in just then, an unwelcome witness to her shivering half-naked body—a foolish sight in her red bra and panties. He stepped towards her and gently placed his hands on her shoulders.

"Honey, I'm sorry, really sorry, about last night. I got caught in this stalemate and—"

She pushed him away and dashed to the bathroom.

He called after her. "Laura, come on. Please don't be like that."

She draped the hotel robe around her body, struggling to get her hands through the armholes. She gave her hair a swift brushing and scrubbed the smudged make-up off with a damp washcloth. When she came out Chris was sitting on the sofa reading the paper, unfazed.

"How do you expect me to be?" she asked, controlling her anger. "Jumping with glee because you've shown up?"

"No, but at least a little bit happy to see me."

"Last night I was looking forward to—"

"I know, I know. I feel terrible. But, Laura, you have to understand. I was stuck, there was nothing I could do. This massive deal...it was on the line."

"And you couldn't call?"

"No, I couldn't. Believe me, it was brutal—and I had to fight tooth and nail for hours to keep the thing alive. You know how nasty these closings can get." The tension in Chris's voice and the sharp lines running across his forehead, further expressed his aggravation. "I was back by nine though, and we still could've had dinner together...but you were asleep, and pretty much out of it from what I saw."

Laura was too nauseous to argue and still embarrassed by her haggard appearance. Sighing, she said, "I'm going to shower and change. Afterwards, let's plan our day, OK?"

He seemed relieved. "Today will be great, I promise."

****

Chris sat down at the desk to work on his computer while Laura showered. He had called the office earlier to pass on the news about his hard-won victory, but he also needed to forward the letter of intent along with supporting documents. He turned on the laptop and checked his incoming messages; an e-mail from Denise eclipsed all the others. He was both thrilled and surprised to receive a note from her as they'd agreed not to communicate during this trip, at his suggestion. 'He'd be preoccupied,' he'd said. In reality, he wanted to give Laura his full attention and focus on their marriage, try to get things back on track. The friendship with Denise had become increasingly distracting and he needed to concentrate more on Laura, especially since work was also consuming his attention. Last night had turned out to be an outright fiasco—he certainly hadn't expected to find Laura flaked out and practically unconscious in the hotel room when he arrived. He listened for the shower running and then read:

Chris,

I apologize for interrupting you on your holiday but I wanted to let you know that my mother died a few days ago. I'm in the throes of making the funeral arrangements, which is keeping me going for now. I still can't believe she's gone, and how abruptly it happened. A heart attack at the cottage. It's an awful time, and I'm functioning on autopilot, in shock I suppose. I've never known loss like this before; they say time heals but I can't imagine how. The funeral is on Monday afternoon — I'm dreading the day.

He pressed reply and tried to write a response.

Dear Denise,

I'm sorry for your loss. No, too generic. He deleted the line and began again.

I was terribly saddened to read your news. Even worse.

How tragic for you to be struck by such an unexpected event.

Why was it so difficult to send a few words of condolence? He raked his hands through his hair and leaned forward, staring at the screen, as if hoping for a revelation, something appropriate to latch on to. He sat in that position, his mind an empty slate, for what seemed a long time. Then he tried again.

Dearest Denise,

I remember the immense loss I felt when faced with first my mother's passing, and then my father's death not long after. The pain was so intense, the world so dark, that I couldn't imagine how light could filter back into my mind. But it did...it always does. Be patient, let yourself mourn.

He sent the message and then regretted it. Reading it again, he felt that he'd been too sentimental. Besides, the words didn't reflect all he felt, didn't provide the support he hoped to offer. Rubbing his eyes, he considered the possibilities. Should he go to the funeral? But that would mean cutting San Francisco short. Laura would be incensed. Besides, he had brought Laura along to spend time together, to make her happy. Going to Montreal at this time was definitely not an option.

****

Laura came out of the bathroom toweling her hair and found Chris hunched over his laptop, oblivious to her presence. "What should we do today?" she asked, trying to convey enthusiasm. "I guess it's too late to drive to Napa Valley."

Chris jumped, as if he'd been jolted by a loud noise. He slammed the laptop shut. "Pardon, what was that?"

"Napa, is it too late to go?"

"It's hardly worth going now, given the long drive. Maybe we should stay in the city today and head out to the valley tomorrow. We could do some sight-seeing."

What a relief. The mere thought of wine-tasting was nauseating. "Whatever makes sense," she said.

"Why don't I run out to a coffee shop and get you some coffee and a bite while you get dressed. We can walk around for a while, see some things, and then have lunch by the bay."

Laura nodded, forcing a smile. "No food thanks, but a coffee would be great. I'll meet you in the lobby in about half and hour."

When Chris left, Laura put on her camel pants and a light-blue blouse. She blow-dried her hair and pulled it back with a coordinating blue satin clip. Fresh make-up and a splash of 'Lily of the Valley' fragrance gave her a further boost. Now that she was dressed and feeling more human, she would try to put last night's incident behind her and enjoy the trip. Since they had decided to stay a second night, she tidied up the room and unpacked her clothes that lay neatly folded in the suitcase.

Short on time, she decided to send a quick e-mail home instead of calling. She sat down at the desk and opened Chris's laptop, finding an e-mail he had written lingering on the screen. Normally, she wouldn't snoop through Chris's communications, but something compelled her to read this message. Since when was Chris sentimental in an e-mail, and why hadn't he mentioned to her that somebody had died? She scrolled down to the original message and read through, twice. Who was this Denise? Perhaps she was a woman on Chris's staff who needed to take a leave because of her mother's death, but was hesitant to come right out and ask. He should definitely give her whatever time she needed, poor woman. Then Laura read Chris's sympathy note again:

"The pain was so intense, the world so dark, that I couldn't imagine how light could filter back into my mind. But it did...it always does."

On the second read, the words struck Laura as even more odd and uncharacteristic of Chris. Usually he treated his staff with respect and consideration, but kept his own personal life private. And he had never expressed to *her* how deeply his parents' loss had affected him, certainly not with such emotion. She remembered his stoic response after the initial blow, his 'life goes on attitude.' Laura closed the laptop, forgetting to write her message to the girls. Unnerved, she picked up her purse and went to meet Chris in the lobby. A young couple holding hands in the elevator greeted her as she entered. "Good morning," Laura replied, collecting herself.

Laura found Chris in the foyer, browsing through sight-seeing brochures. He handed her a coffee in a cardboard cup and held up a San Francisco street map with kid-like glee. "All set," he said.

Glorious sunshine warmed Laura's face when she stepped away from the shade of the hotel awning. They walked along the city streets, admiring the interesting architecture and looking through shop windows.

"Are you sure you wouldn't like a bite to eat? Chris asked when they poked their heads into an upscale bakery.

"Maybe something small," Laura said.

She ordered a ham and cheese filled croissant to go, and ate while they continued walking. They made their way up the steep, narrow city streets to The Dragon's Gate — the impressive portal to Chinatown. There they meandered through the bustling lanes and watched as tourists, locals, and Chinese people intermingled with apparent ease. Herbalists selling ancient remedies, flower shops, laundromats, produce shops, gift stores, and restaurants, lined the crowded commercial avenues. Chris read from his guidebook that San Francisco's Chinatown was the world's largest settlement of Chinese outside Asia. Laura wanted to buy a souvenir for the girls and had each of their names hand-painted in calligraphy by a Chinese street artist. "Beautiful," Laura said to the wrinkled woman, hunched over a rickety wooden table where she worked. The woman's pride was evident as she flashed a toothless, appreciative grin.

From there they took the cable car down the steep incline to Fisherman's Wharf, where they had a light lunch overlooking the picturesque view of San Francisco Bay. Yes, this was what Laura had imagined and hoped for; thankfully, the mood had turned for both of them and Chris was in particularly good humour. Hand-in-hand, they walked along the pier and looked out at the bay.

"There's Alcatraz," Chris said. He pointed to a severe structure on a small patch of land floating on the water. "Imagine being a prisoner there, viewing this breathtaking city, practically in your reach — but it's only there to tantalize you because you have to go back inside to face your world of cold, concrete walls and isolation. Miserable."

Laura shuddered.

"We could take a tour if you'd like," he said. "My book says they're open today."

"Are you serious?"

Chris laughed and she joined in. "Don't worry. It's the antithesis of romance. Not what I had in mind for you."

"Thank goodness," Laura said, laughing. "You had me worried for a moment."

Chris tightened the grip on her hand. "Feeling better?" he asked.

Laura leaned into him. "Much."

"I know this trip had a rough start, but I'll make it up to you, OK?" he said, swinging her around and pulling her close. "I'm sorry to disappoint you, I hate disappointing you."

"You're forgiven," she said, and leaned in to kiss him.

The rest of the day was blissful. As per Laura's wish, they went for High Tea at an elegant downtown hotel and afterwards Chris took her shopping. She had told him about the soiled dress and he insisted on buying her a new one.

"Do you want to go to the bookstore while I shop?" she asked.

"No, I'm coming with you, I'll be your fashion consultant."

Laura laughed. "But you hate shopping."

"Not today. I want to be with you every single minute."

"Then I'll accept the offer." She definitely felt better now.

Laura tried on at least a half-dozen dresses in several stores and more than anything, she enjoyed the attention Chris gave to their mission, to her. She would have been happy with several of the choices but Chris kept saying, "No, I like that but I don't love it—we have to keep shopping until we find the perfect one." Finally, he insisted on buying an outrageously expensive dress that they found in a small French boutique. Laura loved it even more because he had chosen the sleeveless, black silk cocktail dress himself. White brocade edging around the sleeves and the neckline created a stunning effect that made her feel elegant. To complete the outfit Chris bought her a luxurious white pashmina shawl.

"You look like a model," he said. "The most beautiful woman in San Francisco."

"Thank you," she said. "You're spoiling me with clothes and with words."

"And I could go on," Chris said, with a big grin. Now that you have something to wear for dinner tonight, I'm taking you to the best restaurant in the city."

By the time they returned to the hotel it was time to dress for dinner. Chris had managed to get a reservation at a restaurant that usually required booking months in advance. When they arrived, a young hostess with shimmering long blond hair ushered them to a table by the window and offered them drinks. Wearing her new dress — size ten — Laura almost felt like she belonged in the scene.

"What a spectacular view," Laura said. They could see the Golden Gate Bridge covered by thousands of lights, glistening like stars across the expansive skyline. "It's magical." She couldn't remember when she had last been so happy.

The waiter came to tell them about the specials. "We have delectable fresh caviar from—" Laura and Chris exchanged glances and laughed.

"No, not tonight, thank you," Chris said, studying at the menu. "How about some foie gras with raspberry coulis?" he suggested.

"Fabulous," she said.

"And your best Sauternes to go with it."

When the waiter left, Laura gazed over at Chris. "Thank you darling, this has turned out to be such a treasured day."

He took her hand and kissed it gently. "You deserve it."

By the time they arrived back at the hotel it was almost midnight. Laura carefully removed her silk dress and admired it one more time before hanging it in the antique armoire. She had felt very sophisticated that evening, and sexy. And Chris had been particularly attentive, like old times. He came out of the bathroom in his robe, brushing his teeth. Laura watched him check his e-mails on the laptop and wondered if he'd say anything about the one she'd read earlier.

But he didn't.

"By the way," she said. "I noticed a message on the screen this morning, something about someone's mother dying?"

He gestured for her to wait a moment and went to the bathroom to rinse his mouth. He came out in his pajama bottoms and sat on the bed.

"This woman I know from Montreal, actually a friend from my youth, her mother passed away."

"I hope you don't mind, but you left it on the screen and I—"

"No, that's OK. I'm feeling conflicted though. You see, her mother was a close friend of my mother's, her best friend in fact, and I think I should go to the funeral."

"Someone I've met?" Laura asked.

"No. She was at my mother's funeral but I don't think you'd remember her from way back then."

"When is the service?"

"Monday."

"This Monday?"

"Yes, and I'd have to leave first thing in the morning."

"But Chris, we were going to drive down the coast on Monday. We can't leave California without doing that." Her heart sank.

"We could do the coastal drive tomorrow, and skip Napa Valley."

"But that's important too. We can't miss the wine-tasting, the thing you were looking forward to the most."

"But I feel awful for the family and particularly my friend. You can tell how upset she is from her message."

"Who is she, anyway? An old girlfriend?"

"It's nothing like that. We were friends when we were kids, our families were close. I, uh, haven't seen her for years."

Laura sank into the chair. "What can I say? If we have to go, we have to go."

"No, you should stay here, enjoy your last day. There's no point dragging you along when you don't know any of the people, and besides, most of them speak French. You could take a bus tour down to Carmel right from the hotel. I'd hate for you to miss out. You've come all the way here to—"

"To be with you." She couldn't stop the tears from spilling out.

Chris put his arm around her. "I feel awful, I hate to leave you."

Then you shouldn't, she felt like saying. This is our holiday, our special time together. "I'll be fine."

"No, forget about it, I won't go. I'll send some flowers, I'll visit the family another time." He hugged her tightly.

"You have to go," she said, attempting to compose herself. "Funerals are important. I know if one of my parents died, I'd appreciate all the support I could get. If these people are important to you, then it's not fair for me to prevent you from going."

Chris stroked her hair. "Thank you for understanding." He held her face gently, between his large palms, and touched her forehead with his. "You are such a good person, Laura. I'm so lucky to have you."

"It's all right," she said. "I'll be fine."

****

They woke to the sound of rain, drumming heavily on something metal on the building. Chris got out of bed and looked outside.

"Miserable day," he said.

Laura rolled over and put the pillow over her head.

"We might as well make the best of it. Hopefully it'll clear up."

What was he thinking, taking off on his wife during their holiday? When Laura had mentioned Denise's e-mail, the lies had poured out of his mouth as if he had been plotting all day. Yet he hadn't decided anything until that very moment—until she had reminded him of Denise's situation. Should he stay with Laura in San Francisco and forget about his crazy idea? Leaving her behind in such miserable weather felt cruel. But then, if the weather improved tomorrow, she'd have one more decent day. He checked the forecast on the internet and found that sunshine was expected for Monday.

Laura lifted the pillow from her head. "Damn. We should've gone wine-tasting yesterday like we'd planned, the weather was perfect then."

Chris frowned. Those plans were spoiled because of him, because of that damn meeting. "We'll still have fun, rain or no rain. At least we're spending time together. The drive may not be as scenic as we'd hoped but the wine will taste the same."

"I suppose," she said.

"So, let's get going. We can grab a bite downstairs and then be on our way. No point hanging around the hotel."

Driving on the highway was worse than Chris had expected, and the convertible sports car he'd rented for the day was difficult to handle in the heavy winds. Torrential downpours kept teasing them with the promise of letting up and the traffic slowed to a crawl as if they were in the height of rush-hour. Was the whole world going wine-tasting? Chris concentrated on the roads while Laura rested and after driving for four hours instead of the expected two, they reached the first winery. They walked up the long stone stairway to the entrance of the majestic building, a replica of a French chateau. The foyer was crammed with people, umbrellas dripped everywhere, and the leader of a bus tour was yelling over the voices of the crowd, trying to give instructions.

"Who would have thought it would be this packed?" Chris said. "Let's get out of here and move on to somewhere less busy."

They clambered down the slippery stone stairway, descending the precipitous steps with caution. The rain was teeming again and they trudged across the expansive parking lot, packed with cars, without an umbrella because they had forgotten it at the hotel. By the time they got back to their car they were drenched.

The next winery was also busy but they didn't have to wait too long for service. Chris placed an order for a flight of Pinot Noirs, which comprised six glasses of each type. "Nothing special," he said, after tasting the first three and spitting into the spittoon. He pushed the other glasses away.

"I like it," Laura said, "especially this one." She picked up the fourth glass, urging Chris to try some. He shook his head. "No thanks." She drank the entire series, not once using the spittoon.

Continuing on their trek, they visited a couple of smaller wineries and sampled a few more wine selections that Chris considered mediocre at best. Laura was less discerning and enjoyed everything she tried.

"You don't need to drink the entire sample, Laura. The idea is to concentrate on the essence of the wines and to take notes about your observations."

"But I'm not going to waste the rest if I like what I'm trying." She gulped down what remained in her glass.

They couldn't find a decent restaurant along their route to stop for lunch, and settled on a prepackaged sandwich offered at one of the wineries. The lettuce was wilted and the ham had that slimy texture found on old, processed meats. But they were hungry and ate them anyway. Fewer cars wound their way along the country roads, providing some relief from the earlier congestion. By late afternoon, thunder and lightning raged in the sky and the beautiful

Napa Valley landscape depicted in photographs was undetectable. Chris focused on the roads while Laura leaned back in her seat, closing her eyes. At about 5:00, they found a winery that offered dinner and decided to make it their last stop.

"Enjoying this, Laura?" Chris asked, noticing that Laura was still drinking with gusto.

"It's fun," she said. "Here, try this one." She almost spilled the contents while passing the glass to him. "Sorry," she said, giggling. "I'm getting a little bit tipsy, I think."

"Take it easy, Laura."

"Don't worry, I'm in complete control. But I have to go for a wee. I'll be right back." Chris watched with concern as she stumbled in the direction of the ladies room. He checked his watch and scanned the room for the waiter. Feeling tightness in his neck, he rubbed it, wincing when he touched a tender nerve. The enthusiasm he'd felt at the outset of the day had been dashed by the stress of the treacherous driving and the gloomy skies, and he dreaded the drive back to the city.

As Chris had predicted, Laura fell asleep instantly when they were en route and although the rain had let up, a heavy fog hindered his vision. He drove with caution, trying to make out the valley's contours through the rain-splattered windshield. What a shame to be in the middle of some of America's most beautiful countryside and not be able to see it. They would have to come back again for a longer trip, perhaps in a year or two, when they were both in a better frame of mind.

Laura began to snore and Chris glanced at her as she lay slumped back on the reclined seat, her hair frizzy from the rain. He wanted to hold her hand, tell her he was sorry about the day, about everything. The purpose of their trip had been undermined by that e-mail from Denise, but what could he do? Was he making a momentous mistake by leaving early and going to the funeral? Perhaps a substantial flower arrangement with his condolences would have been sufficient. Lying to Laura so blatantly, so unabashedly, had been despicable. What the hell was he doing?

At the hotel, Chris had to practically carry Laura to the room, like a sleepy child. People watched as he guided her one step at a time to the elevator. In the room, he led her to the bed, settled her in, and removed her shoes and slacks. She barely budged as he covered her with the blanket, watching her contemplatively. No, this was definitely not one of their better holidays. If he had been paying more attention at the wineries, he would have urged Laura use the spittoon for tasting rather than consume the entire glass each time. But he wasn't accustomed to monitoring Laura when she drank; she usually had a good head about such things.

He checked his e-mails and found the confirmation for his flight to Montreal—AC612, departing at 6:15 a.m. Fortunately, he'd been able to find Denise's mother's obituary, with the funeral details, on the internet. Considering the three-hour time change, he would arrive in Montreal with little time to spare.

After changing for bed, Chris lay beside Laura, listening to her heavy breathing. Fraught with guilt, he kept asking himself if he was making a terrible mistake. If he slept at all, it couldn't have been for more than a few hours. At 4:30 a.m. the phone rang and Chris picked it up, his heart racing. The recorded voice on the line instantly reminded him of his plans. He crawled out of bed, trying not to waken Laura. Her clothes were strewn on the floor beside the bed, a sign that she had been up in the night, but he hadn't heard a thing, having slept like a beached whale for the short time he did sleep. Daytime seemed distant given the heavy stillness in the dark room, and when he peered outside, there was no sound or movement in the street below, not even the quiet rumble of an early morning cab.

He wrote Laura a note:

Morning Sweetheart,

I don't want to wake you at this ungodly hour, especially since you are in a deep sleep. I've reserved your ticket for the bus tour at the front desk. It leaves at 10:00. And I've asked them to give you a wake-up call at 9:00. Please splurge on yourself in Carmel — buy something extravagant and, of course, presents for the girls. I feel terrible rushing off like this, but I'll see you back home very soon. Love you, Chris

He could still change his mind about the funeral, forget the whole thing and get back into bed with Laura. But remembering Denise's words, "I've never known loss like this before...I'm dreading the day," he felt he had no choice. Lying to Laura was unconscionable, but how could he explain things? No, sometimes white lies were necessary. He gave her a soft kiss and lingered a moment, overcome with guilt-ridden affection, before rushing out the door.

Chapter Twenty-three

Denise's mother's funeral was to take place a week after she'd died, allowing family and friends to make their way to Montreal from all over the continent. Denise made the arrangements quickly and efficiently, determined to create an event that her mother would have appreciated had she attended herself. Her initial shock was overshadowed by all the important details that needed attending to. She ploughed forward as if coordinating a grand function for somebody else: meeting with the funeral director, the florist, the organist, the caterer, and making scores of phone calls to family and friends.

Denise's three siblings arrived one at a time from various parts of the country, bringing along their strong opinions in spite of their dampened spirits. Although Francois had offered to help out, she declined his offer, asking him simply to be there for the children. Relief spilled from his face when she told him she was managing fine — he didn't seem to notice the strain in her voice or her glassy eyes. "I know you need to keep the momentum going on the heritage project," she'd said to him. "Life can't stop because my mother is gone." When Francois didn't protest, Denise wasn't sure whether she should be bothered by his easy submission or not.

The children were exceptionally well-behaved, complying without argument and keeping a low profile amidst the chaos. Clara assisted beyond the call of duty, providing Denise with the reassurance that all would go smoothly with the funeral and the reception afterwards. Requested by her siblings to deliver the eulogy, Denise had agreed, feeling compelled to publically sing her mother's virtues. In life, her mother had always been modest, and had accepted praise with great humility. Today, Denise would shout to the world how loved and revered her mother had been. In less than an hour she had written her first draft, cathartically recounting many cherished memories and listing her mother's numerous accomplishments. Her siblings had insisted that she be the one to speak because of her public-speaking experience. "You're the only one of us who's got the gift for this sort of thing," they'd said. "Besides, you were closest to Mother in recent years."

At the funeral, the church overflowed with mourners. Many of the faces were unfamiliar to Denise, people belonging to a part of her mother's life to which she herself was not connected. How strange to be intertwined with someone's life, yet detached all the same. The sun spilled into the cathedral through the open doors and created a laser-like dance against the stained glass windows. How happy her mother would have been today, on such a magnificent spring afternoon, and how she would have loved the clusters of tulips, lilacs, and peonies gracing the alter. Francois arrived with the children and linking her arm with his, they walked down the aisle together, taking their places in the front pew.

Denise only noticed the organ music after it had stopped. The priest spoke, his words garbled. What was he saying? Was he speaking another language? His arms waved upward, then downward, and then his body appeared to heave. The sounds coming from his mouth seemed to be controlled by a volume dial, the decibel constantly shifting. She couldn't understand what he was saying. Francois held her hand, which lay limply in his. When "Amazing Grace," her mother's favourite hymn, boomed through the sanctuary, Denise began to shiver. She found herself standing, trying to sing, but the words in the hymn book that Francois held open for her made no sense. Her teeth were chattering and she wrapped her arms around herself to stop her body from shaking. When the song ended she heard someone whisper in her ear, "You're next." Then a cough. "Denise, the eulogy." But she couldn't move; her legs were disabled by invisible weights. Dropping into her seat, she felt like a machine shutting down. Heads turned her way and she didn't even try to stand up, knowing how futile the attempt would be. Someone shuffled past her, stepping on her foot. Then a voice bellowed, not the priest's, but her brother's, from the altar. He was saying something about their mother: kindness...dignity...strength...conviction. The words floated around in her mind and then her mother's image appeared amidst the flowers, like a ghost's soft illusion. Denise wept, uncontrollably, inconsolably. Why had her mother been taken from her? It was too soon. Much, much, too soon.

The funeral was over. She walked down the aisle, Francois holding her one hand and Thomas holding the other. Martin and Luc followed at their heels. The intense brightness bothered her eyes and she wondered why lights were on in the middle of the day. But there were no lights, only sunshine. People looked at Denise with sympathy and she nodded back with perfunctory appreciation. All was still; even her pounding heart had restored its gentle rhythm. As she walked toward the back of the church, she caught sight of a man in the last pew, a familiar face, not recognizable at first, in the row of dark-suited mourners. He stood up and watched her approach, wearing a sombre expression. When she got closer, her gasp was a whisper, and her heart's drumming an inaudible roar. She hadn't been expecting Chris.

****

Only an hour earlier, Denise's mother's house had been swarming with people, food passed around and drinks served. The spirited commotion had transformed to solemn stillness, and all traces of a reception had departed with the caterers. Restored to its pristine state, the kitchen was exactly as her mother would have left it before going to bed. Denise and her siblings sat around the kitchen table exhausted, but clinging to each other, the remnants of a family. A tray of leftover tea sandwiches lay in the middle of the table covered with plastic wrap.

"Now what?" asked Denise's sister, Camille.

"Legal issues, sorting through Mom's things, getting the house on the market," Tom said. His tone was flat, pragmatic.

"I can't stay," Jim said. "I've got a conference in Miami on Friday that's been booked for a year. My flight's tomorrow evening."

"What do you mean, 'put the house on the market?' She's gone less than a week and you want to sell the house?" Denise said.

211

"I know it's hard for you, Denise, living closest to Mom and all, but it's hard for everyone." Tom went to the sink and filled a glass with water. "And we don't have much choice. This is the best time to sell, by next month the market will be tapering off."

"He's right," Jim said. "If we all work together we can get a lot done."

Tom sat back down and gave his glass of water to Denise. "We've got a meeting with the lawyer first thing in the morning and then we can come back here to sort through Mom's things."

Denise looked at Camille for support. But she only nodded. "They're right, what choice do we have? We need to do this together and it would be impossible to arrange another time that would work for all of us."

Had a bulldozer come charging through this house? Denise could not believe her ears. She had barely begun grieving and already they wanted to annihilate her mother's material presence. "But we all grew up here. Our souls are in this house. Doesn't that mean anything to you?"

"You're emotional and tired right now," Tom said. "Understandably so. But we also have to be practical. There isn't much time and we have a lot to do."

Denise shot him a scornful look. Where was his humanity? She was being bullied and had nowhere to go. Defeated, she said no more. Tears rolled down her face.

Tom came over to her and put his arm around her shoulder. "If it's too difficult for you to go through Mom's stuff, we'll do it without you. You don't even have to come here again."

He was missing the point. She covered her face with her hands. Tom glanced at the others and went back to his seat. He picked out a sandwich and passed the tray, but Denise ignored the offer and took a sip of water from the glass Tom had placed before her. They continued speaking, making arrangements for the next day, while Chris's image surfaced in her mind. His reassuring expression was the only solace she had gleaned during her distressing day.

Leaving the others to their discussion, Denise went upstairs to her old room. She and her mother had redecorated the bedroom when she'd returned from France after the break-up, the only time her mother had taken an interest in making changes in the house.

She had wanted Denise to feel comfortable, to have a space she could call her own, and together they had pulled down the wallpaper and painted the walls a creamy yellow. How they had fumbled in their efforts to do a perfect job. Denise had been at the peak of her misery then, but her mother had managed to make her laugh.

Camille came into the room and sat on the bed. "Pretty room — although I miss the orange shag rug and the psychedelic wallpaper."

"Lots of memories." Denise removed an old black and white photograph from the wall — a family portrait taken when she was about ten years old. "Look at our mother here, such a pillar of strength the way she stands upright, exuding pride in her brood. The quintessential matriarch."

"A woman who always had her act together," Camille said.

Denise slumped down on the bed beside her sister and leaned her head on Camille's shoulder. "Life will never be the same again," she said, fighting back tears. When she was an adolescent, her older sister was the only one who could provide the wisdom and advice she sought. Camille had known about teenage angst having survived the perils herself.

"You'll be all right, Denise. You've got Francois, and the kids, and a great job. We'll all get through this."

"I suppose." Denise kicked off her black patent shoes and rubbed her foot.

"I'm the one with the big hole in my life. The kids are grown, we're practically empty nesters, and with Mother gone — "

"You can reinvent your marriage, think about retirement together."

Camille grimaced. "I can imagine the scene, Donald watching my every move, listening to my phone calls, telling me how to grocery shop for heaven's sake."

Denise walked over to the bookcase and mindlessly sifted through the shelves. "Why not go back to work? Maybe you should consider a new career."

Camille stood up from the bed and tried to smooth out her now creased dress. "What would I do after all these years at home?"

"Whatever you want. Or better yet, go have yourself a midlife-crisis. Do some traveling, like what's-her-name...Shirley Valentine, or open a bake shop and sell your famous cupcakes, or try parachuting."

"Great advice. Thanks."

Denise went to the window and looked out at the dimly lit street. She could almost hear the clanging of the bell her mother used to ring to round them up at bedtime. One summer, after weeks of frustration trying to locate her children, who had the habit of playing in all directions, she had come upon the idea. When it was time to come in, she would stand at the door and ring that bell with vigour, until her entire brood was safely home. And if you didn't arrive within five minutes the consequences could be severe—no television for a week, or no Sunday dessert, the only time pastries or cakes were served in their house.

"You're lucky to have Francois. Husbands like him are rare," Camille said.

Then why was Chris the man she wanted right now? Why were his arms the place she wanted to bury herself in? "Yes, I'm very fortunate," she said. "He's great."

Francois was putting the younger boys to bed when Denise arrived home. She watched from the doorway, touched by the scene. "I was proud of you guys today," he said to his sons. "Your grandmother would have been impressed by your grown-up behaviour—especially the way you looked people in the eye when you shook their hands. I know it's not easy when you don't know them." He laughed. "It's even hard for me sometimes to talk to people I don't know."

Denise had forgotten how shy Francois could be. Her own busy, people-oriented life was such a part of her existence that she sometimes lost sight of how difficult it could be around strangers. And there was no counting all the public events she had dragged him to over the years.

"Hi," she whispered," and walked into the room.

"Hey," Francois said. "How are you holding up?" He put his arms around her.

214

"I'm good…fine. I'm glad I'm home in time to say good-night to the children."

"I'll leave you to it. If you need me, I'll be at my drawing table." He squeezed her tightly, then left.

Denise kissed Luc and Martin good-night, trying to conceal her distress. Is that what her mother had done? Concealed her anguish during those difficult years after losing her husband? Denise worried about how the children were doing, dealing with the loss; they were taking their grandmother's death like young soldiers, almost in stride. But she would talk to them about their pain another time, when she had more reassurance to impart. She sat down on Martin's bed and began telling the boys their favourite bedtime story, which comforted Denise more than anybody.

Thomas poked his head in the door. "Can I come in?"

"You can come in my bed," Luc said, from across the room. He lifted his covers for his older brother to lie beside him. The boys listened in silence until the story was over and then Denise lay down with Martin until they all fell asleep.

A few hours later she woke with an excruciating headache and went to the kitchen to get some aspirin. Realizing that she hadn't eaten all day, she forced herself to eat some crackers and cheese. Too agitated to go back to bed, she went to the study to check her e-mails. Amongst the deluge of messages she found the one she'd been hoping for.

Dear Denise,
I can't find the words to soothe your grief. You are in my thoughts, my prayers, my heart. Chris

Reading his words was like taking a drug. They calmed her nerves and blunted the edge of her sadness. They meant more to her than any of the well-intentioned condolences she had received that day. People had given her warm hugs and whispered gentle phrases: "I'm sorry…I understand your pain…I wish you didn't have to suffer so…she was a very special person…" But after a while the well-meaning words sound like a familiar refrain. The most poignant moment for her was the flash of empathy on Chris's face at the church. And he had come all the way from San Francisco for that purpose, leaving his holiday and his wife behind. Denise pressed reply.

Dear Chris,

Thank you for your support during this harrowing time. I hope the emptiness I feel will soon pass, but I can't see that far ahead. I couldn't even give the eulogy today, my one last gift to Mother. Your words help a lot, your sentiments even more. Thank you coming. Seeing you there made all the difference. XO Denise

The next day, after meeting with the lawyer, Denise and her siblings met at their mother's house as planned. No one had slept much and they all lumbered ahead with heavy hearts.

"I've arranged for the estate sale to take place next weekend," Tom said. "All we have to do today is go through the house and decide what we want to keep." He handed out corrugated boxes that he had picked up at the local liquor store. "Put your name on the box," he passed out black markers, "and dump in whatever you want to take."

Denise cringed, but succumbed to Tom's instructions. Their mother had already distributed the family heirlooms and valuable items over the years; thankfully they wouldn't have to deal with such things at this time. She gazed into the empty box, wishing she could somehow fill her soul instead. Where was her mother's spirit? Why was it not present in the house providing comfort, helping her get through her unspeakable anguish?

"This shouldn't take too long," Jim said to Denise. "Why don't you and Camille check upstairs and Tom and I will go through her files. We'll also check the basement to see if there's anything important being stored, but I think she did away with most of those boxes a long time ago."

Denise remembered her mother's insistence that they remove all their personal belongings from the basement. She had said, "Now that you have your own homes you can use your own basements for storage. This house is not going to be 'the Gagnon family warehouse.'" The children were in their thirties then, but the request had been met with resistance nonetheless. Jim had teased, "C'mon, Mom, are you trying to get rid of all traces of us?" In response she'd

216

said, "I've had kids' clutter in my house for over thirty years, don't you think at my stage in life I deserve to live clutter-free?" How could anyone take issue with her argument? And then she began giving away most of her treasured pieces; she didn't even keep her good set of china. Was she already thinking of this day?

"Let's have a look in Mother's room," Camille said. "There must be some things worth salvaging."

Denise took a deep breath. Yes, it had to be done, but she couldn't think of anything more depressing. At least Camille was there too. "OK, let's get it over with."

They started with the closet, which housed their mother's sparse summer wardrobe. Denise scanned the contents. As per usual, every piece of clothing was meticulously organized: pants and skirts hung neatly on rods, one row on top of the other; summer dresses and jackets, cleaned and pressed, looked like garments for sale in a clothing boutique. Her shoes were neatly placed in two rows, six pairs in total.

"I suppose we should donate her clothes to Goodwill," Denise said.

"The estate woman said she'd take care of that," Camille said. "Whatever's left behind after the sale will go to charity."

Denise shut the closet door. Her mother's scent lingered on the clothing, intensifying her sadness. "I can't do this." She sat on the bed and swept her hand over the soft quilted cotton. "Mother has had this same bedspread since I can remember, and it's still quite nice." Tiny white daisies, faded but discernible, were sprinkled against a pale green background.

"It's dated," Camille said. "Remember that duvet with the beautiful Egyptian cotton cover I bought her several years ago? She made me return it. 'I don't need it,' she told me. 'Mine is still fine and the right weight.' I couldn't talk Mother into getting anything new."

"She had old-fashioned taste but modern views. Remember that guy you were dating when you were eighteen?"

"Who, Wes Gibbons?"

"I think so. Wasn't he the guy you lost your virginity to?"

Camille blushed. "What about him?"

"I remember hearing Mother give you the 'sex talk.' Contraception, the meaning of it all. But she didn't try to dissuade you from doing it."

"How did you know about that?"

"I was listening at the door. Sorry, but I listened to a lot of your conversations back then. You had four years of juicy experience ahead of me."

Camille gave her a teasing scowl and then laughed. "Oh yes, I remember that conversation very clearly. I couldn't believe how calm Mother was, and she didn't even like Wes."

Denise went to her mother's dresser and rummaged through the drawers. Panty hose, undergarments, scarves, and costume jewelry lay in neatly divided rows. "Here's the scarf I brought Mother from Paris." She unfolded the rich silk fabric, covered with soft swirling brush strokes in deep blue and aquamarine hues, and held it in front of her.

"Now *that* is a beautiful scarf, it reminds me of the Caribbean. And it was stunning on Mother against her blue eyes and fair skin," Camille said. "Do you think she would have liked it as much if she had known what 'Hermès' was? I think she would have *died* if she had known how much it cost you. Excuse the pun." She started to laugh. Then Denise joined in. Suddenly they were laughing so hard they could hardly breathe.

"My gosh we're pathetic," Denise said, sobering herself. She put the scarf in a box. "I'm taking this."

Camille opened their mother's bedside table drawer. "Interesting. Mother was reading *Wuthering Heights*." She flipped through the pages and a folded paper fell to the floor. Denise picked it up and unfolded it.

"A letter." She read to herself. "From a man."

"Let's hear it," Camille said.

Denise sat on the bed again and continued reading in silence.

"Who's it from? What's he saying?"

Denise finished reading and then spoke. "You won't believe this."

She read:

Dear Marie:

I won't pretend to be altogether fine with your response. I suppose I under-stand but it's obviously not what I was hoping to hear. I think we could have built a fine life together, you and me, with or without your children. But I respect your decision and ultimately I must accept that it's probably for the best. As much as I would have tried, I'm not sure I could have adapted to being number five on your list of priorities. I mourn for what might have been, and even though I may not be the love of your life, you are, and always will be, mine.

Your ever devoted, Charles

The sisters looked at each other, perplexed. "Did you know any-thing about this?" Denise asked.

"No, not a thing."

"There's no date here, I wonder when this happened. And who the heck is Charles?"

"I don't remember Mother dating a man called Charles. In fact, I don't remember her dating anyone."

"The paper is so worn," Denise said. "Like she's opened it and folded it hundreds of times." She held it up at the corners and observed the tattered seams.

"Do you think she could have been in love with him?" Camille asked.

"It's hard to know. Mother was always demonstrative with us, but she didn't let us into her own private world very much, did she?"

"And I never saw her cry. Not once."

"Me neither," Denise said. She dropped the letter into her box. "Do you mind if I take this?"

Camille handed her the book. "You can have this too."

After they finished sorting through their mother's room, Camille went downstairs and Denise went to her old bedroom. Books and photo albums lined the shelves, mostly from her childhood and youth. She packed them into her box, stopping intermittently to leaf through some pages. When she came across a photo of her mother, sitting on a beach towel during one of their summer holidays, wear-ing her large brimmed hat, Denise's eyes began to water. She had taken that picture with the new camera she had received for her eleventh birthday. When she opened the gift her mother had told her: "This camera is for you to chronicle your life, to create a visual history of who you are and where you come from. When you're all grown up you can revisit the things and the people who have influenced you, helped you find your true self." Denise closed the album and placed it with the others in the box.

The closet contained mostly her mother's out-of-season clothing—wool slacks and sweaters, a winter coat inside a dry cleaning bag, boots, a hat, and on the top shelf, a shoe bag and two purses protected by see-through plastic. How like her mother to store her winter wear with such care, all ready to go at the first hint of frost next fall. Denise noticed the old black suede purse, the one she'd used in Paris, hanging on a hook, on the back of the closet door. She removed the purse and was about to put it into the box, when she stopped to check inside. Once, when she was a student, she had surprised herself by discovering 500 French francs in a handbag she hadn't used for a long time. What a coup that had been. Denise opened the purse, and a small tear in the bottom seam caught her attention. Poking her fingers through the opening, she felt something like a receipt. She pinched the item between her fingers and pulled out a small piece of paper that looked like a scribbled note. In smudged pencil, barely legible, was Chris's name and phone number, jotted down twenty-five years ago.

Chapter Twenty-four

Camille cleared the table in Denise's kitchen and rinsed the plates. "You've got to eat some breakfast, you've hardly had a bite these past few days and you're wasting away."

Denise pushed her plate to the side. "I *have* been eating, but honestly, Camille, the more you pressure me the less hungry I am."

"Perhaps you should see a doctor," Camille said. "Get some pills, something to calm your nerves. You can't go on like this." She sprayed the counter with disinfectant and wiped.

"You don't have to clean, Camille. Clara will do that when she comes."

She continued to wipe. "What about work, have you been in touch with the station?"

Denise looked out the window with a blank expression. She'd lost count of how many days she'd been off work since her mother's death almost two weeks ago.

"The studio, Denise, do they know your situation?"

Denise brought her plate to the counter. "What situation?"

"That you're not feeling great. I mean, aren't you worried about your show?"

"No, everything's covered. Nicole's doing a great job organizing guest hosts and we've got enough shows lined up for the time being. And Gary's on top of things—he told me to take as much time as I needed."

"Good. I'm glad they're supportive." Camille started stacking the dishwasher. "I've told Donald that I'll be staying here a few extra days."

"You don't have to stay on for me, I don't need a sitter." Feeling light-headed, she sat back down at the table.

"Don't you think it would be nice to spend some time together? I've come all this way...how often do we get this opportunity?"

Denise did not have the energy to battle her sister's good intentions. "All right then," she said, "whatever suits you." She sat motionless except for her fingers, which were tearing a paper napkin into tiny shreds.

"And with Francois working all the time, wouldn't you like the company? I know I would. Besides, with Mother gone, we girls have to stick together, n'est-ce pas?"

"I suppose that's true." The cat rubbed against her legs and she bent down to pet her.

Camille sighed. "I think you need some extra TLC, my dear, and I've got some to spare."

"You're sweet." Denise picked Scruffy up and walked towards the door. "I'm tired, I need to lie down."

In her room, she removed a bottle of sleeping pills from the bedside table and swallowed one with a sip of stagnant water, leftover from the night before. She pulled down the blinds all the way to prevent the light from seeping through. Lying down felt good; if only she could block the intrusive thoughts and images hovering in her brain. Chris's face, with his expression of love and concern at the funeral, was ensconced in her consciousness like an unforgettable song. Wrestling with her thoughts, Denise fell asleep.

The room was still dark when she awoke several hours later. Was it the middle of the night? She felt the other side of the bed for Francois, but his place was empty. Sitting up, she checked the time — 3:25. Where could he be? Muffled voices rose from downstairs. What was going on? When she opened the bedroom door, a stream of light hit her like an electrical shock, and she realized it was daytime. As she slowly descended the stairs, she heard the sounds, more clearly now, of a woman and man in conversation. Halfway down she stopped, and crouched to listen through the banister.

"She's barely eating and all she wants to do is sleep." Camille said.

"Your mother's death has thrown her into a state of shock, knocked the wind right out of her," Francois said. "And she's not ready to face reality."

"But she can't go on like this."

"I'll call the doctor; maybe he can prescribe something to help her."

Denise sat on the step and wrapped her arms around her waist. Why was Francois home in the middle of the day? She didn't want more drugs, just sleep. All she needed was to catch up on her sleep.

"I'm going to stay until she comes out of this," Camille said. "If that's all right with you."

"Yes, good idea. I'd appreciate it. This project I'm working on is taking every moment I can spare, and it'd be a huge help if you stuck around for a while."

Denise went back upstairs. They were treating her like a child and their fussing was ridiculous. She went back to bed, covering her head with the blanket and wishing she could hibernate until life righted itself. Soon, Francois entered the room carrying a tray with a teapot and some toast, which he placed on the bed.

Leaning forward, he pulled the blanket from her face and kissed her forehead. "How are you doing?" he whispered.

She considered feigning sleep, but was afraid that he'd catch on. "I'm okay," she mumbled. "Weary."

"I've called Dr. Stevens to come check on you."

She didn't respond.

"You've got to eat, my love." He helped prop her up and handed her the toast. She looked at it with disgust. "Here's some tea, have a sip." She drank a little. "I have to go back to the site, but I'll be home in a few hours. Try to eat something, please."

When Francois left, Denise went back to sleep and had a dream. She was on her way to the studio, wearing her new outfit. The show was an important one—an interview of a lifetime for a midday talk-show. Her guest was to be Jackie Kennedy and she was going to ask her all about life in the White House. But when Denise arrived at the studio, she couldn't find her dressing room. The hallway that used to lead to her room went in the opposite direction and the taupe walls had been painted a startling maraschino red. Eventually, she found her room but when she went inside, she didn't recognize it.

The floor was marble and the walls were covered with mirrors. The furniture was fuchsia, like her new blouse. Strange people were scurrying around with clipboards, hairdryers, and make-up brushes, like on a movie set, and they all stopped to stare when she approached the woman sitting at her dressing table. A face she'd never seen before. The woman turned toward Denise, a smirk stretched across her face.

"I'm here," Denise proclaimed, but they ignored her and resumed their tasks. Then someone said, "Did you know that Louise is about to interview Jackie Kennedy?" "No she's not, I am!" she tried to shout. But her cry came out as a whisper and everyone ignored her.

Denise woke to the gentle touch of Dr. Stevens taking her pulse.

"I'm sorry to wake you," he said. "How are you feeling?"

"Tired." Pulling herself up, she straightened her nightgown. The room remained dark and eerily quiet.

"It's not unusual to become depressed after the loss of a loved one. The stress can be overwhelming," he said, and placed his stethoscope against her chest.

Strange, she thought, how crushed she was by her mother's death, but at the same time, her mind had been elsewhere during the past few days.

"I'm going to prescribe some pills that should help relieve your stress, but you've got to eat to get your energy back."

Denise nodded.

"Is there anything you'd like to talk about?" the doctor asked.

Denise shook her head. But in her mind she asked, 'If I'm lying here grieving for my mother then why am I consumed with thoughts of Chris?'

The doctor patted her hand. "You'll be fine, Denise. Grieving takes time. These traumas can be difficult for the body and the soul." He smiled warmly. "I'll give the prescription to your sister. You hang in there."

"Thank you, Doctor."

He nodded. "You take care."

Denise heard stifled sounds outside her door. A few seconds later, Camille entered the room, holding the prescription. "I'll get this filled for you." She sat on the end of the bed and patted

Denise's leg. Time passing will take the edge of your misery, Dee. Feeling it now is good, then later we can heal."

Denise forced a smile and nodded. Camille had good intentions but she had no idea what Denise was going through. How could she?

"I'm cooking your favourite dinner and I hope you'll come down to eat with the family."

The thought of dinner repelled her.

"And the boys will be home soon. They'll want to see you."

Denise couldn't have them see her in such a morose and lethargic state; she'd have to make an effort to pull herself together. "All right, I'll come down for dinner. I guess I should shower and get some clothes on."

"Wonderful," Camille said. "We'll eat at 6:30." She opened the blinds and left the room.

After washing her hair and applying lipstick, Denise went downstairs, her summer dress much more cheerful than she could possibly be herself. But the house was empty; even the cat was nowhere to be seen. She went to the study and turned on the computer. Several days had passed since she had last checked her messages and she hoped to find a message from Chris. But who had been the last to write? She couldn't remember. When she opened the e-mail file, dozens of unopened messages lay in waiting. Sifting through, she found three messages from Chris. Her heart raced and her teeth chattered as if she was stuck in the cold with no coat. She closed her study door before reading them.

Dear D, How are you? I'm wondering how you're managing. Let me know, Chris

Then:
Haven't heard from you. Is everything all right? Call me when you have a moment. Chris

And the last:
Denise, still waiting for a reply. Is something wrong? Chris

Denise picked up the phone and dialed Chris's cell number. She hung up after the first ring. What if she came across as frantic as she felt? After contemplating a moment, she dialed again.

"Chris Lambert here."

"Hi, it's me." Denise tried to steady her voice but she could feel the strain passing through the phone line.

"Thank goodness. I've been worried about you. Are you OK?"

"I've had a few rough days but I'm surviving."

"I want to see you. Can I come up? When would be convenient? You name the time."

"No, Chris. It's not a good idea. I'm off work and my sister's here." It was difficult to speak without falling all over her words. "Maybe after Camille leaves."

"How do we do this?" he asked. "I don't want to cause any disruption. But Denise...I've got to see you...soon."

A heavy lull descended on the conversation.

Emboldened by Chris's earnest sounding plea, she said, "I'll come to *you* this time. Maybe next week. I'll find a reason."

"All right, when?"

"Thursday?" She'd have almost a week to pull herself together.

"Fine. I'll book the time off work. Let me know your flight schedule. I'll pick you up at the airport and we'll spend the day together."

"All right."

After their conversation, Denise ran to the bathroom and threw up.

Denise was in the kitchen helping with dinner and talking to Camille when the boys arrived home. They greeted her affectionately, as if she'd been away for a while, and she hugged them tightly, one at a time. Before she knew it, they'd run off in different directions without sharing a word about their day. The phone rang, making her jump.

"I'll get it," Camille said, as she puttered in the kitchen. She picked up the receiver and held it under the crook of her chin while she dried a pot with a dishtowel.

Denise zoned in and out, half listening to the conversation. She'd have to pull herself together fast if she was going to go to

Cleveland in a week's time, and figure out a way to dispel everyone's concerns about her — starting with forcing herself to eat.

"Don't worry, Francois, I'm sure she'll understand. Do you want
to speak to her? OK then, I'll pass the message on." Camille turned
to Denise. "He can't come for dinner. A late night with the architect,
he says. But he's hoping you'll eat."

"Yes, I know. I will, I promise," Denise said. "What are you
making?"

"Tourtière and a green salad. Mother's recipe."

"From scratch?"

"Bien sûr! The crust and all. My objective is to put some meat on
your bones."

Denise got up from the stool at the kitchen island and kissed her
sister on the cheek. "Thank you, Camille. You are absolutely my
favourite sister."

"And you're mine." They both laughed.

After the boys had gone to bed, the two women sat in the family
room drinking tea. "I'm glad to see you up and about again,"
Camille said. "I know it's not easy."

"Nothing like some tough love to shake me out of my apathy."

"What are older sisters for, if not to bully their younger sisters?"

"Camille, the big bully!" Now there's an oxymoron. Denise
hugged the teacup between her palms and took a sip. "I'm not
ready to go back to work, though. I can't face all those people right
now and pretend that everything is normal. Not yet."

"But how long can you afford to be away, "Camille asked,
"without causing disruption and affecting the ratings?"

"A couple of weeks shouldn't hurt. Gary assured me that the
'ship is sailing smoothly' and Nicole said she doesn't mind the extra
load." She put the cup down and wrapped a throw blanket around
her shoulders.

"The girl with the wild curly hair and the raspy voice?"

"That's her — my zany assistant. She's a tough cookie when she
needs to be and she's becoming fairly competent." Denise yawned.
"I had a bizarre dream about the show today. I was supposed to
interview Jackie Kennedy but when I got to the dressing room,

some strange woman had taken my place and no one recognized me."

"Hmm," Camille muttered. "Are you worried, subconsciously, that someone could take over the show?"

"Not possible. *I am* the show. Besides, Nicole can be a pit bull when threatened. She'd never let that happen while she was on guard."

Camille put her feet up on the ottoman. "Even if you did lose your job, I mean hypothetically, it wouldn't be the end of the world. A change could be good for you."

"Like I said — that's impossible. If there's anything I'm good at, it's *Montreal's Alive*. The show needs me as much as I need the show."

"I'm sure that's true," Camille said.

Denise yawned again, like she hadn't slept in days. She turned on the TV and flipped channels until she came across the news. "Let's find out what's happening in the world," she said. "Then I'm going to bed."

Chapter Twenty-five

It took Laura several days to cool off after returning from San Francisco. At first she was livid and couldn't even look at Chris without seething. She snapped at him incessantly, but he didn't argue back or try to defend himself. He let her punish him with her cold shoulder and smoldering eyes, responding only with a guilt-ridden nod. But by the end of the week she wasn't angry anymore, not even disappointed. She was simply numb, and perhaps dumbfounded. Never before had Chris blasted away from her on a holiday like that. Sure, she had told him to go, to do the right thing, but she hadn't expected him to follow through. She thought he'd reconsider after sleeping on it, that she'd wake up in the morning with him lying beside her, affectionate and remorseful. He'd say, "How ridiculous to have considered abandoning you here, on the last day of our vacation." She'd wrap her arms around him and they'd lose themselves in newly revived passion, making love with more intensity than they had in a long time. But none of that had happened.

When she'd awoken that day, the room was cold and unsympathetic with its stark white ceilings and generic furniture. Her head spun from the aftermath of the wine tour (why had she drunk so much—again?) and the sheets beside her were cold. She found the note from Chris and crumpled it in a compact ball after reading it. Oh sure, off she'd go to Carmel with a busload of strangers. How enticing. And he wanted her to buy something special, her own belated Mother's Day gift perhaps? To hell with that. Instead, she had gone back to bed and when the front desk rang with a friendly wake-up call, she politely thanked the woman and asked to be transferred to room-service. She ordered a full breakfast—fried eggs, sausages, hash browns, toast, orange juice and coffee. Then she called back, changing the brown toast order to a croissant. After polishing off the entire meal, she fell back asleep and didn't wake up until noon. She watched three back-to-back pay-per-view movies, which put her through the gamut of emotions: she shed tears, laughed until her stomach hurt, froze with fear and braced herself with anger.

By the end of the day she was spent, as if she had run a marathon. She didn't bother showering or even getting dressed. What was the point? This was her holiday; she could do whatever she damn well pleased. At 6:30, she ordered room-service again—a cheeseburger with fries and a salad for her conscience. The mini-bar contained only small bottles of hard liquor, and nothing to her liking, which prompted her to order a cosmopolitan from the hotel bar. When her drink arrived, she regretted not having ordered two—one as an aperitif and one as a digestif. She consumed her meal while watching the news and then ordered another cosmo, justifying it as dessert. After polishing off her dinner and the last of her drink, she started to cry. She cried with such intensity that she had to press her face against the pillow to prevent the neighbouring room from hearing her uncontrollable sobs.

The next morning she'd had a long shower and got dressed in the beige pants and aqua sweater set she had worn during her one romantic day with Chris. She spent half an hour blow-drying her hair to straighten it and when she checked herself in the mirror, she felt at least ten years younger. A smattering of make-up revitalized her pale skin, at least superficially, and her few wrinkles were hidden by the puffiness produced from last night's heavy bout of crying.

When she'd arrived home, after a long and boring flight, the girls were in school and Chris was at the office. Monique greeted her with a warm hug and inquired about the trip. "It was wonderful," Laura said, "California is an absolutely breathtaking place." How could she admit that in the five days away she had seen nothing but a few San Francisco sights? Virtually nothing of wine country and not even a glimpse of the coast. "One day, I'd love to go back there with all you girls," she said. She went upstairs to unpack her bags and hung the new dress Chris had bought her at the far end of the closet, out of sight, sheathed in its garment bag. Only at the last minute had she remembered the new dress hanging in the armoire at the hotel, and then she considered leaving it behind to languish in the miserable room. But that would be a waste, and rather immature, she decided; instead she had folded it neatly and placed it in the suitcase.

Laura plodded through domestic life on automatic pilot: the morning scramble, followed by domestic errands, volunteering at the school, connecting with friends, church obligations, after school activities, homework, dinner, and bedtime routines. She was too busy to continue lamenting the unfortunate episodes in San Francisco, and had decided not to wallow in anger anymore. Thinking back, she realized how sensitive she'd been after her alcohol binges, and how they tended to skew her perception of events the next day. Perhaps she should monitor her drinking to keep a clearer head.

Chris had been respectful and pleasant since the trip, in spite of her wrath, which helped dissipate her malaise. He'd even given her the overdue Mother's Day gift when she came home — an eighteen-carat gold chain-link bracelet. When he'd handed her the white jewelry box, contrite and endearing, she accepted it with grace. For a while she wondered if the present was an act of guilt rather than love, but then she'd conceded that, of course, it came from his heart.

Now that time had passed since their return, her previous emotional turmoil seemed exaggerated. In addition to the alcohol, maybe her hormones were responsible; could she be perimenopausal already? She busied herself with spring-cleaning chores and redecorating the powder room, which had been on her mind for some time. Wallpaper was back in fashion and she spent hours trying to find a pattern that would suit the small main-floor bathroom. Finally, she settled on a garden motif with soft rose-coloured hydrangea and muted green foliage. Chris was working hard, but he made a concerted effort to come home early enough to spend time with the family and to bring the girls to soccer — one way of making amends. He took Monique out for dinner and the two had come home in great spirits, laughing and teasing each other, bringing a sense of normalcy back to the household.

On soccer night that week, Laura fed Sophie and Tanya dinner at 5:30, rushing to be ready for their practice. But Chris didn't arrive home in time to take them, and as Laura pulled out of the driveway to bring them herself, he appeared.

"Sorry I'm late," he shouted through the open car window.

"No problem. I can take the girls tonight."

"I can still do it, but I need a minute to change."

"Don't worry, we're already on our way."

He waved. "OK, thanks. See you later."

He'd been helpful all week and she certainly didn't mind giving him a break. Besides, she could drop off the girls and use the time to pick up groceries.

Laura delivered the children at the park and watched them scuttle off to the playing field where the coach already had the children doing drills. "Have fun," she called out, "I'll be back in an hour."

She left the windows down to enjoy the comfortable breeze. Driving by the local tennis courts, she noticed a group of middle-aged women playing doubles. Stopped at a red light, she watched them play, the ball flying with speed and power. Perhaps she should take up tennis again and get a doubles group going. Monique had offered numerous times to practice with her, but after a ten-year hiatus, Laura was reluctant. And she didn't have the right equipment anymore; she'd have to buy a new racquet, new tennis shoes, and new tennis clothes. Realistically, when would she have the time to play enough to get back to her previous level? Maybe next year.

After buying groceries, with ten minutes to spare before the practice ended, Laura shot home to put the ice cream into the freezer before it melted. As she drove along Shaker Boulevard, past Sonya's house, she noticed the SOLD sign jutting from the front lawn. Sonya was standing at her front door talking to a man wearing a baseball cap backwards. Laura almost stopped to wave when she saw that from behind, the man looked like Chris in his running clothes. Remembering that she was pressed for time, she continued on her way, but then decided to drive around the block to satisfy her curiosity. This time she approached at a slower speed, cranking her neck to see if it was indeed Chris. The two were still in conversation, but now the man was standing inside the doorway. Tall cedars lining the walkway obstructed her view. She slowed down some more and thought about calling out to get their attention, when Sonya and the man suddenly embraced. Not a friendly, 'you take care' kind of embrace, but more like a lingering, 'I wish you could stay longer' kind of embrace. When they let go, they continued talking, standing less than an arm's length from one another. What was that all about? Laura didn't get out of the car, and didn't make her presence known, hoping they hadn't seen her spying. Ducking her head, she drove away, mystified by the possibilities presented by the scene. She shook her head. Impossible. That was certainly not her husband.

Back at her house, she lugged the groceries inside, quickly put the ice cream in the refrigerator beside the milk, leaving the rest of the items on the counter. She was the last parent to pick up her children at the soccer practice, and arrived to find the girls petting a passerby's golden retriever puppy, while the coach loaded his trunk with soccer balls and pylons. Still flushed from running, Tanya and Sophie jumped into the car.

"Can we go for ice cream?" Tanya pleaded.

"Please, just a teensy one?" Sophie continued.

"It's late, girls. You have to take a bath and get to bed. Tomorrow's a school day."

"Daddy always takes us to Dairy Delight," Sophie said.

"Shhhhh," Tanya said, as if trying to protect some secret they had with their father.

"I bought some ice cream at the store, you can have some at home."

Placated, the girls turned their conversation to Wendy Harrison's temper tantrum over not getting to wear the number four blue pinny during practice.

After the girls had had their runny chocolate ice cream, which had melted from sitting in the fridge instead of the freezer, they rushed upstairs for their baths. When they were settled in bed, Laura went downstairs and found Chris on the patio in the backyard.

"How was your run?" she asked.

He closed the file he'd been reading and said, "Good. I did the usual circuit." His hair was still wet from his shower and he smelled of lavender soap.

"I'm thinking of taking up tennis again," she said. "I need to get fit, be more active."

"Fantastic. I'll play with you anytime."

"No, I need to get myself into shape first." She lifted her arms to show him her slight muscles. "I've got to build up some strength before I take you on." They used to play before they were married, and although he usually won, she could at one time, give him a good game.

"I'd be happy to hit the ball with you. It'd be great to get you back on the courts."

He'd been trying to convince her for a few years to get back into sports. Golf was his biggest push, but that took too much time. "We'll get a sitter once a week," he'd said. "You can do a clinic during the day when the girls are in school, and in the summer we can play while they're in camp." She'd liked the idea, but somehow never got around to it. Sonya was probably and excellent golfer.

"Maybe I'll give it a try—go out with Monique for starters."

"Way to go," he said.

"Good run?" she asked again.

"Yeah, great."

"And you did your 3k?"

He nodded.

"Without stopping?"

"Uh huh. It felt good." He drank from his glass of water. "How was the soccer practice?"

"Fine, I think. The girls were happy when I picked them up."

"I'm glad the girls are into the game. Soccer's a great team sport."

She couldn't refrain from saying something about Sonya, to feel him out. "I noticed Sonya sold her house. Did you know that?"

"Yes. In fact, I was running by her place earlier and she called out to give me the baseball cap. Remember? The one she gave me as a thank you for helping her after the accident? I'd left it at her house. Pretty lousy after she'd gone to the effort of getting it for me."

234

"Hmm," Laura said.

"She told me she'd had three offers on the house and ended up with more than she'd expected."

"That's great news." And the hug? Was it to congratulate Sonya on the house sale? To thank her for the hat? She checked his face for clues, but all she saw was his usual post-run fatigue.

"And she said something about a house she's considering in Chagrin Falls, to make a clean break, to start fresh."

"Now that's interesting." Chagrin Falls was only about fifteen minutes away, yet in a different world altogether—a quaint village known for its natural setting and charming century homes. "I'll give her a call to see if she needs help packing. What a shame for her to move away when we're getting reacquainted." She thought she saw a flash of melancholy in Chris's eyes, as if he had his own reasons for being disappointed.

Chapter Twenty-six

Denise arrived in Cleveland at 10:30 a.m. Getting away for the day had been easy, almost too easy. Nobody had questioned her explanation—that she needed to follow-up with the wine-producers who wanted to collaborate on a show about Eastern State regional wines. "Great," Francois had said. "I'm glad you're eager to get back into gear." Camille had stayed on, in spite of Denise's efforts to persuade her to go home, and Clara had taken a few days off. Camille had practically pushed her out the door in the morning, "Have a great day," she had said, "Go do your stuff."

Although Denise had been taking the anti-anxiety pills prescribed by Dr. Green, she could not attribute her mental boost to the pills alone. In fact, he had said they would take at least two weeks to kick in. The most effective drug, if she could call it that, was the renewed connection with Chris. Since they had talked, she had managed to pull herself out of the grey zone. Maybe she didn't need the pills at all. Three days ago she couldn't get out of bed, and here she was, heading to the airport. Thank goodness the cloud had passed and the light was finally seeping back into her mind.

After passing through customs in Cleveland, Denise called Chris on her cell phone. He said he was circling in his car around the terminal and they agreed to meet outside, at the end of the building by the curb. During the flight she'd been questioning her impetuous decision to come and for a while, she was in a state of near panic. The only way to control her urge to flee had been to meditate, and now that she'd arrived, Chris's calm voice reassured her.

Denise rushed to the restroom to freshen up, but when she observed herself in the mirror, the cool fluorescent lighting highlighted every wrinkle and every blemish on her pale face, causing her further distress. She applied some powder and some lipstick, but still looked sallow and miserably thin. Would Chris notice how emaciated she had become? With the help of Camille's superb cooking, she had replaced some of the shed pounds, but her hip bones still protruded—an unsightly image when she was naked. She wore a flared skirt with a loose white blouse, hoping that the flowing fabric and the bold pattern concealed her fragile figure. The day before, she'd had her hair cut shorter to create the illusion of a fuller face, and bangs for the first time in years.

When she stepped outside the terminal, Denise immediately saw Chris standing by the curb at their meeting place, hands in his pockets, pacing the sidewalk. She considered retreating, heading back into the building, undoing this whole charade, but she kept on walking with shoulders erect, trying to appear poised. He was indeed a handsome man, standing tall in his casual summer attire— beige slacks and a royal blue polo shirt. Dark sunglasses gave him a mysterious allure and when he caught her gaze, she almost tripped. Where was her confident stride, her self-possession? She continued walking self-consciously, driven by a determination beyond her control.

They kissed on both cheeks, French style, and Chris opened the passenger door for her. The car, though cool inside, felt stifling. Denise opened her window to get some air. "I've got a touch of a headache," she said, and reached into her purse.

Chris glanced over, looking concerned.

"I'm fine. An aspirin will get rid of the edge." She popped one of Dr. Green's pills in her mouth and swallowed it dry, hoping it would provide relief.

Chris's phone rang but he didn't answer it. "For this special occasion, I'm not taking calls," he said, and turned the ringer off. "I think business will survive for a few hours without me."

"Same here." Denise turned her phone off and dropped it in her purse. "That's why we have voice mail."

"How was your flight?" Chris asked. "No problems getting out of Montreal?"

"Easy. No line-ups, no delays. Couldn't have been simpler."

"I can imagine your fans pushing and shoving to get a better glimpse of you, or begging for an autograph."

She laughed. "I'm no rock star, Chris." In truth, she did get a lot of attention in Montreal, and until recently she'd enjoyed it. But since her mother died, she wished she could wear a burka and hide from the public altogether. The attention was too exhausting these days, and she didn't have the energy to play the game. In Cleveland she would be anonymous, a pleasant reprieve from unwanted intrusions.

"I remember the way people stared at you at the Realitz, like you were quite a phenomenon."

"Oh, I don't know about that." She felt like a charlatan. Granted she had fans, but her audience base was limited, and in reality, she was no more than a small-town celebrity. Chris had placed her on an inflated pedestal, as did many of her fans. She didn't know what to say next and that painful first-date awkwardness overcame her. Clasping and unclasping her hands, she said, "Lovely day today."

"A nice day for a drive. I thought we'd coast along the country-side, get out of the city. Is that all right?"

"Whatever you think is best."

"And maybe go for a walk somewhere."

"Wonderful. Sounds perfect." More platitudes. She felt sixteen, tongue-tied and self-conscious. And she was a talk-show host, for God's sake.

"There's a country restaurant north of here. We could find a place to walk and then have lunch. Are you up for that?"

"Anything." The acute sensation of her pulse tapping, and blood charging through her veins was unnerving. Calm down, she kept telling herself. Calm down! What on earth was she doing, running away from home for the day, engaging in some clandestine liaison with a man she barely knew? Chris took her hand and squeezed it, as if he sensed what she was thinking. She checked his reaction to her sweaty, cold palms. He appeared pensive.

"Thank you for coming," he said. "I think we both needed to do this."

Denise nodded. He was right, they had to do something. They couldn't communicate perpetually through e-mails and phone calls.

But she wasn't ready to enter into a heavy discussion about the future, not yet. Instead, she probed him about Cleveland, a city she didn't know much about.

Chris told her about the world-class Cleveland Orchestra, the Rock and Roll Hall of Fame, and the vast effort to clean the ecologically devastated Lake Erie. The lake had become so sanitary, he told her, that fish thrived in it and children now swam in it.

"Didn't the lake catch fire once upon a time?" Denise asked. That was one of the few facts she remembered learning about Cleveland long ago. She also recalled the city being referred to as 'the mistake by the lake,' but she didn't mention that.

"The Cuyahoga River actually caught fire, not the lake — in 1969. But those days are long over and the lake is the cleanest of the five Great Lakes." Chris sounded proud, as if he was directly responsible for its transformation. He continued to tell her about the racial integration experiment in the fifties that took place in his neighbourhood, Shaker Heights, and how culturally diverse the city was.

"Cleveland's one of America's best kept secrets, you know." He shot her a conspiring glance. "Don't tell anyone."

"You couldn't be biased, could you?" she said, grinning.

"Perhaps. But no kidding, the quality of life here is outstanding and real estate prices are reasonable. I should show you some of our spectacular neighbourhoods." He laughed. "First I sound like a tour-guide and now a real-estate agent."

"You've sold me on the place," Denise said, in her 'Montreal's Alive' talk-show voice. "When do I move here?" Then she realized how foolhardy she sounded, as if she'd drop her life and start all over in Cleveland.

"When I first came here to join Kendra I thought we'd move on in a couple of years to a place where we could have a 'bigger life.' Somewhere like Chicago, or Boston, or even New York. But here I am, twenty-one years later, feeling more entrenched than ever."

They stopped at an old-fashioned coffee shop in a small town, which offered brewed coffee and tea, and the choice of donuts or muffins. Rickety pine chairs and small tables, covered by red and white checkered tablecloths, produced a charming, homey atmosphere. Denise ordered tea and a blueberry muffin and Chris ordered a coffee. They were alone except for the lady who worked behind the counter.

When they sat down, Chris said in a solemn voice, "I don't know where to begin, Denise. Your mother, Paris, or simply, what you're thinking about these days?"

She took a sip of tea, then smiled at him. "How about San Francisco? Let's start with that. How was your trip?"

"Not a remarkable holiday, to be honest. Weather wasn't great, had a few mishaps—"

"And then you left early to come to Mother's funeral. I'm sorry the time with your wife was cut short because of me. I didn't intend for you to—"

"I know you were extremely close to your mother...I wanted to be there."

"Your presence meant a lot to me." Her eyes swelled with tears. "You have no idea."

"I know what it's like to lose a mother. I still think of mine all the time."

"I'd forgotten about that," she said. Much of Chris's life was still a mystery and she knew virtually nothing about his parents.

"Mom supported my decision to marry Kendra despite her disappointment in my leaving school, and she played a significant role in Monique's childhood. We both miss her a great deal. But life goes on. I promise, the pain will subside over time."

"I hope you're right." Denise became aware of the woman behind the counter whose lingering presence made her uncomfortable. She lowered her voice. "Sometimes I don't believe my mother is gone. I half-expect for her to call me to say that she isn't dead after all, that the hospital had it wrong and that it was all a big misunderstanding."

"She was a special woman, wasn't she?"

"My anchor." The tears began to flow.

Chris took her hand across the table and they both noticed the woman watching them from the counter, straining to hear their conversation.

"Let's go," Chris said.

When they were outside, Denise blew her nose. "I'm sorry. I didn't mean to make this visit a mournful one."

"I don't care what kind of visit this is, having you here is all that matters." He drew her close to him and hugged her.

She was nineteen again, being comforted by a stranger's embrace. Her convoluted emotions were oddly familiar and, as in the past, she didn't know what to do with them.

After they disengaged they didn't speak, and Denise couldn't look at Chris for fear of crying again. They walked to the car and got in, a heavy silence wedged between them. Chris drove for about fifteen minutes before he said, "There's a Reservation area not too far from here, part of what's called the 'Emerald Necklace.' Cleveland is encircled by these protected green spaces — nice for hiking or walking. How would you feel about going for a nature walk?"

She looked down at her shoes. Thankfully, she'd worn her flats. "That would be fine."

"We bring the kids there sometimes because they love to come for picnics and play on the moss covered rocks." He laughed. "You should see them slipping and sliding and trying not to fall. And sometimes we take them through the trails in the fall. It's like walking through a tunnel of flames."

Denise noticed a kind of nostalgic expression on Chris's face, as if he was basking in the memory. How strange to have forgotten that Chris had a family, and to have flagrantly disregarded her own. To temporarily erase that part of her life was unconscionable and alarming. Jabbed by shame, she closed her eyes and asked for forgiveness, feeling further distressed because she didn't know where to direct her thoughts.

They drove into the Reservation, past an unmanned security booth and a wooded area, until they reached a large parking lot, vacant except for a pick-up truck and a shiny yellow Volkswagen Beetle. Chris parked next to the trail entrance and when they got out of the car, Denise relaxed. It was the same feeling she experienced when she arrived at her cottage — the smells and sounds of nature immediately connecting her to her surroundings. Inhaling the fresh air, she observed the birds and insects scurrying around with purpose. Wild flowers sprouted from the mossy ground, reminding Denise of how her mother always tried to identify each particular species when they came across the fragile blooms at the cottage.

Chris put his arm around her. "How are you doing?" His voice was low, his touch, soothing.

"At this particular moment, I feel good," she said. "Strangely at peace."

"Me too." He squeezed her shoulder.

"Soon, we'll have to return to reality." She put her arm around his waist.

"I don't want to think about it. We're together at last, in a simple universe. Let's enjoy the tranquility."

They came to a bench, which had been strategically placed as a rest point, facing a river. A fish leapt in the air as if to make its presence known, and the birds chattered overhead. Denise watched a mother duck swimming with the current, followed by seven fuzzy ducklings. She and Chris sat on the bench holding hands, observing nature's activity like an old married couple—a snapshot of what they could have been, might have become.

"You and me," Chris said, his voice contemplative. "This could have been our reality, Denise."

"But it's not," she said.

"No."

"Now what? What do we do with this illusion of happiness?" She swept her hand through the air as if waving a wand.

"I don't know. I'm at a loss." he said, standing up, agitated. "Something bizarre is happening here. I can't get you out of my head or my..." He slammed his palm against his heart.

Denise's own heart plummeted. This new level of interaction was a bad idea; she never should have come to see Chris. But how could she accept that truth, and how could they turn back now? Holding hands, they retraced their steps to the car, her mind wandering into places it shouldn't go.

For lunch, Chris had chosen a restaurant nestled on the outskirts of a small town, catering to cross-country skiers in the winter and to hikers and golfers in the summer. At this time in the spring, the place was all but abandoned. Only three tables in the dining room were occupied and Chris asked to be seated by the window, far away from the other patrons. Tall wooden beams, a cathedral ceiling and a wood-burning fireplace in the centre, created a casual ambience. Cream linen table clothes and sterling silver cutlery added a touch of formality.

"Charming," Denise said.

"I thought you'd like this place. I'm glad they're open today."

The waiter came to greet them. "Would you like a drink?" he asked Denise in a friendly tone. "A glass of wine perhaps?"

"I'll have some sparkling water, please," Denise said, "with a twist of lime."

Chris asked for the same. They placed their orders—angel hair pasta with baby shrimp, asparagus and dill—the special of the day.

"So, here we are," Chris said.

"Here we are," Denise repeated.

"About your life in Paris—your letter read like fiction, loaded with drama. I still can't believe what happened to you."

"Thank goodness that life is behind me."

"Is it?"

"Of course." She fiddled with the salt shaker.

"But you liked Paris?"

"I loved the city, although you have to differentiate between the place and the people."

"You didn't like the people?"

Hmm. Did she like the people? "Actually, I did like them, for the most part. But I've always been haunted by the mass deceit. Of all our friends and acquaintances, I don't know who knew and who didn't know about Jacques' wife, but there seemed to be some kind of conspiracy…'let's see how long we can keep Denise in the dark.'" She could feel the blood rushing to her face and tried to dispel the brewing anger by taking quick imperceptible breaths. Then she drank from her water glass before continuing. "To find out that you're the only one who doesn't know the truth about your own life is rather disconcerting."

The food arrived and the waiter poured more water. Denise twisted the pasta around her fork but didn't bring it to her mouth. "Trust has become a valuable commodity, something I don't dispense easily," she said, her eyes hardening.

"I can understand why." Chris passed Denise the bread basket. "But you've moved beyond that experience, to another country, a new life."

"Different country, different life. Problems nonetheless."

"Are you not happy, Denise? I mean, apart from the fact that you've lost your mother."

She noticed that Chris wasn't eating either. "That depends. How do you define happiness? I'm not sure I've figured that out yet. Have you?"

He cleared his throat. "I suppose happiness is different things to different people. For instance, what I feel sitting here, speaking with you and gazing at your beautiful face, is beyond happiness."

"But that's a snapshot in time, a moment's pleasure. What about your life? What constitutes happiness in your day-to-day existence?"

Chris leaned back and caressed his scalp, as if massaging his brain. "Wow. I don't usually think in those terms. I mean, life is hectic. You work, you play, you engage with your kids, you try to feed your mind...geez...I don't really know what true happiness means. The word contentment — *that*, I can define."

A husky voice interrupted them. "Hey, Chris, good to see ya."

Surprised, Chris and Denise exchanged glances.

Chris jumped up from his seat. "How are you doing?" he said, and shook hands with a sturdy man with a receding hairline, wearing jeans and a leather sports jacket. "What brings you out here today?"

"Rhonda and I placed an offer on a piece of property. Five acres at the bottom of the hill. Don't know if we'll get it, but we're hoping." He crossed his fingers.

"Good luck with that," Chris said. "You planning to build?"

"That's the idea — Rhonda's dream house." He put his arm around his wife's waist and smiled at Denise.

Chris introduced Denise, as if he'd suddenly realized she was there too. "This is Denise Gagnon, a journalist friend from Montreal. She's doing an investigative report on some...umm... environmental issues out here. I'm showing her around the area."

"How interesting. Nice to meet you," he said, shaking her hand. "I'm Bob Warden and this is my wife Rhonda. What exactly are you — "

"Hey, I hope you get that property," Chris interrupted, shutting down further discussion.

"Thanks." Bob grinned, giving Chris a pat on the back. "We'll let you folks get on with your lunch."

"Damn it," Chris whispered to Denise when they were out of earshot, "I wasn't expecting to bump into anyone out here. He's a lawyer my firm uses and his name completely escaped me. I hope he didn't notice."

"Don't worry, you handled it with aplomb," Denise said.

"He came right out of left field."

Denise ate what she could of her meal, but left more than half. When she glanced at the Wardens' table she noticed them quickly looking away. "Your friends are keeping an eye on us."

"I don't want to have to watch over our shoulders and whisper like we're in a library," Chris said. "Let's go."

"What do we have to hide? We haven't done anything wrong," Denise said. "I can imagine the complications, the entanglements that could arise if we were actually involved in an affair. It's ridiculous that two old friends can't have lunch together without feeling like fugitives."

Chris laughed. "You're right. It's not like we're sleeping together. I don't know why I made up that bit about you being here to study the environment when I could have told the truth — that you're a friend visiting from Montreal."

Declining coffee and tea, they rushed out of the restaurant, waving to the Wardens from the entrance. Chris opened the car door for Denise and shut it when she was seated. Slipping into the driver's seat, he turned on the engine and faced her. "Here we are in the middle of nowhere on a weekday, trying to share some uninterrupted time, and I have to come across someone I know. What rotten luck. I guess there's no true escape for us." He took her hand and smiled. "Good thing no one was lurking behind the bushes earlier."

They had only held hands but if anyone had been watching them together, the scene would certainly not have appeared platonic. Denise closed her eyes and relived those few intimate moments by the river. She wanted to hold on to the feeling forever.

After driving for about ten minutes they came to a small picture-book village with quaint antique stores and art galleries. "Would you like to stop here and poke around?"

"Sure," Denise said. "It'd be like sneaking into candy shops when we're supposed to be in school."

The antique stores were mostly filled with country relics that didn't have great appeal or much value, probably the unwanted contents of old farmhouses and family heirlooms that children didn't have use for when their parents passed on.

"These stores are like mini museums," Denise whispered, when they entered a small art gallery packed with more used furniture and knick-knacks than art.

"Yes, but they could use a better curator," Chris said. He pointed to an old pine table piled high with teapots, old books, unusual kitchen utensils, and old-fashioned electric appliances.

Paintings were displayed above the tattered sofas, while others were stacked like lumber against the wall. Denise inspected the wares while Chris checked out an old doctor's case, filled with anti-quated medical tools.

"Chris, come see this painting, it's like the scene from earlier today." She pointed to a small painting depicting a river, bordered by budding vegetation, and a mother duck swimming with her ducklings trailing behind her.

"It has an impressionistic quality," Chris said. "I like it."

"The artist captured the serenity of the moment perfectly. Don't you think the picture belongs on a proper wall, where it can be appreciated?" Denise said.

"Absolutely. And I want you to have it. I'm going to buy it for you," Chris said.

"That's not necessary." She was suddenly embarrassed.

"As a souvenir. Please let me do this small thing."

"Then, thank you," she said. "I'll cherish it."

Back in the car, Denise began to relax. Chris played a CD and they listened to classical music in comfortable silence. Studying Chris's face as he focused on the road, Denise imagined that he was her husband. He was easy to be with, genial and calming, and already, she felt like she'd known him for years. She thought of Francois and his frantic intensity when he became consumed by his work, and how she sometimes avoided him during his big projects. With Francois she often felt disjointed, with Chris she felt whole.

"Chris," she suddenly said. "Can we go back to the Conserva-tion area, to the river? Maybe I'm foolish, but I'd love to recapture that peaceful sensation. There's nothing like getting swept away by nature." Or by love, she thought.

"Why not?" he said. "We still have a couple of hours before your flight."

The parking lot was vacant when they arrived, and the seclusion gave Denise a new sense of freedom. They walked along the bumpy path until they reached the bench by the water. Denise embraced the solitude, her nerves finally soothed. When they sat down, she leaned her head against Chris's shoulder and felt nineteen again, propelled by forces beyond her control to be spontaneous. She wanted to burst into laughter or perhaps tears, or run along the river as fast as she could. What would she do if he kissed her? She wouldn't stop him, she couldn't. Her head started to spin, her body began to ache, and at that instant she would have done anything – she didn't care about the repercussions, nothing and nobody else mattered.

A pair of mallard ducks swooped down from the sky and landed on the bank, close to their feet, unfettered by human intru-sion. The female plunged into the water and the male followed. "Are they mates for life?" Denise said.

"I'm not sure." Chris took her hand and she caressed his palm. His wedding band seemed to grip his finger as she moved her hand across his.

Chapter Twenty-seven

Chris watched Denise walk through the airport's automatic doors, her purse swinging against her hip, and the painting, wrapped in brown paper, tucked under her arm. His mind wandered to the time he had dropped her off at the library twenty-five years ago, after sharing the night together. Back then, like now, she didn't turn around to catch his gaze or wave good-bye. The sinking feeling in his gut, or his heart, was identical to the way he had felt when he was nineteen.

He suddenly realized that they hadn't even discussed when, or if, they would see each other again. Staring at the doors opening and shutting as people entered and exited, Chris was unaware of the tow-away sign and the traffic guard, who unceremoniously waved him off. Where to go from here, was the question hammering his mind. What could possibly become of this reconnection with Denise? The traffic guard knocked at his window and flashed his ticket pad with impatience. Yes, yes, Chris gestured, his irritation swelling, and then drove away.

In spite of his heavy heart, he felt invigorated—strange to be depleted yet revitalized at the same time. Instead of taking the exit towards home, he headed in the direction of the office. How could he face Laura after a day like that? If he went to the office and powered through some work he might calm down, stabilize. He should check in anyway, see what was happening with the guys from Chicago. Weren't they supposed to come tomorrow for a meeting? He'd better confirm the agenda and review the material. But for now, he needed some time alone to decompress. Spending the day with Denise had been like rock climbing—each advance forward gave him a rush, but one false move, one fumble, would risk the entire ascent. But there had been no fall and the thrill of reaching a new plateau with Denise had left his adrenaline pumping.

Chris arrived to a barrage of voicemail and e-mail messages, twice the usual volume. Turning off his cell phone had been a bad idea in the end. He hadn't expected much to happen during his absence—a dead day with no meetings, no conference calls, and no pressing issues.

"Chris, where the hell are you? We've got a fuckin' crisis here," Tony's voice hollered into his voicemail. "Call me as soon as you get this!"

A message from Laura: "Everyone's looking for you, there's some emergency at work. Where are you?"

He stopped listening to the messages and checked his e-mails. Same thing. Since when was he so indispensable? Another diatribe from Tony. The San Francisco deal had crashed again; the client was backing out, implying circumstances had changed, and they needed to talk to him immediately.

Chris kicked the side of his desk. Why the hell did everything have to fall apart when he had taken a few measly hours off? And why was it always him who had to save the world? Tony should've handled it—he was there—why hadn't he covered for him? And then to involve Laura...shit. He checked his watch. 6:00 p.m. in Cleveland and 3:00 p.m. in California. Picking up the phone, he drew a heavy breath and punched in the numbers.

"Hank Davis, please," he said to the assistant.

"I'm sorry, he's not available, can I take a mess—"

"Tell him it's Chris Lambert calling, he'll want to speak with me."

"I'm sorry, like I said, he's not—"

"You get him on the phone right away. This is urgent." His tone was controlled but threatening, on the edge of erupting.

"One moment," she said.

Chris pulled out the paperwork as he waited. He reviewed the contract—iron clad as far as he was concerned.

Hank came on the line. "So, *now* you surface. No such thing as cell phones on your side of the country?"

"What's going on, Hank?"

"Deal's dead."

"What are you talking about? You got what you wanted. You signed, you shook." He had nailed it, made them feel it was their victory. What had happened?

"Your company misrepresented some of the figures. Gotta do our due diligence, you know."

Chris whipped his pen across the room. "Impossible! I checked those figures myself—had them verified by accounting. They're irrefutable."

"Sorry man. Deal's dead."

Come to think about it, there had been a strange expression on Hank's face that night, like he had a scheme going. But they had closed the deal—Hank even wanted to go out and celebrate afterwards. "You went with Dean & Scott, didn't you?"

"I can't discuss it with you now, Lambert. All I can say is, too bad you weren't available earlier, there was a window—"

"Bullshit!"

"I've gotta get back to my meeting. We'll be in touch."

"Right!" Chris slammed down the phone. A burning sensation surged through his body and he wanted to hurl the phone across the room, smash it into pieces. But he didn't move. He stared at the wall in front of him, too incensed to act.

On the way home from the office, Chris called Laura.

"Now you call. How convenient after we've had dinner and the girls have gone to bed."

Her harsh tone came at him like a sledgehammer. "I don't need this, Laura. It's been a nightmare of a day."

"Is that right? Rough day on the golf course?"

If that's where she thought he was, he wouldn't deny it. "I'm getting it from all directions today, I don't need guff from you too."

"I don't care if you play golf, I don't care if you work late. But what I do care about is you making us wonder when you're going to show up," she said.

"I'm sorry. I didn't expect things to run into the evening. It happens."

"It certainly does. I thought *things* were changing — last week you were great, making the big effort. Now you're incommunicado. I knew your sudden transformation was too good to be true."

Not the ranting again. Chris's head throbbed and he felt his throat tightening up. "C'mon Laura, be reasonable."

"You mean, be a doormat, Laura. Take everything as it comes and have no expectations of your husband."

She hadn't been this angry since he'd forgotten about the girls' ballet recital over a year ago. "You have no idea what kind of day I've had," he said, conquered.

"Right now, I don't care." She hung up.

Shit, shit, shit. He couldn't go home to that. Changing direction at the next opportunity, he headed back downtown. Would Denise be home yet? He wanted to rewind his day, go back to the river and watch the ducks. If life were only that simple. The thought of Denise sitting across from him at the restaurant relaxed him for a moment and helped him escape from his troubles. Those deep, alluring eyes never failed to mesmerize him. What was it about her that provoked this wild obsession? Everything about her captivated him — if only they could be together…a little longer. He wouldn't trade the time they had shared that day for anything, not for that bloody deal, not even to avoid Laura's wrath.

He parked the car on the street and went into a bar, where people were watching the ball game. The bartender pointed to the over-sized television when he sat on the stool at the bar. "Good game. Tied three-all in the seventh." Chris ordered a beer and planted his eyes on the screen, while his mind tried to untangle the knots in his day.

****

"Was that Dad you were talking to?" Monique asked Laura.

"Yes," she said.

"I heard you arguing. What was that all about?"

Laura folded the wet dishtowel she had used to dry pots and hung it on a rod. She poured herself a glass of wine from the half-empty bottle sitting on the counter. "I'm getting frustrated with your father these days, Monique. He's got his own agenda, which doesn't seem to involve us."

"He's been working lots."

"That's a fact." She took a big sip of wine.

"Is he coming home now?" Monique asked

"Who knows? We didn't exactly end our conversation on a good note."

"Oh."

"Don't worry, he'll be home eventually." Laura knew she was being harsh with him, but she couldn't get rid of the vision in her head of Sonya and Chris locked in an intimate embrace. Sonya sold her house for a good price…big deal. Was that enough of a reason to lunge into his arms? And although Laura had thought she'd forgiven Chris for leaving her alone in San Francisco, now she wasn't feeling as magnanimous.

"I uh…need to…ask you something," Monique said, staring at the floor.

"What is it?"

"I need to find a doctor. A gynecologist."

"A gynecologist—specifically?"

"Yes." Monique poured herself a glass of water, her back facing Laura.

"Our family doctor won't do?"

Monique mumbled, "I think I have a problem."

"Do you want to tell me about it?" Laura asked with concern.

"No." Her voice was so faint that Laura could hardly hear her. "It's personal."

"OK. I'll get my doctor's number for you." She had never seen Monique appear in such a vulnerable state.

"Thanks."

When Laura returned to the kitchen with the number, Monique was sitting at the kitchen table sobbing. "What is it Monique, what's wrong?" Laura asked. She sat down and put her arm around Monique's quivering shoulders. Monique was crying with such vehemence that she couldn't speak; all she could surrender were gasps and broken words.

Laura waited. She glanced at her watch. Where the heck was Chris? She used the consoling voice that was usually effective with her younger daughters. "Monique, honey, tell me what's the matter. I can't help you unless I know."

Monique looked up, her face almost unrecognizable. "I think I'm—" She started to sob again.

Don't say it, Laura said to herself. Please don't tell me you're pregnant. She passed Monique a box of tissues.

Monique blew her nose and wiped her face. "I messed up," she whispered through her tear-stained face. "I think I'm pregnant."

Laura knew it was coming but the words shocked her nonetheless. "Are you sure?" Chris should be the one dealing with this; where could he be?

"I think I'm sure." She dropped her head on the table over her folded arms and said, in a muffled voice between sobs, "I don't know what to do."

Laura considered who the father might be. Andrew was the only guy Monique had been hanging around with, but wasn't he just a friend? Should she ask? No, she would leave the questions to Chris. "Monique, it's going to be all right. I'll make the doctor's appointment for you tomorrow and I'll come with you, if you'd like."

"Thank you," Monique said, covering her swollen face again.

"Maybe it's a false alarm," Laura said.

"But I've never been late before," Monique said, still sniffling.

"It can happen." Laura got up to pour herself some more wine, emptying the bottle and shaking it to capture the last drops. She picked it up and read the label; the French words meant nothing to her.

Chris arrived home a few hours later and Laura was waiting for him upstairs. She had read the same paragraph of her book over and over again, had gone through all 102 channels on TV several times, and had opened another bottle of wine. He came into the room and walked directly to the closet.

"You don't say hello anymore?" she said.

"I thought you weren't talking to me. Hanging up on me is a pretty strong indication that you're not interested in conversation."

"Do you blame me for being angry? Seriously?" She tried to control her fury.

"No, Laura, I don't blame you for anything."

She watched absentmindedly as he stripped down to his boxers. He sat on the bed and removed his socks. How could she tell him, when should she tell him? Monique had asked her not to say anything, but Laura had said it wouldn't be right to keep such a serious matter from Chris. She wondered if telling him now was the right thing to do considering his cranky mood. Perhaps the news should be left to another day, at least until it was official. Monique should be the one to tell him at any rate — in her own way.

"We lost a hundred million dollars today. The San Francisco deal," he said.

"Oh no," Laura said. "Is that why everyone was trying to hunt you down?"

"Yup."

"But can't it be salvaged? Broken deals can come back to life, right?"

"Not this time."

"I'm sorry," she said.

"Me too."

The next day, Laura and Monique returned from the doctor's appointment in a state of disbelief. Laura had assumed the results would be positive, but she'd clung to her faint hope that they'd leave the doctor's office giddy with relief. When they arrived at the house, Monique followed Laura inside and ran upstairs to her room. The whole way home neither had spoken in the car. What was there to say?

Laura punched in Chris's work number and hung up. No, now was not the time. She thought about Sophie and Tanya, coming into their own. Could this happen to them one day? If it could happen to Monique, it could happen to anyone. For that matter, she herself had risked pregnancy in her naïve, invincible youth. But she had gotten through that period of life unscathed, by pure luck she realized. She went to the kitchen and flipped through the cards in her recipe box. Chocolate chip cookies. How ridiculous to think that cookies could possibly make Monique feel better, but at least she herself might feel better. And the girls would be thrilled to walk in to the sweet aroma of cookies baking in the oven when they arrived from school.

Laura took the butter and eggs out of the fridge. What else did she need? Sugar, flour, baking soda, vanilla. She put the items on the counter and combined the ingredients, sifting flour all over her black pants. When she tried to brush the powder off, it smudged into the fabric, creating large white, cloudy patches on her legs. She turned the oven on and lined the cookie sheets with parchment paper. Rummaging through the cupboard, she searched for the chocolate chips, and scavenged around every cupboard, top to bottom. Hadn't she seen them the other day? Then she remembered that they'd used the last of the chips when she and Tanya had made chocolate chip banana muffins for the school's bake sale. Since the girls would be home soon, she didn't have time to run out to the store. As tears pushed their way out of her eyes, she picked up the bowl and dumped the batter into the trash.

****

Hunger gripped Chris for the first time that day when he walked through the door. Something smelled good. From the kitchen doorway he watched Laura serve dinner to the younger girls at the table and then to herself, noticing that there was no place set for him. When he entered Laura got up from the table and approached him with a conciliatory kiss, which magically relieved the ache in his chest. Then she attempted a smile, the kind that was not quite forced but summoned by will. This unexpected gesture brought welcome comfort and he smiled back, hoping that his eyes did not betray his burdened spirit.

"Yay, you're home!" the girls cried in unison.

"Hey kiddettes, whatcha eating?" Chris gave each daughter a light kiss on the top of their heads. "I'm starving; I hope you've saved some food for me."

Laura brought him a plate. "Voila," she said, "your dinner, Monsieur—chicken à la mashed potatoes and broccoli. Bon appétit!"

Knowing how the girls felt about broccoli he scrunched his nose at it, making them laugh. Like old times, they ate together as a family and shared stories about their day.

"Where's Monique," Chris asked. "Out with Andrew again?"

"No," Laura said. "She's in her room, not feeling so great today."

"She's crying," said Sophie. "We think she has a broken heart." Tanya nodded in agreement.

Chris moved his chair back and was about to leave the table when Laura motioned for him to sit down, "Let her be. Why don't you finish your dinner and check on her afterwards?"

The girls began discussing the benefits of owning a hamster, their enthusiasm augmented with each point. Chris stayed to deliver his views — the disadvantages of owning any rodent, period.

"You're a party pooper," Sophie said.

"No he's a hamster pooper," Tanya piped in. Both girls laughed hysterically and Chris and Laura looked at each other and smiled.

After dinner, Chris stood at Monique's door and listened but he heard nothing. When he knocked, there was no answer. Opening the door slowly, he peered in and found her lying on the bed, wearing earphones, listening to music. Her eyes were bloodshot, gazing upwards, empty. Maybe he should come back later, he thought, let her spend some time alone, but that would be cowardly; he should at least offer his support.

Monique caught sight of him and pulled off her earphones. "Did Laura tell you?" she asked in a hoarse voice.

"She told me you weren't feeling well."

"She didn't tell you why?"

"No, should she have?" Loosening his tie, he walked over to her.

"Oh, God," Monique said. She wailed like a sick cat and pulled the pillow over her face.

Chris gathered Monique's disheveled clothes piled upon the chair, placed them on the end of the bed and sat down. He'd never seen his daughter that upset and was unsure how to approach her. His instinct was to give her a hug, as he did when she was a child, but this didn't seem the kind of grief that could be consoled by a mere hug. Leaning forward, with his elbows on his knees and hands clasped tightly, he said, "Monique, what's going on?" But she didn't respond. He would sit there all night if that's what it took for her to open up to him.

She grabbed some tissues from her bedside table, blew her nose with a vengeance and wiped her wet face on her duvet cover. With a raspy voice, she finally spoke. "The worst thing has happened." Her sobbing resumed and she couldn't continue.

Chris leaned back, shaking his head in both frustration and worry. Did she get dumped? But who was she dating? Not that Andrew guy; at least they didn't appear that serious. Did she fail some exams? Get in trouble with the law? Smash the car? What could possibly warrant such misery?

Then she blurted out, "I'm pregnant!" Her strained voice cracked between heavy sobs.

No, not possible! What was she talking about? She didn't even have a boyfriend. Chris stared at her in disbelief and breathed in deeply. "What was that? Did I hear you right? Did you say you're pregnant?" For the second time in his life, those words hit him with the force of a blow to the head. She nodded, clenching her teeth. "How did that happen?" What a stupid question, he immediately realized. "I mean, Monique, where was your head? I assume you know about birth control."

She eyed him fearfully, as if he'd slapped her.

"You, of all people," he continued. "One of the smartest young women around, how could you be so—"

Her pensive gaze transformed to anger. "Stupid, irresponsible, crazy, thoughtless, corrupt, brain-dead? You don't need to tell me, Dad."

"I was going to say, negligent." Chris tried to summon his self-control, to calm himself. He walked to the window and put his hand on the glass. Shaking his head, he said, "You're no different than Ken...," he stopped short.

"You mean I'm a flake like my ditsy mother? That woman who dumped you with someone else's child and took off? Is that what you're trying to tell me?" A fire ignited in her eyes.

"That's not what I'm saying." He threw his hands in the air.

"But I know what you're feeling. You despise me as much as you despise her."

"I don't hate your mother."

"You never talk about her. Since the day she left you've acted like she doesn't exist. You want her wiped from our memory."

"That's not true, Monique. It wouldn't even be possible because every time I look at you and every time you speak, I'm reminded of Kendra."

"And it's miserable for you, isn't it?"

Chris struggled to calm his voice. "Listen to me, Monique. First of all, it's not possible to wipe those years from my mind. Secondly, I don't want to. Your mother gave me a gift when I became your father, and believe it or not, I'm grateful to her for that. You have always been the biggest light in my life."

Monique erupted in tears again. "But I don't want to be like her, and I don't want to do to this baby what she did to me, and to you."

Chris sat back down in the chair. "Who's the father?"

"Andrew."

"How do you feel about him?" Chris struggled to refrain from saying what he thought, that she could have at least picked a guy with more substance, more backbone, someone who didn't follow at her heels, hiding behind his shaggy long hair.

"We like each other; he's a good guy but—"

"Have you told him?"

"No."

"You should."

"He'll freak out, Dad. It would ruin his tennis career."

"What tennis career? I thought he went to college with you?"

"He did, but he dropped out. He's on the tennis circuit and goes to tournaments all around the country. Since he doesn't have much money he kind of lives in his van when he travels. We couldn't be together—it would be stupid. And he wants to become professional—it's his dream."

Chris saw his own life flash by: stopping his education, moving back east, and struggling to be a parent far too soon.

"Tell me what to do, Dad? I can't think straight."

He wished he could wrap her in a blanket and carry her to his bed as he had done when she was a little girl, crying from nightmares. But this nightmare was not one he could alleviate with a snuggle and a glass of warm milk. "I'd like to give you advice on this," he said, "but sometimes we have to make life decisions that no one can help us with, Chickpea. You'll have to dig deep to figure things out for yourself. Whatever you decide, I'll support you."

Monique thrust her face against the pillow and wept.

Chris stayed by her side, trying to contain his own emotions. His life seemed to be taking an unforeseen turn towards inexorable failure.

Chapter Twenty-eight

Waiting for the cab to take Camille to the airport, Denise noted how smart her sister looked in her new suit—a grey tailored pinstripe that Denise had insisted on buying her as a thank you. She had also taken Camille to the spa and to have her hair done, a makeover of sorts. The new polished style dispensed with her matronly appearance and Denise couldn't help but take pride in this transformation.

"Donald is going to wonder who the stunning woman is in his house when he gets home from work today," Denise said.

Camille laughed. "Maybe I'll scare him away."

"The total opposite," Denise said with teasing eyes. "I bet he'll be chasing you to the bedroom." She grazed Camille's hair with the tip of her fingers. "You're about ten years younger with these highlights. I don't know why you let the gray take over, and a touch of lipstick makes all the difference."

"You know me, I'm not fussy about appearances."

Denise appreciated that fact about her sister, but she wished she wouldn't take it to such an extreme. Her face was lovely with her mother's smooth skin and warm eyes, and she still had a trim, well-defined figure. To witness such physical potential being obscured by ambivalence was disheartening. "You're gorgeous, Camille. Don't be timid, don't let your looks languish in midlife obscurity," she said, and then realized she had stolen those words, verbatim, from Mimi, *Montreal's Alive's* regular fashion guru.

Camille shrugged, smiling self-consciously. "I'm not a glamour-queen like you. At any rate, I'm pleased that you're doing better,

Denise. I was concerned for a while." She stretched her neck to look out the window for the cab.

"Thanks to your wonderful cooking and care-giving, I feel great. What would I have done without you?" Denise hugged her. "I'm going to miss you, Sis." She had certainly helped her get out of that awful slump. But was Camille now going home to her own slump?

"There's my cab." Camille opened the screen door and waved at the driver. "You give those boys another big hug for me, OK? And take care of yourself." They embraced one more time and she was off.

Sadness engulfed Denise as she watched the cab drive away. The house would be empty without Camille, and less cheery. She stepped outside, locked the front door and walked to the car, thinking about the joyful moments they had shared while reminiscing about their childhood, and the darker moments, when they had wept together, lamenting their newly orphaned state. Camille was like her mother, solid and forthright, and had brought reassurance with her; but she didn't fully understand the extent of Denise's pain. How could she be as connected to their mother, living way over in Wisconsin? Camille had been gone all but a minute and Denise's spirit was already sinking. Thank goodness she had her show to keep her preoccupied; she couldn't be more ready to plunge back into the fray.

When Denise arrived at work, she performed the perfunctory task of greeting the staff and accepting condolences. Finally seated behind her desk, she began to think about life's strange turns. So much had happened in the last two weeks, yet here she was, reviewing the show schedule, clearing messages, making calls – like any normal day. She'd slipped on her talk-show persona the moment she walked into the studio, the place where she'd always been most comfortable.

After she'd dealt with the most pressing issues, she glanced at the topics that had been arranged during her absence. Good. They had gone ahead with the interview with the Mayor of Montreal and his wife – she'd watch that segment later on – and they'd done the Spring Wedding theme and the Seniors in the City' piece. Why was the Readers' Forum' cancelled? The viewers counted on that show the first Monday of every month and would surely be upset if it were cancelled. What book were they going to discuss again? Oh, yes, "The Great Gatsby." And wasn't the well-known literary critic, Professor Johnston, going to be the guest? She had been pleased when he'd agreed to come to share his insights. The theme was going to be 'The decline of Western Civilization then and now" — a topic that was sure to have elicited an interesting discussion. Denise checked the agenda for tomorrow's show. 'Spring and summer fashion trends,' a small fashion show with the regular experts, including Mimi, giving their commentary. No problem; little preparation would be required, and instead she could focus on the upcoming agenda. A knock at the door broke her contemplation and shifted her attention to Nicole, standing in the doorway, uncharacteristically pensive.

"Hello, Nicole," Denise said. "Come on in."

Nicole stood at the doorway with unusual reserve. "How are you doing? I know you've had a rough ride with your mother's passing and...oh, you must be raked."

"It hasn't been the greatest time of my life, but the best remedy for me is to get back to work."

Nicole nodded empathetically. "Your mother was a cool lady. She always had something nice to say to me when she came to the studio."

"She was a positive person." Denise noticed Nicole fidgeting with her bracelet and gestured for her to sit down. "Your hair is different, more sophisticated."

"They've been straightening it for the show." She laughed. "Gary thought my locks were too out-of-control for TV." She swept her hair to the side, playfully striking a movie-star pose. "I've had a lot of fun on the set. I never knew interviewing would be such a blast."

Denise stared at her, incredulous.

"Don't get me wrong," Nicole continued. "I take it all very seriously and I spend hours preparing."

Until recently, Nicole would come on stage during tapings to make an occasional introduction, or to lend a hand when one was needed, but she hadn't full-out hosted the show. When Denise had spoken to Gary about taking some time off, he'd said that they'd hire various Montreal 'personalities' to guest-host during her absence. There had been no mention of Nicole filling in. Denise stood up and leaned against her desk, wishing she had a cigarette for the first time in years. "Good for you," she said. "I'm glad you've had a chance to gain some experience."

"Tomorrow we've got the fashionistas on. I can't wait to do that show."

Denise shuffled her papers and looked at Nicole, stone-faced. "But Nicole, I'm back now. I'll be doing the show tomorrow."

Nicole avoided Denise's eyes. "But I've worked really hard on this segment. I even had a hand in the clothing selection. It's all been arranged. We weren't expecting you back quite yet and—"

"I see." Denise thought for a moment. Maybe it wouldn't be such a terrible thing to take a few days to access the situation. Nicole could have Mimi and the mindless banter. "All right, you can host tomorrow since you've done all the groundwork."

"Thank you, Denise." Nicole seemed enormously relieved.

"You're welcome. Before you go, Nicole, a quick question— what happened to the Readers' Forum?"

Nicole got up from her seat. "Oh, it was cancelled because we needed some fresh material, the other stuff was getting stale. I suggested doing a segment on 'Trampolining, the New Fitness Rage' instead. It was awesome!"

Denise stopped herself from scowling. Why would they chop a piece so integral to the show to fill it with fluffy fitness antics? "How inventive," she said, and feigned a smile. When Nicole left her office, Denise called Gary. Things hadn't gone quite as smoothly as she had been led to believe. She had been gone less than two weeks and in that short period, 'Montreal's Alive' had become a circus.

"Hey, Denise. Good to have you back," Gary said.

"Thanks. And thank you for the beautiful flower arrangement you sent on behalf of the network for my mother's funeral. It was very thoughtful."

"Don't mention it. I feel for you—damn lousy thing to happen."

"But I'm back, and I want to get to work immediately, before this show falls into complete disarray. I had time to think while I was gone and I've come up with interesting new ideas to—"

"That's great. That's really great. Glad to hear it, Denise." She could hear him tapping on his computer keyboard as they spoke. "And it's cool to have you back. I mean, the place doesn't rock as much without you."

Could he not speak with a little more sophistication than a sophomore? He was beginning to sound like Nicole. And he was in his thirties, for heaven's sake. "Can we meet to discuss next week's topics? I'd like to start preparing—"

"Well, you see, Denise," he cleared his throat, "we didn't know when you were coming back and we went ahead and designed next week's programming with Nicole in mind."

"OK. I understand that. But I'm back now and I'm not going anywhere. You can keep this week's plan in place but there's plenty of time to change the items for next week." Wonderful. Not only did he plan to keep Nicole in the limelight, but he was buying into her ridiculous ideas. Trampolining! What was he thinking?

There was silence on the other end of the phone. Then Gary coughed. "Listen, Denise, I'd like to keep her out there a while longer, while she's got this momentum thing happening."

"Excuse me?" Denise said, gritting her teeth

"We're already reaching a wider audience, a younger crowd. It's a good thing for the show." He coughed again. "Look, I'm surprised too. I had no idea that Nicole would be such a wild hit. But I tell you, they loved her, lapped her up."

Another bombshell. "What's going on here, Gary?" She laughed with purposeful insincerity. "This is all too much. I think a serious meeting is—"

"I gotta go, I'm swamped here. I'll come by your office early next week and we can discuss it further, OK?"

Denise took a deep breath. "Fine, I'll talk to you later." She set down the phone and sat motionless. What was he talking about? Absolutely, they should branch out to attract a younger audience, but Nicole didn't have the experience to host the show on her own. Denise's eyes darted around the room. Where was her purse? She found it behind the door, which Nicole had left open. She closed the door, resisting her temptation to slam it. Something strange was happening and she'd have to get to the bottom of it right away. She rifled through her purse and found her pills. After taking one, she slumped back down in her chair.

Feeling the urge to speak to Chris, she picked up the phone, but didn't dial; it was almost noon, probably not a good time for him. They hadn't been in contact since their rendezvous in Cleveland four days earlier, except for one quick phone call the next day. His soothing and restorative voice was what she needed, a mental massage that would get her through the rest of the day. But would that be enough? Now that their relationship had escalated, her need for him was more intense. She wanted him this instant, at least a part of him—a moment of him. But she knew that a brief conversation would not satiate her; it would wear off within a few hours and then she'd crave him again, like a drug. Did he feel the same way? She scrolled through her messages.

Nothing from Chris.

She would not contact him. She would wait for him to make the next move.

She sat for five minutes, then wrote:

Hi Chris. My first day back at the studio has hardly been splendid. I'd never have expected that my short absence could result in such turmoil. I hope your day is going better than mine. Write me when you have a minute. I'm still thinking of last Thursday and I'm wondering how we should follow up. D.

Hmm. Should she dare be that presumptuous? But then, he had been as emotionally involved as she, hadn't he? She closed her eyes and imagined herself with Chris sitting on that bench in the middle of nowhere, in their surreal world. Recalling that scene was like a form of meditation—she could almost smell the trees and the fresh air, and see the river ripple in the gentle breeze. When she opened her eyes, she pressed 'send.'

Denise left the TV studio earlier than she'd planned because there was no point staying around when the itinerary had been set for the week. Gary was clearly unwilling to make any revisions and she didn't have the energy to fight him—not today. By next week, she'd get them all back on track. Deciding to drop in on Francois at the construction site, she left the building without saying good-bye to anyone. Francois would appreciate the visit since she hadn't been to the site yet, which he'd pointed out to her more than once. She'd surprise him with a double espresso and an apple tart, and he could give her a tour and explain the plans. And if she still had time, she would surprise the boys by picking them up after school, something she'd not yet managed to do that year, despite her intentions. She'd take them out for pizza and hear all about their day. Once in the car, Denise was bolstered by her mission. With windows down and a gentle cross-draft sweeping her hair against her neck, she momentarily felt free and unencumbered.

Buying coffees was not the simple task she had anticipated. Having been out of the public eye since her mother's death, and being unknown in Cleveland, she'd almost forgotten how intrusive people could be. Some days they'd merely glance her way, respecting her privacy, and other days they'd bombard her with friendly chatter. As she walked along the street, one person asked where she'd been in the last two weeks, and another stopped her to say, "I like your haircut. Makes you look younger." Denise tried to be gracious and receptive to the remarks, but inwardly she was irritated by the interruptions, much more than usual.

An elderly woman wouldn't let her out the door of the coffee shop. "You are even lovelier in real life," she said, with a strong brogue. "You remind me of my best friend in Ireland, from my youth. She had shoulder-length hair like yours, the same charcoal colour, exactly." The woman swept her hand through Denise's hair. "And she had a blazing personality, everybody loved her. She'd be eighty if she were alive, you know. But she was killed by a bomb on her way to the shop one day." The lady's eyes darted around as if to see if anyone was listening. "IRA," she whispered. "My, she was a beauty."

Not having the heart to interrupt the woman's monologue, Denise nodded with sympathy. Eventually, she tried to extricate herself by interjecting, "Maybe we'll do a segment on the effects of Northern Ireland's struggles on women. These kinds of issues are important to bring to the forefront."

"Yes, dear," the lady said. "You are a splitting image of my friend. What a fine lass she was."

Denise said good-bye and made her escape, but when she reached her car a middle-aged woman addressed her.

"Denise Gagnon, is that you?" The woman stepped between Denise and her car door and pulled a younger woman to her side. "We love you! This is my daughter." She took the girl's arm and shoved her towards Denise. "We went to see your show the other day, waited weeks for tickets you know, but then you weren't there. We were awfully disappointed, weren't we, Simone?" The girl nodded, embarrassed. "Instead, that Nicole gal came out and I thought, who on earth is that? But she was hilarious. We laughed the whole time. Now my daughter wants to buy one of those trampolines. Maybe I'll even try it!" She winked at the girl.

"Excuse me, but I have to run," Denise said, holding up the cooling coffees as evidence. She had hoped that one of the women would open the car door for her since her hands were full, but the mother pulled her daughter along and waved good-bye.

When Denise arrived at the building site she was surprised by the extent to which the structure had been demolished. Scaffolding surrounded the exterior, now a mere shell. Inside, sheets of wood, tools, and various building materials were strewn about, forcing her to navigate her way carefully towards the back corner, where Francois was speaking to some workers in hard hats. Building plans were spread out on a huge makeshift table and the men huddled around, in serious discussion. Francois didn't notice her presence until she tripped over some two-by-fours, causing an enormous crash with boards falling against her. One of the workers ran to help her recover from her near-fall and another removed the planks surrounding her.

"Are you all right?" he asked. He took the coffees, which had hardly spilled thanks to the plastic lids, and she brushed the dust and dirt from her pants.

"I'm fine. Thank you," she said to the worker, taking the coffees from him. She gestured to Francois who was watching the commotion from the back of the building. "How did you like my grand entrance?" she shouted across the room.

He didn't say anything until she approached. "This is a surprise, what brings you by?"

She detected a slight tone of annoyance in his voice. "I thought I'd come to encourage a coffee break, can you take a moment?"

The men he'd been talking to dispersed, but stood in earshot as they waited for instructions. Francois smiled at Denise when she passed him the coffee.

"Thanks. I guess I could use a break. What's up?"

"Apart from the fact that Nicole has usurped my job, nothing much."

Francois gesticulated to the men to give him two minutes. "How'd that come about?"

"Gary said that she's on a roll, playing host, and that she's tapping into a new, younger market. He wants to see if she can maintain the momentum. Frankly, I think she'll fall flat on her face. I can't believe that their new, shallow, approach will hold ground." She took a sip and made a face. "This is awful, it's cold," she said as her eyes searched for a garbage bin.

"I have to get back to work, Denise, the guys are waiting. We'll talk more when I get home, all right?"

"Yes, of course. I'm sorry. I guess I intruded here. The renovation is coming along nicely." She glanced around, feeling out of place. "See you tonight." She was conscious of the men's curious stares as she passed by, carefully making her way through construction maze.

If traffic was still moving well, Denise could get to the school in time to greet the children. She looked forward to catching the boys off-guard and seeing their reaction. A free afternoon was a luxury, which is how, she suddenly decided, she would try to view her imposed absence.

When she arrived, the school bus was parked at the side entrance, the same place as the year before. Denise parked the car across the street and walked towards the school gates to wait for the boys to emerge. The bell rang and she congratulated herself for being on time. From one moment to the next, the empty school yard transformed into a bustling field of noisy children running every-which-way, like ants scurrying about. She searched for familiar faces amongst the swarm of uniformed boys.

After waiting and watching for ten minutes, she turned her attention to the school bus. Many children had already boarded, and after the remaining stragglers climbed in, the driver shut the doors. Where were her boys? Through the windows she caught sight of Thomas, then Martin. How had she missed them? Realizing the bus was about to leave, she tried to catch the driver's attention as he yelled at the students to sit down. She tapped on the door but he didn't notice; he was preoccupied watching for cars in his side-view mirror. When the bus pulled away, Denise ran in front and waved frantically, causing him to slam on the brakes. He opened the door and threw up his hands.

"Lady, you try' in to get yourself killed?" he said, in a rough Quebecois dialect.

She was out of breath. "My children. I came to pick them up to-day, but I must have missed them," she said in Parisian French. "They somehow got on the bus without me seeing them."

"Quoi?" he snapped.

Her accent must have caught him unawares. She repeated her words, speaking slowly.

"All right, get them off, but make it quick, will you? I'm on a tight schedule here."

Denise climbed aboard and stood at the front. The noise level was so high, and the children so rambunctious that she felt like she was in a sports arena. Since she couldn't get her sons' attention, she called out, "Thomas, Martin!" Neither responded. Instead of raising her voice even louder, she walked towards the back of the bus until they saw her.

"Mom," Luc said. "What are you doing here?"

"I came to pick you up, let's go." They collected their backpacks, following her with reluctance.

When they got to the car, Thomas said, "I can't believe what you just did, Mom. That was the worst thing ever." He threw his back-pack in the car and got in.

"Yeah, Mom. That was sooo embarrassing. Mothers don't come on the bus," Luc said.

"Sorry, but I thought you'd be happy if I came to pick you up." She fastened Martin's seat belt and gave him a kiss, the only kid not complaining—her baby.

"You should have told us you were coming," Thomas said. "You made us look stupid in front of all the other kids. Now we're gonna get it tomorrow." He crossed his arms and stared out the window.

"What do mean, 'get it?"

"They're gonna call us Momma's boys. I'm not taking the bus ever again," Luc said.

Denise clutched the steering wheel and clenched her teeth. This had turned out to be a fine day indeed. The pizza idea was out. No, they certainly didn't deserve a treat. Not after that unpleasant episode. When they got home, the boys raced to the house, dumped their bags on the floor at the entrance, leaving Denise standing in the foyer, alone.

Clara walked by, carrying a load of laundry. "Oh, hello. You startled me. You're home earlier than I expected."

Even Clara seemed disturbed by her presence today. Denise dropped her work tote on the heap of backpacks. "I'm not feeling great. Would you mind getting the boys an early dinner and supervising their homework? I think I'll lie down for a while." She walked past Clara without waiting for a reply. Instead of going upstairs, she went to the study, closed the door and checked for messages on the computer. Her mood lifted when she saw an e-mail from Chris. She opened it with anticipation, hoping for some friendly words from someone in her corner.

Hi Denise, we need to talk. Please call me. Chris

What an odd message. Denise read it several times in an attempt to decipher the tone. He'd still be at work, perhaps now would be a good time to call. She punched in his cell phone number.

"Chris Lambert here." He sounded stressed.

"It's Denise. I got your e-mail. Do you have time to talk?" She felt a pinching sensation, like tweezers plucking at her nerves.

"Yes, but I was about to go to a meeting, we'll have to be quick."

"How are things?" she asked.

"Not good. Not good at all."

His serious tone took her aback. "What is it? What's wrong?"

"I've got some problems."

"Oh?"

"It's my daughter, Monique. She's pregnant."

Phew. For a moment she thought he was going say that it was over between them. Then the gravity of his situation struck her. "Oh, no. What's she going to do?"

"Who knows? Frankly, I don't have a clue how to advise her. She's just finishing college and this could blow her whole future."

Denise held her breath while her mind raced. What if Monique had the baby and Denise and Chris raised it together? They could be like surrogate parents. Monique could finish school and still see the baby whenever she wanted. They could move away somewhere, where no one knew them, like Seattle. Was she going crazy?

"What a difficult situation for you all," she said. "There's no easy answer in a case like this. She must be petrified."

"She's beside herself. I told her I'd support her, no matter what."

"Which is all you can do," Denise said.

"And that brings me to another point, Denise." His voice faltered. "I think it would be for the best if we didn't communicate for a while. I mean, I want to talk to you, and especially see you, but things are getting out of control on the home front—I've got to focus on my family right now. Do you know what I mean?"

Denise dropped the phone. She was not expecting this. Was he calling it quits? Hardly able to breathe, she stared at the phone on the floor for a second and then picked it up. In a clear and composed voice she said, "I suppose."

Chris didn't respond right away. She could hear him breathing on the other end, and then a weary sigh. "You're very important to me... shit, this is hard to say, but I'm getting too...uh...attached or something. It's getting complicated...we're getting complicated."

He was right, how could she not agree? But to sever all communications? She felt as if she had been stabbed. He was jilting her and they weren't even lovers, at least not technically.

"I've been thinking the same thing. My life is overwhelming too, it's probably wise to back off from this—well, whatever it is we have going." Don't cry, don't cry, she kept repeating to herself.

"So you agree? We should take a breather, at least for a while?"

'What's a while?' she wanted to ask. A few days, a few weeks, a year? Or was this his way of saying they were finished? "Yes, right, no more communication, it's for the best." Meanwhile, her heart plummeted and her entire body seized up. Perhaps this was his way of casting her off, gently. "Good luck with your daughter, I hope things work out for her." She couldn't talk a second longer. "Take care, Chris," she said with as much composure as possible. She hung up the phone. Now what? How was she going to face tomorrow and the day after that? She stared at the phone with loathing.

Chapter Twenty-nine

Laura reviewed the credit card bill one more time and circled an item. Those flowers couldn't have been for the funeral because they had been purchased several weeks earlier. Who had they sent flowers to in Montreal? $200 to 'La Maison du Jardin?' Hmm, that would be quite the bouquet. She'd have to ask Chris about the charge; but then, maybe the credit card company had made a mistake. She pushed the bill aside and continued with her accounting, something she did at the beginning of each month. Covering her mouth, she yawned. Paying the bills and doing the household accounting had become the most challenging thing she did these days. How had she let her brainpower slip away into domestic oblivion? The parent council at the school had been interesting at first, but after a while, those fundraising events had become redundant and too political. She'd thought office politics were behind her when she left the workforce, but no, they were as rampant as ever — at school, at church, even at her book club.

Perhaps she should contemplate going back to work; the girls were becoming more independent and the house was as renovated as it would ever get. Something part-time. Management-consulting was not an option given the long hours and constant travel. Traipsing around the country on business had been exciting at the beginning of her career, but after a few years, it had become grueling. By then she had welcomed the possibility of settling down with Chris and starting a family. After ten years at home, though, she was finding domestic life almost as taxing. Chris and she had developed a division of labour that made perfect sense, was efficient, but ultimately left her unsatisfied. She could hardly blame him; he'd always been supportive, offering to hire a housekeeper, a babysitter, a gardener—whatever she needed. Somehow the thought of strange people in her house wandering about, performing tasks that she knew she could do better herself, had been unthinkable. She had more than she could ask for: wonderful children, a beautiful home, and a lifestyle to be envied; however, none of those things fulfilled her any more. Laura pulled her fingers through her hair, as if raking away her shameful thoughts.

Monique entered the kitchen and went to the fridge. Laura watched her get a drink from the fridge and a bowl from the cupboard and wondered if Monique's slight stomach bulge was purely her imagination. Lately, they had both avoided the topic, going about their days as if nothing had changed. What could she possibly say to Monique, her step-daughter? But how long could they ignore the elephant in the room? Laura bit down on her lip and asked, "How are you feeling?"

Monique turned with a start. "Laura, hi. I didn't see you there. I guess I'm OK. I get a little nauseous in the mornings and tired some days."

"Do you need anything, I mean, can I help in any way?" Laura couldn't begin to imagine Monique's inner turmoil, but what could *she* do about it, how could *she* diminish the anguish?

"No, but thanks."

"Have you come closer to making a decision?"

"According to the doctor, I'm not even two months pregnant, which means I still have some time to decide. This might sound wonky, but I'm hoping I'll wake up one morning with the answer."

Laura moved her chair to face Monique. "You think you'll have some kind of epiphany in your sleep and that's how you'll make your decision, a decision that will affect you for the rest of your life?"

"Uh-huh. That's why I'm not fretting too much."

How naïve, Laura thought. Either Monique was in denial or she was paralyzed with fear. Chris would have to talk to her. "If there's anything I can do to help, please let me know." She tried to convey compassion while hiding her frustration.

"Thank you," Monique said. She poured a bowl of cereal, and was about to leave the kitchen with it, but then put it back down on the counter. "Not enough milk," she said, and poured so generously that the milk almost overflowed. "Oops, too much." She bent her head over the bowl and slurped from the edge.

Laura watched with wonder. How on earth would this girl manage as a mother? At times she was like a fourteen-year-old in a twenty-one-year-old body. Yet other times Laura was amazed at Monique's maturity—at her clarity of mind. She was at that age of coming into one's own, feeling confusion, yet exuding incredible confidence.

Monique wiped the counter with a cloth, where she had spilled a few drops of milk. "I'm watching a video of the talk show that Dad's going to be on, for that wine discussion. Have you seen it?"

"What talk show? He didn't mention anything to me."

"I can't believe he didn't tell you. He was asked to be a guest on this show in Montreal, to talk about wine collecting or something. The network sent him some tapes to check out the show's format."

"Interesting."

"I think it would be cool for him to be on TV, don't you? Do you want to watch with me?"

"I don't know. I've got the bills to finish and grocery shopping to do before the girls get home."

"Oh, come on. It'll be fun." She put her cereal bowl on a tray and walked out of the kitchen. Laura followed.

"I'll rewind it back to the beginning," Monique said.

Laura sat on the sofa and made herself comfortable, nestling into the over-stuffed cushions. Spending time together was rare these days because Monique was always running out the door. With the girls at school, and peace in the house, Laura quite liked the notion of lounging in front of the television, something she'd never do on her own. Playing daytime hooky, taking a hiatus from her house-keeping chores and her to-do list, felt decadent.

"That's the host of the show," Monique said, pointing at the television screen. "Denise something."

An attractive woman with dark brown shoulder length hair stood behind a counter beside a man wearing a white apron, cook-ing on a make-shift stove. She was striking in a crisp white blouse with an over-sized collar. A string of white pearls drew Laura's attention to her long, lean neck and her classic features. Laura thought she looked European, perhaps Italian.

"They're making crêpes," Monique said. "He's a chef from some fancy restaurant in Montreal. 'Le Papipon or Papillion' or something like that."

Laura watched as the attractive woman laughed in response to the chef's insistence that she make the next crêpe. "I lived in France for many years but I never mastered the art of crêpe making," she said. She tied her hair back with a clip, rolled up her long white sleeves and changed places with the chef. "Here goes," she said as she poured batter into the pan.

"Too much, too much!" the chef shouted. "You're not making a giant pancake here, you're making a crêpe.

"I knew this wasn't a good idea," the woman said sheepishly. "How about we ask a member from the audience to come up and try."

Laura noticed a large dimple on her right cheek when she smiled. There was something very glamorous yet good-natured about the woman. "Not your father's type though," she said.

"Pardon me?" Monique said.

"Oh, nothing. I was just thinking out loud."

For the rest of the program Laura watched the woman's movements, particularly her facial expressions. The sounds fell to the background of her mind as she half-observed the rest of the cooking segment. Something like sliced apples or pears was simmering with lemon and sugar and then the chef assembled the dessert, asking her to scoop some vanilla ice cream onto the finished product. "This I can do," she said.

"Yumm," Monique said. "Doesn't that apple crêpe look amazing, Laura? I can almost smell the cinnamon."

"Pardon?...Oh, yes. Delicious."

Monique stopped the tape. "So, what do you think? Should Dad go on that show? He could do like a wine-tasting thing. I think it would be a hoot."

"I've never heard of this show before. How did your dad get mixed up with it?"

"I think that lady, the host of the show, is an old friend from school or something, I'm not entirely clear on the story."

"What's her name again?"

"Denise something. But did you like it?"

"I suppose." She had to admit that she liked the woman's style—intelligent and good-humoured. And there was something very classy about her.

While the theme music played, Laura watched the credits and saw the name Denise Gagnon spelled out on the screen. Why was it familiar?

"If Dad does do the show, then you should go to cheer him on. In fact, we should all go." Monique turned off the television with the remote and scanned the TV guide.

"We'll see." Laura stood up and gazed at the blank screen. Then it clicked. That was the woman whose mother had died; she was the reason Chris had left San Francisco early. But why hadn't Chris mentioned that she had asked him to appear on her show? He hadn't said a word about it.

"Back to my bills," Laura said to Monique. "The girls will be home from school soon." She went to the kitchen to get a cold drink and to finish her administrative work, but instead of opening the fridge, she pulled a bottle of red wine from the wine rack, opened it, and poured herself a generous glass.

****

When Chris arrived home, Pepper leaped at his knees, playfully nipping at his trousers. Chris leaned over and rubbed behind the dog's ears. "Hey pup," he said, "where is everybody?" He found the girls watching television in the family room, but they were too preoccupied with their show to pay him much attention. Expecting to find Laura in the kitchen cleaning up after dinner, he instead found an uncharacteristic mess. Dirty dishes covered the counters and a pot sat on the stove containing macaroni and cheese remnants, caked to the bottom. Chris checked the fridge, wondering if Laura had prepared a plate for him as she often did when he worked late, but he found nothing.

"Where's Mom?" he called to the children over the TV racket.

"In her room," Tanya said.

He went upstairs and discovered Laura in the brightly lit bedroom, lying on the bed, fully dressed and asleep. Quietly, he changed from his work clothes and turned all the lights off. She hadn't been sick in the morning but maybe she was overtired, or had caught a bug. Many people at the office had colds; it was that time of year, and Marnie had just gotten over her flu. Chris rounded up the girls and read them a story after tucking them in bed. They thanked him profusely, which made him realize how important this ritual was, and how neglectful he'd been of late. After lying with each daughter for a short time, he went back to the kitchen to get some dinner. The counter was so cluttered that he couldn't find space to make a sandwich. Cleaning up took longer than he antici-pated because he had to unload the dishwasher before he could load the dirty dishes. He didn't know where half the items belonged and spent a great deal of time going through the cupboards, attempting to put each item in its rightful place. When he dropped an apple juice can into the recycle bin, he noticed an empty red wine bottle with a familiar label. He removed the bottle and stared at it in disbelief. "Holy shit!" The Margaux that he was supposed to store for Tony. Where could he find a replacement? New York? Boston perhaps? Not likely in Cleveland. He'd have to phone around. And he'd have to shell out a good $700 for that vintage, maybe more. Chris had noticed the bottle on the kitchen wine rack numerous times and had intended to bring it to the cellar, but somehow he'd never got around to it. Damn!

When it came to making his dinner, he was faced with another challenge. The bread in the breadbox was moldy and there was only one egg left in the egg carton—so much for a sandwich or scram-bled eggs and toast. He decided on cereal, but when he went to pour the milk, about a tablespoon trickled out of the container. Laura must be really unwell, he thought. Mess everywhere, nothing good to eat. Checking the pantry, he found a can of baked beans, not his first choice, but better than nothing. After polishing off the entire can of cold beans with a glass of orange juice, he tossed the can into the bin and put his dirty dishes in the dishwasher. At least there weren't any more pots and pans to clean. Not in the mood to work, Chris dragged himself to the study to prepare for an early morning meeting.

How long had it been since he had last spoken to Denise? Less than two weeks he calculated, but it seemed like months. He thought he'd be able to will his mind away from her, but he couldn't do it. He just couldn't do it. What if he called her and left her a short message, saying that he was thinking of her? No. He'd been the one to cut off contact, after all. But he longed to connect, to hear how she was doing and to find out if she was missing him too. His mind wandered back to their afternoon together in the country and he tried to push those thoughts away. The effort was futile, for the more he tried, the more persistent they were. He hadn't slept with Denise for twenty-five years but in a strange way, he felt as though they'd made love during their last encounter. His desire wasn't merely physical; it was the compilation of powerful, inexplicable emotions that kept pulling him back to her. What was he to do with those feelings, pack them up and put them aside? No solution was at hand, and no respite. He opened his e-mail file and began typing.

Dear D,

I know I said we shouldn't be in contact, but the last couple of weeks have been brutal not being able to communicate with you. I think of you all the time, in spite of myself. I know this break is the right thing to do, but I don't know if I can continue this way. My love for you is...

How could he possibly send this? He sounded like a love-sick teenager, pining over an unattainable girl. Humiliated, he closed the document. Why had he entered into this undefined relationship with Denise, and let her soak into his soul, when she had no justifiable place in his life? Attempting to address his paperwork, his stubborn mind kept wandering off to places it had not right to go. Eventually, having made insignificant progress with his work, he went to bed.

Chris woke to the piercing sound of his alarm clock at 6:00 a.m. and turned towards Laura, lying beside him on her back, unfazed by the noise. Her pale and lifeless form brought to mind the image of his dead cousin's body exposed in a casket. Terror ripped through him as he recalled hearing how she had died one night, in her sleep, after suffering a brain aneurysm. He nudged Laura's shoulder, which caused her to grumble and roll on her side. Immense relief released him from his sense of foreboding; for a swift moment, his wife was dead. He reached for his glasses on the night table and, before getting out of bed, watched Laura sleep, tempted to wrap his arms around her and feel the rhythm of her breathing against his chest.

Chris carefully slipped out of bed, not wanting to disturb her just yet—she'd be up before long to get the girls ready for school. But after he'd showered and dressed, and reviewed his agenda in the study, Laura had not made an appearance. As gently as he could, he tried to wake her by whispering her name and tapping her gently. Pulling the covers over her head, she muttered, "I have a migraine." Laura had never suffered from migraines before, but Chris knew how debilitating they could be. He looked at his watch—7:10 a.m., twenty minutes to get to the office for the strategy meeting. No way would he make it with Laura out of commission.

Tanya and Sophie came into their parents' room, sleepy-eyed and hungry. Chris told them that their mother was unwell and instructed them to get dressed. They scurried away without argument. He considered waking Monique to get the girls breakfast and off to school, but remembering how weary she'd been lately, he refrained.

In the kitchen, Chris rummaged through the cupboards thinking cereal would be quick and simple, but then recalled that there was no milk. A few individual packages of oatmeal lay loosely on a shelf—oatmeal, it would have to be. Since the orange juice container in the fridge was almost empty, he grabbed a can of frozen juice from the freezer and thawed it out in the microwave. By the time he had found the pitcher, mixed the juice up and prepared the oatmeal, the girls were dressed and sitting at the table. They had to be out the door in twenty minutes.

"Yuck, I hate porridge," Sophie said.

"It's not porridge, it's oatmeal," Chris said, hoping to create a diversion.

"I hate that too!"

"Eat it and don't complain, you don't have much time."

"This juice is too watery," Tanya complained.

280

"Tough!" he said.

Within seconds, orange juice was flooding the table and dripping onto the floor. "Don't be mad, don't be mad!" Tanya cried, squeezing her eyes shut, "It was an accident."

His cell phone rang from another room and Chris rushed about, trying to locate it. When he found the phone in yesterday's jacket pocket, the ringing had stopped. Checking the menu, he noticed he'd missed several calls. Already, they were hunting him down. With all that was happening at work, he couldn't afford to be late. When the girls had finished picking at their breakfast, and Tanya had mopped up the spill with paper towels, Chris corralled them to the bathroom to brush their teeth.

"Why aren't you girls wearing your uniforms?" he asked.

"It's freestyle day today," Tanya said.

"But isn't your dress a bit fancy for school?" he asked Sophie.

"Yeah, Soph, you're not going to a birthday party," Tanya said.

"I don't care, I like this dress. Mommy would let me wear it!"

"No way, she would," Tanya countered. She suddenly noticed that juice had spilled down the front of her top. "I have to change," she said, fretfully.

"There's no time. Brush your teeth and get your backpacks," Chris said, exasperated. "You'll miss the bus if you don't hurry."

The bus arrived at precisely 7:40, when they were putting on their shoes, and Chris kissed them as they ran out the door. His cell phone rang again. Where the heck had he put it? This time he caught the call.

"Where are you, Lambert? We're waiting for you?"

"Go ahead without me, Tony, I've been detained. Fill me in later, OK?"

Monique walked into the kitchen, her face blotchy and her hair disheveled. "Hey, Dad."

"Morning. How are you?"

"OK, I guess."

"I need to talk to you about your plans."

She made a face. "Now?"

"Yes."

"It's too early in the morning," she groaned.

"Then when do you suggest we talk? You're never here in the evenings and I hardly ever see you. Do I need to book an appointment with you?"

"Good idea."

Chris banged his hand on the counter. "Don't be snarky with me. Sit down and talk to me."

She sat down at the kitchen table and crossed her arms.

"First of all, have you told Andrew yet?"

She shook her head.

"And when do you propose to do so?"

"When the time feels right."

"Have you made any decisions as to what you're going to do?"

Again she shook her head. Chris pulled out the chair across from her and sat down. "You can't be complacent about this, Monique, you have to make some serious decisions — and soon."

"I know, Dad, you don't have to tell me that." She started stacking the dishes on the table.

"What about the counsellor the doctor recommended, have you seen her yet?"

"No."

Chris was about to yell but held back. Cursing under his breath, he got up from the table and said as calmly as he could, "You can't ignore what's happening, Monique. This is your life we're talking about, and another life."

Monique sniffled and Chris's phone rang again. He grabbed it from the counter, checked to see who was calling and slammed it down, unanswered. "I don't want to upset you, but you're running out of time."

"No, I'm not, I still have a few weeks," she said, whimpering like a child. "Just leave me alone." She got up from the table and ran out of the kitchen. Chris grabbed his briefcase and marched out the front door.

****

By the time Laura dragged herself downstairs it was almost noon. Her housecoat hung open over her pajamas and she hadn't brushed her hair. She couldn't even bear to look in the mirror. The aspirins she had taken, when she first awoke, had relieved some of the pain shooting through her head while she lay in bed feeling like a wreck. The breakfast mess in the kitchen confronted her like a rude assault making her want to retreat to her bed. She put on some coffee and slowly cleared the table, the soles of her slippers sticking to the juice-splattered floor. Spotting Chris's cell phone on the table amidst the breakfast dishes, she had the fleeting thought of throwing on some clothes and rushing it over to his office. But her throbbing head squelched the idea.

She poured herself a cup of coffee and popped a piece of bread in the toaster, ignoring the light green spots on the crust. The milk carton was empty, compelling her to drink her coffee black, which she'd normally consider repugnant. She sat down on a stool at the kitchen island, about to read the newspaper, when Chris's phone rang. Picking it up, she debated whether or not to answer, but it stopped ringing before she had decided. She pressed the menu button to view the names and numbers programmed into the phone and found hers at the top of the list. She scrolled through the other names and numbers, most of which were unfamiliar. Then she came across 'Denise Gagnon.' That name was appearing a little too often these days—first the funeral, then the TV show, and now programmed into his phone? What was going on? Laura dropped the phone on the counter and stared into space. Chris's behaviour had been strange lately, and his mood uncharacteristically volatile. And what about that cozy little hug with Sonya? No, she couldn't deny any longer that something was going on with him.

Chapter Thirty

Denise sat in the front row, listening to the energetic buzz around her as the audience anticipated Nicole's stage entrance. She had arrived early to avoid attention, an unnecessary tactic given the excitement surrounding the 'celebrity' theme that day. She had even worn a baseball cap with her hair tucked underneath, sunglasses, jeans and an 'I Love New York' tee-shirt, in an attempt to conceal her identity. While she waited for 'Montreal's Alive' to begin, she couldn't help overhearing a conversation in the second row.

"I can't wait to see Donna Douglas in person," the woman behind her said.

"Me too. It's one thing to read her column in 'The Montreal Sunrise,' but quite another to see her live," said her friend.

"I wonder if she'll be as crude and sassy as she is in her articles."

Denise had met Donna Douglas only once. She wrote a gossip column for a tabloid that claimed to be a serious newspaper with an edge—a rag that Denise had no respect for, with its bizarre and misleading slants on current events. Donna D, as she was often called, claimed to have inside information on celebrities' lives and her observations were often scathing and callous.

"Shhhh," someone murmured in Denise's row, "I think it's about to start."

Unrecognizable theme music played and the announcer bellowed his introduction. "Welcome to "Montreal Living!"

Denise gripped the arms of her seat. *Montreal Living*? What happened to *Montreal's Alive*? Bernard must have made a mistake, must be losing his marbles. She looked around but didn't see a reaction from anyone else in the audience. Her list of items to discuss with Gary was expanding by the minute.

Nicole scampered to the front of the stage. She wore a funky outfit: tight black pants and a zebra-striped halter top. Her hair was tied back with a matching ribbon and she wore black shoes with heels that Denise couldn't imagine standing in, let alone walking in. The audience exploded with applause.

"Hey!" Nicole yelled over the clapping. "How y'all doin' today?"

Denise cringed.

"Aren't you a hip group!" She spoke for a few minutes about a silly incident that had happened to her at a bistro the night before and the audience howled. Then she told a few jokes, like a stand-up comedienne, gesticulating with her body as she spoke.

Denise stared at the stage, incredulous; Nicole was making a mockery of her show. Nicole introduced Donna Douglas, who strutted in wearing a bright orange body suit and black stilettos. Her long black hair hung loosely, which, along with her performance make-up and outfit, reminded Denise of the costumes worn in the musical production, 'Cats.' This had to be a farce. The two women sat down on stools facing the audience, and began bantering about who wore the funkiest outfit. After a few minutes they solicited the audience's opinion, asking for a show of hands.

This was too much. Denise scanned the exits, nausea inciting her to flee. All the doors were at the back and escape was impossible without drawing attention to herself. Watching such a spectacle for an entire hour would be torture. But she had no choice; she was captive. The rest of the show focused on celebrity gossip, most of which was denigrating and obviously exaggerated. The audience lapped it up, reacting with claps and hisses at various sensationalist revelations. Denise scanned the crowd. These were not her people, her audience. Who were they? When the show ended, Denise was the first person to dash out the door, and in a near frenzy, she rushed to her office to call Gary. When he didn't answer, she called his cell.

"Gary Evans."

Noise and commotion filtered through the connection, indicating that he was still backstage. "Gary, it's Denise. I have to talk to you."

"Can't talk now. How 'bout you call Jane and make an appointment."

"You have got to be kidding. I need to talk to you, immediately!" She could feel her face burning.

"You caught me at a bad time, Denise. Can't it wait?"

"If you don't come to my office immediately then I will come find you," she said, gritting her teeth. "And if you'd like to avoid a public confrontation, I'd advise you to get a move on it."

"All right, all right. But it'll have to be quick."

She hung up the phone and sat at her desk, barely moving a muscle, waiting.

A few minutes later, Gary came to her office and walked in without knocking. He didn't bother to sit down. "Don't get me wrong, Denise. You're a great daytime talk-show host and you've had a really good run."

"You mean to tell me that this is permanent? You're going to take this ridiculous low road because of a minor improvement in the ratings?"

He leaned forward, as if to let her in on a secret. "We can't ignore the upswing, it's been staggering, and the network is not going to backtrack now." He lowered his voice. "You're a smart woman, Denise, you know it's all about the ratings."

She didn't like his patronizing tone. "But you must be aware that this is a short term surge, Gary. It won't be long before people tire of Nicole's shtick."

"We'll deal with that when and if it happens. For now we gotta ride the current."

Stupid, stupid people. But what could she do? Her contract was in the process of being renegotiated, the timing was terrible.

Gary stood up and put his hands in his pockets. "Listen, it's the end of June and we're about to wind down for the summer. How about we let Nicole finish the season and we'll talk some more next month." His apologetic expression implied that they would *not* be talking next month, or any other time.

****

Laura sat in the waiting room flipping through a magazine. Monique had experienced cramping all morning and then she had started spotting, which wasn't alarming at first, but the discomfort had become more and more severe. In spite of the pain, she stubbornly refused to go to the doctor and Laura practically dragged her to the clinic. Thankfully, the doctor could see them right away. When Monique emerged from the examining room, her head hanging low, Laura guessed the prognosis. The pregnancy was no more. A nurse approached Laura and asked her to come, along with Monique, to the doctor's office. Monique slumped down in a chair on the opposite side of the room, her head turned away, her eyes downcast.

Laura addressed Monique "Aren't you coming?"

"No."

"I think you'd better," Laura said, her voice firm.

Laura followed the nurse into the doctor's office and sat in the stiff leather chair facing his desk. He was hunched over his notes and all she could see was a white doctor's coat and a thick mass of white hair. Monique had dragged behind and was leaning against the door, her arms crossed, her eyes fixated on the tiled floor. Laura couldn't take her eyes off the doctor's orange and yellow striped tie against the backdrop of a purple shirt; the combination striking her as incongruous with his serious expression.

"Spontaneous abortion," he said. "Miscarriage."

"Why? How did this happen?" Laura asked.

"It's a very common thing," he said. "Often such a miscarriage will occur before a woman realizes she's pregnant. But not to worry, this incident will have no bearing on any future pregnancies." He gave Monique a reassuring nod. "You'll be fine. Go home and take it easy for the rest of the day and by tomorrow you'll already be feeling better."

When they arrived home, Monique headed straight to her room and Laura went to the kitchen to call Chris. With charged nerves, she sat on a stool at the island and dialed.

"I've got some important news for you," she said, when he answered the phone.

"I hope it's good, I've had enough downers this week."

"Monique had a miscarriage this morning. There's no baby and no more big decisions to make."

"Are you serious?"

"It's the first time I've ever considered a miscarriage to be a happy event," she said. "I know people who were heartbroken when it happened to them. Remember how devastated Cindy Travis was?"

"Yes, I remember, but how's Monique?"

"She was quiet on the way home from the doctor's, but I think she's relieved. As much as she's been trying to be stoic about it, this thing has been weighing heavily on her."

"I'll try to wrap my day up early to be with her. Thanks for helping her, Laura — and for all your support."

Tears came to Laura's eyes. "I'm glad it's over. See you at home shortly." Now that Monique's problem was resolved, they'd have to confront their own issues. Since viewing that talk show video, she'd been watching Chris carefully. But he hadn't done anything to elicit further concern. Maybe she was becoming delusional and stupidly paranoid.

Laura made some tea and brought it upstairs with some biscuits. Monique appeared to be sleeping, so she set the tray on her bedside table and left the room. The girls wouldn't be home for another hour, which allowed enough time to work on her résumé and to pick up a few groceries. She sat down at her kitchen nook and tried to open a new document on the computer, but the system was frozen and rebooting didn't help. She'd noticed Chris's laptop on his desk earlier, which he'd probably forgotten in the morning rush. Figuring he wouldn't mind if she created a file for herself, she settled into his office chair. As she waited for the computer to start up, she reviewed one of her old résumés that she'd retrieved from the filing cabinet in the basement. She thought hard about what she could add to her last entry over ten years ago: raising daughters, renovating houses, managing a household? Not likely. Perhaps she could at least include her parent council involvement at the school and mention the fundraising events that she had co-chaired.

While trying to access the word processing program, Laura noticed Chris's e-mail folder. She hesitated, but then opened the file, spurred on by her recent malaise. Not that she didn't trust Chris, but her inkling of doubt persuaded her to scroll through the messages. She found a message from Denise and opened it:

Dear Chris,

How are you? Hope you're keeping all right and that your family is fine. It's a busy season here at the TV station because spring is the most exciting time for our show. Lots of interesting topics in the works. Any chance you'll be coming back to Montreal soon?

Denise

Early May, before their trip to San Francisco. Hmm. Laura found another note.

Hi Chris,

Thank you for the spectacular flowers. What a lovely surprise. They made my day! Denise

So that's what the flowers were all about. Then she found the message sent to Chris in San Francisco, about the funeral. But how come Chris had never mentioned the Gagnon family before, given that they were old family friends? Laura grabbed a throw blanket from the wing chair and wrapped it around her shoulders, pulling it tight. She thought back on how she had naively accepted his explanation—all that nonsense about feeling an obligation to attend this woman's funeral, and how quick he was to leave her behind in San Francisco. With trepidation she opened the 'Sent Items' folder:

Life is busy here too. Springtime comes with all kinds of surprises. Enjoy the nice weather. Chris

PS. Let me know your flight info. Chris

Laura let go of the blanket over her shoulders, feeling minor relief. The messages were innocuous; she would definitely have to get to the bottom of the flowers, though. Maybe she was reading too much into everything; the e-mails could be nothing more than friendly banter leading up to his guest appearance on her show. After all, he would make a charming guest; perhaps Denise was courting him for that.

Pepper's frenzied barking startled Laura; she found him in the kitchen, anxious to go outside. "I'm sorry, doggy boy, have I been neglecting you?" She opened the screen door and watched him race out to the garden. He sniffed the grass, meandered about, lost interest, and then came back to the house, beseeching a biscuit. "But you didn't do your business, fella. You know the rules—no business, no biscuit." The dog gazed up at her with sappy, hopeful eyes, panting and pleading. "All right, you little rascal, you always get the better of me." Wasn't it the same way with Chris? Whenever she started experiencing doubts, he'd somehow slip into his most endearing self and she'd feel contrite for ever having entertained negative thoughts about him. She opened the cupboard door and removed the box of dog biscuits. Pepper wagged his tail with glee as she pulled one out. "Here you go, boy," she said.

Tanya and Sophie charged into the kitchen. "Hi, Mom. I'm starved," Tanya said. "Can I have a snack?"

****

Chris leaned back in his chair, dumbfounded. Monique was no longer pregnant. He was shocked beyond elation and felt guilty for his desire to celebrate. Since his last conversation with Monique, he'd been trying to figure out a way to get through to her, to shake her into action. His plan had been to give her a few more days and if she still hadn't decided what to do, he would bring her to a counsellor, kicking and screaming if necessary. Now, it was all a moot point.

He turned to his computer and opened his e-mail file, hardly allowing himself time to think.

Hi Denise,

Monique had a miscarriage. She's fine, but shaken up. I feel an incredible sense of relief and wanted to share the news with you. I'm so sorry for cutting you off, but I didn't know what else to do given all the chaos in my life. Please forgive me for being such a louse. I'd really like to end our communication moratorium now that Monique's situation is resolved. If you'll accept me back, that is. What do you think? Is it all right to be in touch again? Please write, or better yet, call me. I hope you're doing all right. Love, Chris

He pressed 'send' before he could change his mind. The tides were changing, even work was picking up again. The San Francisco deal had been lost for good, but he had a new piece of business equally significant in the works. In fact, he needed to be in New York the following week to meet with the client. And he could pick up a replacement bottle of Chateaux Margaux for Tony while he was there; find something as good, if not superior. Chris still hadn't mentioned to Laura that he'd found the empty bottle, thinking it would be better to sweep that incident under the carpet considering all the turmoil in the house.

He opened his day-timer and considered his travel options. The need to stay close to home because of Monique was no longer an issue, and the sooner he could schedule the meetings in New York, the better. He wrote a quick note to his assistant:

Please arrange for me to meet with Freeman Group in New York next Thursday and Friday. Book me a room for Thursday night at The Pierrot. Thanks

Chris chewed the top of his pen, an old college habit. What if Denise were to meet him down there for a couple of days? Would she be open to that, or was he nuts? No, it was a completely irrational idea—what was he thinking? He put his pen down and packed up for the day. Flowers might cheer Monique up, and some jujubes; he'd make a quick stop at the store on his way home.

After buying a large spring bouquet a local forist, Chris called Denise from the parking lot. He had to speak to her.

"Denise! I'm so glad I caught you," he said when she answered.

"Hello, Chris."

For a second, he didn't recognize the voice. It sounded stiff, mildly hostile. He thought back to his e-mail. Had he offended her? "How are you? It's only been a couple of weeks since we've spoken but it feels like a century."

"Yes, it does."

He didn't know what to say next. His body tensed the same way it did when Laura was annoyed with him. "Did you get my e-mail?" he asked.

"Yes."

Stony silence. Then she said, "I'm glad to hear that Monique is all right, that things have worked out for you all."

"A huge relief. I can't tell you the half of it. I had visions of having another baby in the house. Laura and I are too far beyond that stage." The words shot out in rapid succession, as if he had to unload his angst.

"I can imagine."

"Listen, Denise. I'm sorry about what happened. I mean, I know it was abrupt of me to cut things off like I did. Life became crazy all at once. Forgive me?"

"No need to apologize. I've got a lot going on in my life too."

She still sounded cool. "Tell me how you've been, what's going on with you these days?" he asked.

"Apart from getting unceremoniously ejected from my show, not much."

"What do you mean? What happened?"

"My trusted assistant, Nicole, pulled a strategic stunt during my absence. Basically, she usurped my job."

"But how could that be? Everyone loves you. You're a star."

"Not anymore."

Now he understood why her voice was stilted. "I'm sorry to hear that, Denise. What are you going to do? You've got to sue them for starters."

"My contract is up for renegotiation in the fall—this could have been brewing for a long time, for all I know. I'm still in shock, quite frankly, and I don't know how it will all play out."

"I wish I could help you out. What can I do?"

"Nothing. But thanks."

Chris didn't stop to consider his next words before they poured out of his mouth. "I've got business in New York at the end of next week. How about joining me there for the weekend? I think I read that there's a wine-tasting event at The Pierrot—French wines, I believe—which I'd love to take you to, especially since you're such a connoisseur. And we could talk, away from everything and every-body, and maybe I could help you figure out your next move."

"Why not?" she said. "I don't have much else on my agenda."

Chris hardly heard her response. The only thing that registered was that she had said yes. He took a deep breath. "I'll e-mail you my schedule. I'll be staying at the Pierrot—do you want me to—"

"No, I'll book my hotel, thanks."

After their telephone conversation, Chris called his assistant and left her a voice mail message:

Andrea, could you please also reserve Friday and Saturday at The Pierrot for me? Thanks. Oh, could you book me a couple of tickets for the wine-tasting event at the hotel on Sunday.

****

Chris and Monique relaxed by the tennis courts drinking Cokes while they watched people hit balls in the sweltering humidity.

"I'm getting too old to play tennis in this heat," Chris said. "I'm glad we're not playing today." He wiped his brow with a napkin. "What's with this kind of weather in June?"

"C'mon Dad, you're only forty-four. I think you're a bit young to be such a fair-weather tennis player." Monique slurped the last of her Coke through a straw.

"Maybe I just can't bear the humiliation of my daughter defeat-ing me. What was the score last time? 6-1 and 6-2? I'm lucky to get just one game from you these days. Is your buddy Andrew to blame? Has he been giving you lessons on the sly?"

"Yup, I can give him partial credit, he's come out to hit with me on occasion."

"I knew it!" Chris pretended to pound the table. "There had to be some kind of conspiracy going on, how else could I have been pummeled so miserably by my gentle, kind-hearted, daughter?"

Monique laughed. "Now you know my true objective—to crush your over-inflated, tennis ego."

The waiter came by and handed them menus; a slight breeze provided momentary relief from the stifling heat. Chris watched Monique study the lunch menu, and listened with amusement as she joked with the waiter, relieved to see that she had reverted to her old self. It had been a while since she had been so cheerful. They ordered burgers and another round of Cokes, and sat back in their chairs, enjoying the simple pleasure of being together. He almost didn't broach the sensitive subject of her pregnancy, but then changed his mind.

"Did you ever speak to Andrew about your predicament?"

Monique's cheerfulness vanished like a layer of dust smothering the mood. Chris regretted raising the topic.

"I told him after the miscarriage," she said.

"What did he say?"

"He told me he loved me." Her face and voice were devoid of expression.

"Interesting."

"Yup, interesting. He was pretty angry that I hadn't mentioned being pregnant, said it wasn't fair to keep him out of the loop."

"He has a point." Chris wondered if he had misjudged the kid.

"Then Andrew told me he would have dropped his tennis aspirations if I had wanted to keep the baby, that he would have married me in a flash and found a regular job."

"Sounds decent. Do you believe he meant it?"

"Yeah, I think so."

"Would you have wanted that?"

"No." She removed her cap and then replaced it backwards on her head. "He reminds me of you, you know."

Chris raised his eyebrow. "Really?"

"Yes. He's decent to the core and would want to do the right thing. But I know how much you've sacrificed for me and I've always felt guilty about it. I couldn't see myself doing the same thing to Andrew."

"I've told you before, Chickpea, you were a gift, not a sacrifice." He touched her hand gently.

"I know. But I also know it wasn't easy for you, all that stuff you had to deal with. I've watched you all my life and I've tried to model after you, and make you proud." The drinks arrived and Monique took a big sip. Her intensity deepened when she continued. "You have no idea how much I admire the way you handle problems. You're always so calm and smart about things. You really are a great dad, and the best role model. The most crushing part of this nightmare was disappointing you."

"I never knew you felt that way."

"Sometimes I wonder if I'll ever get married 'cause I don't know if I'll even find a man with as much integrity and backbone as you have. And even though I care for Andrew, as devoted as he is, I don't know if he could ever measure up."

Chris put his sunglasses on and glanced over at the tennis courts. How could he look his daughter in the eye after that tribute? Shit. What had he been thinking, asking Denise to meet him in New York? All that Monique respected about him felt like a pathetic sham.

Chapter Thirty-one

When Laura tried to round up the girls for bed they ignored her, or didn't hear her calling. She looked up at the cloudless sky, still boasting daylight though night-time was fast approaching.

"Girls, are you listening? It's time to go in," she said again, her voice slightly raised.

"But, Mommy, it's not nearly dark yet," Tanya said.

"I'm not tired. Not one bit," Sophie said.

Laura checked the time. 8:30. Tomorrow was their first day of Gymnastics camp and if they didn't get a good night's sleep, they'd be out of sorts before the day even began, especially Sophie, who always had difficulty with the first day of anything. Laura shook her head as she peeled off her gardening gloves. "I've already given you an extra fifteen minutes, now hustle your bustles."

"Five more minutes, pleeeeze," Sophie pleaded.

Laura sighed. "All right, five more minutes." If Chris were here, there'd be no arguing and they'd march to his first command. But he was away on another business trip—New York this time. Monique had been such a doll, offering to care of the girls during the weekend again and encouraging her to surprise him there. "Once I start my job at the pool I won't be around as much," she had said. "You should use me while you can." Chris had mentioned he'd be at meetings on Saturday and Laura considered surprising him in the hotel room. On Sunday she'd tag along to the wine-tasting event, not her idea of a great time in New York, but Chris would be sure to be pleased. And there was always Saturday night. A fantasy flashed through her mind involving the red lingerie she had bought for San Francisco and she wondered if this could be another chance to play-out her previously botched romantic intentions. Now that time had passed since the San Francisco fiasco, she was tempted to put their recent conflicts aside and take a chance at resurrecting their passion and their marital equilibrium. How could Chris not be receptive?

Laura walked across the garden searching for weeds while the girls continued playing hopscotch on the driveway. She was tired of being the grumpy bedtime sergeant, always directing and repeating, scolding and screaming. When would they ever respond the first time she asked them to do something? Sitting on the front steps, she picked off the dead azalea heads from the bush beside her. The prolific bright pink blooms failed to boost her mood as she plucked the faded ones. When she glanced toward the street she saw a young couple pushing a baby stroller with a golden retriever pulling them along. They waved at her and she waved back. Not long ago Chris and she were just like that young family, with Pepper tugging in all directions as they walked and Tanya cooing in her pram; how quickly the years had passed and how strange to have lost that sense of joy. Perhaps the novelty of motherhood and the excitement of burgeoning love had driven her spirits at the beginning, but now…well now, life had somehow lost its punch. She watched the girls play and listened to their banter, remembering her own uncomplicated childhood. Life had become cumbersome lately, with its routines and domestic drudgery. Tomorrow she'd work on her résumé some more, perhaps make a few calls to investigate the professional world she'd abandoned.

"Oww," Tanya wailed. She was lying on her back holding her knee.

Laura rushed over to her side. "What happened?"

"She fell when she was jumping…like this." Sophie hopped on one foot, from one square to another, and fell to the ground with dramatic emphasis.

"Let me see, sweetie." Laura bent down and removed Tanya's hand from her leg. "It's a nasty scratch all right. But not too deep. Let's go inside to wash it and put on a bandage." She helped Tanya up and held on to her waist as she limped to the house.

After settling the girls in bed, Laura went down to the kitchen. All evening she'd been self-restrained and hadn't opened a bottle of wine. But she disregarded her earlier resolve and looked in the fridge for a crisp bottle of white. Darn, she'd forgotten to replace the one she'd drunk the other day. She found a Sauvignon Blanc on the wine rack, opened it, poured a half-glass and plopped in two ice cubes. She smiled as Chris's chastising voice popped in her head: "Putting ice in your wine is sacrilegious, Laura. It's like putting salt in your coffee!" Pepper barked, startling her. Then she heard a tap, tap, tap at the front door. She looked through the living room window and saw Tony's convertible. Didn't Tony know that Chris was in New York?

"Hey, Laura," he said, when she opened the door. "I'm sorry to bother you, but I was on my way home from work and thought I'd drop by to pick up my Margaux."

"No bother at all. Come on in, Tony."

He followed her to the kitchen.

"I was just pouring myself some wine. Would you like to join me?"

"Sure, thanks." He sat on the stool and Laura handed him a generous glass. "I've got a big date on Saturday— I'm making dinner for my new lady friend."

Laura noticed an edge of shyness in Tony's voice. She liked the way his soft side came through when he talked about his personal life. When Belinda left him a year ago, he'd been a mess. Laura recalled the scene in the living room when Tony recounted how it had all ended. His eyes had been bloodshot when he told them in a broken voice, "Belinda's gone. She left me."

At first Laura couldn't believe it. Belinda was ten years younger than Tony and such a sweet soul. Chris and Laura had been there during the wooing stage, the dating stage, the living-together stage, and then the marriage stage. Tony doted on Belinda and she idolized him. They had always been affectionate and playful with one another and Laura had secretly envied their relationship.

Laura remembered Chris saying to Tony, "She'll be back, she loves you."

"No, she won't. *This* time it's over"

Laura hadn't known there'd been 'other times.'

"She wasn't even sad," he'd continued. Didn't shed one tear." As he spoke, his own tears flowed. "I blew it, and there's no turning back."

He told them how Belinda was fed up with his long hours and unpredictable schedule. That she wanted to have children, but not with someone she couldn't rely on to be there. She was tired of being alone in the relationship and had come to the realization that he would never change. She walked out the door and flew back to her family home in New Mexico.

"So, tell me about your new woman," Laura said, passing him a bowl of mixed nuts.

"She's great. Smart, attractive, level-headed."

"How old is she?"

"My age. A year older actually — forty-one to be exact." He took a sip of wine. "She's divorced, has two kids." He laughed, "Maybe I'm over my head but I promised to make her a lavish Italian dinner."

"What are you making?"

"Veal Parmesan. But if I ruin it, at least I'll have my fancy wine to impress her with."

"Oh yes. The wine. Come to the cellar with me, I wouldn't begin to know which one it was."

Chris's wine cellar was a small room in the basement with a mahogany interior and floor-to-ceiling redwood wine racks. It housed eight hundred bottles of wine but was only half full, the reds on one side and the whites on the other. Tony described the bottle to Laura and they both began to look for it. Laura shivered in the cool room as she sifted through the racks. After a thorough search, they came out empty-handed.

"That's strange," Tony said. "I dropped it by a few weeks ago, remember?"

"Yes I do, but if it's not here, I don't know what to tell you."

"I'll phone him," Tony said.

They went back upstairs to the kitchen and Tony called on his Blackberry. "I'm getting his voicemail." With irritation in his voice, he finished his message saying, "And you'd better not have drunk it, Lambert."

"Don't worry," Laura said, "If Chris had opened it, I'm sure I'd be in on it." They laughed.

"What's up with you these days?" Tony asked, taking a seat at the kitchen island. "And how are the kids?"

"We're all great." Laura couldn't bring herself to mention the episode with Monique, nor her own domestic frustration. "How about you? Still working like a maniac?"

"It's busy in the world of buy-outs and take-overs, that's for sure." His voice became concerned. "How's Chris doing? He's a bit on edge at the office."

Laura opened the fridge and searched for something to serve. She found some cheddar cheese and a jar of olives and put them on the counter. "Well," she said, as she reached in the cupboard for a platter, "I think he's stressed. That San Francisco deal caused him a lot of grief."

"No kidding. What a debacle. By the way, did he tell you where he was that day when we were all trying to find him?"

"Wasn't he playing golf?" She put the cheese on a plate and scattered crackers around, adding a few grapes from the fruit bowl.

"Don't think so. You've met Bob Warden, our corporate lawyer, haven't you?"

Laura shook her head. "Maybe."

"He said he bumped into Chris having lunch with a woman out in Cedar Falls that day."

"Really?" Laura said. She felt a sharp sensation in her head, as if a blood vessel had burst. "Who?"

"Beats me. He didn't mention it to me either." Tony drank his wine.

"Must have been a business thing," Laura said.

"Yeah, probably."

Tony's phone rang. He looked at the call display and answered, "Hey, bud, I'm still at your house."

Sipping her wine, Laura watched Tony speak to her husband.

"What? You busted my Margaux? Come on!"

Laura winced. When had that happened? Why hadn't he said anything? She went upstairs to check on the girls...and to escape for a minute. Hadn't Tony said that the wine was worth $700? It wasn't like Chris to be so careless. Thoughts of Chris drinking the wine on a clandestine rendezvous with some mystery woman rushed through her head. She imagined him sitting across the table from Sonya, delighting in the prized vintage together. Then the image was replaced by that other woman, Denise, the talk-show host. Laura went to the bathroom to splash cold water over her face. Then she brushed her hair, put on lipstick, and went downstairs, clutching the banister as she walked.

"How do you like that? He smashed my Margaux to smithereens."

Laura checked the floor for any tell-tale signs. She didn't see any chips in the ceramic tile or stains in the grout. "What an unfortunate waste," she said.

"He was planning to replace it in New York. Didn't want to admit what he'd done."

What else wasn't he admitting? Laura shrugged her shoulders. "Well, it's only wine," she said.

"Yup, only wine," he said.

The next day was Friday and Laura had promised Sonya that she would go over to pack up boxes. Why had she been so effusive with her offers to help? Jumping to everyone's rescue was becoming tiresome; she'd much rather go to bed early and read her book. However, this would be a good opportunity to find out more about Sonya, to get to know what lay beneath that optimistic exterior. And although she didn't want to believe that Sonya and Chris had anything between them, part of her needed to find out definitively and to once-and-for-all annihilate that silly notion. She had always prided herself in her ability to read people, to scope out what they were about, but somehow she couldn't determine Sonya's 'truth.' Furthermore, she wanted to find out what had really happened between Sonya and her ex-husband, Jack. Sonya's mother had led Laura to believe that the break-up had been entirely due to Jack's philandering, but was there more to the story? Wasn't there always two sides?

Monique had offered to watch the girls that night, and Sonya had enticed her with take-out Thai and a bottle of Riesling; in the end, how could Laura resist? A night out would be a good diversion and it would be interesting to learn what it's like to run solo with two kids, a mortgage, and a temporary disability.

All day, Laura had been ruminating about flying to New York to meet Chris. But she couldn't decide what do. In the end, no decision was the final decision because now it was too late to make plans.

Laura selected a pair of jeans from her closet and surveyed her bedroom while she undressed, admiring her own good taste. The four poster-bed and antique bedside tables looked like a picture from 'Dream House Magazine.' On cold winter nights she and Chris would sometimes snuggle in bed with a fire blazing across the room and watch the dancing flames make the painting come alive above the hearth. They'd listen to jazz or classic pop and make love while the snow fell and the children slept. She had it good most of the time, relatively speaking, and she should be grateful. A bump here and there was normal; every marriage had its occasional glitches. She plumped a cushion on the bed. Then why did she have knots in her gut?

Laura cringed with dismay when she couldn't zip up her jeans. Only a few weeks ago they had fit her like a glove. She'd bought them when her new bathroom scale revealed seven pounds less than when she'd first stood on it in the store, two months earlier. She ran to the bathroom and jumped on the scale, convinced that there was a mistake; the pants must have shrunk. But she hadn't washed them yet. She shrieked to herself when she saw the cruel reality—up ten pounds. Damn, she'd have to go back to her 'fat' pants. The idea of romance in New York had definitely lost its appeal.

When Laura arrived at Sonya's, she noticed that every light in the entire house was on. She hadn't been there since their afternoon tea and it felt like an entirely different place. The walls were bare and the window treatments had been removed, making her feel exposed to the world outside.

"I've sent my curtains to be dry-cleaned," Sonya said, when she noticed Laura looking at the naked windows.

"I can't believe how different your house feels. It's like I'm seeing it for the first time," Laura said.

"I barely recognize it myself. But that's a good thing. Makes it easier to leave."

Laura handed Sonya the bottle of wine she'd brought. "Will you leave with some happy memories?"

"I don't know. A mix of good and bad ones, I suppose." She showed Laura the packing tape and the flat cardboard boxes stacked behind the sofa. "First we need to assemble some boxes and then we can start packing. I'm finished upstairs and tonight I'd like to make some headway in the kitchen and the living room."

Laura sat on a chair and began to unfold a box. "Are you looking forward to your new life?" she asked.

"It's been new for a while, but yes, I'm anxious to move out and move on. I never realized it would be liberating to leave this house."

"I heard you got a good price. Congratulations," she said, remembering the embrace she'd witnessed between Sonya and Chris in front of the house that day.

"I'm ecstatic. I got $30,000 over asking." Sonya stacked four empty boxes that she had assembled and the top box fell to the ground. "C'mon, let's tackle the kitchen."

Laura grabbed the box that Sonya had dropped and followed her into the kitchen. Piles of old newspapers sat on the kitchen counter to be used for wrapping and she noticed the headline on one of the front pages when she picked up a bunch. 'Popular congressman comes clean and loses wife, girlfriend, and possibly his job.' She recognized the face, the once confident politician now looking haggard and defeated. 'Is this the age of perceived entitlement?' the caption went on to say.

"I ordered our dinner before you came, it should be here any time. Would you like a glass of wine?" Sonya asked.

"Yes, thanks," Laura said, without hesitation.

They worked hard, speaking little, and packing with care while they waited for the food to arrive. Laura was cautious with her wine, afraid of becoming unproductive and clumsy; she didn't want to risk breaking anything. Sonya had many beautiful, fragile items in her kitchen: handmade stoneware platters, crystal glasses, and porcelain coffee mugs. When dinner arrived, they put all the steaming food containers on a tray and sat at the kitchen table to eat. Spring rolls, pad Thai, stir-fried vegetables, skewered chicken with peanut sauce and spicy shrimp produced a blend of enticing aromas, intensifying Laura's hunger. Sonya re-filled Laura's wine glass and poured two glasses of water. She lit some candles on the table and switched off the lights, reminding Laura of how Chris and she used to end the week together before Tanya and Sophie came along.

They served themselves and launched into the meal, "So, where's Chris tonight?" Sonya said.

Laura dipped a spring roll into the spicy sauce. "New York."

"On a Friday night?"

Why was she curious? "He's there till Monday. It seems that in his business, weekends don't exist in New York." She took a bite and savored the crunchy sweetness in her mouth. "And he said something about a wine-tasting event he wanted to attend on Sunday."

"Why didn't you go with him?"

"Now wasn't the best time. Besides, I'm not into the wine-tasting thing. Not like Chris."

Topping up their glasses, Sonya said, "And we'd rather be drinking than tasting, right?" They both giggled like schoolgirls.

"Last year I ran the New York Marathon," Sonya said. "I came in 109th."

Laura would have preferred not to talk about Sonya's athletic accomplishments, but then felt guilty, knowing that her running days may be over. "What a feat. Must have been grueling."

"Yes, but I loved it. I can't wait to do my next one." She dipped a chicken skewer into the peanut sauce and took a small bite.

"That's great. I didn't know you'd be able to run again."

Sonya's face tightened. "My doctor hasn't exactly cleared me on that front yet, but I know I'll get back to it eventually. If not next year, there's always the year after that."

Laura held up her wine glass. "To your next marathon."

"Thank you." Her solemn tone left Laura wondering if Sonya honestly believed her own prediction.

By the time they had finished eating, the wine bottle was empty. Laura noticed a slight limp as Sonya cleared the table and felt bad for the negative thoughts she'd been harbouring towards her. She rinsed the plates and put them in the dishwasher while Sonya opened the bottle of wine Laura had brought, and filled Laura's glass before she had a chance to decline.

They worked for a couple more hours in the kitchen, listening to Billy Joel, Carole King, and James Taylor CDs as they carefully wrapped the breakable items and filled the boxes. Laura undid the top button of her jeans, wondering if Thai food was fattening or just bloating. When all the cupboards were empty and they had stacked the packed boxes in the corner of the kitchen, they moved to the living room, bringing their wine glasses with them.

"Cheers," Sonya said, holding up her glass. "Thanks for coming over and helping me tonight."

"My pleasure," Laura said. And she meant it. She was having a pleasant time after all.

They assembled several more boxes, laughing at their fumbling. "Nothing like a little vino to make a task more fun," Sonya said.

"Absolutely." Laura laughed as she taped her finger to the box.

Sonya went into the kitchen and emerged with two popsicles. "Dessert."

They sat cross-legged on the floor in the living room and Laura unwrapped her grape popsicle. "I'll try not to drip on your carpet."

"This rug has seen a lot worse than dyed sugar-water," Sonya said. "I remember one night when Jack and I had quite the rollicking time right where we're sitting."

Laura shuffled over a few inches.

"We started with martinis and shrimp cocktails and ended with all kinds of kitchen condiments."

Laura winced while she laughed. "Sounds adventurous."

"We had some good times back then...and great sex!" Her face flushed as she spoke, and after a short pause, she continued, "Did I mention that I'm seeing someone?"

"No, you didn't."

"It's a new thing and I don't want to say too much and risk jinxing it."

"What's he like?"

"He's sexy as hell."

"Good for you, Sonya. I'm glad for you." Laura chastised herself for feeling glum. She knew she should be happy for her, but all of Sonya's misfortunes seemed to get rectified rather easily; there was something unjust about that.

The image of Sonya being intimate with Chris jumped into Laura's consciousness again. Sonya couldn't possibly be referring to Chris when she said she had a new man—no, she couldn't be that evil. But how well did she know Sonya? Hardly at all, in truth. Was Sonya the type to offer a good time to handsome non-suspecting neighbours? Was that her intent when she had called Chris to the front door the other day?

"How about you?" Sonya continued, "I'll bet that you and Chris have great sex."

No one had ever asked Laura a question like that before. She had no idea what to say. Blushing, she said, "It's fine."

"I can't believe how radically things change over time." Sonya looked reflective. "Jack and I went from whooping it up to…nothing. I don't even know how we reached the beginning of the end."

Laura watched Sonya lick her popsicle and felt sickened by the sight. After drinking almost an entire bottle of wine, the effects were messing with her imagination. Sonya was a beautiful woman with magnetic sex appeal—would Chris have had the wherewithal to rebuff her? Especially since there hadn't been a whole lot of action in their own bedroom lately. Laura chewed the last of her popsicle and jumped to her feet. "Better get back to work or we'll never be done," she said.

Sonya worked in the living room, packing up family photos and books from the built-in shelves, while Laura tackled the hall closet, which was stuffed with winter hats and gloves and kids' sports paraphernalia. She packed one full box and then began to fold the spring jackets. When she came across a man's navy blazer she was about to ask Sonya if she should pack it, but then stopped short. She inspected the label and checked the pockets, finding a crumpled credit card receipt with Chris's signature. Her head pounded and she could feel her blood pressure rising. Why would Chris's jacket be in Sonya's closet? Was this her way of divulging that she and Chris were…? No, it couldn't be true. She thought back on the embrace she had witnessed—a lovers' embrace. And now the jacket. How many times could they have been together? Was it a physical thing? A true passion? Laura wanted to throw up. She glanced over at the living room where Sonya was wrapping photographs and humming the James Taylor song, 'You've Got a Friend.' Suddenly, her world was caving in. She grabbed her purse at the front entrance, bolted out the door, and ran the four blocks home.

When Laura woke up early the next morning, her head was still spinning with incredulity. How could she have been so blind? She'd ignored the signs—at least dismissed them—for weeks. And there Sonya was, taking advantage of her, making a mockery of her, by manipulating her into helping with the packing and then probing about her marriage; she'd even asked Laura about their sex life.

Laura put on her robe and pulled her hair back with a clip. Damn, Chris. Damn them all! When she went downstairs she realized it wasn't quite light outside. She'd had a restless night, barely sleeping, and now she had to face a busy day: meeting friends with the children at the Science Centre, having lunch together, and then to Shaker Square, where she'd promised to take Tanya and Sophie to the bookstore. Just thinking about their plans made her nauseous. As she poured ground coffee into the filter, she felt a tickling sensation on her ankle and looked down to find Pepper licking her.

"Oh, Pepper," she said, dropping on the floor to pet him. "What am I going to do?"

The dog jumped into her lap and nuzzled against her neck, as if sensing her distress. She hugged him tight.

By 9:00 the girls were up, full of energy and asking for breakfast. To their amazement, Laura let them eat in the family room in front of the TV. "Don't worry," Tanya said, "we'll be careful with crumbs and we won't spill anything." Sophie nodded in agreement. Laura watched them as they sat on the carpet in front of the television, gleefully indulging in their breakfast of Froot Loops, lemonade, and leftover chips from the night before. Let them have fun, she thought; after Chris came home, their lives would never be quite the same again.

The doorbell rang, causing Pepper to jump from his slumber and to frantically bark. Laura tightened the belt of her robe as she approached the front entrance, expecting one of the neighbourhood kids. Opening the door, she grabbed Pepper's collar to prevent him from running out onto the street.

Tony stood there, with his hands deep in his pockets and hunched shoulders, as if bringing bad news. "Hey, Laura," he said.

"Come in," she said. "What's up?"

He pulled his hands out of his pockets and stepped inside. "I came by to talk to you. Do you have a few minutes?"

"Uh huh. I've got some coffee going in the kitchen. Come join me for my fourth cup this morning." Her laugh was strained.

They sat down at the kitchen table and Laura felt self-conscious about her disheveled appearance.

"I uh...I was wondering...you see, Laura..." Tony took a gulp of his coffee.

"What's going on, Tony?"

He stood up. "I got a call from your friend Sonya last night."

"Sonya? How do you know her?"

"You'll think this is weird. I mean, we didn't want to say anything yet because—"

"What are you talking about?"

"Sonya and I have been seeing each other. For about two weeks."

Laura couldn't hide her shock. "What?"

"We didn't tell you guys 'cause we didn't want to make a big deal out of it, in case things didn't work out. The whole blind-date thing can be embarrassing." He sat back down in his chair.

"Now that's an interesting bit of news." Laura got up from the table and walked to the counter, hoping that Tony didn't notice her red face. She grabbed the coffee pot and offered Tony some more coffee even though his cup was full. "I'm glad you're seeing her, she's a great gal."

"That brings me to why I'm here. She called me last night and told me about what happened at her place last night. She was worried. Called you three times and left messages but you didn't pick up or call back."

Laura's face went crimson and this time she couldn't hide it. "I guess I had a bit of a meltdown last night. When I was packing up Sonya's hall closet I found Chris's jacket, and I assumed...I don't know...I jumped to conclusions."

"You thought Chris and she were..."

Laura nodded.

Tony laughed. "But Laura, do you know how preposterous that sounds? Chris is the one who gave me her number. He thought we could be good together."

"He never mentioned it to me."

"I told him, no thanks, that I didn't need any help meeting women. But a couple of weeks ago I called her on a whim and we went out—hit it off right away. I didn't tell Chris. Like I said, we wanted to wait to see if what was happening was for real." Tony's face was flushed.

"But Chris's jacket?"

"Sonya said he left it there that day you went over for tea. She reminded him when she saw him out for a run and he said he'd swing by to pick it up, but he never did."

"Oh." Laura remembered making him wear that jacket to Sonya's that day, in spite of the heat. "Tony, I'm such a fool. I thought they were having an affair. I must be going crazy." Suddenly she felt light-headed, almost giddy. Fuel seemed to pour through her veins, lifting her fatigue, giving her life again. "I'll call Sonya right away to explain, to apologize. She must think I'm nuts."

They both laughed.

"Can I get you something to eat?" Laura asked, resuming hostess mode.

"No thanks, I've got to run. By the way, I spoke to Chris yesterday and he's got some heavy things happening with this New York deal. He'll be going there a lot in the next while." Tony stood up and put his mug on the counter. "I'm glad we've cleared things up here. But do me a favour? Keep my relationship with Sonya quiet, OK? I don't want to jinx it."

"You like her a lot, don't you?"

His face broke into a wide grin. "Yeah, I guess I do."

When Laura saw Tony off, he ran back up the steps before she closed the door. "I forgot to ask if you could do something for me. I need an e-mail that Chris wrote to the guys in Montreal, which they said they never got. He said it may be on his home office computer but I need to get it to them by Monday morning; would you mind checking for it when you have a moment, and then forwarding it to me?" Tony wrote down the company's name and e-mail address on the back of his business card.

"No problem, Tony. I'll be on it right away." She took the card and waved good-bye.

Chapter Thirty-two

Denise was glad she'd taken an early morning flight to New York City, allowing for plenty of time to get ready before meeting Chris. The comfortable limo ride from LaGuardia and the impressive skyline view helped temper her simmering anxiety. The weather was perfect with the sun shining and a mellow breeze cooling the air. After checking into her room at the hotel and freshening up, she changed into a sleeveless lilac top, tied the matching cardigan over her shoulders and straightened her pants. She brushed her hair in front of the full-length mirror and studied her appearance; not bad considering all the sleepless nights and her struggle to gain weight. This was the vacation she had craved for a long time, a couple of days away from the stresses weighing her down at home—the getaway that she could be enjoying with Francois, had he been amenable.

Francois would barely even notice her absence, given his focus on work these days. He'd spent the last few weekends at the site and hadn't been up to the cottage once that spring. When Denise announced that she needed to go to New York for the weekend, he hadn't even asked her why. He'd merely said, "That's great. It will be good for you to get away." And Clara was eager to stay with the children—making the arrangements had been almost too easy.

Denise was to meet Chris at the Frick Collection on 5th Avenue and 70th Street at 11:00. She still had time to walk there from the hotel and look around before Chris arrived. How long had it been since she had been to New York for anything but work? Fifteen years? She and Francois had come shortly after they'd met for a whirlwind, sightseeing frenzy. They'd gone to shows, on a boat tour to see the Statue of Liberty, and to the top of the Empire State Building. She remembered leisurely mornings with breakfast in bed at the hotel, but which hotel? They had walked through Central Park in the rain and had taken a horse-and-buggy ride after dinner, wrapped in blankets, sipping hot chocolate. It must have been fall because she had a vague recollection of leaves crunching under the carriage wheels. The only other times she had been in New York were for quick turnaround trips, meeting prospective guests for her show. Montrealers loved Manhattan and about once a year Denise would bring home a taste of the city for those who couldn't go there themselves.

Walking up Fifth Avenue, with Central Park on one side and luxurious apartment buildings on the other, she felt an odd sense of comfort, like she belonged there, in the city of contrasts. When she arrived at the Frick Collection, once the home of the wealthy industrialist, Henry Frick, she took her time poking around the collections of paintings, sculptures, and antiques. She imagined living amongst such treasures, like Mr. Frick and his wife had done in the early 1900s. The museum served as a grand monument to a man who was described in the brochure as 'one of America's most notable art collectors.'

Denise took particular interest in the sculptures, and when she came across a delicate and intricate terracotta statuette of a young woman and man embracing, she couldn't take her eyes off it. The couple was surrounded by three cherubs pushing them together and scattering roses from a basket. The plaque read: ZEPHYRUS AND FLORA, by Clodion—1799.

She recalled the damaged Henry Moore piece in her living room back home, cracked where the mother lovingly held her child, and she flinched with guilt, thinking how utterly careless she had been to drop it. As if her mind were a movie screen, she saw herself pick up the museum piece and smash it on the floor, then watch the pieces scatter across the room. The image made her shudder. Suddenly, the statue appeared to vibrate, as if provoked by the early trembles of an earthquake. She took a few steps backwards, afraid that somehow she was responsible. Then it stopped. Why was her mind playing tricks on her? Something swept across her back and for a second she was disconnected from her surroundings. She drifted outside of herself and sensed lips skimming her cheek.

A quiet voice reverberated in her ear. "Hello."

Denise turned around, startled. "Chris, you're here early."

"As are you. I was planning on greeting you at the entrance, but you beat me here."

Why did her body ache? Her head was spinning and pounding at the same time. "I'm sorry, I need to sit down for a moment, I'm feeling a little light-headed."

He took her arm and led her to a bench.

"I feel like an old lady."

"If you're an old lady, then I'm an old man."

The idea of being old together appealed to Denise — better yet, *growing* old together. She sat for a few seconds and then stood up. "I'm all right now."

"Are you sure?"

Denise nodded. Feeling like a schoolgirl dizzy with puppy-love, she struggled to regain her composure.

"OK then. Where should we begin?"

"I've already seen almost everything."

Chris laughed. "Me too. You'd think we'd have bumped into each other before now. How about walking around the Garden Court?" He took her hand and they walked in silence until they came across a Dégas painting.

"Beautiful," Denise said. "I love his ballerina paintings. Such elegance and fluidity." She pointed to a man playing the violin on the edge of the frame. "Dégas often includes a violinist, like him, who's detached from the dancers — playing his instrument with sombre disinterest."

"The girls in the painting remind me of my daughters," Chris said. "Tanya and Sophie love ballet. They played mice in the 'Nutcracker Suite' last Christmas."

"Adorable." Denise smiled at him.

"Monique used to dance too, but she gave it up for basketball and hockey." He laughed. "You never know what's going to grab their interest."

Denise thought about her own boys and how different they all were. "You have an active brood," she said.

"That's for sure."

Denise could tell that Chris's daughters brought immense pleasure to his life. She wondered how he would take to sons — step-sons.

They moved on to the indoor garden, a tranquil room surrounded by lush vegetation with the soothing murmur of water flowing from a massive fountain in the centre, and they sat on a stone bench facing the water.

"I wish I had a room like this," Denise said, "a place to escape."

"You can't beat the soothing influence of nature," Chris said. "Once in a while I fantasize about buying a bunch of land and packing in the job, the grind of city life."

Denise envisioned herself living with Chris in the country, protected by nature, tucked away from everything and everyone. But all she said was, "It's a nice dream." She'd come to New York prepared for an adventure and had convinced herself that this trip would help her put things back in perspective, and revitalize her diminishing energy. But the opposite was happening and she was feeling vulnerable and mentally drained. Her head pounding, she poked around in her purse and pulled out her pills. "Tylenol," she said, and popped one in her mouth.

"Maybe you need to eat," Chris said. "How about walking across the park and having a bite at The Tavern on the Green?" He looked at her with concern. "Or we could take a cab if you're not up to it."

"Walking will do me good. Let's go."

Holding hands, they took their time crossing Central Park, enjoying the pleasant weather and the lush grounds, still vividly green after a wet spring. The weather was too beautiful and the mood too agreeable to rush. Runners and rollerbladers whizzed by them, and mothers and nannies ambled along, pushing strollers. Dog walkers tramped in all directions, the oddest combinations of masters and pets. A little old lady walked a massive Great Dane, as tall as she, while a slight young man with arms stretched outward, walked six dogs on each side. Running past them, a man in a business suit yelled after his fleeing Dalmatian, the leash dragging behind in the dirt. Denise and Chris laughed.

"I think every resident of New York City owns a dog," Denise said.

"You'd think they'd be busy enough here chasing after cabs, kids, and money."

"Human beings seem to be programmed to complicate their lives, and in the meantime, sabotage their own happiness."

"I'm all for simplicity." Chris said.

"Simplicity. A concept to aspire to."

Jazz musicians played in the distance and they walked toward the music. A crowd had gathered to listen to the trio performing with gusto.

"They're good," Denise said. "I'd like to bring them to Montreal for my show. I could do a segment on 'Central Park Musicians." Then she remembered that she didn't have a show because it had been stolen from her.

Chris cocked his head inquisitively.

"You know, that show I *used* to host?"

He put his arm around her shoulder and they continued walking. "You've had a nasty blow. Is there anything you can do to challenge the network?"

"Even if there was, I don't have the energy to fight. And I'm still incredulous that Nicole and Gary would betray me like that—they switched from my allies to adversaries in a matter of weeks. My fair-weather colleagues pulled quite the number on me." Her voice cracked. "Let's talk about something else."

Chris stopped walking and pulled her close to him. They were inches apart, and she could feel his breath as he stared fixedly at her. Suddenly they were kissing and she was nineteen again, melting in his arms. She couldn't break away, didn't have the will. They kissed like teenagers—tongues, saliva, smothering faces, devouring. As abruptly as it started, it was over. Denise wasn't sure who pulled back first.

"I'm sorry," Chris said. "I shouldn't have done that. I don't know what came over me."

Why was he apologizing? To kiss her like that and then tell her he regretted it was more than offensive. She didn't know what to say.

They continued walking, detached and in silence until Chris spoke. "I *do* know what came over me." He stopped walking and faced her. "I'm so in love with you, it's ridiculous. And I've done too much, even said too much, without knowing what you think and feel." He looked desperate, almost pathetic.

"The same," she said. "God, help us." She shook her head and he pulled her into his arms, kissing her again with unconstrained passion.

Releasing their embrace, they stepped back, dumbfounded. Denise saw trepidation in Chris's face, perhaps from his audacity, perhaps from her own lack of restraint. They were crossing a precarious bridge, one that could collapse beneath them at any time. Stunned by what had occurred, they continued walking toward their destination in murky silence.

By the time they arrived at the restaurant, they had somehow found a way to recover their composure. Lunch was heavenly — oysters, champagne, lobster bisque and fresh-baked breads. The glass-enclosed room had a whimsical atmosphere, creating for Denise, an illusionary perception; was she acting in her own dream? Was Chris a figment of her imagination? When they had been together a few weeks earlier, strolling carefree along the river bank back in Cleveland, and then meandering amidst the countryside shops, she had thought she was experiencing the epitome of happiness, but she had been wrong. Life couldn't be better than now — sitting here with the man of her dreams, as if the world had opened a secret passage that only they had access to. Knowing that Chris shared her feelings was the only drug she needed; as soon as she got back to her hotel she'd flush Dr. Steven's sedatives down the toilet.

After lunch they walked down Central Park West to the south end of the park. "Would you like to check out some Fifth Avenue stores since we happen to be in one of the best shopping neighbourhoods in the world?" Chris asked, putting his arm around Denise's shoulders.

She didn't care what they did, as long as Chris was holding on to her. Her head swirled with giddiness and she had to keep reminding herself that she was in her forties, not her twenties. "Sure," she said.

"I want to buy you something spectacular."

"No, Chris, that's not necessary. Your company is enough of a gift. It's better than anything you could possibly buy me."

"But I think it should be my prerogative to get you something special, to make up for twenty-five years of deprivation." He swung in front of her and pulled her close. Whispering in her ear, he said, "Did I tell you how stunning I think you are?"

She threw her head back like a teenager and laughed. "But I'm not nineteen."

"You could be seventy and I'd still think you were gorgeous." They walked a few more blocks and when they reached Tiffany's, Chris stopped. "Let's go in."

Denise was confronted with an uneasy feeling—a cheapness, like she was about to become a mistress. "No, I can't possibly let you buy me something here."

He pulled her hand. "Then let's just browse, for fun. C'mon, it's 'Tiffany's.'"

She followed him in with reluctance. The store was empty compared to the hordes of pedestrians on the streets. They scanned the glass countertops, which showcased everything from watches to diamonds. When they came to a section that displayed exotic gems, Chris stopped to study the pieces.

"I found it...exactly what I had in mind." A salesperson magically appeared. "That green pendant,"—he pointed through the case—"I'd like to see it."

The man unlocked the sliding glass compartment and carefully removed a necklace with a solitary emerald in the shape of a tear-drop. "Remember our day together in Cleveland, walking in the reservation area?"

"Of course."

"We were in the Emerald Necklace. I know it sounds corny, but this stone will symbolize that day. When you wear it, you'll think of me—I hope." He gently attached the gold chain around her neck, his hand sending tremors through her body as it grazed her skin.

She looked in the mirror and touched the gem resting slightly above the neckline of her shirt. It was small enough not to be ostentatious, but sizable enough to stand out against her olive toned skin.

"It's beautiful. But, Chris—"

"I'm buying you this necklace and please don't argue with me." He undid the clasp and handed it to the salesman with a nod.

Lifting her hand to her neck, she touched the spot where the pendant had been and swallowed back tears. "Thank you, it's beyond generous." She leaned over and kissed Chris on the cheek.

"I don't ever want to let you go," he whispered in her ear.

"Then, don't," she whispered back.

After their shopping expedition, they walked to the hotel where Denise was staying, a few blocks from where Chris had checked in. She had made the decision to stay in a different hotel, naively thinking that a separate location would safeguard against temptation. Whether she had the strength to uphold the arrangement at night was becoming questionable, but she didn't want to think about that now. They made plans to meet in the lobby at 7:00, allowing some time to rest and freshen up for the evening ahead.

Chris walked her to the elevator when they arrived. "Let me come up."

Denise was tempted by his pleading eyes and her own euphoria. "No, Chris. We both know it wouldn't be wise." The elevator came, interrupting his chance to protest, and Denise hurried in before she could change her mind.

She lay on the bed, trying to relax; an impossible endeavour with her mind racing and her heart hammering. She turned on the television and then turned it off. She closed the curtains and put on some soft music to help her settle down. Her adrenaline flowed. All she wanted was to be with Chris. If she had let him come up, they would be making love right now. Why hadn't she? She thought of her mother's words: "Careful, now." But how could her mother have foreshadowed this? And why hadn't she seen it coming, herself? Would it have made any difference? *What could I have done, Mother? How could I have stopped this from happening? From the instant I saw Chris again, it was too late. I love him more than any man I have ever loved. What am I supposed to do with these feelings?*

Instead of flushing the sedatives away, as was her earlier intention, Denise took one and lay down under the covers, rolling herself in a ball. She thought of the Henry Moore sculpture she had dropped in her living room back home, and recalled the fracture, exactly where the mother held her child. Did that crack represent her mother's broken hold on her? Or was it her own failure to maintain attachment to her three children? Denise fell asleep with the image of the three cherubs at the Frick Museum pushing the man and woman towards each other; but then the man and woman became Francois and her, and Thomas, Luc, and Martin were the cherubs pressing them together.

****

Chris headed toward his hotel, frustrated that Denise had rebuffed him, yet relieved at the same time. What was he doing? When he had asked Denise to meet him in New York, it was a fantasy. Now that the fantasy had become reality his life was exploding—whether the explosion was dynamite or fireworks was difficult to discern. The last thing he wanted to do was to sit in a room by himself dreaming about Denise instead of being with her. He shoved his hands deep into his pockets and walked to Madison Avenue, thinking back to when he was nineteen and had first met Denise in Montreal. Why was she penetrating his psyche with such intensity, and why was she still embedded in his heart? Not speaking to Denise while Monique was having her troubles had been brutal, and the more time he spent with her, the more inextricable the relationship was becoming. For the first time in his life, he didn't know what to do.

Stepping off the curb to cross the street, Chris was oblivious to a cab's screeching breaks, but he became aware of his mistake when the driver shouted obscenities at him for jaywalking. Chris waved in an apologetic gesture and continued walking, picking up his pace while dodging pedestrians. If only he and Denise had understood back then what they knew now. The missed opportunity was beyond measure and now they were trying to...what? Recapture something? Make up for lost time?

He tried to focus on his surroundings as he bumped shoulders with people of various shapes, sizes, and nationalities. The one thing they all had in common was their intensity—all running to catch cabs, buses, the subway, or perhaps scrambling to meet someone. He suddenly felt out of place in this crowd of resolute pedestrians. But he kept his pace, preoccupying himself with the storefront windows. When he came across a wine boutique on Madison Avenue, he stopped to examine a display of vintage wines in the window. The store's facade was vaguely familiar and he backed up to view the sign above the red awning: Livingstone Wine and Spirits. Ah, yes. He had been here before, years ago, with Laura. At the time, he had already developed an interest in wine-collecting but had to put a hold on his hobby because Laura was expecting their first child, and they had recently bought their new house, overextending themselves financially. In fact, Laura had been about six months pregnant with Tanya when they were together in New York, their last romantic getaway before the baby arrived. He remembered Laura's enthusiasm when they'd stumbled across the store.

"We have to get you something here, Chris — a souvenir for your collection," she said.

"No frivolous expenditures. Remember our pact?" he replied.

They had agreed before taking the trip that they would do New York on a budget. No shopping, no expensive meals and no Broadway shows. Instead, they were going to walk as much as their energy and feet would permit, and visit as many museums as they could manage. They were to stay at a friend's apartment, eat in, and take the bus or subway instead of cabs.

"Let's go in and see what they have — out of interest." She nudged him towards the door.

Of course, once they were inside, he became enthralled with the quality of the wines and impressed by the diverse selection. There had been one bottle in particular that had caught his eye, a vintage Burgundy, a rare find. Chris remembered the exact expression on Laura's face, the excitement radiating from her eyes.

"Let's get it," she said.

"No way, this is over the top, we can't afford it."

"I'm buying if for you, even if I have to cash in some bonds. Let's think of it as an investment, like gold."

There was no talking her out of it. She took the bottle out of his hands, brought it to the cash register and handed the man her credit card. He could see her now, in his mind's eye, stomach protruding under her loose maternity blouse, the animated glow exuding from her contented face.

He didn't argue further, not wanting to disappoint her, but also because he was thrilled with the gift. "The salesman says the wine will be perfect in about ten years—how about we keep it until our twelfth anniversary?" he said. "Even better, let's plan to come back here to celebrate and I promise you, by then we won't be skimping."

"Fabulous idea! We have a date in ten years then, right back here in New York City." They shook hands to seal the pact.

Chris's thoughts jumped back to the present when he noticed an empty bottle of Margaux propped against an old wine crate in the window display. Tony's wine! He charged into the shop and darted up and down the narrow aisles looking for a salesperson. "Can I help you?" a woman asked. He turned toward the voice and found a young woman whom he'd mistaken for a customer. "Yes, I'm wondering if you would have a 1989 Chateaux Margaux in stock." Without hesitating she said, "No, we don't, but we do have the 1990. It's in the cellar, shall I get it for you?" Chris couldn't believe his good fortune—that he'd stumbled upon a wine store that had Tony's Margaux, a superior vintage no less.

Leaving the store, he looked up at the storefront once more and thought of Laura. Not only was she pregnant and not drinking when she had splurged on that bottle for him, but wine held little interest for her. She merely wanted to indulge him, do something special for him. When they had returned to their friend's apartment that day, they spent the rest of the afternoon, evening, and night in bed, oblivious to the fact that they were in New York City.

Chris smiled at the memory and then guilt smacked his conscience like a blow to the head. Here he was—ten years later—in New York City...but with Denise.

****

Denise woke to shrieking sounds coming from the speakers. The classical station she had been listening to had moved on to opera. She jumped out of bed, turned the radio off, and checked the time— 6:45—only fifteen minutes to get ready. The new skirt and fuchsia blouse hung in the closet with the tags still attached. Getting

321

dressed, Denise suddenly regretted her choice of outfit. She hadn't worn it since Francois' negative reaction, and now she questioned whether it was appropriate for tonight. But it was too late; nothing else she had brought would do. The skirt was slightly loose because of her recent weight loss but the blouse covered the waistband, hiding her skeletal frame. Nicole had said the outfit was smashing on her, sexy even, and she hoped Chris would see it that way too. All she needed was some make-up, a spray of perfume, shoes, and her purse. Lingering in front of the mirror, she studied herself more closely. No amount of make-up could hide the lines that had been creeping across her face during the past few years. The emerald necklace lay elegantly against her neck, but her collar bone protruded. Old-lady bones. Then she looked at her once beautiful hands, inspecting them from all angles. Her long fingers and lean bone structure, previously touted as 'the hands of royalty' by the fashion set, now seemed unsightly with protruding veins. Even her French manicure could not conceal the fact that these hands were passed their glory.

In the hotel lobby, Denise found Chris pacing the floor as if waiting for news of a loved one in a hospital. Every time she saw Chris he appeared more handsome. Tonight he wore black from head to toe—black jacket, black shirt, black pants, no tie. His graying hair added to his sophistication, like one of those middle-aged news broadcasters. When he turned her way she tried to appear self-possessed, but inwardly she was painfully self-conscious.

"You look sensational," Chris said when she was close enough to hear. He kissed her on the lips and then pulled back, placing his hands on her shoulders, and staring at her as if penetrating her soul. They went outside and waited for the doorman to hail a cab.

"What do you think of New York?" Chris asked.

"Blissful." She edged closer to him.

Sipping champagne on the 65th floor bar in Rockefeller Plaza, Denise was barely able to believe where she was and who she was with. She felt like she was playing a role in her own movie. The view of Manhattan from their table was spellbinding but the view across the table was hypnotic.

"Doesn't it feel odd to you that we're together like this after so many years?" she asked.

"This is exactly where we should be," he said with assurance.

"I can't disagree." She picked up her evening bag and searched inside. "I have something to show you. Here's your name and phone number from that fateful day, twenty-five years ago, when we parted ways."

Chris took the scrap of paper and studied it. "I thought you'd lost this."

"I came across it recently when I was clearing out my mother's house. It had somehow slipped through a torn seam in my old purse."

"Hmm," he said. "How different our lives would have been if you had found it, and found me, earlier."

"Maybe I wasn't supposed to find you until now."

"D'you think fate has thrown us together?"

"I do."

"Like I've said before, I don't believe in destiny. We make choices and then we live with the consequences."

"I agree to an extent. I mean, we've chosen to come here and to spend time with one another, but I don't think we can choose how we feel." She watched him watching her, and she took a sip of her drink.

"I can't deny how I feel about you, Denise. You bring out emotions in me that I didn't even know existed."

She loved what she was hearing. For the last month and a half she had never been quite sure what all those cryptic e-mails and phone calls would amount to—what was hidden beneath the layers of polite conversations and friendly communications. She had found it difficult to read between the lines, especially when Chris had broken their contact. At last, her doubts were alleviated.

"Sometimes I wonder how I've existed for a quarter of a century without you," he said.

"I suppose we both could have avoided a lot of hardships had we understood our feelings back then."

"Our lives would have been entirely different." He took her hand. "We would have made a great team."

Denise hadn't noticed the slow transformation of daylight to dusk until now. The skyline shimmered with flickering lights as far as the eye could see. More people had arrived at the bar and the mellow ambiance was becoming charged with nightclub vivacity. She looked at Chris across the table and drew a deep breath when he leaned in closer. She tried to say something but the words scattered in her mind, making speech impossible.

The heavy moment broke and Chris let go of her hand to spoon some caviar onto a toast wedge. He handed it to her, "You've got to try this."

"Thank you. Krug and Beluga caviar make the most divine combination."

A strange look swept across Chris's face, a vacant sadness. "You all right?" she asked.

He blinked, as if he'd mentally left her for a second. "Fantastic." He smiled and held his glass up as if to make a toast. "I still can't believe that I'm sitting here with you—that we're actually doing this."

They spoke about politics, religion, and philosophy—subjects to avoid in general company. They did not speak of their spouses, their families or anything else that could interfere with the evening's glow. When the waiter poured the last of the champagne into their glasses, Chris told Denise about the Margaux he had purchased earlier.

"Such a coup," he said. "A vintage like that is rare, and almost impossible to find."

"I know exactly what you're talking about," Denise said. "When I lived in Paris, I had the opportunity to try that particular wine. It was a memorable vintage, probably the best I've ever tasted."

Chris broke into a broad smile, his entire face brimming with enthusiasm. "I have an idea. Why not go to my hotel and break open the bottle. We can order up some Chateaubriand to go with it. Wouldn't that be a great way to end the day?"

Denise laughed. "We are certainly going over the top today. But what can I say? That's a difficult offer to refuse." In a way, she felt like she did when she was nineteen, agreeing to go to Chris's parents' home, even though she knew she was walking into a potentially loaded situation. Would going up to his room bring her to the point of no return, or had that point already been passed?

"Is that a yes?"

"Absolutely." The answer had slipped out before she had finished deliberating.

Chapter Thirty-three

The lobby at The Pierrot was bustling with activity when Denise and Chris arrived. Men in black-tie and women in colourful formal gowns decorated the room like streamers and balloons at a birthday party.

"I wonder what's going on here," Denise said.

"Probably a wedding," Chris said.

Denise approached a woman who was standing alone, fanning herself with a booklet. "Excuse me, what's happening here tonight?"

The woman, wearing a red sequined gown, stared at Denise. Then she perked up, "You caught me off-guard, I was keeping an eye on the entrance. I'm waiting for someone."

Denise repeated the question. "What's the event?"

"Oh, yes, sorry. It's a vintner's dinner. Something to do with French wines. I've been invited as a guest, so I don't know the details." Continuing to watch the entrance, she leaned over and whispered to Denise, "At a thousand dollars a plate, I'm expecting a grand to-do."

"Indeed," Denise said. "This must be connected to the wine-tasting event tomorrow afternoon, which my...husband and I are attending." She motioned toward Chris and he nodded in greeting.

The woman smiled at him. "I wouldn't know anything about that, or about wine, to tell you the truth," she whispered. "I'm an imposter here. All I know is that wine comes in two colours—red and white."

Denise laughed. "Your standards might go up a notch or two after this evening." She glanced at the woman's program, "I imagine you'll be drinking some of the best that France has to offer."

"Take my program, if you're interested," the woman said. "I can get another one inside." She turned away once more and fixed her gaze towards the front.

Denise flipped the pages of the booklet. "Oh my goodness," she said to Chris. "I know this man." She pointed to a black and white photograph of a distinguished-looking gentleman holding his wine glass toward the sky, observing its contents. "That's Monsieur Charest, one of the most renowned vintners in France. When I lived in Paris he was very good to me, a fatherly figure." She scanned the crowd. "I'd love to say hello if I can find him. Would you mind?"

"Not at all. I'll go up to the room and wait for you there," Chris said. He kissed her on the cheek, whispered the room number in her ear, and left.

Denise leafed through the program again and gasped when she came across another familiar face.

Jacques' image leapt off the page. The last time she'd seen the man was during their awful confrontation in Paris, fourteen years ago. In the photograph he appeared almost regal, sitting upright in a leather chair, staring intensely at the camera. The only thing that had changed was his hair colour, which had transformed from stark black to salt and pepper grey.

She followed a group to the Doulton Room where the dinner was being held. Two women stood behind a podium welcoming the guests and collecting tickets. Denise watched people flow into a resplendent ballroom where ornate crown moldings edged the twenty-foot walls, and massive crystal chandeliers hung from a sky-blue ceiling scattered with life-like clouds. Tables dressed with white linen tablecloths and fine china dominated the room. Denise clenched the program as she surveyed the crowd, hoping to catch a glimpse Jacques. Since all the men were in black-tie, it was difficult to spot him. She approached a staff person with a nametag pinned to his dinner jacket.

"Excuse me, Mr. Gordon, can you tell me where I might find Jacques Chevalier?"

"I believe he's already inside," the man replied.

"I'm not attending this dinner, but he's an old acquaintance from Paris, and I was wondering if I could have a quick word with him?" Was she out of her mind to seek Jacques out?

The man gave her a card and asked her to write down her name. "I'll see what I can do," he said, courteously. He then passed the card to a server and whispered something that Denise could not hear.

She waited outside the dining room, reading the text beneath Jacques' picture.

Jacques Chevalier, one of the world's leading Burgundy winemakers, shares with us tonight the insights and experiences that have brought him to the world stage. He has taken a small family vineyard to unsurpassed heights despite regional challenges, and his winery has produced some of the finest Burgundies that connoisseurs have ever had the privilege to enjoy. To some, he is known as the Lord of Burgundy.

He was probably sitting alone in his lofty tower, or at best with a wife he didn't love. Denise smoothed back her hair and adjusted her outfit. Walking by a large mirror, the backdrop for an enormous flower display, she caught a glimpse of herself. Why hadn't she used the ladies' room before asking for him? She should have at least freshened up her makeup and brushed her hair. Never mind, Chris had said she was ravishing tonight; a few hairs out of place would hardly matter. Poised to afflict him with regret, she smiled. He would see how his own arrogance destroyed the best thing he ever had.

Jacques emerged from the banquet room with a young woman, many years his junior, at his side. Probably his daughter, Denise speculated.

"Jacques," she said in her gracious talk-show host voice, holding out her hand. "How nice to see you."

He took her hand and kissed it. "It's been a long time," he said, his French accent heavier than she remembered. "This is my wife, Adrienne." They shook hands and Denise noticed the huge diamond ring glistening on her left hand.

Words swirled in her head and she had trouble putting them together. "When I found out that you were here, I thought I should say hello." But she regretted the decision. What on earth was there to say, especially with that child-woman on his arm? She looked about the same age that Denise had been when she had first met Jacques, and she could not help but view her as competition.

"I came across the information quite by accident in the lobby...that you were here, I mean." He was even more handsome than she remembered with his graying hair and black-tie ensemble.

He smiled, his eyes piercing her. "You've been keeping well?"

"Yes. Wonderful. I have three children and I work in television and I—"

"Congratulations," he said with vague interest. "Adrienne and I have a two-year-old daughter, Arielle. Children bring much joy, n'est-ce pas?" He beamed at his young wife.

Denise had to stop herself from glaring at him. Had he not told her many years ago, in no uncertain terms, that children would be an impediment to his lifestyle? She remembered pleading with him to consider having one child with her. When she'd found out about his existing family she'd assumed that the real reason for his lack of interest was that he already had children and didn't want any more. But now she knew that even that was not the case. He just didn't want to have children with her.

Denise stumbled back into the conversation. "Yes, children are wonderful." She was about to tell him about *Montreal's Alive* but stopped herself, convinced nothing would impress him. "Your winery is thriving, I see." She held up the page describing its success.

His wife gazed at Jacques adoringly and Denise noticed him squeeze her hand. "Yes, in fact, we moved there some time ago. We've built a new chateau on the property, which has become our main residence. The country air is good for Arielle...for all of us."

"How wonderful." That woman, who couldn't be more than twenty-two, was living out Denise's past dreams. How many times had she told Jacques that she wished they could settle in Burgundy and run the winery together? And how often had he spurned her fantasy? She smiled as charming a smile as she could extract and said, "I'll let you get back to your function. Lovely to see you both."

"Likewise," Jacques said, and kissed her hand again. "We must keep in touch."

Like hell.

Denise found the ladies room and entered one of the stalls. She sat down on the seat. Of course things would have worked out for Jacques, why wouldn't they? He was the kind of man who could have, or take, anything he wanted—a player with a penchant for excitement, and young women. Denise ripped the page with Jacques' bio from the program and tore it to shreds, letting the pieces fall to the floor.

Now, more than ever, it was clear that she had been a mere accessory in his life, a prop to make him shine. When she created her own television show, she finally had a chance to shine in her own spotlight, and the affirmation of her worth had felt wonderful. But all that was gone. At home she had different roles, different objectives—mother and wife—roles that seemed less and less appreciated these days. With Chris, the layers fell away and for once she was free to be herself. How could she harness that new sense of being? Beginning a new life with Chris was the only chance she'd have to realize her true self. With trembling hands, she reached into her bag for her pills. Jacques was completely irrelevant to her life and there was no reason to feel wretched. She had enough drama in her life as it was.

****

After Chris had placed the room service order, he called home with a nudging sense of guilt because he had neglected to call earlier.

"Hello, Tanya speaking."

"Hi, doll. It's Daddy."

"DADDY! Something terrible happened today!"

He could hear Laura chastising in the background. "Tanya, no, you weren't supposed to tell him."

"I forgot," she said, whimpering into the phone.

"What's the matter, sweetheart, what happened?"

"Pepper got hit by a car." She cried harder.

Laura came on the line. "I'm sorry, Chris. We weren't going to say anything until you got home."

"He's all right, though?"

The reply came slowly. "No, he's not."

Chris's legs went numb and he had to sit down. Gripping the phone harder, he said, "What happened?"

"The front door wasn't shut properly and the wind blew it open. Pepper saw a squirrel and ran outside, chasing it across the street. You know what he's like with cars...has no clue." Chris heard a faint sniffle. "When the car hit him, he flew about ten feet in the air."

"Did he suffer? Was it quick?" He swallowed hard.

"He died almost immediately, before we were able to get him to the vet."

"I can't believe *my* dog is dead."

"Our dog." He could hear her blowing her nose. "We loved him too, you know," she said between sobs. "But I know how much he meant to you and how hard this is to hear. I'm sorry you had to learn about it like this."

His tone softened. "Accidents happen. At least it wasn't a child." He had visions of one of the girls running after Pepper onto the street and being struck instead. "We'll talk some more about it when I come home, OK?"

"OK," she said, still sniffling. "Bye."

It's only an animal he told himself; it's only an animal.

Chris tried to distract himself by making the room hospitable. He found a classical station on the radio and turned down the lights. Candles would complete the ambience but there weren't any to be found; maybe they could bring some up with the food. The room appeared pleasant, comfortably intimate—he was ready. But where was Denise? It had been ages since he'd left her in the lobby.

Visions of Pepper jumping up to greet him dampened his spirit and caused his eyes to burn with suppressed tears. He sat down, then stood up. Feeling the stubble on his face, he wondered if he'd have time to shave again. When he scrutinized his image in the bathroom mirror, he was shocked; his eyes were bloodshot and his complexion was deathly pale. He rinsed his face with cold water, brushed his teeth, and slapped on some aftershave, trying to imagine what he had looked like when he was nineteen, meeting Denise for the first time. Twenty-five years was a long time. At least he was physically fit thanks to his regular squash games with Tony, and the running, and the power walks with Pepper. He grabbed a towel and whipped it against the wall. Pepper's death was his fault. If he hadn't stayed in New York to be with Denise, Pepper probably wouldn't be dead. Everything going wrong seemed like his fault these days.

The knock at the door forced him to restore his composure. But it wasn't Denise, it was dinner. A valet, withered and wrinkled, entered the room and set up a table by the window, overlooking Central Park. He moved in slow motion as he laid the tablecloth, straightened it, and then placed the china and the silverware on the table with painstaking precision. He had trouble with the matches, but finally succeeded to light the candles. Taking a step back, he examined his table-setting, as if it were a work of art, then slowly rolled the trolley with the food to the tableside. He noticed the bottle of wine on the dresser and asked if Chris would like him to open it. Chris nodded. In helpless frustration, he watched the man try to tear the foil from the wine bottle neck, his fingers working slowly as he pulled the edge of the foil.

"Don't worry about it, I can do that," Chris said, reaching for the bottle. He handed the old man a few bills and ushered him to the door. About to close it, Chris caught sight of Denise walking along the narrow corridor.

"I was beginning to worry," Chris said. "Did you find your friend?"

"Someone else, actually. Another blast from the past."

"Who?"

"Jacques Chevalier."

Chris had read Denise's letter about her life in Paris so many times that he felt as though he knew the man. "Small world. What happened?"

"Not much. We spoke briefly and he introduced me to his lovely young wife."

"He divorced the other one in the end?"

"I suppose." Denise took off her shoes and walked over to the window. "Beautiful view."

Chris sensed her disinclination to discuss Jacques further. "Are you ready to try the wine?" he asked, picking up the bottle and showing it to her.

"Love to," she said, barely paying attention to the prized wine. She pointed to the small round table covered with crisp white linen and set with bone china. "We have quite the intimate set-up here."

Realizing that the man hadn't left his corkscrew, Chris searched around the bar area while Denise stared outside. After rummaging through cupboards and drawers, he found one behind the ice bucket. "You must be starved." He motioned for her to sit down and pulled out the chair for her.

"Everything looks perfect," she said.

"A beautiful setting for a beautiful woman." Chris cringed after he spoke, realizing how corny he sounded. Like the old man, he fiddled with the rigid foil encasing around the bottle neck.

"So, where does fantasy end and reality begin?" Denise asked.

He removed the cork and filled their wine glasses. "Such a heavy question over dinner? Let's eat first and ponder life's quandaries later."

She lifted the warming lid off her plate. "This beef looks delicious."

"I ordered medium rare, I hope that's OK."

She nodded. "Wonderful food, fabulous wine, being alone with you...what a scenario. I can hardly believe I'm here."

"I hope the wine meets your expectations." He lifted his glass to his nose, closed his eyes and inhaled the aromas. Denise did the same. Enraptured by the rich, dense, smoky bouquet, Chris let his senses take over. "Wow," he said when he opened his eyes. "I haven't even tasted it yet and I'm in heaven." He lifted his glass. "Santé."

"And to you." They clinked glasses and drank. "Sublime," Denise said.

Chris held his glass to the light and studied the deep red colour. "They say that this is the most famous wine in the world, and it has yet to be surpassed in greatness. Wines like this are meant to be consumed by those who appreciate excellence."

"Our relationship is just like the wine," Denise said. "It's been quietly fermenting until it was ready to be enjoyed. Don't you think?"

"Wine and romance are sweet companions." Thoughts of Laura and the precious bottle of Burgundy she had bought for him during *their* visit to New York crept into Chris's mind as he drank. If only he could close that compartment and fully enjoy the present moment.

During dinner, they conversed casually about their impressions of New York, which helped take his mind off Laura. Talking to Denise was easy and comfortable; she was knowledgeable about many subjects and her opinions were well-founded. Chris loved sharing a meal like this — good food, fine wine, and scintillating company. Intermittently, he stopped listening to her words and simply watched her movements — the way she swept her hair behind her ear, or raised her eyes to the ceiling when she was pondering a question.

Soon, the subject she had raised at the beginning of the meal began to infiltrate his mind and meddle with the evening's serenity. How real was their relationship? What was its place in their lives? When he was with Denise he could barely think of anything else; even when he wasn't with her, she dominated his thoughts. But what about the rest of his life? Laura, the kids, his job, the world he had painstakingly chiseled out of nothing. Interesting how blindsided he was when it came to Denise. Interesting and frightening.

"Chris, did you hear me?"

"I'm sorry, Laura, what did you say?"

There was a crash of silence. Then, "You called me Laura."

"I'm sorry, I don't know what I was thinking. Here, let me pour you some more wine." He felt his face flush. What an imbecile.

"I was asking you if you ever went to the symphony." Denise's voice had an edge of annoyance.

"We used to, on our date nights, until Laura caught me falling asleep once too often and said we were wasting our money." He laughed. "How about you?" This was not the time to be mentioning Laura, especially after the last gaffe. What a cad. Chris drank some more wine, trying to focus on its rich silky finish.

"One of my job's perks was to get tickets for cultural events. I was fortunate to have the opportunity to go to the opera, or ballet, or concerts, as often as I wished, courtesy of the network. But that's all over."

Chris reached for Denise's hand, the first physical contact they'd had since she came to his room. "You'll find something better, I guarantee. You're too special to fall by the wayside, I'm certain you'll be getting all kinds of offers when the news gets out."

"Are we in the world of fiction now or the world of reality?" She pulled her hand away.

There was something definitely bothering her. "Is something wrong, Denise? Did I offend you?"

She got up from the table. "No, I'm not offended. I'm…I don't know, afraid, I suppose. I mean, look at us. When we're together, it's as if we've always been together, like it's the most natural thing in the world. But it's a tease, because then we have to go back to our lives and act like everything's normal."

"I know."

"What do we do about it? We can't go on like this. At least I can't."

Chris walked over to Denise and embraced her. "I love you. In truth, I've always loved you."

Denise started to cry. "This is ripping me apart."

"I wish I could be with you all the time, till the day I die." he said, stroking her hair.

Imploringly, she said, "Then let's do it, Chris. Take what we have and build a future out of it. It's not too late, we still have half our lives ahead of us."

"But our families — it's not straightforward."

"Other people get divorces. It happens all the time. Kids adjust, they're resilient."

Chris couldn't say it, but there was something else stopping him, pulling him backwards. He still cared for Laura, he loved them both. What could he do? The price was too high to do what Denise was suggesting. When he didn't answer right away, he saw dread in her eyes.

"You say you love me, you want to be with me, and that it was a mistake not to stay together all those years ago. Now it's in your power to give yourself that chance, to be happy, in a new life." She walked across the room as if she was going to walk out the door, but she swung around and stared intensely at Chris, like she was willing him to say what she needed him to say.

Chris wanted to agree. He wanted to say, yes, let's go for it, build a new life, take back the lost time and fill it up. But he couldn't because he had filled those years with other things, other people. The image of Monique, sitting across from him at the tennis club, came to his mind. *You have no idea how much I admire the way you handle problems. You're always so calm and smart about things. You really are a great dad, and the best role model*, she had said. Then Laura—the sound of her voice, crying about Pepper, not for her own sake but for his; the snapshot in his mind of Laura snuggling with nine-year-old Monique in front of a fire on the coldest day of the year. And his sweet girls, like the little ballerinas in the painting he had seen earlier in the day, innocently dancing through their lives. He didn't want to be like that violinist in the picture, in the background, excluded from the action. No, he couldn't destroy his family; they needed him, *he* needed *them*.

Denise sat on the bed and lowered her head. "I can't go on like this. You have to make a decision."

Chris froze.

"What do you want from me?" Denise asked, her voice cracking.

To admit his confusion would be torturous. It would mean letting her go forever, with the knowledge that he would never see her again. But he had to be honest; to mislead her into thinking he would leave his family would be despicable. How did it come to this? He wasn't sure he had the strength to let her go—to move back into life without her. Watching Denise as she sat on the edge of the bed, dejected, made him want nothing more at that moment than to take her in his arms and make love to her, to say that he was hers completely. But when he saw Laura in his mind's eye, standing in the wine store with her big stomach, buying him that special gift, he became paralyzed. He loved them both and now Denise was forcing him to choose. "I'm sorry," he said, tears spilling out, "I can't leave my family, I could never leave them." The truth caved in on him at that moment. In his heart he had the capacity to love two women, but in life, in the real world, he knew he could only devote himself to one.

Denise stood up and walked slowly to the door. Picking up her purse from the floor, she turned to face him, her eyes sadder than he'd ever seen. "These past two months have been like walking on a minefield, Chris. I'm tired of dodging the inevitable." Her face was strange, almost contorted, but Chris couldn't fully absorb her grief because he had enough difficulty dealing with his own. It wasn't until later that night that he realized she'd left without her shoes.

Chapter Thirty-four

The next day, Denise paid the cab driver and teetered up the flagstone path toward her front door. The late morning sun beamed down on the east-facing garden and the buds on the rose-bushes looked as if they would explode into a profusion of beauty at any moment. But the sight brought no pleasure; instead she had an urge to clip the buds before they had a chance to bloom. Her black linen slacks were wrinkled and her lilac cardigan, tied over her shoulders, lay askew around her neck. She'd left the rest of her clothes and toiletries back at the hotel in New York. She wouldn't miss that new outfit—it had been a mistake to buy it in the first place, and a mistake to wear it. Every decision in her life had turned out to be a catastrophic mistake.

The flight was a blur. Denise couldn't remember whether she had spoken to anyone during the course of the trip and she barely recalled the cab ride home. All she wanted to do was to crawl into bed and obliterate the memory of the last two months. She fiddled with her key, trying to get the door open, but it jammed inside the lock. Tears of frustration welled in her eyes as she struggled with it, and suddenly, Francois opened the door, a wide smile on his face.

"Welcome home," he said, and kissed her. "How was New York? I missed you."

What did he care about her trip? She recalled how he'd barely paid attention when she told him that she needed to get away for a few days to clear her head. She'd even suggested he come along, knowing full well that he wouldn't.

"Terrific," she said, her voice flat.

"Are you all right?" he asked.

Francois looked like the Francois from the past in his black denim trousers, crisp white button-down shirt, and black loafers. With his rectangular glasses and his short blond hair swept back, he had that artsy look she'd always found attractive. And today he came across uncharacteristically relaxed.

"I'm fine, I'm great," she said, sobs erupting.

Francois took her in his arms and held her tight. "What's the matter, what's the matter?"

She broke away from his hold, staring at him through saturated eyes, and blurted out, "I was in New York with another man." The words spilled without warning, with no time to edit them.

Francois stepped back, away from her. "Are you telling me that you're having an affair?" His expression transformed from concern to disbelief.

"No, I'm not having an affair. And whatever it was, it's over." A powerful sense of calm engulfed her and her thoughts became clear, for the first time in days.

"You just said you were in New York with a man, did you not?"

"That's right. But I'm not going to see him again." Her sudden composure surprised her.

"And that makes it all right?"

"We didn't sleep together, Francois. It wasn't like that."

"Then what *was* it like?" His eyes narrowed.

"He was someone I knew when I was nineteen, we bumped into each other recently and became friends."

"You don't go off to New York innocently with a male friend. Tell me what's going on, Denise."

"Nothing. It's nothing. I told you, it's over."

"What a fool I am! I was so worried about you, thinking you were going through a rough time. I didn't go into work today because I wanted to be here for you when you came home." He slammed his hand against the wall at the bottom of the stairs.

"You're overreacting. Nothing happened. I'm telling you all this because I want to move on, deal with this together, and move on."

"Move on? You've got to be kidding. Sorry, what I think you need to do is *move out*. How can I be with someone I can't trust, who has a relationship on the side, while I'm working 24/7?"

"Don't be unreasonable, let me explain. Listen to me for once!"

"What kind of marriage is this?" He pointed to the stairs. "Get your things and go!"

"But the boys, I want to see them."

"They're not here. Clara's taken them to her place for the day, to give us time alone." His eyes spewed loathing as he took something out of his back pocket. "See these," he said, waving papers in her face. "Tickets to Bermuda. I was going to surprise you with them today." He ripped them in half and dropped them on the ground. "Surprise."

Denise walked past him and stopped at the living room, her favourite sanctuary in the house. The Henry Moore statue was back on its pedestal, the mother figure glaring at her with hatred. Then all of the objects they had collected together over the years — the paintings, the antiques, the knick knacks, and the gorgeous rug — became useless relics. Denise clutched the railing as she climbed the stairs and when she reached the landing, she ran to the bathroom and vomited. Her heaving was so fierce that she had to steady herself by grasping the toilet seat.

When she was finished, she rinsed her mouth and spat the vile taste into the sink. The woman she saw in the mirror was someone else, not Denise Gagnon, accomplished wife and mother of three, host of *Montreal's Alive*. She brushed her teeth, washed her face, and combed the knots from her hair, realizing she hadn't brushed her hair since yesterday. Staring at her reflection, she barely recognized herself; two puffy slits sunken into sallow and blotchy skin, and a face etched with misery. The hollowness she felt inside was facing her in the form of an eerie, ghost-like vision of her former self. Francois was right; she was a failure on all accounts, useless and undeserving, and they'd be better off without her. What had she expected when she divulged her secret? Maybe his response was what she was waiting for, the truth she needed to hear. She couldn't do anything right these days, couldn't keep her job, couldn't even keep a man.

She stuffed random pieces of clothing into a large gym bag. The small painting Chris had bought for her was leaning against the closet wall, still wrapped in brown paper. She placed it on top of her clothes, along with a pair of canvas shoes, and a few pairs of underwear. From her bedside table drawer, she removed a newly prescribed bottle of sleeping pills and threw them into the bag. Before zipping it closed, she noticed the copy of *Wuthering Heights* that Camille had found at her mother's house and tossed it in.

When Denise came down the stairs, Francois was still there, sitting on the middle of the third step, hunched over, with his hands covering his face. "Denise," he whispered as she squeezed by him. But she didn't answer, and she didn't say good-bye when she slipped out the door.

Chapter Thirty-five

Denise drove away, her mind swirling with Francois' caustic words, and her heart numb with remorse. Lush maple trees, lining the boulevard with their new growth, looked like gnarling overgrown weeds to her darkened spirit. When a neighbour waved, she averted her eyes and didn't wave back. All she could focus on was the street ahead of her, the dark pavement — the path to her mother's house. It was only a few miles away but she had no sense of distance as she drove along the same route that she had taken thousands of times before. The minutes passed like hours as she weaved through the city streets. This would be the last visit to the house, the last journey into her past, and the last time she would ever smell the scent of the only place she could truly call home. Her mother's absence had left behind a vacuous world, one that now seemed uninhabitable.

When she arrived, she was pleased to see that the impatiens and the begonias, planted by her mother, were blossoming with unrestrained splendor. She imagined her mother kneeling there in her large brimmed hat, meticulously planting the flowers and then watering them with the same metal watering can she'd used for thirty years. But the soothing scene vanished when she noticed the 'Sold' sign puncturing the manicured lawn. Before entering the house, she stared at the building from the driveway, trying to capture the image like a photograph in her mind. From the corner of her eye she noticed movement next door, in Mrs. Peterson's front window. A silhouette peered out between the curtains, two snooping eyes and the edge of a shoulder, and then the face was gone, the curtains left swaying. The one thing her mother would certainly not miss in this world was Mrs. Peterson's busybody antics.

Bracing herself, Denise trudged toward the front door, crushed by the weight of her own misery. The key turned easily in the well-worn lock and she half-expected to be greeted by her mother's warm embrace. But to her chagrin, the place was cavernous and gloomy, with only a few odd pieces remaining—a down-filled armchair and the piano in the living room—Camille's things. Boxes, with Camille's name printed in thick black marker across the front, were piled in the corner. The walls were bare except for the dark rectangular shadows, where paintings and photographs had once hung. Dust had settled on the hardwood floors, now barren without the richly coloured area rugs scattered throughout the rooms. The warm, bright sun, shining through the naked windows, reminded Denise of happier times, when laughter and chaos had filled the rooms. Holiday celebrations from her childhood, to more recent family gatherings, raced through her mind like a movie in fast-forward. There had been good times here, plenty of memories to cherish.

Denise walked into the empty living room, an eerie echo follow-ing each step. The comforting thoughts from a moment ago now provoked sadness. When her mother died, Denise's inner child died too; no longer was she somebody's daughter, but merely a mother herself, bearing a responsibility that she felt ill-equipped to handle. Shouldn't her own children bring her comfort and give her purpose? But when she saw the floors and walls in her mother's house stripped of their trimmings, she saw her own empty life, and an empty future.

Denise fell back into Camille's chair, causing it to slide back and scratch the floor. She could imagine her mother flinching as she heard the scraping sound from her grave. Chris's emerald necklace, still hanging around her neck, felt cold against her skin and she fiddled with it nervously. With a sharp tug, she ripped it off and stared at the green gem in the palm of her hand. Was it only yesterday when he'd presented her with this symbol of his enduring love? Ha! She threw it at her feet and watched it sparkle in a sea of dust.

She unzipped the gym bag and removed the painting Chris had purchased for her. She'd intended to hang it at the cottage on the empty space between the hearth and the pine armoire, but that had been a bad idea. As if unwrapping a birthday present, she tore off the brown paper, letting the shreds fall to the ground. Why had she been captivated by the image of a mother duck swimming down the river with her chicks? Now, she felt nothing. It was a silly painting. Silly and trivial. Closing her eyes, she tried to re-enact her walk with Chris along the river bank, in one of the gems of Cleveland's Emerald Necklace. But conjuring up the blissful feelings of surrender that she had experienced that day was impossible, and her head ached from the effort. Leaning over, she picked up the broken necklace and stood up, the painting nestled under her arm.

Denise headed out the back door, down the deck stairs and towards the north-west corner of the yard, where her mother kept a stash of gardening tools hidden under a lilac shrub. Sure enough the basket was still there, covered by a green garbage bag and camouflaged by the bushy, low branches. A gardening magazine was wedged between the trowel and the fork, and her mother's garden gloves and a pair of shears were there too. Denise slipped the gloves on her hands, picked up the trowel, and kneeled in the dirt to dig beneath the lilac bush. Before long, she had dug a large enough hole to bury the objects. She put the painting, the necklace and the piece of paper with Chris's name and phone number into the plastic garbage bag, twisting the top and tying a knot.

She dropped the bag into the grave-like crevice and covered it up with dirt, her movements slow and solemn. Leaving the gardening tools in the basket under the bush, she returned to the house, covered in dirt and perspiration. With robotic movements, she walked back to the living room, tracking muddy footsteps behind her. While searching for the sleeping pills in her gym bag, she noticed the slightly tattered and discoloured jacket cover of *Wuthering Heights*. The shaded image depicted a young couple embracing, while blades of lightning flashed against the darkened moors in the background. Denise couldn't imagine her mother having an interest in a tragic tale about two people at the mercy of love's destructive forces. Biographies, gardening books and National Geographic were more her thing. Was she trying to send a message to Denise through this sordid tale? Was that why the novel had ended up in her hands, to warn her of her own demise? Denise laughed out loud. Her mother was the last person to believe in psychic babble.

Denise found Dr. Stephen's sedatives in her purse, almost a full bottle. Between the two medications, she should have enough to do the job. She went to the kitchen and searched in the cupboards for a glass, but they had all been packed. The only drinking vessels were the pill containers, so she poured out their contents on the counter and filled the bottles with water. Picking up a small mixture of pills, she popped them into the back of her throat and tried to wash them down with the miniature cup. Because there was barely enough water in the tiny bottle for one swallow, she turned on the faucet and used her hands as cups. Water spilled down her shirt and onto the floor, creating puddles at her feet. For a moment she coughed and gagged, but then she took the next bunch into her hands and repeated the procedure, continuing until all the pills were gone.

Hello, darling, she heard from behind. She turned around and saw her mother sitting in a kitchen chair at the end of the table, her usual spot, wearing a pale blue blouse and the Hermès scarf draped over her shoulder. Denise wasn't surprised to see her. In fact, she had expected, or at least hoped, to see her again, one more time. *Why do you want to die?* She asked matter-of-factly.

"There's nothing left for me here, Mother. Nobody wants me. Nobody loves me. Even my children don't need me anymore. You were the only one who ever understood me, and now you're gone."

Even if you think that way, you mustn't give up. You're a strong woman and you can rebuild your life, just as you did before.

"No, you're wrong, Mother. I'm not strong like you. I'm a failure and a disappointment. I can't hold on to anything."

Now, now, dear, you know that's not true. You've always moved on from disappointments. Search deep inside and you'll find your courage.

Denise shook her head. It was too difficult to explain that she was utterly depleted.

Didn't I always teach you that when one door closes another one opens?

Denise sighed. "Yes, you did tell me that, many times. But I've walked out my last door, and I don't have the strength to go through any more."

Nonsense. Tell me, dear, what were you doing out there in the back with my gardening tools?

"Burying some pieces of my past, the ones that destroyed my life." The words came out slurred and she was getting dizzy. "You were right, Mother, I never should have continued having contact with Chris. It was a terrible idea."

And you think hiding those items in the ground will somehow make things better?

"It doesn't matter. I needed to do it."

Sometimes we make mistakes, but then we need to fix them, not bury them.

Denise noticed the disappointment in her mother's eyes. "Don't worry, Mother, next time you see me, everything will be fixed. Everybody will be better off." She closed her eyes, the shame sickening her spirit. When she opened her eyes, her mother was gone. How strange for her to appear like that and then disappear without even saying good-bye. She didn't even have the chance to ask her mother about *Wuthering Heights* or about the letter from Charles.

The house was too warm, almost suffocating. Denise ran her fingers through her messy hair and noticed that her white shirt was soiled with earthy smudges. She dragged herself to the living room and sat down in the chair to rest. Unable to get comfortable, she went to get a box to use as a footrest. The carton at the top of the pile was labeled 'family photo albums.' Attempting to lift the heavy box from the heap, Denise staggered backwards and it crashed to the ground, ripping open, revealing several binders of neatly labeled albums. The one at the top read: 1964 – 1968 / EARLY YEARS IN THE NEW HOUSE. Denise sat on the floor with her back leaning against the wall, and began to sift through pages filled with shots of family gatherings, birthday celebrations, and pictures of her father – a handsome young man with dark sideburns and short black hair, pictures she hadn't seen in years. Perspiration poured from her body and her breathing was laboured as she concentrated on the photographs.

When she came to a sweet photo of eight children sitting around a table, happily eating birthday cake, she stopped and stared, focusing on the small faces. Heather Winter's eighth birthday party. Denise closed her eyes, remembering that day. The kids were only vaguely familiar because the birthday girl lived far away, and she only saw her once or twice a year. Mrs. Winters and her mother were long-time friends. Heather was the only child at that party whom she had known, but all the kids had been friendly. Denise had even been given the first piece of cake because she came all the way from the West Island to the South Shore, and she was considered a special guest.

She recalled a little boy there who had been particularly attentive, making her laugh and showing her the good hiding spots when they played hide-and-seek. And then he gave her the coveted quarter hidden in his piece of cake while everyone else received dimes. His curly-headed image was a blur in Denise's mind, but when she opened her eyes and read the inscription her mother had written underneath the photograph, it all became clear. *Heather Winter's 8th birthday party – June 1970.* The children's names were listed in order: *Heather, Celine, Denise, Chris, Louis, Carole, Amy, Robert.*

Denise studied the face of the boy sitting next to her at the table. He had a broad, large-toothed grin, and was leaning sideways, touching her shoulder with his. Could that possibly be Chris Lambert? Another image came to her mind; the childhood photograph she had seen at Chris's parent's house that night they met at the bar. A school picture from grade two, he had told her. Why hadn't she made the connection before? Denise started to convulse and she keeled over, holding her stomach. She lay down on the floor and closed her eyes, pain running up her legs and into her head. Children's laughter, playful music and women's chatter comforted her, while colourful balloons, bubbles and sunshine flashed through her mind.

****

Someone was holding her, cradling her head in their arms. She couldn't see, could barely hear, but the whispers, "hush, hush, it's all right," eased her soul. "Mother, is that you?" she whispered. Then the shrill sirens, coming closer, penetrated her consciousness with unrelenting hostility. The unbearable pain in her head intensified and her lungs would not accept air. But the gentle, soothing voice continued, "You'll be fine, sweet girl, you'll be fine."

Chapter Thirty-six

Pepper's death had left the family despondent and Laura still couldn't believe that he was actually gone. She blamed herself for never having trained him to stop chasing every squirrel in sight. If she could only turn back the clock twenty-four hours and lock the door after coming home yesterday, then life would be peaceful and normal. When Tanya asked if they could bury Pepper in the back-yard and have a funeral for him, Laura found it difficult to respond. She didn't know exactly what the vet did with dead animals and in truth, didn't want to know. Instead they went to church to pray for him, which didn't help much. Even Monique had come along, hoping for a spiritual boost. Afterwards, Laura offered to order pizza for lunch but nobody was hungry. Instead, they all sat around the kitchen table struggling to eat tomato soup and crackers.

In the evening, Monique and Andrew took the girls to see a Disney movie, as a distraction more than anything, but Laura stayed behind to put the house in order. Chris would be back the next day and he should come home to a warm, welcoming sight, not a cavern of sadness and clutter. Then Tony called, reminding her about the e-mail he'd asked her to forward.

"Oh, no," she said. "I completely forgot." She told him about Pepper's accident and felt even more depressed after their conversation.

Sitting at Chris's desk, she turned on his computer and waited for the screen to light up. She looked at the randomly displayed items, between the books and photographs on the office book-shelves, that the children had made for Chris over the years: a ceramic plate covered with Tanya's five-year-old handprints; a glass jam jar filled with seashells, a small flowerpot painted in primary colours; and a blue leather CD case that Monique had made for him when she was twelve. Then she studied the pictures: Monique standing proud, holding a trophy; Sophie dressed as a fairy one Halloween, grinning toothlessly; Tanya on Chris's shoulders reaching for an apple at Porter's Farm; and Chris with Laura at her brother's wedding—all precious memories.

Laura scrolled through Chris's e-mail file, searching for *Banque Lafayette*. When she didn't find the name she opened the 'sent' file to see if she'd find it there. Nothing. She typed the name in the search and find bar—still no luck. Then she noticed Denise Gagnon's name and her chest tightened. But there was nothing new. Seeing those e-mails again unsettled her, but nothing written was inappropriate, nothing she could justifiably object to.

Before shutting off the computer, Laura saw the draft file, on the side bar, holding two documents. Perhaps the Montreal e-mail would be there. When she opened the file she found the missing message, unsent, which would explain why the company complained they hadn't received it. The other message was to that woman, Denise. Laura opened it and the words: *my love for you is* sprung from the screen, pummeling her like a fist in the face. She re-read the message five times before the crushing words sank in. Chris was in love with another woman. Chris was indeed having an affair. Not with Sonya, but with that Quebec talk-show host. Why hadn't she listened to her instincts? Of course he was having an affair with her. All that 'childhood friend' business was hogwash. He'd been lying and cheating for who knows how long. She sat motionless, staring at the screen, until she heard footsteps and voices in the front hall.

Laura sent the girls upstairs to change into pajamas and brush their teeth, her voice calm but her head swimming in near-madness. When she read them a chapter of *Charlie and the Chocolate Factory* in her king-size bed, someone else seemed to be speaking. She heard a voice rise and fall with narrative inflections, but the words made no sense. While Tanya and Sophie were lost in Charlie's world, she was lost in her own miserable story: Chris and Denise making love, whispering passionate endearments to each other, and Chris sneaking phone calls to his lover while Laura was waiting for him to come to bed.

When she finished reading, the girls began to sniffle because of Pepper and she let them stay with her, snuggling together until they fell asleep. While she lay motionless, wedged between her two daughters, she put her hand over her mouth to stop herself from screaming.

Once the girls had dozed off, Laura crawled out from the bed and went downstairs, desperate for a drink. Monique and Andrew were in the family room watching TV.

"How was the movie?" she asked.

"Good," Monique said. "Funny. You should have come."

"Yes, maybe I should have."

"And great music," Andrew said. "I think I'm gonna get the CD."

"Nice haircut, Andrew," Laura said, "now we can see your handsome face." She was amazed at how pleasant and coherent she sounded, even to her own ears.

"Thanks," he said, blushing.

"He chopped it off for his tennis scholarship interview," Monique said.

"How did that go?" Laura asked. She crossed her arms to hide her trembling hands.

"He got the scholarship." Monique squeezed Andrew's arm. "He's going to Georgetown University in the fall."

"Congratulations, that's wonderful."

"Thanks," he said, brimming with pride.

"You won't be living in your van anymore?" Laura asked.

"Nope. The van will be my guest room. Like when Monique comes to visit."

Monique hit him with a cushion.

"I look forward to watching you play at the US Open some day," Laura said.

"I'm already too old for that, but maybe you'll see me on the sidelines as a coach."

"I can't believe that twenty-one is too old for anything. But that's great news, Andrew, I'm happy for you." Coherent, smooth, unflappable—a good actress.

Laura went to the basement and switched on the light in Chris's wine cellar. Where was that bottle she'd come across the other day when Tony was there? She scanned a few shelves until she found the Burgundy, dusty with age.

In the kitchen, she carefully removed the cork and smelled the contents. Gorgeous—plums, chocolate, raspberries, and a touch of oak. Picking up the bottle, she slowly tilted it, and watched the deep red liquid flow into the stainless steel sink and down the drain. When it was empty, she placed the bottle on the counter—the last bottle of wine she would open in her kitchen, the last bottle she would ever touch. Her days of drinking, of drowning her problems in alcohol were officially over. Now that she was off the tormenting emotional roller coaster she'd been on during the past few months, it was time to deal head-on with her life.

If Sonya could do it, why couldn't she? It may have been a long time since she worked, but there had to be something out there for her. Her business degree and ten years of management-consulting experience must account for something. She wouldn't move out of the area like Sonya, but there were many lovely homes in Shaker that she and the girls could move into, close enough to their school and to their friends; perhaps a townhouse or a three-bedroom condominium.

Laura tidied up the kitchen and swept the floor. She couldn't explain it, but somehow the truth had liberated her. The rejection she felt, the betrayal and the shock, were stinging her core, but she wanted that pain, needed to feel it, in order to come out of it. This was not the end of the world—no, it was the beginning of a new one.

Chapter Thirty-seven

When Chris arrived home after his Monday morning meeting in New York, his nerves were stripped raw. He hadn't been able to concentrate on anything in the airplane, not even the newspaper, and he could hardly recall what had transpired at the meeting. There was no point going to the office as he'd intended, even though it was only 3:15; what could he possibly accomplish in his state of mind? But when he opened the front door to his house, his sickened heart plunged into further despondency. Pepper did not come to greet him as he had done for the past nine years, jumping at his knees, forcing Chris to put down his briefcase to pet him. Chris used to joke with his family that the only living soul that truly appreciated him was the dog.

Slamming the door shut and dropping his keys noisily on the front dresser, he hoped to summon Laura's attention, somehow afraid to seek her out himself. When she emerged from the kitchen her face was blank, as if she didn't quite recognize him.

"I know what you're thinking," she said. "It feels strange to come home and not get the 'Pepper' greeting."

"That's right," he said, putting his bag down. "It'll be tough to get used to. How is everybody?"

"Sad. Missing Pepper. You don't look yourself, though, are you unwell?"

"Not so hot, actually."

"Come to the kitchen, I'll make you some tea."

He advanced, intending to kiss Laura, but she walked away as he approached. Following her, he said, "It's quiet here. Where are the girls?"

"At gymnastics camp, and Monique's life-guarding today."

Chris stared into the backyard, picturing his younger daughters laughing while Monique pushed them on the swings on their jungle-gym. He could hear Pepper running around them, yapping excitedly, wanting to get in on the fun. Everything was different now; the familiarity of his surroundings was gone, his spirit disconnected and empty. Even Laura seemed strange to him, aloof. He went to the kitchen sink, washed his hands and splashed cold water on his face. Grabbing a paper towel from the roller, he noticed an empty bottle of Burgundy sitting on the counter. It couldn't be their anniversary wine from New York, could it? He picked up the bottle and studied the label: "Cote de Beaune, 1989, Coche-Dury," remembering the salesperson's description, 'a near perfect wine.' The wine would have more than quadrupled in price since they'd bought it ten years ago, and it had been an extravagance to them back then.

"Laura, is this the wine you bought me in New York? Our anniversary wine?"

She didn't respond.

"It's empty. Did you drink it?" He smelled deep inside the bottle's opening as if hoping to prove himself wrong. "I can't believe you drank our wine," he continued. "Why would you do that?"

"I didn't drink it. I poured it down the sink."

"What?" He glared at her as if she were out of her mind. "Did you dump Tony's wine too?"

"What are you talking about?" Laura said.

"You know, the Chateaux Margaux. The bottle he asked me to cellar for him."

"But you broke it. I was standing right here when you confessed to Tony on the phone."

"No, Laura, I didn't break it." He shook his head, incredulous. "I found it in the recycle bin."

She gasped. "I didn't know…I didn't realize. If I had known, I never would have…"

"What the hell's going on here?" He picked up the empty bottle and shook it in front of her face.

"In case you haven't noticed, Chris. I've been drinking a little too much lately."

"I did notice, but if I ever mentioned it, you'd tear a piece out of me."

"Then you'll be pleased to learn that I'm not drinking any more. It's over." She pointed to the bottle, as if pouring the expensive Burgundy down the sink was proof of her resolution.

Chris read the label again and swallowed hard. Why did he feel betrayed? He ran his hand along the smooth surface of the aged glass, unable to find the words to protest further. "I'm glad you've made that decision, Laura. But I still don't understand why —"

"Another thing I've decided is to go back to work."

"OK," Chris said. "I didn't know you wanted to." Something bizarre was happening and he could not make sense of Laura's behaviour.

Laura brought the tea to the table and they sat down across from each other.

"How was your trip?" she asked in a casual tone, as if all was normal. "Did things work out as you had hoped?"

Her hard stare made him uncomfortable. "Work was good. This deal I'm scraping together is coming along. Could be the big one." He took a sip of tea.

"That's great."

A suffocating aura descended and nobody spoke for a moment.

"You look haggard." Laura spoke with concern, but her body was rigid, her face tight.

"We have to talk. I need to tell you something," he blurted out.

Laura got up and went to the fridge for some milk, then rummaged through the cupboard, pulling out the sugar bowl, although neither of them took milk or sugar in their tea. When she sat down again, Chris gently touched her hand.

"There's been another woman, Laura." He could feel the blood rush to his face. "I don't know how else to say it." She tried to pull her arm away but he wouldn't let go.

Then with eyes blazing she said, "I know."

"You know? How?"

"I've known something wasn't right for a while, but I couldn't figure it out. I thought maybe you had a thing going with Sonya and —"

"That's absurd. What gave you that idea?"

"It doesn't matter. Everything has become clear...that woman Denise...you rushing off to her mother's funeral and buying her flowers."

Chris wanted to give an explanation, but his mind scrambled in all directions.

"And I read your e-mails, the love letters."

What could she possibly have read that was incriminating? He'd been so careful. He looked at her, mystified.

She got up from the table and went to her corner desk, grabbing a file marked 'bills', from which she pulled out a sheet of paper. She threw it down if front of him.

Dear D,

I know I said we shouldn't be in contact, but the last couple of weeks have been brutal not being able to communicate with you. I think of you all the time, in spite of myself. I know this break is the right thing to do, but I don't know if I can continue this way. My love for you is...

"My God, how'd you find that? I never even sent that message."

"But you wrote it, you felt those things." Her voice cracked.

"I don't know what I was thinking at the time." Cornered by her accusation, he turned away, feeling ashamed and exposed. "But Laura, you have to believe me, it's *you* I want to be with, it's *you* that I want to be married to." The words came out fragmented, feeble.

She buried her head in her hands. "How did this happen? How could you do this?"

"I don't know. She landed in my life out of nowhere, after twenty-five years. My first love...I can't explain how it happened." What a mess, what a frigging disaster. "Laura, please listen to me. It sounds worse than it is." He went over to her and put his hands on her shoulders. Laura's body stiffened upon his touch, and in a shaky voice she asked, "Was she in New York with you?"

"Yes, but—"

She stood up to face him and screamed, "How can you say that it sounds worse than it is? This is the worst thing you could have done to me!"

Chris's diaphragm collapsed and he slouched over, holding his stomach. She'd belted him and he hadn't seen it coming.

"You're a liar and a cheat! I hate you!"

Chris grabbed the back of a chair and sat down, gasping for breath. "I never slept with her. I didn't cheat on you, Laura."

"Right."

"I never crossed the line. I'm telling you the truth."

"You damn well crossed the line, Chris, big time!"

"I know what I did was wrong and I'm sorry. I also know you won't forgive me right away, but I hope you will eventually. I want to fight for this family, for us. Please don't make me fight alone." For the first time since they'd been together, Chris cried in her presence.

"Do you still love her?" she asked.

"What's important, most important," he said, "is that I love you, and I will never leave you — you and the girls are my life."

Tears flowed down Laura's cheeks but she made no sound.

"Please tell me you'll try to forgive me, that you'll give me a chance." Chris waited for her reply, but she said nothing. Had he lost both Laura and Denise, all at once? He stepped forward and extended his arms, but Laura retreated.

"No, Chris. This is all too much for me right now. *You're* too much."

"Are we over, then? he said, shuddering.

She wiped her eyes with her wrist and said, "Twelve years together and three daughters — some things can never be over."

"Are you saying there's hope?"

She looked away. "I don't know."

****

When Denise opened her eyes she couldn't focus. Excruciating pain pulsed in her head, causing her to want to vomit. Slowly, other sensations began to present themselves: legs that wouldn't move, needles in her arms, a knife in her throat, bricks crushing her chest. The only soothing sensation was in the palm of her left hand, a gentle gust running along her fingers and settling at the bottom of her wrist. Slowly, her vision began to sharpen; she saw a white ceiling, machines, wires, a window, and pale green walls. The smell was antiseptic, sterile. Then she heard a voice, a whisper, "Denise."

Again, "Denise." She slowly moved her head toward the sounds. The pain, the pain. The voice spoke again, "Thank God." Looking at the soft hand holding hers in its own, she saw long fingers, smooth nails, and weathered skin. Her mother's hand. But when she saw the face belonging to the hand, she saw her sister's gentle eyes with tears trickling out.

"Denise," she whispered. "You scared us. My God, you scared us."

"I'm sorry," Denise replied in her mind, her lips too numb to speak.

Camille squeezed her hand. "You've been unconscious for two days, and breathing like a sick little bird."

Denise squeezed her hand back and tried to smile at her sister's sad face.

"Francois has been here day and night. He's sick with despair."

Denise cringed. She remembered how she'd left him at the house, keeled over on the stairs, pulverized by her treachery.

Camille continued, her voice like a feather brushing against Denise's ears. "He told me what happened and he blames himself. Something was terribly wrong, he said, and he was too busy to see."

Looking at Camille, Denise mouthed the words, "I betrayed him."

Camille stood up and walked to the end of the bed. "He says he let *you* down, that he failed *you* by not being there for you. And now he's quit the project, wants to focus on the boys, and you, if it's not too late."

Denise listened to the words, shocked by what she was hearing. That Francois could forgive her, and take responsibility himself for what *she* had done, intensified her shame.

Camille sat at the end of the bed and Denise could see the strain in her face. The creases in her forehead and her grave eyes said it all. "You didn't really want to die, did you?" Camille whispered.

Denise closed her eyes and shook her head. Everything had caved in on her so fast—her mother's death, losing her job, and then this thing with Chris. In spite of her foggy mind, she could see with such clarity now. Chris had been a crutch while her life was crumbling beneath her. Could they realistically have fulfilled their romantic destiny? Maybe, but at what cost? With Francois she had built a family, a life of substance, a world that mattered. No, she did not want to die and she didn't want to lose her family. Her priorities would have to be redefined, her life rectified. She thought of her mother's message, about fixing mistakes and not burying them. Was it too late? Had Francois and she destroyed their own happiness? Maybe there was a chance. One thing she knew for sure was that she had to repair her relationship with her children, learn to be there for them in a way she hadn't been before. They were every-thing to her — everything.

In her mind's ear, she heard her mother's voice telling her how strong she was, and how courageous. For the first time in her life, she believed those words could be true. And she realized she hadn't even allowed herself to properly mourn her mother's passing. Until she came to terms with the loss she would not be able to move forward. But she must also allow herself to mourn what Chris and she would never have together; it was time to let go of that dream.

When Denise opened her eyes, Camille was standing by the window sill, repositioning flower arrangements. She picked up an overflowing bouquet of pink peonies.

"Those are beautiful," Denise said

Camille turned around. "I thought you'd fallen asleep." She placed the peonies in the centre of the ledge. "They're from Mrs. Peterson. She's been awfully concerned since she found you on the floor in Mother's house."

Denise recalled the loving voice, the warm embrace, while lying half-conscious on the living room floor.

"She told me how happy she was to have finally done some-thing helpful for Mother."

Denise broke into a smile and felt herself laugh. "Yes, I think Mother might appreciate the fact that Mrs. Peterson saved my life." Camille began to laugh too, and they both laughed until tears rolled down their cheeks.

ACKNOWLEDGEMENTS

Thank you to Paul, Matthew and Ryan for supporting and encouraging my writing projects over the years. They have always believed that my books were worthy of publication and have given me the push I needed to make it happen. My gratitude also goes out to my parents and siblings for their constant love and support.

Special thanks to Trish Feehan and Beth Pollock, my two very talented writer friends, whose feedback and insights have always been invaluable. I also want to give my appreciation to Andrea Vander Vliet, my literary cheerleader and wonderful friend, and to Julie Otto, who helped with the final revisions, finding glitches and foibles with her very keen editorial eye.

AUTHOR BIO

Carla (Bethlenfalvy) Sandrin was born and raised in Montreal, Quebec. After receiving her Finance degree from McGill University in 1985, she moved to Toronto, Ontario to start a career in business.

Later she completed a degree in English Literature at the University of Toronto and a Certificate in Creative Writing at Humber College.

A LICIT AFFAIR is her first novel.

Carla currently lives in Toronto with her husband and two teenage boys.

15236988R00214

Made in the USA
Charleston, SC
24 October 2012